GARY L. STUART

HIDE AND BE

BOOK 1

A DR. LISBETH SOCORRO NOVEL

For information about this title or to order other books and/or electronic media, contact the publisher:
Gleason & Wall Publishers
2039 E. Glenn Dr., Phoenix AZ, 85020
www.garylstuart.com
gary@garylstuart.com

ISBNs: 978-1-7368946-6-8 (print)
        978-1-7368946-7-5 (eBook)

Printed in the United States of America

Cover and Interior design: 1106 Design, Phoenix, AZ

To Kathleen and Kara

OTHER BOOKS BY GARY L. STUART

"He doesn't know which of us I am these days, but they know one truth. You must own nothing but yourself. You must make your own life, live your own life, and die your own death . . . or else you will die another's."

—*Fondly Fahrenheit* by Alfred Bester,
Fantasy House, Inc. (1954)

CONTENTS

CHAPTER ONE

WHO ARE YOU?

Magistrate Judge Eli Hightower's courtroom was the smallest in the US District Court's 567,000-square-foot building in downtown San Diego. Like all federal courtrooms, his was open daily. He serves justice and deserves respect from those in the pit, as well as everyone in the pews behind the court rail. As federal judges go, he might best be described as a bulldog with a sense of humor. Prosecutors saw him as fair but neutral. Defense lawyers saw him as open and patient.

As is the case for many federal buildings in California, this one was designed in New York. Even so, San Diego loves it. Natural lighting in all interior spaces. The San Diego Bay and the Pacific Ocean provide year-round natural ventilation. One well-known local critic said, "The federal court building triumphs as a graceful departure from the lumpish mediocrity of its neighbors, as a guardian of green space at the heart of

1

the city, and by transforming public perceptions of the law in action."

United States Magistrate Judge Eli Hightower's entrance into the courtroom had instantly hushed the small group of lawyers huddled near the podium. A plain but hardly simple man, he always walked to his bench without the usual pomp attached to the comings and goings of judges. As he climbed the single step up to the clerk's platform and then the second step up onto the judge's bench, everyone in the room could hear him wheeze. At two-hundred and fifty-five pounds, Judge Hightower was a force to reckon with, both physically and intellectually. His long-standing battle with cigars accounted for the wheeze, and his fondness for Snickers bars and A&W Root Beer mocked his daily promise to lose weight.

"Take your seats, please," he said in a voice that softened the scowl on his face. "I thought, with sixteen years under my belt, or should I say under my robe, I'd heard it all. But the docket calendar says we're here to conduct an *identity* hearing. Whose identity is at question here? And better yet, why is there nothing in my bench book that lends the slightest clue as to what an identity hearing is? My clerk tells me that this is a joint request by the government and the defendant."

Looking first over the rim of his store-bought reading glasses at the prosecutor, Stran Cabelson, and then across at the defense lawyer, Gordon Kemper, he turned back to the prosecutor and nodded his head.

"Your Honor, we are here because we are not in agreement about the identity of the defendant. If I might, Judge, maybe I could summarize the situation. I represent the government in its case against Martin Cheshire on the arson murder of his brother, Arthur Cheshire. Martin Cheshire was initially arrested by the FBI in Portland, Maine, seven weeks ago on an embezzlement charge. His statement in that case led the FBI to open a second investigation. The defendant denied he was Martin Cheshire. He told them he was Arthur Cheshire, Martin's twin brother. But Arthur Cheshire died, as we contend, in an arson fire in Mexico, fifty-six miles from here, eight weeks ago. The FBI believes that Martin Cheshire killed his brother, Arthur, to cover up the embezzlement in Maine. But before we can proceed with an indictment, Mr. Kemper and I agreed that the confusion and doubt about exactly who the defendant is warrants this court's intervention. We've discussed it in chambers with Chief Judge Sharp, to whom this case is assigned. He sent us to you. We need this court to order a psychiatric evaluation to establish the actual identity of the defendant. That's why we agreed with the defense that the first person you should hear from in this case is Dr. Lisbeth Socorro."

"Hold up, Mr. Cabelson," the judge wheezed. "Who arrested him and under what name?"

"He was arrested as Martin Cheshire and initially admitted his identity to the FBI. He denied the underlying embezzlement, but when confronted with the allegations regarding the suspicious death of his brother, Arthur, he changed his statement and said he *was* Arthur. If that's the case, then the charges in Maine, as well as here in California, must be re-examined. Perhaps the only thing the government and the defense agree on is that none of us are confident about *who* Mr. Cheshire is. Is he Arthur, as he now claims to be, or is he Martin, as he originally admitted he was? As I said, Chief Judge Winthrop does not want an arraignment and a plea to the charge until we can give him some assurance as to whom he's arraigning and who is entering a plea. Mr. Kemper and I agreed to ask this court to conduct an *identity* hearing."

Mr. Cabelson, walking stick-legged due to a heavy fiberglass boot on his right foot, lumbered back to his desk.

Deputy US Marshal Gentry, sitting next to the man whose identity was at issue, got up and walked up to the podium.

"Judge, my role in this case started when Mr. Cheshire, sitting next to me, agreed to extradition from Maine to California. I went to Portland, secured his custody, and brought him here, in handcuffs. He's what I would call non-conversational. For the airplane trip back here from Portland, Maine, he only used two words, yes and no. He only answered when asked about the bathroom, his seat belt, and his handcuffs. He's listed as Martin Cheshire in the transfer order, and I signed a receipt for him under that name. But once we got him into custody, he insisted he is Arthur Cheshire and that his brother Martin is dead. So, I asked Dr. Lisbeth to give me some guidance. That's about all I know about the case."

Judge Hightower moved his head back toward the defense lawyer and nodded at him.

Mr. Kemper charged out of his chair. Dressed in a dark blue pinstripe suit, he had a face like a hatchet and a courtroom demeanor that always drew attention to whatever he was about to say. He used his large steely grey eyes to project a state of concentration, suggesting his audience should pay close attention to what he was about to say. "Because my client says he is Arthur Cheshire, my first duty is to him. The confusion about identity stems from my client's statement in court in Maine. He admitted there that he'd been sort of play-acting as his brother Martin, even holding himself out to be Martin, at least in Maine. But simultaneously, he's been holding himself out as Arthur, here in California. I cannot in good faith represent the man the government insists is Martin Cheshire if in fact Martin is dead, as my client, Arthur Cheshire, insists. What we have here is a double identity problem—who is the defendant—who is the decedent? Those two answers will tell us whether a crime was committed at all, or whether this is just a simple wrong man, wrong place, and no crime case."

Turning his attention to Dr. Lisabeth Socorro, Judge Hightower motioned her to come forward. She gathered her notes from the prosecutor's table and took her place at the podium. The judge, lawyers, court staff, FBI agents, and the US Marshal knew her well. The defendant did not. They all watched her. He did not. She was short with laugh wrinkles at the edge of her dark blue eyes. Her blondish, silverish hair was cut in a business-like fringe. She was accustomed to courtrooms, even though she spent most of her time listening to deranged and depressed prisoners brought to her office by uniformed jail guards who never had a sense of humor.

Reaching the podium, she nodded politely and said, "Your Honor, I've spent about a half-hour with Mr. Cheshire, the defendant. And I've looked at his file, such as it is. There is enough ambiguity here to warrant a psychiatric evaluation. Martin and Arthur Cheshire are identical twins. Among other things that means that photographs and historical records could be misleading. And DNA is of little value. In my initial session with Mr. Cheshire, I noted a third, much more serious problem than the one outlined by the lawyers today."

"What would that be, Doctor?" the judge asked.

"Mr. Cheshire may not, himself, know the answer to the question about his identity. If my initial suspicions prove to be the case, this man, the defendant in this case, has been playacting all his life. Sometimes he's Arthur and sometimes he's Martin. He slides easily from one role to the other. There is a psychiatric possibility that even now, he doesn't know. In that case, Your Honor, it's not just identity that's in question, it's sanity."

Judge Hightower held up a cautionary hand.

"Let's hold that thought a moment, Doctor. Mr. Kemper, are you inserting a sanity defense in this case, or is the issue at this moment limited to identity?"

"That, Your Honor, depends entirely on my client's identity. I can't assess possible defenses to a crime until I know whether it was ever committed. That question will resolve

whether an insanity defense is appropriate. But until someone figures out which Mr. Cheshire is here in court, we are
deadlocked."

"All right, let's take this one step at a time. Is your client
willing to undergo a court-ordered psychiatric evaluation for the
express purpose of establishing his identity?"

"Yes, Your Honor."

"So ordered."

"Gentlemen, and Dr. Socorro, I want a briefing statement
from each of you giving me the jurisdictional basis to establish
identity. I would think that's the government's principal problem.
It has to know whom it's charging, right? The public defender's
office is likewise burdened. Is Arthur Cheshire dead? The US
Marshal's office obviously wants to know whom it picked up in
Maine and transported three thousand miles to face charges for a
murder that may or may not have ever occurred. So, if there ever
was a case for Psychiatric Evaluation Services to intervene, this
seems to be it. Dr. Socorro, is it within the realm of psychiatry
to actually identify a human being?"

Dr. Socorro returned to the podium. "Your Honor, a person's
identity, in psychiatric terms, is a person's role in life. It's both
perception and a sense of self. It's often described as a sense of
individuality, that is, distinct personality, talents, abilities, and
flaws. But often, patients see themselves as the sum of charac-
teristics by which they are self-recognized, as well as how others
see them."

"Thank you, Doctor," the judge wheezed. "But from this
side of the bench it seems to me that identity is usually a factual
determination based on historical records, DNA, photographs,
dental charts, fingerprints, and maybe polygraphs. Where does
psychiatry come in?"

"Your Honor, psychiatrists and psychologists see patients
and help them understand and live with identity disorders."

"That what you think we have here? A defendant with an identity disorder?"

"No, Your Honor. I have not yet begun to evaluate the defendant's mental state and . . ."

As usual, Judge Hightower didn't adjourn the hearing. He said, "OK, let us know what you think after your evaluation of him." Then he pushed himself away from the bench, wheezed, and stepped down onto the courtroom floor. He didn't walk—he lumbered his way to the narrow door to his chambers.

ARTHUR CHESHIRE—DR. SOCORRO—A WEEK LATER

Medical clinics smell, especially ones tucked into jails. This one was only four years old and had a highbrow name—the *Angus Witherspoon Federal Corrections Medical Center*. The inmates called it The Psych Tank. Whatever it was, Arthur hated it. His nose itched, his eyes watered, and his spleen bulged unmercifully against his rib cage.

The detention officer, Officer Billy Martinez, nudged his prisoner through the first plate steel door and waited until the door buzzed closed behind them. Flashing his electronic ID on the second door's entry box, he tightened his vice-like hold on Arthur's elbow and guided his way through the three-by-six holding area between the two doors separating the jail section from clinical services. Windows on both sides of this short hallway gave prisoners, at least those lucky enough to cross over, a right-side glance at downtown San Diego and a left side look at San Diego Bay. Today, the huge body of water claimed bragging rights to a gigantic US Navy carrier, docked at Coronado Island on the far side of the bay.

They walked to the clearing window, under the glare of black security cameras, to the far end of the walkway and stopped at the Plexiglas gatekeeper.

"This here's Martin Cheshire," the guard said. Arthur shook his head from side to side but said nothing.

"Prisoner Number A-1113-2039—to see Dr. Socorro."

"Appointment time and transfer number?" asked someone behind the Plexiglas, through the small speaker embedded in the lower right corner.

"Zero nine forty-five hours. Lemme see, yeah, here it's at—transfer order number twenty-five sixty-two. We got a match?"

"Hold one . . . Yeah, on the list. Push him through."

As they moved through the second set of doors, Arthur, knowing how futile it was, said, "Wrong again, Mister, whatever *your* real name is. *Mine's* Arthur Cheshire. Been mistaking me for my brother for three weeks now."

Martinez, unarmed except for a club, two pepper spray canisters, and 220 pounds of muscle and attitude, prodded Arthur into what looked like an emergency room waiting area—doctors, nurse practitioners, cops, staffers, lawyers, inmates, and patients. They all looked tired. Two overpowering odors wafted through and over the vinyl chairs and Formica tables—Lysol and sweat. Hushed conversations buzzed, eyes looked up, and then just as quickly down. Nobody paid heed to anyone else here. Everybody in here had clinical issues. No need paying attention to anyone's but your own.

Arthur, or Martin, whichever one he was today, had been in lock-up for fourteen days. He knew the drill.

Glancing at his ridiculously large, black, official Navy Seal watch, the guard stopped in front of one of the dozen doors covering two walls of the reception area. The government-issued removable sign said "Lisbeth Socorro, M.D., *Psychiatric Evaluation Service.*" Pushing Arthur inside, he mouthed the required warning. Behave. She'll be right in.

The far wall of her little evaluation room had a one-way mirror, next to a two-way door. Dr. Socorro came in, took her seat, and smiled.

"How are you, Mr. Cheshire?"

Arthur looked at her; he took his time, and decided the question was merely rhetorical.

She tried again.

"Anything new since we last talked? If not, let's try something new, all right with you?"

"We're fine, thanks. You?"

Today, like every Monday, Wednesday, and Friday since his identity hearing before Judge Hightower, two weeks ago, Arthur alternated between his truth and theirs. Leaning back into the vinyl mesh panel on the back of his chair and tapping out a steady beat on the table, he mumbled, "I'm Arthur. Martin's dead. I told you that already, right? Any chance you'll believe us today? If not, let's just talk about you. You hiding anything? Anything we ought to know about your life?"

His blue shirt darkened at his armpits. She looked away but dutifully took a note. Or a doodle. He couldn't tell. She wrote in a black cardboard-bound lab book. Made him feel like a lab rat. Leaning forward into the table, her face four feet from his, she moved the fledging conversation to something more abstract. Abstract is good for delusional inmates. And Cheshire fit that, she thought.

"Why do you see yourself in the plural; you know, the royal 'we,' some would call it? I mean sometimes, when we talk, you respond in person, but for the last two, three, sessions you seem to be a little outside yourself. Maybe I could understand your situation better if you let me inside. Can we try that?"

"You're doing it too, Doc. Can *we* try that? Which *we* are you? I mean you know I'm Arthur, no matter what your little lab book says. Hell with the polygraph, and double hell with some ignorant Mexican who mistook me for my brother. If you can be we, why can't Martin and I be we? Explain me that."

His sweat made her nervous. Even though she worked for state wages, and mixed with prisoners every day, it still made her nervous to see them sweat. She couldn't decide whether it was a symptom, or just an odor.

It seemed longer, but four days later they made me go see her again, after lunch, before my nap. But right away she got in my face, just when I was thinking she was on my side.

"All right, Arthur, as you know, I'm required by law to remind you that the federal government has identified you as Martin Cheshire, but that, as a licensed therapist, I will call you by whatever name makes you comfortable. We've talked now, what is it, six sessions? Whatever, it's enough for me to understand your reality. I've read all the charging documents in your murder case here in federal court, and the embezzlement charges back in Maine. So, I'm rich in what's happened to you in the last year or so, but still poor in the real *you*. You and your brother. So, if you don't mind, I'd like to return to a subject we touched on in your second session with me. Let's go back to your formative years."

"Formative years? That's what you think they were? Hell, you know?"

She was like all the others. Cept now I was in San Diego, not Maine. There's a harbor here too. But different, you know. Warm all the time. Wind from San Diego Bay, since it's sheltered by Coronado Island. Back in Portland, the wind came in straight off the Atlantic. Colder'n shit. Please don't evade, she said. I had to be straight with her. Straight? Hell, you say. My brother never knew her. That's good. He wouldn't have liked her. Hell, she know about forming anything. Back then, when Martin was hiding, and I was out in front, she'd have never got it. I coudda told her I was him. Hell, she knew. Only thing different this time was they took me into her real office, not just that little evaluation room Martinez stuck me in last time.

"Nice office you got," I said.

She scratched that into the lab book.

"It's OK," she said. "Take your time."

I would have told her more, but then I had to look at her. Rather see the clouds—out her window—nice window, I said. They didn't have windows in the cells—had a steel toilet, bout where your window is, I said. Alongside two spring-iron cots hanging from chains bolted to the wall. Three-inch mattress pads, two sheets, a polyester blanket. But this, this is real nice, I told her. Wall to wall carpeting. Back in the cells, I had a towel on the floor, to pretend. She had books, on shelves, and pictures in frames. I had one book, only one per day, from Hanford, the book-cart guy.

"Did I have any pictures?" she asked, trying to be nice.

I had one picture of Martin and me, but it got taken away. It was bad for me to look at it, they said. Hell, they know.

She was older, but still firm, best as I could tell under her white jacket, which she had on every time they brought me to see her. Lots of questions. True answers. Back then and now. But hell, she know. Sixty minutes down the tube, she buzzed the guard.

"All right, Arthur," she said, closing her book, capping the pen, arching her back.

Then, like he was lurking outside, the guard came in the back door. Or was it the front door? Depends, I guess. I shuffled to my feet. He said something about nice seeing the doc.

"We had fun. Next time my place," I said to her, over my shoulder.

She never took offense. Just notes. Same jacket. Same time, three days a week. Eval. Eval is what she called it. I knew better. She was writing down Martin and me. So, she could say give me the needle. Or not. Hell, she know.

FIRST FOSTER MOTHER—PORTLAND, MAINE—TEN YEARS EARLIER

Like I said, me and Marty were from Maine. Born, bred, and fed. By foster parents mostly. Always hated the cold.

We lived in drafty houses in winter, wore cheap coats in spring and fall, but not knowing any better, just accepted it. Lived our lives wherever the caseworkers said. You know, go here, stay there, new doctors, and interchangeable houses.

A general practitioner, whose first name was Doctor, talked to our first foster mother, but not us.

"Don't worry, Mrs. Greyson," the doctor said.

That's what he always called her—Missus—she didn't have a first name, and he didn't have a last. He was Doctor and she was Mrs. Us? We were just two little jellybeans sitting in one chair. Doctor had three chairs in his office. One for her, one for him, and the third for us. I remember liking that—same chair, same us.

"Autonomous language is common, harmless, really. It'll go away in time," he told her. Not us. He never said anything to us. We don't remember the exact words, but who cares? Fumbuck, he knew. You? How can you tell? Autonomous, dummy. Marty told me.

"They will always be hard to tell apart. Dress them differently. They will want to be together, with their family gone and all, but treat them like regular brothers, even if they are identical twins."

That's what he told Mrs. Greyson. And she told it to our caseworker. But it didn't take. They always thought we were so funny, just because we looked exactly alike. We had to be alike, as it turned out. Even if it wasn't funny. Even now, here in the jail, people talk about me as though I was a jar of jellybeans. No need to talk *to* him. We can talk *about* him. But I was telling you about that office, the doctor's office.

They always said, "We're going to the doctors."

Not the doctor's office, or the doctor. It was always plural. Not like you, or your office.

DR. SOCORRO and ARTHUR

"Why did they take you to the doctor in Maine? Were you sick? Or was it something about your brother? Do you remember?"

"Remember? Maybe. We had bumps and scrapes. Marty fell out of a tree, on top of me. And another time he hit his face on a rock and might have broken a cheekbone. But X-rays were expensive."

"Why was he climbing the tree? Did you tell the doctor?"

"Nope. Didn't fess up then. No need to do it now. Martin said he'd been up the tree. Hide and be, ya know? We lived that way. For one another. And as one another."

"I'm sorry, Arthur, but I wonder why you keep recalling these little stories about fooling people back when you were a small child in Maine. Did you and your twin brother think if you could fool people then, you can fool people now? Is that it? Sometimes I don't think you distinguish between what happened to you and what happened to your brother. That's one thing I'm trying to establish, remember? We talked about the charges against you, now that you are here in California. Remember—embezzlement in Maine but something more serious here—murder, right? You understand how serious murder is, right? Do you remember why they thought you were Martin and that you'd killed your own brother? Why do you think they asked you all those questions about growing up in Maine? Was it the same as I'm asking you now—about growing up in Maine?"

"Why? You always wanna know why—all the time. Fumbucked! Martin asked me once if they had twin doctors. No one ever said. But back there, in Maine, it wasn't like this. Those doctors' offices were sam-o sam-o—never changed, always a man doctor, a second-story office, even when a different doctor was in it, never changed. Maybe they had twin doctors but only one of them saw us. Maybe they were exactly like us. We couldn't tell. What do you think? Framed papers up on the wall. Now I'm older, I know about degrees and licenses. Back then, we wondered where the pictures were. No pictures of people—a brown desk very tidy—three chairs—but me and Martin shared the same one, every time—smelled like it was mopped with acid or something—I held my nose with my thumb and the knuckle on my first finger. So did Martin."

ARTHUR IN CELL BLOCK 9

Ya know, I said to the sink in my cell, you're just like me. Some days you swallow soapy water, other days I puke. My life as a twin was not like this. Now I'm a singleton, and I'm slowly unwinding like silk from a spool. Dr. Socorro ain't really trying to diagnose me. Fumbuck that. She's trying to tag me with a name, like in hide and seek. Well, that's not the game—it's Hide and Be.

I yanked from side to side the fourteen-inch square cardboard box under my bunk, to get it out. It held what the freakin guards called my "particulars." It had my dopp kit minus my razor, socks, shorts, tee shirts, Levis, boots, and papers the police in Portland gave me. Damn thing weighed ten pounds. It had the stupid arrest report in Maine, yakking about the embezzlement plan Martin started and told me about way too freakin late. Even those dumb shit cops didn't know which of us followed and which led. But I betcha that doctor who testified in my hearing and now is riddling me with questions knows. She's got a form-fitting white jacket, that's what I like about her. Like it or lump it, she's getting used to me. She's guessing but it's toot suite, ya know.

She told me she read the whole damn file including that indictment crap back in Maine based on what some dude told some other dude. Just talk, not what my lawyers call "evidence." Shit, they already know me and Martin shared everything fifty-fifty, cept for booties. Well, at least before our fishing boat crashed. She knows we could fool doctors, cops, bosses, booties, and whoever we in hell wanted to. Just like when we got wacked and strapped when the fosters got the wrong twin every god-damn time, every goddamn time.

She laid that psycho logo stuff on me plenty of times. What 'n hell she know? That's not true about one twin dying and the other losing it. Hell, she know?

Officer Billy Martinez brought Arthur in. He was OK, Dr. Socorro thought, watching him hand Arthur a freshly popped Coke can. Arthur looked at it, smiled when Martinez left.

Not looking directly at her, he said, "That Martinez, he's OK. Brought me my Coke. Never took a sip. See?" he said, pointing to the straw poked down into the hole in the top of the can, "It's still in the paper tube. Ya know, Doc, I think he likes you. He didn't say so, but we can tell."

Looking up, Doctor Socorro frowned, but only for a moment.

"We can tell? Who are you referring when you use the plural rather than the singular? Are you speaking for your brother—or are you talking about you and Officer Martinez?"

"Well, me and my brother think sam-o sam-o, but me and Martinez don't, ya know."

"All right let's talk about when you were a child in Maine, and someone took both of you to see a doctor. We started that yesterday but got interrupted. You and he were what, five, or six? Do you remember the doctor's name?"

"The doctor's name? Dunno. But his label said M.D. He was right about lots of things, but he still missed the big stuff. It was more than just our secret language that disappeared. He told our foster mother we were auto noms or something like that. Over the next ten years, from when the fosters died, or pulled the plug on us, like maybe when we hit sixteen, Mrs. Simonson moved us three times."

"Sorry to interrupt, Arthur, but tell me again, who was Mrs. Simonson? I started a note here about Mrs. Greyson."

"Doc, you gotta focus on us. Greyson was our first foster *mother*. Simonson was our first *caseworker*. We lived with Mrs. Greyson, but we only saw Mrs. Simonson when she came to visit. That's what she called it, 'visiting.' Sometimes we weren't sure, but Marty figured it out for us. Caseworkers didn't have houses. Foster mothers did. Maine didn't have men caseworkers just like California doesn't have women guards. Or men shrinks. Why is that, Dr. Socorro?"

Dr. Socorro waived her pen at me and pushed her chair a little bit back. Arthur knew what that meant.

"Right, back to the question. Counting the first fosters, we did time in three foster homes, all with the same freezing, god-damn six-month-long winter. Colder'n hell. Or here. A Maine winter can eat you alive. San Diego's never tasted winter. That's what they say about us."

"All right, Arthur. Let's go back a little. How much do you remember about your first foster home? Did your foster mother treat both of you the same? I know you looked alike and all, but were your foster parents, the man and the woman, unable to tell you apart?"

"Martin, Doc. That was his name. Is his name. Can't you use his real name? Quit calling him my brother. We never did. Sometimes we went by one name, then just like that, it was the other. See, that was part of the game. I'd hide. He'd be me. Martin, Arthur, me, him, us, what difference did it really make? Oh, right, I see it on your face. You think by being the same then that now, when it's even more important, the cops got it right. Just because they say I'm Martin don't make it so! Write that down. We are never getting anywhere if you don't know which is which."

"OK," she said. "You talk, I write it down. But you have to be clear about who you're talking about."

She watched as he took slow, long breaths and teetered slightly from side to side in his chair. He gripped the arms on the government-issue chair like he was riding a buck board wagon. She counted his breath intakes by watching him breathe through his mouth rather than his nose. He looked out the window, back at her, and then down at the floor, as though truth was in the air, on her face, or caught up in the dust of seeing six patients a day.

After a couple of minutes, she thought he'd fainted. The eval room, constantly tracked on an automatic audio system, but not video, was kept at a constant sixty-eight degrees. As she looked at him over the rim of her reading glasses, she could see him focusing on the nameplate on her desk. Her name was stenciled in black. He scanned the room as though he was taking inventory; a metal filing cabinet, two wastepaper baskets, a table behind her side of the desk—books mostly. Files here, and there. His file, about two inches thick, was always placed corner to corner on the lower left side of the table. The lab book, with his name on it, captured the right-hand corner.

"Hey Doc," he said, "how come, if you believe me, you have the wrong name on that little cardboard book you write stuff in? I ain't Martin Cheshire, although I pretended I was. Lots of times. But not now. I'm Arthur. Hell, they know? I see only black ballpoints in that black jar—upper right quadrant. Why so much black?"

"Does that bother you, Arthur, that I take notes in black ball point ink?"

"Well, yeah," he said, in a low growl. "Me and Martin lived in the dark a lot and there was always something black back then. Moods. Future. Past. All black. Just like Mrs. Simonson's long black coat. And our parents' caskets—they were black too. Both of them. We remember, no matter what Martin says now, if he had anything to say, that is. Both caskets were black. Wood or metal, no, never mind. Just black. That's what sticks. Yeah, it was a hellva long time ago. Martin's? What are you saying exactly? Trick question? He drowned. I buried him. I told you bout that. Never had a casket. Buried him in the fall in Maine. Burned his body in the summer in Mexico. No casket. Either time. Again? You want it again? What's the point?"

CHILDHOOD

Marty used to say, what's "placed"? The *boys*, as their caseworkers knew them by, were often placed in some new place. As the memories of their parents dimmed, meeting new foster parents became a routine.

Arty answered Marty. "Placed means sticking us with new fosters, but they don't own us. They just take care of us, till we're big."

Mrs. Simonson, the lady caseworker in the long black coat, was in control. She'd come to whichever foster had them. They'd pack our stuff in two boxes, a pillowcase apiece, and an old leather suitcase with frayed straps tightly buckled. Then she'd place them somewhere else. The old fosters hid out while they were being replaced. The new fosters smiled, at least at first. There was always something to sign, then a room to look over, then usually good things, cookies, or candy bars. OK with us.

In winter, she had big boots, but in summer, brown shoes. We had shoes too. Same color, same size. That's still true. Well, sort of true. Then? I already told you that. Long black coat, with big boots. She never took it off, just asked us how it was. At first, we told her. Then we didn't. She moved us anyhow.

Mrs. Simonson figured it out, bout when we turned thirteen. Maybe. Can't be sure. But here's something that year was different. By then we knew stuff. "Boys," she said, "it's time to go."

One time Mrs. Simonson brought another woman who worked for the government, or maybe the police. She had a uniform. Gray pants and shirt and a badge but no gun. She told us her name. Can't remember it now. But she was different. She looked different. Spicy. What's that mean? Nothing, just how she looked. She visited us in our room on the back porch. She visited the fosters in the kitchen. She took notes, just like you do. She was not old. She had a jacket, like you, but I don't remember the colors—not black, I remember that. And she took hers off. I remember she had real boobs; Martin liked that. He wanted her to hang around just to watch 'em jiggle. I guess I liked it too, not for myself, but because he did. We did the same things, you know.

PORTLAND, MAINE—FOSTER HOME

"Boys are you under there?" Mrs. Greyson hollered.

She was always hollering at us. Why'd she have to be like that? But we didn't talk; we just sat there, huddled back-to-back so we could watch both ways, front and back, real quiet, trying not to let her hear us breathe. My back on his, chin tucked in between my knees. He was doing the same, like always. We just waited.

"I know where you are, don't think just cause I can't see you; I don't know you're under there. You come out right now, or when he gets home, I'll tell on you. You know what that means, don't you?"

I just stayed put. Yeah, scared. Damn straight. But Marty knew what to do. He kicked some dirt on me as he turned around and crawled like crazy—back through the opening in the porch wall, headed for the trap door—up into the broom closet. He could always crawl faster than me. I could run faster.

Marty found the trap door in the broom closet. The foster put us in there with the brooms, a sorry excuse for a mop, and a tin bucket with a broken handle. She did it cause we were bad.

It was not too bad once we were inside. We held onto each other. It was dark, but he never hit us once the door got locked on us. No hitting in there. It was not too big, and there was this box, a big ole wooden box, which used to have toys in it until we got there. He took them out one day. Burned them.

We'd been bad again. That was how Marty found the trap door, in the back of the closet, under the wooden box. Yeah, it had colors. But no name I can remember. Green, like bark gets after winter is gone, and white, but dirty white, all around the top. Probably more. Who cares?

The first time, when he found that trap door in the floor, Marty made me go first. I was brave then. Lying on my stomach, I reached down far as I could where the dirt was. I could feel it. Under the house. And I could see some light toward the front. Ya know, under the front porch. So, I just dropped down, not even thinking about it. He followed. We could see light at the front, where the porch was. There was a hole in the porch wall. A little hole. Just right for us. It was knocked out for pipes, or something. It went out under the front porch, but then a dead end. You couldn't crawl outside to the front yard, or the street, or anything because those boards under the porch were pretty good boards. But you could sit under the porch, and hear folks come in, and spy on them, and everything.

We used to crawl out there after he, Mrs. Greyson's husband, left to go to work. Then when he'd come back pretty near dark, we'd hear him walking across the gravel to the house, scraping and dragging his bum leg. Don't know how he got it. Usually, before he came up the front steps, he'd spit. We could hear him gag first, then spit, then wheeze, and start up the porch steps. We'd crawl right on back and be up in the closet before he got there to check on us.

Sometimes, she heard us under there after he left. She didn't care if we were there, but she was not supposed to let us out of the broom closet if we'd been bad. She never could figure how we got under there, under the porch, when he'd put us in the broom closet, way at the back of the house. But here's the thing. She knew she'd be in trouble if we were not there when he got home. She was safe as long as he thought we were locked inside the closet. Looking back on it, how could he not know? His broom closet—his big ole wooden box, his trap door to the crawl space under his own goddamn house? No, I don't know. It got pretty cold in the broom closet. That's why he put us in there when we were bad. He'd give us a few licks with his strap. "That'll warm you up. This'll cool you off," he said. Then he'd point inside. We'd do what he said, he'd slam the door, and turn the big lock on the outside. Stupid. Even when he didn't put us in the broom closet, we went in there to get to our hiding place under the front porch. He never knew. Like I said, no one really knew us, much less anything important about us.

Marty was gone for a while, then I heard him up over my head on top the porch. I was still sitting down underneath with my chin in between my knees and my arms holding tight. It felt really good to sit like that. No one could see me. I didn't shake so much. Marty was up there, on top the porch. I could have touched his feet cept for the floorboards between us. Up on the porch. Right on top of me. Shuffling his feet. I guess.

She must have heard him.

"How'd you get up there?" she hollered from down in the front yard. "I heard you down here, under the porch. And where's your brother? Is he under there? You tell him to get on out here, right now."

"No, Mama, he's not under there." She made us call her Mama, even though she wasn't.

"He's upstairs in the bathroom. I heard you calling for us from the backyard. I came through the kitchen."

That was a signal, I guess. So, I crawled as fast as I could under the house, hit my knee on a big rock, then scrambled up the trap door and into the broom closet, just in time. Listening, real careful like, I scooted up the back stairs to the bathroom. Bout a minute passed. Then she came in, holding on to Marty's ear between her thumb and that big knuckle on her first finger. She was mad at me.

"I see you. You got the same dirt on your clothes as your brother. I think both of you was under that damn porch again, and you scampered out. You boys are lying to me again. I'm going to tell on you soon he gets home."

He came home just before dark, like always. We were back in the broom closet, like we were supposed to be.

"Evening, Father," which was what she always called him.

"The boys have something to tell you, maybe you'd best let them out so you can hear for yourself what I already know."

"Mother, you supposed to be watchin' them boys. What do they have to tell me that you can't?" he asked, as he fished in his vest pocket for the key. Course we couldn't see him, but we could hear his wheezing, the rustle of his black coat as he hung it on the hook, and then the key squeaking itself into the lock, and clickin'. We liked to hear that click. Marty covered his eyes cause the bright light on the back porch always hurt a little when it first jumped into the closet with us. Soon the door opened.

We didn't say nothing. Just stayed there. He never liked us talkin' until we was asked. So, we just stayed.

"They have figured out how to open the door, and get outside," she whispered to him.

"Then they go under the front porch. They did it just this afternoon, isn't that right, boys?" she said, in her low mouse voice. That's what Arty called it, a mouse voice. Father was a bobcat. Mama a mouse. Mouse never hurt us. Just told on us.

"Well, now, you boys got something to tell me. Something that you know I won't like, and neither will Jesus."

"We didn't do nothing bad, I promise," I said, but then Marty, came out from behind me. He'd been holding onto my shirt, and Mama just backed away into the kitchen.

It was like he didn't even care what we said. Marty told him it was him that got out, by just pushing on the door, and that I was too scared to come out, and so he went and hid under the front porch, where Mama found him.

"No, Arty, that ain't right—I saw you and I heard you," Mama said, but she was looking at Father out of the side of her face, like she did when she was as scared as us.

"But, Mama, I'm Marty, and I'm telling you the truth."

Like always, that was enough for Father. He took ahold of my ear, squeezed it till I got some tears. He'd stop if you cried real tears. Then he grabbed Marty, thinking he was me, and marched us both right into the front room, where the crucifix was. It was his, he said, but it was older than anyone. I bet it came from a grave. And he got the strap from the hook beside the crucifix. Two hooks on the wall. One for Jesus' crucifix and one for Father's braided neck strap, the one he hooked on the back of the crucifix, when he walked around the room praying to all four of the windows. God's windows, he told us.

"You boys been bad again, haven't you. Don't look at the floor. Look at Jesus, up there on the wall. He can see you been bad. He wants me to give you ten licks, but I ain't had my supper yet."

We stood there just looking up at Jesus, except Marty, like always, looked up from behind me, and I could tell his eyes were closed. He never looked right at Jesus. Then he got one lick from the strap, and I got the other. He cried. I didn't, but I wanted to. One of us was not supposed to cry. This time was my turn.

"So, boys, is one strap enough? Just one of you snuck out, that's what Mama says. Now you go on upstairs to your room. Mama will be up soon enough with your food. I don't abide sneaking out after you've been bad, and neither does Jesus. But He fed the birds and the beasts, and I'll always feed you, even if you've been bad."

See, that was it. We didn't have to say for what. Just bad. Then he'd put us in the broom closet. Sometimes he gave us the strap right there in front of the cross, like now. Sometimes not. But the strap didn't hurt much. He called it the good boy strap and said Jesus knew when we were bad. We hated the dark in the closet more than the strap. That's why being under the porch was good, you see? Little slivers of light all around. It was like the light from out in the front yard, down the path and the way to the road. That good light snuck under the porch just for us. So we could see each other, not the road, but we could hear whenever anybody came up the road.

Dark was bad. Strap was not too bad. Light helped. Light with dirt felt especially good to us. I do not remember why, but I sure remember feeling safe under that porch. We thought maybe our mom and dad would come back and find us under the porch, whenever we pretended they didn't die.

"But Arty, they are dead; they can't come back. Can they?"

"No, you goose," I told him. "Jesus came back, that's what Mama says."

"But Arty, if they did come back, would they be able to see us under the porch? We are hiding but not from them. Are we?"

We didn't care, I guess. Dirt was our friend. It felt soft. Me and Marty must have believed back then that dropping out of the broom closet was escaping, sort of. As long as we got back before they went to the broom closet, things were OK. We would not have to go to the crucifix.

PORTLAND, MAINE—MARTY AND ARTY'S FISHING CAMP

Their fishing camp was up on the Damariscotta River, about fifty miles north of Portland. They called it Jones Point, maybe two miles from South Bristol. It was weather beaten and rickety, like every other third-rate fishing camp in Maine. Jack and Melinda Porter owned the camp. The Porters turned out to be the boys' last foster parents. They had the Cheshire twins for four years, from twelve to sixteen. In their own way, they loved the boys, and took them to the fishing camp every other weekend from May to October. They did not have crucifixes in the house, or at the camp.

Jack Porter turned sixty-five the year the boys turned sixteen. He and Melinda decided to sell the house in town and move to Florida. Since the boys were "of age" they could live on their own, didn't have to go to school, but needed a place to live. The caseworker said, OK, just tell the judge. The judge said OK, just deed the fishing camp up on the Damariscotta to a court guardian, who will sign it over to the boys on their eighteenth birthday.

"But why, Arty, why'd they give it to us?"

"Marty, you dumb shit, who cares? They just did, that's all. So, as long as we got gas for the truck, and we can sneak off, we can fish for our dinner all the time. And if we ever get girls, we can bring them up here and . . . You know."

PORTLAND, MAINE—MARTIN AND ROSIE—THREE MONTHS AGO

I'm Martin. Yeah, I'm the other twin—the younger one, by about a minute. Where in hell are my duck boots? Where, goddamn it? Not under the bed, where they should be. Or on the back porch, where I left them last weekend. This rental house, the one I rented when AmHull sent Arthur to live in San Diego, it was a three-story dump but had nice furniture. It needed fixing up. In our world of ship's insurance this house was a freakin' shipwreck.

Old as Maine, that's how they talk up here. It seems like everything and everyone is old here. This house hides my duck boots pretty good, though, I'll give it that. Besides, who wants to live on Brighton Lane anyhow? Not on the water, not in the woods—what good is it? Arthur says Portland, down home Maine, is the state where "life is the way it ought to be." At least it was until fumbucking AmHull sent Arthur out west and left me here to look for my duck boots.

"Fumbucking AmHull," I said to no one in particular.

"Whad' you say, love?" Rosie answered.

When she moved in here with me two weeks ago, I was over-the-top happy. Not wanting to screw it up, but being the cautious twin, I asked, "Why, Babe? How'd I get so lucky as to snag you?"

"'Cause you need me, that's why. You're the spittin' image of your brother, who I've never seen. But everyone says you are. He's coming home next week; I want to be here when he walks in. Surprise, twin brother, I snagged Martin, I'm gonna say the second he walks in. Now, whad' you lose? Fuck boots?"

"Duck boots. Arthur hates 'em. I wear 'em cause he don't. Christ, my brother probably took 'em to San Diego. Just to needle me, I suppose. No ducks out there. Hell, they don't even have ponds, much less ducks. But lacoponds never bothered him."

"Lack-o-ponds? That's got to be another one of those secret words you and your twin have, right? When are you going to give me a dictionary of Cheshire twin talk? Or is it an oral language known only to the twin of you? Damn, you've got me making up words now. Is it your boots you want, or is it AmHull that you're still cussing?"

Rosie's mighty easy on the eyes. I leaned into the refrigerator, looking for a cold beer, against the back wall past the yogurt, soymilk, and a bag full of arugula big enough to smother a cat.

"You think the duck boots are in there, or are you looking for your brother?"

She clicked on the overhead light, a 150-watt bare bulb hanging from a twisted piece of electrical cord that was as old as the house. This tiny woman had an irritating way of asking the right question.

"Damn straight, nothing's where it's supposed to be. I'm pissed at AmHull. My duck boots are gone, my brother is gone, and my job is about as secure as clam sand, and it's all their shitty fault. But I'm working on getting even. Besides, my boots will probably show up around the time Arthur walks in here Friday night."

"Dandy, love, I know you'll get even. What time Friday night?"

"Eight maybe? His flight gets in about seven twenty. He'll be dry and thirsty. Been eating San Diego string beans and tofu and the like—he'll want down home Maine lobsta and icy cold Sam Adams beer. How about Sweeties? You can meet us there. We'll down a few, and you can check him out in person. He's different in person. You've been talking to him on the phone, but you gotta see him to believe him, so they say. As I been telling you, know me—know my brother."

"Seen my extra book bag while you've been searching for the boots? I need it for class tonight."

"No, maybe my boots are in your bag. Maybe I'm in the bag."

I found a beer and offered her one. She said no thanks and closed her book. Said she'd help with the duck boot search. A month ago, Rosie was living up north in Augusta trying to shake the last lingering bit of mourning over the death of her husband—which happened two years ago. She'd mourned for too long. She said I was good for her, but that still didn't explain moving in with a man she hardly knew. What was she thinking?

"Here they are, down under the mud shelf. Now, where do you suppose my other book bag is?"

As I watched her walk up the stairs, I could not believe my luck. She was a dream come true for me. Of course, I was still flabbergasted that she'd move in after knowing me for such a short time, and not knowing my brother at all. How could she know me without knowing my brother? I showed her some pictures of me and him together, and two of him by himself, one up at the fishing camp, and another standing next to some big statute in Boston, when we went down there last year for a Sox game.

"Yeah, you look alike. But you're from Maine. Everyone in Maine looks pretty much alike. Lots of inbreeding up here," she said.

She's right. New people didn't move here all that much. Old families stuck with Maine like the statues on Easter Island. A look-alike mystery. Mainers were born here, grew up, married, or sometimes not, and had babies with other Mainers. It made for a lot of blue-eyed, ruddy faced, wholesome-looking people like Arthur and me; strong bones, in various sizes, round eyes, generally well-spaced, and flat foreheads, showcasing light to dusty dark hair. Maine women never dyed their hair. Dying away the gray was fine for Boston, but in Maine, well, the natural look was the only look. That's the way it's always been. That's the way it'll stay. It's the way things ought to be. It says that in the Maine chamber of commerce.

Except for Rosie. Blond to the bone, with one dyed black streak down the right side. Get that? She dyed one little streak black as coal. Big green eyes, an untroubled brow, two dimples in her left cheek, one in the right. "That's where I smile," she explained.

Oh, and not all that big boned, either. Little, like I said, but wiry, like a slinky, and always in motion. She could outrun, outthink, and make me holler uncle if you know what I mean. And she liked tickling.

New Hampshire across the harbor is different. They have a law against tickling. They are straight sticks, those New Hamps. But Rosie, who was born down in Foyes Corner, ain't no straight stick, like everyone else down there. She has this long, convoluted story about living there twenty-two years, then a year in Florida, then back up to Augusta, our fair capital, then Bangor, and now here.

"Searching for a hum," she said.

"Wait till you meet Arthur. We'll hum you, Babe."

"Yeah, wait. That's what they all say. Tell me again, what are mirror twins?" she asked.

"We're monozygotic twins, the result of the union of one egg and one sperm, Babe," I answered, settling into her office chair and holding the too-damn-hot coffee she'd mixed with two hands.

"Do you guys feel the same? I don't mean like emotions and stuff; I mean does your skin feel like his, and does he have knots on the top of his head like you do?"

"No, my skin feels like liquid bananas and his feels like tree bark. Are you crazy or what? Those are not knots on my head, they are scars from getting banged on, which is, none of your business about who did the banging. Don't go there."

Come Friday night, she'd find out what Arthur felt like. He'd hug her like a lamppost in a blizzard, and he'd whisker her face while twirling her around the floor in Sweeties. No doubt he'd get a boner from that hug. I did almost every time we hugged. I'd known her for a month now, and she was a month-long hard on.

DR. SOCORRO and ARTHUR

Sure Doc, you wanna know about when I met Martin's girl, Rosie? Figured you'd get around to that. But she was always Martin's girl, never mine, you gotta remember that. And take good notes in your little lab book. It's complicated.

All the way from San Diego to Portland, rerouted through Pittsburgh, I thought about meeting her. Rosie, Martin's latest bootie, sounded hanbo to the max. We'd always shared even the smallest details of our love lives—Rosie would be no exception. Two things, maybe three stood out. He liked her. He respected her. And he loved sleeping with her.

High-class babe. Bamber, he called her.

The door from the Boeing 770 opened into a round tube connecting the plane to the terminal—Portland International. As I moved through the crowd, past the slow ones, past the security gate and passengers coming into the gate area, I kept thinking about Rosie. Strange. I'd seen pictures and we'd talked on the phone. Kidding around stuff. You know that, right? No one in the crowd paid any attention to me, or to Martin, standing there on the other side of the security area. Not until we grabbed one another and jumped up and down like idiots. Then people did the usual double take.

My travel clothes, picked out in San Diego nine hours ago, matched Martin's picked out two hours ago at the Brighton Lane house. For me, khaki pants, a blue cotton button-down, leather jacket with buttons, not zippers. Martin's cotton twill pants were different but looked the same. His blue cotton button-down was mine. Came from the same store. It might have been his. As we walked down the painted concrete floor, up the little escalator to baggage, we stopped at the men's room door.

"Back in one," I quipped, sorta California dude style.

"Be here when you are," he bounced back. Life was good again.

As we passed the glass-covered signs on the walls of the tunnel, headed for baggage, our mirror images bounced off the glass back and forth. Cheshire boys must of all had stick-out chins, thin noses, and ears tucked in tight. We weighed around 175 but were always within three pounds of one another. Diets don't matter. Somehow, without trying, we both went on moderate fast-food binges. Gained five or six pounds. Then, just as fast, we lost it. Fat gram destiny? Dunno.

Martin carried my gym bag, with his left hand, like always. I carried my computer bag, and a paper sack with black jellybeans, and gum with my right hand. That was the thing about us. Me right-handed. Martin left-handed. Martin wrote like a lefty. He'd pretty much trained himself to be ambidextrous in other things, but he couldn't shake the left-handed style of writing. I figured it was because he was second in line in the birth canal. Right was right. I wrote right-handed like everyone else I knew, except for Martin.

"So, how's the booty, buddy? Bamber, I bet," I said, passing by the rental car desks. One clerk, a tall blonde with big teeth, huge lips, and a come-get-me grin, gave us a peace sign.

Walking on to the baggage carousel, we got the usual looks. Twins, aren't they? Always on their faces. "Nice to be home, Bud," I said.

"Twice as nice," he echoed. Indistinguishable looks, indecipherable language. Bamber was one of our first words—we used it interchangeably with good, better, and best—always in context. Bamber meant *best* when we intended it that way. Alternatively, if whoever used it said it in a way that implied merely "good" that was the way we took it. Hard to explain, yes; but easy for us.

We got to the parking lot. Dumped my bag in the back of Martin's beat-to-death Ford Explorer. Buckling up, I asked, "So, what's she like down deep inside—you said she had a sweet pair, but you stopped describing her at chest level. You never told me how she was below the belly button. Is she tight?"

Martin squinted a little. Unusual for him. Took his time.

"Hey, why are you focusing on Rosie? I thought you'd want to talk about Alice Blue Gown. She has been bugging me lately about you, like when you're comin' back and all that—what you got going with Alice that I don't know about?"

"Nada, man. Marcella's all I can handle. What'd Alice Blue Gown say?"

Martin smiled and ignored my question as we headed off the short freeway, down the ramp to Sweeties Bar & Grill.

Rosie had steeled herself for what she felt would be both a shock and a pleasure—seeing two of Martin. She'd spent a half-hour with her make-up, then more picking out the right silk blouse, off-white slacks, and shoes to match. Her auburn hair made most colors look brighter, but the mauve blouse shimmered in the subdued lighting in Sweeties. Her unbuttoned top-two buttons showed a faint image of a maroon lace bra. The rope belt snuggled tightly around her small waist made her long legs look longer. Big surprise. Those legs. Nothing Martin had said prepared me for those beauties. Long legs were his weakness. He'd made some foolish but memorable mistakes with women who had long legs. Marcella's legs were medium long, but Rosie's were by-God l-o-n-g.

Rosie got to Sweeties before they did, found an empty bar-stool, sipped on a pint of Guinness, and fixed a steady watch on the front door, about twenty feet from her end of the bar. As the boys, as she'd already begun to think about us, pushed through the small crowd at the door, Martin pointed at her. Too late. I spotted her by the look on her face. A big girl smile, but more than that. Like most people, she did a double take at seeing absolutely identical twins. But unlike most people, it seemed to delight her. Rosie's lower jaw dropped a little, and she moved forward on the bar stool but seemed stuck to it. Like a video on pause, she was caught on hold. Not in focus. Not out.

Then, as if on rewind, her mouth flew open. Arching her eyebrows, a grin spread from one dangling earring to the other. You could all but see it on her face. She couldn't tell. Who do I kiss, and who do I shake hands with?

"Hey Babe, did you get us a table?" I said, as I encircled her waist and kissed her lightly on the lips.

"No," she said, looking behind me at the man awkwardly holding out his hand to her. A quick look of disapproval took over as she waited for Martin's introduction of his twin brother. Instead, the man took her hand somewhat formally and said, "Rosie, I know you only just met Arthur, but don't get in the habit of kissing him, and shaking my hand. You'll diminish my self-confidence and boost his."

Hide and Be. Worked again. Just like always. Rosie had no idea that she was part of the game or that she was about to become the best game we'd ever played. She was hugely pissed. She knew that she'd made a small fool of herself in mistaking me for him—but she also suspected this was likely to happen sooner or later. It never occurred to her we would try to fool her before she could do it to herself.

She recovered nicely. "Martin, is that you? Arthur, is that you? Who gives a shit, let's get a table, and you two juveniles can sort yourselves out over lobsta and sweet potatoes. I'm going to the ladies' room where grown women are not subjected to pranks," she said, pointing a fire-engine-red fingernail at Arthur.

Turning sideways to Martin, she added, "Or pricks."

DAMARISCOTTA RIVER—SOUTH BRISTOL, MAINE—THREE MONTHS AGO

Martin drove his old beater of a truck from the Brighton Avenue house in Portland to our fishing camp on the Damariscotta. He unlocked the boat house while I hosed down the ramp and winched the landlines down to the river's edge. He spotted a new hornet's nest up under the eave; I flushed it. Then we launched the boat together, like always. It had this little rail thing, and with the little electric motor at the top of the ramp, the boat slid down and into the river like a sluice. We stored the rods, snugged the bait box, popped two beers, and motored downriver.

"So, what's going on in the accounting room at AmHull, Martin? Is that where you are hatching this secret get-even plan for us?"

"It's not the accounting room, Bud, it's the accounting department. Jeez, you've been away from Harold Hull too long. You're forgetting his piss-ant insistence on how things look—as versus how they really are."

Mimicking Harold's New England baritone, sounding proper as hell, Martin said, "AmHull has a by-God accounting department—don't you dare minimize it by calling it a room. But I'll forgive you, considering . . ."

"Cut the copycat, Martin, you just ain't got the voice for it. You can mimic my voice—hell, you do it better than me. Tell me bout this plan. The one you been spoon-feeding to me on the phone for three weeks. Give it up, bub."

"Ah, do I ever have a plan. I've been dying to tell you about it. Little skimming. Little cream scraped off the top of the AmHull coffee pot once, twice, a week."

"What coffee pot, Martin—God, you're becoming obtuse in your old age."

"We age together, Bud, so be careful what you say about me—I'm your mirror. I mean the coffeepot that perks up those dandy little premium checks three times a week. I've figured out a way to dilute the coffee just a little bit—it's simple. We move 10 percent of some premium checks from AmHull's bank account to ours. I cook the accounts receivable ledger to match the accounts payable ledger. Hell, man. It's Hide and Be the Money. Hanbo to the max. Remember?"

Two hours later, four medium-size fish in the tank, and . . . "Watch it! Shit, Martin, you almost hit the buoy—you better back off on the throttle, or the beer—the combination is gonna get us wet."

I veered back out into the widest part of the river as we watched some weather come up from the northeast. Maine weather. Slate gray clouds bunched up, blowing down on us. Rain in the air. Temperature dropping. Zip-up time.

An icy spray sprouted over the bow. Sucking on salty Atlantic air was not the homecoming I had in mind. Sky closed in. Waves got choppy. White caps downriver. Yeah, Marty was driving—one hand on the rudder, the other wrapped around a beer. Been on the river for about two hours, maybe four beers, coudda been five. Christ, I don't know.

Our twenty-six-foot Pemaquid open launch was drawing maybe two feet of water. Middle of the day fishing never was good.

Martin loved to talk about Rosie Anderson, his new squeeze. Chapter and verse; everything from brainpower, manners, good judgment, interests, habits, quirks, preferred sexual positions, foreplay preferences, family history, and, well, you get the picture. As I pieced it together, she had no idea about Martin's Hide-and-Be-the-Money plan—or anything about AmHull's splitting us up. Bastards.

"You're gonna love it, Bud, it's get even time with AmHull. And Rosie, man, you're gonna love her." He popped the tab on another Sam Adams.

"Actually, I have been beside myself—no pun intended—in planning this. Here's the deal—but it's a little complicated, so why don't you take the rudder, and I'll warm up with a cold beer. But watch your head, we are getting close to those damn out-rocks. See 'em? Wind pushing hard to starboard."

Bored with beer, Rosie stories, and fishing, I switched seats, grabbed the rudder, and angled her into the wind. Right, Martin was the better boat driver, particularly in weather, but we were only about two miles from the Cheshire Dock. As Martin settled on the mid-boat oar-seat, his left foot hooked on a life vest strap under the seat. Neither of us wore the damn things, even in weather, once we got close to camp. Kicking the bloody thing back under the seat, he went back to his Hide-and-Be-the-Money story.

"Fuck AmHull's auditors. They ain't gonna get it either. Remember, I'm the only one with both ends of the spreadsheet. Premium in—premium out—long as they balance—nobody's gonna know, not even Alice Blue Gown. What a ditz she is."

Looking to port, and reaching for the padded seat cushion, I felt the boat dip hard to starboard.

"Martin, what the . . ."

He never said a word.

Sickening sound—the aluminum bottom of the boat grinding on slick, barely submerged granite. Bow lurching up high in front. Bang, bang, slamming back down. Rudder flew out of my hand. I was hanging on by the rope tiedown closest to me. But the upswing of the bow wrenched my shoulder then it got worse. The ice chest flew back at me, along with the bait bucket. Both knocked me back to the stern almost into Martin. 'Cept he wasn't there. I was alone in the boat.

How long? Hell I know.

What? Oh, yeah—backed up, slid back to the stern bench, grabbed the rudder, and swung to port. Nothing there.

Why? Cause the propeller and drive shaft were up and all the way out of the water. That's why. Slammed down a second time, leaning 40 degrees to starboard. Now drifting back out into the current, but engine still pulling. Slipped her into full throttle, spinning, squealing, boiling water. Then, nothing. Engine died. Couldn't believe it. Just dead. Stalled in foaming water.

Martin gone.

How in fuck? The last I saw of him was he'd leaned over the starboard side for something. I don't know what. Right when the bow shot up, hung in the salt air, and then came crashing back down. Martin went out—out and over the starboard side—facing the middle of the river. It wasn't dark yet, but the sun was down. Light fading fast. I could see Martin for a second in the water, right there next to the boat. Pulled and pulled the freakin' engine cord. Rip it—set the idle—pull again, more throttle—pull, pull. Drifting back out into the outgoing tide. Finally, heard the engine sputter, then the caught-fire sound. Throttled back, stabilized idle, looked at his seat. Nothing. He was gone.

We were taking on water up front.

"Fuckin rock, fucking, piss, goddamn rock. Martin, where are you, come up dammit! Come up right now!"

Maybe Martin was really hurt—not just thrown overboard, but really hurt. Could he swim? Yeah, a little. You didn't really swim in Maine—not like they do in San Diego. You jump in on purpose. We stay in the damn boat. Except for this once. Now that I had ahold of the rudder, I put the engine in neutral and stopped the downriver drift.

We weren't still on the submerged granite shelf, maybe ten to twelve feet from the tree-lined bank. Grabbed an oar. Tried to change position while at the same time looking ahead, and all around, corkscrew-like, for Martin.

Gagging on vomit, I almost quit breathing, but not really. Hard to remember.

Where was Martin?

Like a giant gas mask plastered on my face. Sucking all the air out of me.

"Martin? . . . Hey, Martin. You answer right goddamn now, Martin!"

I don't know how many times. He never answered. I screamed his name. Begged him, cussed him. Damned him. Me too. All the while trying to keep the stupid boat from moving back out into the current or crashing again up onto the submerged granite shelf. Ten feet from the bank. Throttling down to idle, looking, looking all around. Three-hundred and sixty degrees—no Martin.

Upriver—no, that was stupid. He had to be down river, with the current, didn't he? Tide's going out. He's downriver. Right? Has to be.

A fog, wispy, settling. Sound sucking up into fog. How could he hear me in this? I couldn't hear my own words. Could he? Martin, I mean. Shaking my head. Not at Martin, at myself. I wanted to sit up, higher in the boat. Felt like a soaked rag in a bucket. Knees sank down into the well of the boat. They hurt, hand too. Holding on too tight. Jerking throttle did not help. Just cool it.

Oh shit, I do not want to find him. No, not that way. I mean I didn't want to be the *one* that found him. If someone else did, I could stop, stop screaming.

River water. Not blue any more. Almost black now. Heavy with foam, and oil slick. Bubbling, swirling around. Black coffee spilling over onto stove. Hissing. Burning. Me too. Everything started to hiss, all around me.

"Martin, goddamn you to hell, you come up, right now."

As stupid as it seemed later, at the time it seemed the only thing to do. I tied off the rudder. Throttle to idle. Quiet down. Think. Hit my chest to slow it down. Can't think because my heart is not in my chest anymore. Where? Up in my throat. No air, just spittle. And snot. And crust around my eyes. Who's screaming? Me? Do something! How deep? Maybe five or six feet of water, in the lee of the tidal flow. Wind? Ten—knot wind, gusting to twenty or more. But it seemed my only choice.

Reached under the bench for a life vest. Cork screwed arms to get the damn thing on.

What else? Oh, right. The anchor. Dropped it over the port side, heard the chain lock snap to. Over the port side, with my legs up, over the gunnel, then sliding down on my belly. Water rushing in. Everywhere. Jacket, boots. Too heavy. Too cold. No use, but no choice. Pushed out two feet from boat. Treading water, trying not to sink, no shelf here to gain traction.

Time? Dunno how many times. Less than an hour while I dog paddled back to the boat, around the stern, looking to shore. One hand on rail, like ice now, other arm flailing the water. Then, later. No, dammit, I don't know how long!

How long was I in the water? Your guess. I remember my knees wouldn't work. Couldn't even lift my arms up anymore. And gritting my teeth. Gums bleeding, skin aching. Shivering frantically. Made boat rock. Face bleeding, no not bleeding, just wet, but oily. Wiped it off. Made it worse. What? Oh, the only dry thing in the boat. We had an engine box, tools, stuff. And rags. Spilled the box into the bilge but held onto the eight-pack of boat rags. Kept blinking, wiping off snot, salt on lips. Eyes hurting.

Then. Maybe ten minutes later. I saw him.

Take a breath. Right. Hulking brown thing floating. Maybe ten yards away. Max, fifteen. Off the port side. Yeah, toward the shore. We were still facing upriver. On the lee side. Could it have been later? Dunno. Closer? No, maybe further in, but not closer. Yes. Once, I went swimming right there. Right there. Hulk not there then. Several times. Nothing there then, but damn sure there now.

Used oars to get the boat over there, one boat length maybe. He was right goddamn there. Same freakin submerged granite shelf that Martin had yelled at a few minutes ago—or was it a few hours? But different now.

Martin always wore duck boots. Ankle length. Waterproof. Solid rubber sole and half-upper. Leather top, but water-resistant. Socks? How'n hell I know. My left duck boot was stuck. Stupid, right? Stuck into the crack, you know a crevice thing. In the granite shelf. I already told you. A little bit—maybe six inches. Maybe a foot. But he was not just floating—he was stuck.

He didn't say anything. Not drowned. Just not talking. Floating side to side, ignoring me. Get in the fuckin boat! No answer. Bastard! Tried to hook onto him with the oar. No good. No, we did not have a hook. Net, yes, but so what? He seemed to want to stay there, in the water. Floating.

Now I think about it, sure, there was an explanation. There was this narrow crack in the granite, like I already said—a crevice. Maybe six, eight inches wide, but not the same along its length. Wider some places and not wide enough others. Dunno how long.

It grabbed and trapped him. Below the water line. Now with the tide going out, I could see better. His duck boot seemed locked into the split in the granite shelf on the port side of the river. Not him, just his boot. And only one leg, the left one. From the boat, I could reach down into the water. Could see it plain as day. Long time. Got boot untied. Not too hard. Simple, actually. Yanked his foot out of the fuckin duck boot. Drug him into our boat.

No, I don't know which side. Damn near swamped the boat. Might have drowned us both. Cussed the river. Myself. My brother. Lot of cussing going on. Him? Not moving the whole time.

We hadn't moved twenty feet, but I was out of strength, out of my mind, and ready to just float down to wherever fishermen go when they give up. The current was ready to take me, and I was ready to go. Arms decayed. My throat shriveled up like a half-inch rubber hose. No air in me. I sucked in more salt. I remember being thirsty. Yes, we had water in the boat, somewhere. My ears were ringing. But I couldn't hear him.

What? Was he there all the time? What do you mean, all the time? Damn right, I can swim. Swam all over the place. Already told you. He must have been hiding from me. No, that's not the game. It's what happened. No damn game.

Martin and the river looked alike. I couldn't tell the grey granite or the black water from him. They were twins, not him and me. Couldn't tell him from the river. Maybe he couldn't tell the boat from me. Everything blended into us. Me. The river. The fog. Us.

No, I wasn't paralyzed. Paralyzed? How do you mean that? Fear? Yeah sure, maybe. Terrorized is a better word. Write that one down. Terrorized, not paralyzed. I moved. I looked and looked. I hollered and hollered; I swam and hit the water with an oar. Paralyzed is a severed spinal cord. Martin was severed from me, but he was still my brother.

All in my head? Yeah. My brain is in my head. I was brain dead, at least for a while. I could move but couldn't think. Otherwise, I'd have found him. Right? That's what you're saying? Alive in the water—hell you asking? Hell yes! Somebody else—someone inside me—wrenched his body—water-soaked, flaccid, oily, 175-pounds. Up and over the side, into the belly of the boat.

Just laid there. Waddya you mean? I said I laid there beside him for a long, long time. At first, we slept. Everything will be OK. Let's just sleep a little bit. OK. No, not dead. Not dead because I could feel his body moving. Mine? No, mine was definitely not moving. Breathing? Maybe not later, but at first, yes. While we slept in the boat, I breathed in, and he breathed out. His breath was mine. I was alive—so he must be too.

Compute? Think it through? Then or later, when we got to the camp. There. I dunno. I didn't accept, I didn't do anything— I laid there, in the bilge, in that black oily water, holding him, us, tight. It seemed the most important thing at the time—just hold on, I told us. Later, maybe an hour, I don't know, it struck me. Feel for a pulse. On me first, then on Martin. I had one— really big pulse—in my brain, and chest, and feet too. But he didn't. No, ma'am, doctor or whatever n' hell you are. No pulse for Martin. I shoulda let him use mine.

Yeah, we took boat safety courses. He would have already been giving me CPR, if I'd gotten thrown overboard. I knew that. But at the time, no working brains. You know?

Martin wasn't dead. He couldn't be, not as long as I was alive. We used to trade places all the time. I'd be him, he'd be me, who knew? Who cared? I never before wanted to take my brother's place as much as I did then. For the first time in my life, I wanted nothing. I didn't want to exist. I wanted to die and have Martin live. It was that simple—but this time I couldn't just hide and let Martin be. Lying there in that boat, I came to it—or at least I talked myself into it—Martin would somehow "be" again. As odd as it sounds now, I slept some more. Dreamt a little.

CHAPTER TWO
WHO AM I?

I don't know why, but the guards would not take me to Dr. Socorro's office for a week and a half. Not even Officer Martinez. We need her, I told him.

"You ain't going," he said.

"Why?"

"Fuck it man, I get a take-over order, I take you. I don't, you stay here."

But then, the next day, he took me to her office.

"Doc, got any ideas for me? Here's one—call the judge. Call the morgue. Bang my head against the bars. Wait. Already did that. Right. Nothing works."

The rest of the story? You serious? Didn't believe the first part, so tell me why I should keep talking. Well, that's a point. You write it down—I talk—then you either believe me, or you don't.

OK, here goes. The river. I'm driving our boat back upriver. I'm dead. OK, Martin's dead. Same thing. Only black sky now. Full dark straight up. Straight down. The water in the bottom of the boat was greasy, mixed gas, salt water, rainwater. Fluids.

Maybe piss too. Empty beer cans floating. Bait box overturned. Fish? Can't remember. But I remember the toolbox. And screaming. Seems like I wet myself some time ago.

No, I did not want to get up. The boat was lodged in the rocks. Safe from the tidal flow, ebbing out. Safe from drowning. Me. Not him. He already drowned. What difference did it make if we just stayed there forever? Wanted to. Come to think of it, I wish I had stayed there. Well, OK, not right there. But I coudda pulled the anchor and let the tide do its work. Out into the current. Down to the sea. The boat would have righted itself, stern to sea. Just two miles. Easy to slip over the side, grab Martin, and let us both float. On the top at first. Then wherever drowned people go. Good thing is they never come back. Why hide in the boat? Why not be in the sea? Why didn't I think of that?

Choices? Yeah, sure. Back downriver to Boothbay Harbor, and the coast-guard station. Brain struck, Martin struck, boat struck, hey here's a thought I didn't think of then—why not just be an anchor, like Martin? He went over the side like an anchor without a chain. I should have been the chain. There was one in the bottom of the boat. Anchors away instead of anchor away—get it, Doc? But no, I pissed around trying to get unstuck. The boat was stuck, Martin too. Boat too. Why not me? Got to unstick to decide anything, I thought. The boat's nose turned upriver. The tide headed out—down river. Which way? Pulled the anchor. Ripped the engine and eased off idle to spin the screw. Settled on the wet seat. Wetter than me. Or Martin. This way I could not see his face. Headed for the Cheshire Dock, I guess. Not really a decision, more a direction.

Boat rocking side to side and felt good. Real good. Helped with my shaking. What's the plan? Did I have one? Sure. It's only two and a half miles. No one else around. I knew for damn sure I could make it there. Then what? Well, that can wait, can't it?

Muck, bilge water, Martin's blood. All pooling. So, I looked upriver. Funny thing about that blood. His blood. I'd seen blood before, several times. It was always black, never red. But now, the blood from Martin's head was red, at first, as it slowly seeped out, then turned black when it hit the bilge in the bottom of the boat. Propped his head up with my life vest. Got blood all over that too. It's OK. We always share. Blood. Lives.

Why am I yelling? The blood! Not red anymore. Black as coal. I already told you that. It seemed outrageous at the time. And besides, it was a pool, not just spilled blood, but pools of it. No, it did not smell. But the river smells, salt, trees, seabirds, and the damn boat itself. It all smelled except for the blood. I thought the blood meant that he was not dead. Dead men don't bleed. Drowned does not bleed. But if he's not dead, he couldn't have drowned. But, he bled, and bled, and bled, and I could see all that blood, and none of it was mine.

Was he dead? I cursed myself for asking—so I just said it. But I'm not mad at you. Only me. Yes, you murdering bastard, I said. He is. But he didn't drown; he bled to death. He bled to death because his own worthless fuck of a brother didn't pull him out of the water right away. Right when he went over the starboard side. Right when I should have been looking but was fucking with the boat, trying to hold on myself, not taking care of my brother.

What could I have done? Well, how about sticking a simple rag on his head when I had the chance to, right there when I saw him just over the edge of the boat?

Then the pier. Our pier. The Cheshire Dock. Solid posts, strong planks. Not rotting. We kept it that way. Creosote, tar, spar wax. The Cheshire Dock. We owned it. Was our only anchor. We liked it because no one else was there. But not now. Now someone should have been there. The police. The Coast Guard. Somebody. I felt like a shell. Stiff. With moss or seaweed strung on me. Why? How would I know, then or now?

But that shell saved me. I know that now. I curled up inside the shell. Martin was the shell. Can you understand that? In a way that I'd practiced for years. My whole life, really. I could think like him. Like Martin. No, not like Martin—as Martin. No, Arthur, it's not your fault, you keep saying. It's my dumb shit fault for downing one beer too many—slows the reflexes, you know. I can't remember why I leaned over the side. Does it matter now? Maybe something I saw. Or heard. Dunno. I leaned over the side when the boat hit the shelf. Solid granite. Wood slides through water. Granite crushes wood. We die.

No, you bastard. Not that simple. I didn't just die. I saw you—trying to find me. You tried to save me, but I was under the water for a minute there, and when I came up, you went the other way. I tried to call out. Mouth was full of water, or blood. Tasted cold. Probably water. But it tasted black. Did you know that black tastes different then red, or gray? My own fault. I think I told you that. Instead of spitting water out, I kept on tasting that black taste. Then it was too late. My fault, not yours.

Who's talking? Martin. To me. Like now I'm talking to you. Hide and Be. The game. Yeah, maybe. I thought maybe I was you, and that we were playing the game again, but I forgot who was who. So, I died. Not your fault, Bud. Take care of my booty, she's bamber.

What's that, Doc? Oh. We're done for the day. Same time next week, right?

"Doc, it's awful early in the morning, isn't it? How come you changed my 3:00 pm session this afternoon? I like those, after my nap and all. You know if you get me over here at 7:30 in the morning, the guards are jumpy, especially Martinez, he ain't had his chorizo yet, if you know what I mean. You don't. OK, don't matter. What's on the plate this morning? We gonna talk about formative years or what happened to Martin, or what?"

"Arthur, we had a good session on Friday, but I am unclear on what happened after you went to sleep in the boat. I know what happened before, you don't have to go into that. But take it from there. How did you get the boat back upriver? You were going upriver, right?"

"He told me. Martin. Not in words, you understand. But I was thinking his thoughts, there in the bottom of the boat. It was easy from then on. We went back to the dock and took it one step at a time from there. Take care of the boat, clean it out, put the stuff away, take care of Rosie, be me. That's what he told me to do."

I wanted Martin to be, and I would hide. No more kid stuff. Not the Jesus strap. This was real. We had to do what we had to do.

No change, Doc. Same day. Martin and I were one person. There weren't two of us—especially now. Finally, now. Only one of us. The river we loved for so long had finally done what we really wanted—Martin and me. It made us one, the one that everyone always thought we were anyhow. I quit calling his name, but I whispered mine to him. I swear he twitched. At the sound of my name. "Arthur, we are the same." Martin is alive because I am. I saved him.

The logistics? What logistics? Not hard. Took some time, that's all. Pulled Martin's body up out of the boat. Drug him into our boathouse. Cleaned up the boat in the dark. Him too. Used a gas lamp inside. It was the floorboards. See. Three hours digging a shallow grave below the floorboards of the boathouse. Somebody, a long time ago, filled in what was a basement, in the original boathouse. Probably to keep out the river at high tide from seeping in below the boathouse. Just fill dirt beneath the second set of floorboards.

"Two sets of floorboards, Arthur?" she asked. She'd been looking down at her pad the whole time. Writing like a machine. Like she was scared to look up, or I'd stop. Felt good to have someone listen to me, not Martin, me.

Right. Two sets of floorboards.

How deep? Maybe three, four feet. Two floors in the boat-house was a secret; just like us. Two of us. We were a secret until Mexico. Right, we'll get to that later. Two floors in our boathouse.

How'd I know? Martin told me. He found it when he pulled up a broken board. Gonna fix it. I guess.

Sun came up next morning. Surprised me. Hoped it wouldn't. No close neighbors on our side. West side of the river—two houses quarter mile down river. Not close enough to see but could hear them at night. Sometimes they party late. Bothers the frogs. And us. But it was quiet that Sunday morning. You live someplace quiet, Doc?

Right. No personal questions.

Had anybody looked they'd see only one twin. But, like always, which one? Nobody was around so far as I could see. But if they'd been there, they'd have seen me dressed in Martin's hand-washed, stove-dried clothes. Suppose no one bothered to look. Maine's not just quiet. It's private, ya know.

Folded up the iron cots. Used the electric winch and the overhead tow to haul the boat inside. Stopped 'er over the floor-boards, right over Martin. That's inside the boathouse, remember. But even if someone was standing on the road, looking at the open double doors, they couldn't tell it was me or my brother. Course they'd see only one. But that was normal too. One of us would hide and the other would be. Did it all the time. Had my clothes on by now—all washed and stove dried.

Closed up the house just like always. Nothing changed.

How'd I feel? You tell me. Not bad. Scared but OK. Racking my Martin brain—my side of his brain—for ways to carry it off.

Be Martin from now on. I was paying attention to him, not me. "Arthur, look at me, please," she said, cause I was over at the window then. Talking to the San Diego Bay, watching the birds fly away. A song, right? Remembering.

"Why don't you come back to your seat? I have a hard question for you. Tell me about your plan, after you moved here. How did you fool everyone in Portland. Didn't they miss Martin?"

Sure, I had a plan. Simple. Concentrate. Be him. Put on his skin. Felt like mine. Drove back to Portland for the first test. Told Rosie that Arthur drove up Bangor way. Gonna see an old girlfriend. That was the plan. No, no sex that night. I slept downstairs on the couch, oh no, didn't sleep, just kept thinking what we'd have for breakfast. That's not complicated, right?

Afternoon. Bout the same, Doc, thanks for asking. You? It's another clear day, the hundredth and something this year in San Diego. Tell me, you lived here long? Doesn't it get to you, perfect weather, every fricken' day? Right, sorry. But fricken' ain't cussing. Close, but you otta get out of here and visit the cells sometimes. You'd hear what fricken' means.

"All right, she said, but I'm not at all clear on why or when you moved from Portland to San Diego."

"Jeeze Louise. I told you about Harold Hull, the boss, right? About his worthless sons and how they hated Portland? I remember the first day he changed our lives forever—me and Martin's whole life—down the shitter that day."

"Mr. Cheshire, you've mentioned him, but you've never been clear about your brother staying in Maine and you moving out here to San Diego."

"OK, Doc. You gotta be patient with me. I hated the bastard, remember? I told you that already, but lemme try again.

"You know how someone's voice can drive you crazy? Well, I gotta tell you, Harold Hull's monologue was stupid. He insisted that we, me and Martin, had to help his boys add to our insurance business by opening an office on the West Coast. He said San Diego had a fine harbor, with splendid docking. He said the boys told him they had the same kind of fishing trade out there that we had in Portland. The boys had thought of everything, but they would need staff out there to start our West Coast franchise. He actually asked me and Martin if we agreed!

"No, we didn't. We said we're staying here, or we quit. We told him we quit. But listen to us? Hell, he care about us. His plan? It was never his. It was his clueless sons' plan. They hated him, Portland, the business, and everything about their lives. Those silver spoons were, I dunno, too small, I guess."

"What was their plan, Mr. Hull's sons?"

"They had no plan. It was a trick. His boys wanted to live in San Diego. That's all. Just play in a new yacht club, find some new West Coast booties, play with them, make somebody else do the work. Those snotty little bastards had it all and now wanted to mess up our lives so we'd be as screwed up as they were."

"Was the new business out here successful?"

"Mr. Hull was a good businessman, I guess, when it came to business. But with his boys, he was fumbucked. They were supposed to join the local boating organizations, the yacht club, the chamber of commerce, and network for hull coverage.

"Christ all mighty, I had to do the actual underwriting and, when the claims started coming in, he insisted, I would do the adjusting as well . . .

"I said hell no. Well, not 'hell' no. Just no. The boys were both employed by the company already, but they never learned about underwriting, claims adjusting, or office management. We could teach 'em, Harold Hull said. You and Martin. Martin stays here but you have to move to San Diego. If you need help, Martin can come out occasionally and give you a hand. Mr. Hull thought it would only take a few months to set up the office and get the business rolling. Hell, he knew! We could do that, he said, then in a few months, we could hire a clerical to sit the office, you know—one just like Alice. And the West Coast office would be all set."

"All right, Arthur, that helps me, but why didn't it work?"

"Because his precious boys insisted, they had to become part of the 'larger boating community in San Diego.' That's how they put it to him. He was too stupid to know they had no intention of working for a living."

"But," she said, "you went along with it—moved out here and ran the business without them, right?"

"Right, me *and* Martin did—we pulled a Hide and Be on him, on Alice, on everybody in Maine. I told him what if I go out there for, say six months to give them a good start? But Martin would have to come out there and work with me for at least one week every month. He would teach me all the underwriting, log-in procedures, and office stuff that he and Alice do here. And I would have to come back here, say one week a month, to help Martin take over the claims work here and get used to the outside sales reps, their problems, and all. We could be like a *transition team*."

Dr. Socorro shook her head and held up her hand for Arthur to stop talking while she wrote a long note. Then she asked, "Did Mr. Hull agree to start the business out here your way—you know, with you and Martin both coming back and forth from the West Coast?"

"He didn't like it. We didn't like it. But it was a truce. We should never have agreed; we should have quit. He knew it. So, that's how it started. Me here. Martin back home. The boys, total no-shows. They only came to the office down on lower Broadway two times in three months. Harold himself never even visited, although he got telephone reports and bills from the San Diego Yacht Club."

"All right, Arthur, why didn't your plan work? You went out there, rented an apartment and space in an office building.

Martin came out and helped, and you went back to Maine a few times. Right? Up until the boating accident?"

"No, that ain't right. It was just us doing here in San Diego what we did back home in Portland. We'd been doing both jobs, switching places for three years in Portland by then. Nobody could tell us apart and here's the thing—Harold didn't care which of us he was talking too. He didn't mind paying both of us and never knew that only one of us worked at a time. He was a dumb shit, and his boys didn't give a shit. They just wanted their monthly allowances deposited on time. The rest was for show. Martin and I named our San Diego job 'Unnerchucking.' One of us could hide, in plain sight as usual, and unnerchuck. The other twin, as the world thought of us, showed up one week out of the month, and 'be' the unnerchucker. Get it? Good. Now can we talk about me? For a change? That's it, Doc, take a note. Good."

"Arthur, thank you. You give good summaries, and they help me put all the pegs into the board. We've got a few more minutes, would you mind painting a word picture for me of how the office in Portland worked? You know, before Mr. Hull sent you out here?"

Dr. Socorro turned to a fresh page in her lab book. I gave her an earful.

"Sure. American Hull Insurance, started by Harold's grandfather, who was something important, I guess. What exactly do you want to know?"

While she didn't tell Arthur, Dr. Socorro used a few minutes of each session to test his reality. Was he grounded in the present and could he relate past events without wandering off in his mind? Could he stay in the present? She'd ask about recent events but tie them to his current reality.

"Tell me about Portland."

"You want the tourist version? Right, I'm into that. AmHull was at the corner of Commercial and High streets. In just under twelve minutes, across the Casco Bay Bridge, you can take your visitors to snap a shot of the Portland Head Light, photographed by every visitor since 1791, when George Washington personally ordered its construction. Unlike some of the bigger companies, AmHull, as Mr. Hull insisted that everyone call the agency his grandfather started, was on the second floor of a walk-up two blocks from Cus Ho Pier. Mr. Hull, known as Harold to a few, but 'Mister' to those who didn't really like him, was a duck. A sea duck but still a duck. He actually liked the play on words that AmHull stood for."

"Thank you, Arthur. Tell me about marine insurance. I don't know anything about that business."

"Sure, Doc. We sold marine insurance to family-owned fishing fleets in New England. What I mean is we underwrote and sold *hull* insurance, including cargo and salvage endorsements for over one hundred years. Hull insurance is the kind of coverage that attached to the ship itself, known as a 'hull' in the trade. The fact that Harold Hull's grandfather wrote hull coverage in the late 1800s gave him a double play on the family name."

"Good tourist version, Arthur, now tell me about a typical day in the Portland office, after the fishing boat accident."

"What for?" Arthur asked.

"Just so I can understand how your life in Portland was before you were arrested there and extradited here to California."

"OK, I'll start with our boss, Harold Hull. One day he stopped me in the hallway, not about business, but about his sons—the 'boys' he called them. He stopped me in the *dull hull* hallway. That's what we called it. He wanted to give me another chicken-shit lecture on how important he was to a company he inherited from his dad. So far, he had not quite managed to sink the company. He wanted news from San Diego, how things were 'shaping up' out there, you know."

'Martin, since the end of the month is nearly on us, be sure, will you, to have Arthur in the office first thing Saturday morning. I'm anxious to hear firsthand how things are shaping up out there in California. I get his reports, and I get phone calls from my sons, but I can't say I'm really on top of how we're doing out there.'

"No, sir, Arthur will not be in on Saturday morning. This is the end of the season, so we just have this last weekend to fish the shit out of the river. Arthur will fill you in Monday morning."

Harold Hull never cussed but loved gossip. Odd combination, I thought, but I took a little perverse pleasure dropping in a "bad" word, or two, just to get his goat. Old bastard should not have split us up by sending Arthur out to babysit his two worthless kids. Shit. Their foray, as he called it, into the marine insurance business in Southern California, was big-time stupid. Didn't Harold get it? Didn't he know those boys picked San Diego because it was the farthest harbor away from here? All the freakin' way across America. Just so they could get away from Portland and him. What a crock—a new branch office in San Diego? Yeah, right. Those boys had not sold a single policy and the branch had been open for four months. Fortunately, Harold paid little attention to little details, like how much money the office was losing. If he paid attention, he might stumble on to the fact that San Diego wasn't the only hole sucking his money down.

'Oh, dear. That's not what I wanted. I need Arthur's report on Saturday, not Monday. And by the way, will you be in all morning, or will you be out adjusting this afternoon?'

"In for a few, out for a few. Gone by five, just like always, Mr. Hull."

PORTLAND—AMHULL OFFICE—A YEAR AGO

"All right then, Martin, mind the books, and tell Alice as soon your brother Arthur gets here," Harold said, more over his shoulder than directly. Alice Blue Gown was to the front office what I was to the back. She the gatekeeper. I the gate closer. Harold liked everything tidy. Front and back, in an out, as though the office were some perpetual-motion machine. Tick-tock, tick-tock—Alice out front, me in the back. We had other clerks, mostly transient. Outside agents sold the policies, outside adjusters handled most claims. Out of sight, out of mind; no matter. Just let him know when Arthur was back. And Alice. Did she even know he was gone?

"Alice, my dear," I muttered, on my way past her desk, past her receptionist's mood, and past her squinty look, "I'm going to adjust a claim or two, and won't be back till after two, OK with you?"

"As if it mattered, Martin."

She was pretty, in a way. Prettier sitting down than standing up. Flat chested, square hips, but high cheekbones, and nearly flawless skin. Small black expensive glasses, a little jewelry, but not showy, made her the perfect gatekeeper. She answered the phones, made everybody's calendar work, knew about computers, and kept our Linksys network up. She could reboot, and restore the mail server, and our 1999 Blackberry Enterprise server. That alone made her indispensable, and we knew it.

"You think I'm just part of the furniture here. You ought to think about that. You'd be dead if I couldn't fix your computer and keep you connected to Arthur, out there in la la land. Other times you don't think of me at all. But you should know that nothing escapes my attention. I'm onto you—you're headed for *Sweeties*. Right? In the middle of the day? Tsk, tsk. Whatever will Mr. Hull think, when I tell on you?"

"Don't you dare, Alice, my dear. He won't believe you. Besides, you will have to introduce yourself as an employee here. That might not be in your best interest. Just cash the paycheck and hide here in plain sight. It's been working for three years, at this rate you will retire in a decade or two, and none of us will ever know."

Smoothing down my fall hat, I zipped through the double doors, and out into Portland, in all its bluster. Afternoons were for me what yard release was for prisoners. A time to breathe, loosen up stifled limbs, and plan an escape. Ocean air, squawking gulls, diving pelicans made a forty-five-minute walk through the docks a pleasure. I talked to deck hands, took notes about the nicks and bangs that all ships get, and filled out claim forms, damage estimates, and witness notes. Sure in hell beats my dreary mornings, playing underwriter, assessing coverage changes, premium ranges, and futzing around with policy endorsements so every policy is as incomprehensible as we can make it.

"Jimmy, my boy," I said, dropping three quarters down on the stack of papers at his news stand on the corner of Dock Street and Twentieth, "what's in?"

He slid the quarters off, looked at me through rummy eyes, and pushed forward the *Dockside News* and a Snickers bar. "Bout the same, Marty, cept for a new sixty-five-footer over there on Pier 12. You seen her yet? She's got a woman at the helm, so's I hear. Ain't seen her though. Been watchin'. You?"

Jimmy the newsboy, a Steady Eddy if there ever was one, sold papers, candy, cigs, and dirty books from under the counter. He was older than anyone around; gnarled like a coastal root pushed up out of a rocky crevice. Everybody liked him, but we avoided touching his hand. He was one of the few that still called me Marty. Once I thought asking him nice to call me Martin, but what the hell. He called my brother Marty too. So that worked. We liked it when we could hide as one another.

"Jimmy, no, I ain't seen her. Captain, you say? Well, there's a lot of 'em I hear. Just not around here. Tomorrow, I expect some skinny on her. You keep watch, you hear," I said, and walked down the oily cement toward Pier 12.

Every boat in the harbor was familiar. Two that were tied up at Pier 12, a coal barge and a sixty-five-footer sorely needing paint, had been here before. I don't know how many times. Her foredeck was busy, taking on cargo, the bridge was open, far as I could tell from fifty feet away, but saw no sign of a female captain, or the slightest hint of a female touch on that going-to-rust old bucket. Casco Bay was full of women doing all kinds of ship work; no doubt captaining too, just not out in the open where you could see them. No steam up, boilers quiet, so neither boat was headed out. Neither carried AmHull coverage. That's all I cared about.

It took me just over an hour to climb up the dock ramp onto them. Both had engine room damage. One broke boiler. The other with damaged bilge pumps and electrical shorts. What the hell kind of a job is this? Taking notes, not talking much; that's my idea of adjusting claims.

Sweet Alice Blue Gown pestered me when I got back four hours later. "How long did it take to duck out the back door of Sweeties, adjust two little claims, and slip back in, Martin?" At least she didn't call me Marty.

"How long were you watching, Alice?"

"Not watching you, Martin. But I get lunchtime too, ya know. Besides, Harold's looking for ya, you know? I told him just hold it, he's got engine rooms to visit. So, I guess you owe me, right Martin?"

"Thanks, Alice, you just keep a running tab on my bill, won't you?"

Harold was waiting outside his own double door. AmHull had two double doors: one in front for customers and one inside, for Mr. Hull. His office was not much bigger than the reception area, but those matching double doors were his thing. Soon as I headed down the hall his way, he crooked the first finger on his right hand, motioning me in, while his left fist gripped the brass handle like it was going to run away.

"Martin, where have you been? Step in, will you. I got a call from my boys."

The boys were always plural. Like he could never separate them, by name, or number. They had names but Harold never said Thorndyke, or Palmer. He just said boys.

"What's up with the boys, Mr. Hall?" I asked, as I scissored into his office.

"They say business is slow but picking up."

"So, picking up is not bad, right? I mean that sounds like they sold a policy right?"

"No, not exactly. But they are networking and getting a solid feel for AmHull's entry into the West Coast market. You know the boys, they are always optimistic, always marketing. But that's why I sent your brother out there, you know, to help the boys. Their eternal optimism and the way they meet people; sometimes doesn't get to the closing part of business. Arthur's a closer, isn't he? He's the one in your family that can tap the lid on the deal. There's one in every family, right?"

Now Harold was not what you call a mind reader. He was more of a mind ignorer. Carrying not one whit what I thought, he only wanted reassurance that Arthur, the closer in our family, was on his way back from the Pacific theater, to report on the war. He thought of marketing as a war. His boys, no-name runts, thought marketing was something they could sell to their dad.

We'd been with AmHull for four years. The company was still a sole proprietorship. As Harold put it, "My father didn't need a corporation, and neither do I."

Actually, he did, but he didn't know it. A corporation might have given him a lawyer, an accountant, maybe even an auditor. Had that been the case, he might not have made that arrogant decision to split up Arthur and me. What's he mean, "the closer in your family?" We closed more deals together than he could ever remember. We knew the agency business inside out; each of us covered the other's job, with Harold none the wiser. Harold thought Arthur was his underwriter, with some experience in office procedure. When he thought of me, he saw a bookkeeper, with some experience in the low-end parts of underwriting and claims. He probably suspected that we'd more or less cross-trained one another on our jobs, but he had no idea how interchangeable we were.

Leaving Harold's office, on the way back to mine, Alice's piercing little voice reached me, forty feet down the hall, "Martin, wait up, your favorite salesman, Rondo Short, is here."

Rondo was one of AmHull's five outside sales reps. Sales reps didn't like coming into the office—down time, they called it. Their world, pounding the docks, hitting the keyboard, and selling, selling, was what got them out of bed in the morning. They were what made AmHull, without any inside sales force, a huge profit maker. And Rondo knew it.

"Martin, how's tricks? Where's your bro, or are you the bro? Got a minute?"

I said sure, told him about Arthur's move to San Diego, chewed the fat for a while, and then he got to why he was here.

"Was down Portsmouth way two weeks ago. Talked to one of the Fontaine brothers. They got five boats now, you know. Wrote a policy on number five last year, right, you know that, don't you?"

"Sure, Rondo. Portsmouth. Fontaine brothers. Your gravy train, right, or should I say gravy boat?"

"Got it. Those guys know fish, they know boats, they know how to fish up a ton of money. But they don't know shit about insurance, which makes 'em just perfect for me. I know nothing about the fish business. And apparently, neither do you."

"Me? Who said I did? I know about dec pages, endorsements, and premiums. I don't sell policies, but I sure as hell check 'em.

Including Fontaine. What are you saying? A problem with their policies, endorsements, dec page problems, what?"

"Don't go all female on me, Martin. But we got a little problem with the Fontaine policies, that's all I mean."

"Shouldn't you be talking about policy stuff with Mr. Hull? He's the boss, remember?"

"Yeah, he is, but I got a feeling this is a problem I ought to be talking to you about first, OK?"

I looked at Rondo hard. What did he know? Saying something about Alice and her big ears, I got up, closed my door, and dug the Fontaine policy file out of a wooden cabinet that was over sixty years old. It creaked like eighty, but the drawers still slid out on command. Stepping back to the desk, I took a big breath, pulled out a note pad, clicked my Bic, and leaned back.

"What's on your mind, Rondo?"

"Seems like Fontaine Brothers got plenty of coverage; they are happy, I'm happy, premiums are good, my cut is good, but then there's this little oddity that I noticed when I was down Portsmouth way last week. I saw your brother Arthur down there; at least it looked like him, or you. I still get you guys mixed up, right? Anyhows, I was in Bruno's coffee shop. Your brother was coming out of the bank, like I said, sort of rushing-like. I thought he was in San Diego. That's what Harold told us in an email a month ago. But then it hit me. I don't know Arthur from you. So maybe I got it ass backwards. Was you down there, last week, or did I see somebody looks like the two of you?"

Alice Blue Gown, front office queen, opened the mail, futzed with the files, and did Harold's bidding. Her view of the front door—through the looking glass—and out onto Water Street, was the envy of all who happened to be stuck further back, all the way to my domain. A 125-year-old Hemlock desk, always neat and tidy, fronted her, with its seemingly endless supply of drawers, moldings, and flat space, was as much throne as it was workspace. With ears like a red-tail fox, nothing said, except behind closed doors, was a secret from her. And her tidy little hand, wrapped around a fountain pen that never lacked ink, logged every entrance and exit, by the minute. It was an old habit, started by Harold's grandfather, who insisted, so we're told, on knowing exactly who came in, who went out, and how long they were here. Alice was gate-keeper, note taker, and chief tattletale. Harold may not have liked Alice all that much, but he trusted her log. Hell, if it said he had not come in when he actually did, he'd take the log's word over his own.

The occasional policyholder or tradesman hawking office supplies all said she was pretty, in a mousey sort of way. Her signature feature, the thing that defined her character, was an endless supply of blueprint dresses in various shades of blue. She did not always look the same, but she did, you know what I mean? Arthur gave her that name, "Alice Blue Gown." She knew it, blamed him for it, and looked down her nose at him. Me, she gave a bad time, but Arthur, she had it in for him. Or maybe she had a thing for him. Who knows?

"Where ya been, Martin? I logged you out two hours and ten ago; mind telling me, just for the log, you know?"

"Nah," I said, "just log me here. Besides, we don't get paid by the hour, so what's to log?"

"Logs tell more than time, Martin; they tell fortunes too."

I bantered with her a little more, but then escaped when a fix-the-printer guy saved me. Nudging his way between me and the big front desk, it seemed like he was here for the first time. Alice questioned his *bona fides* before she let him even look at her printer. Jeez, it ain't the company jewels, I thought as I headed on back to my little space.

PORTLAND, SEVEN YEARS AGO

"Slow down, Martin, you're gonna kill us—watch the road. Dammit. You know this road is curvy. Don't do that!"

"Va va voom, Arthur! Lighten up, Bud, this is our birthday, we're eighteen today, Bud—the big one eight. And we're legal now—we can buy and drink all the 3.1 beer we can hold. So, slide another Pabst Blue Ribbon over and I'll tell you a . . ."

"Legal my ass. You're not getting another beer from me, or anyone else. I told you. Let me drive. Now pull over, damn it, before some trooper sees you sliding all over the road like it was goose shit. Then you jam the pedal to the metal just so you can smash the brake pedal like it was a snake after you. Watch out, damn it, can't you see—oh shit, the brakes on this bucket are like water. I said slow down. Now."

"Don't piss your pants, Arthur. I'm slowing down. Hate to tell you this, Bud, but we got 5.0 behind us—those are red lights back there. Oh, shit. Hide and Be, Bud. That's a trooper for sure back there—I'm going to turn into Forest Grove—see it—right up there on our right—half a block—there, do you see it on the right? When I swing past the big elm, he won't see us for a few seconds. I'll slam on the brakes, and you jump over here, and sit behind the wheel, you're sober—you dumb shit, dumb but sober."

"I can't, Martin. He'll see us. Besides, I had a beer too, he'll smell it and . . ."

"Just do it, Bud, my ass is grass if you don't. One stinking beer don't make you DUI. I've had four. They'll nail my ass for sure—come on, Bud, be me—this time it's important."

DR. SOCORRO

Officer Martinez deposited Arthur on the bench outside Dr. Socorro's office. "Hold yourself, right here, Cheshire, I wanna talk to my bud over there, with his take-over," he said, pointing to a guard pushing and a new inmate by the elbow. The newbie was old with a limp and a runny nose.

"I'll just be a minute or two. Jones owes me some bucks on the Chargers game yesterday. You bet on those games, Cheshire? No, I didn't think so. Not your game, right?"

While Martinez was collecting his winnings, Arthur used the time to smell the air. There was an open-barred window on the far end of the room, and although there were two dozen smelly inmates and five or six guards, the air was sea air. Not like in the cell blocks—used human air there. He remembered an early morning phone call from Martin just three months ago.

"Hey, Bud, glad to see you're up so early in the morning. Is it dawn out there yet?"

We talked about sleeping girls. Man, Rosie can sleep, he said. Marcella, no. She's not a sleeper. She's always half-awake. Like a fox. Always ready to pounce or run.

"Hey yourself, Bud, what needs saying before even the damn seals are up out here?"

"Well, I'm gonna lay it on old Harold this morning, that needs saying."

"Lay what on him?"

"Here's the scoop, Bud. I saved his ass this morning while you were fast asleep mismanaging the way-the-hell-out-there San Diego branch of this chicken shit company. It's part of my Hide and Be the Money scam. Ain't you interested?"

"No way. I resemble that remark. I'm the loyal twin. Remember? I never sleep. Why would you go out of your way to save his ass, miserable as it is?"

"Arthur, my man, you speak some truth when you say you *lie awake*. You lie awake and you lie in your sleep. You lie even when you try to tell the truth. That's what I love about you—you lie to the world, but never to me. Your focus on lying is phenomenal.

Speaking of focused, are you still focusing on Marcella nightly? And every other lunch hour? How's your sperm count, Bud, any drop there yet?"

Arthur jolted when Officer Martinez poked him with his baton and told him not to slump down like he was sick or something. Gotta keep your head up, dude, he said, as he headed back across the waiting room to the other guard. Arthur closed his eyes to narrow slits, tugged his collar up, and slid back into his memory about that conversation with Martin—the only one about his scamming AmHull.

"Martin, you are straying from the scam story. I need coffee. It really is still dark here, on the bottom of the United States of America.

"OK, Bud, here's the deal. You remember that new account we got last spring, that five-boat fishing fleet steaming out of Portsmouth? A Russian family owns it now. Name of Fontaine— don't sound Russian to me, but Bobby Bellemear—whose dad used to own four of those boats—told me the new owners were from Russia or maybe it was Ukraine. Same difference, right? Anyhow, this family came over to the US in the last century, man. Well, it turns out that all is not well financially, if you know what I mean. They tried a little creative accounting by claiming two docking accidents on two different boats. I got the claims forms in the mail two weeks ago. So-called fumbucking docking accidents were three days apart. Funny thing, though. The dollar losses were within pennies of each other. Odd, don't you think? How could they be so close in amount but still be on different boats, in different ports, and on two different dates?"

Arthur tried to shake himself into paying attention to his brother's zero-dark-fifty phone call. "Well, looking odd and proving odd are two different things, bro. What did you do, go to the port, and inspect the mooring posts for recent paint smears?"

"No way, Martin. The ports are in a part of the Atlantic that I don't care to visit, even to discover fraud against our chicken-shit employer. I just called the port authority in both ports. They checked the harbor logs. Confirmed the berthing times and gave me pier-docking numbers for each boat. Turns out that the dumb shits thought I was such a dumb shit that I would not notice identical docking numbers, but the berth times were an hour apart. And get this. The harbor log in Portsmouth shows one of those boats in dry-dock refitting an engine the day before the claimed date of loss. So, genius twin, how could it steam north to St. John, New Brunswick, in thirteen hours, just in time to run into the bloody pier? Shit, Bud, they would have had to crank up 120 knots over a flat sea to do that. It's a fishing boat, not a hydroplane."

Martin said hold the line, Bud, I gotta scratch something, just take a sec.

Arthur waited two minutes and then yelled, "Martin, you still there? What's the matter?"

Martin burped into the phone and said, "Sorry bro, something caught in my throat. OK, here's what really happened. One of the boats did hit the Canadian pier in St. John. Banged up pretty damn good, too. Those Ruskie boys just decided to get clever by filing duplicate claims. They faked the second claim, but on the wrong boat! Christ, Bud, talk about low-end fraud. All they did was scan the damage estimates from the salvage guys. Then, like we wouldn't spot it, change the numbers to fit two boats instead of one."

"So, you're saying that you're gonna lay this on old Harold this morning, and he's gonna promote you for your little theory? Fat chance. Harold's not motivated by theory. You gotta have more than a good theory, bro, you gotta have proof. What does the crew say? What does the port authority say about damage to the pier? You got a nice theory but no proof."

"Well, that's the other part, Bud. I just got off the phone with one of them Ruskie boys, name of Rob or Bob, something like that. Took just a few innocent questions. Not a single accusation did I make. I promise. The Ruskies decided that it'd be best if neither one of their claims was processed. They practically begged me to shit-can both claims. And they said that they just instituted new safety procedures. And no way, they said, would they be making any *new* claims for the next full year. Of course, Rob or Bob, whichever, wanted my assurance that this little mistake, on the part of some unknown relative of theirs, would be buried in the same shit-can as the claims forms. Naturally, I gave in—but I made 'em sweat a little."

"So, let me get this straight, you eliminated some piss ant little claim, and . . ."

"Piss ant, my ass. The legitimate claim was for almost forty-two thou. If I had not discovered the fraud, it would have been forty-two thou times two. And more to come, I bet. I figure this is worth a hundred and fifty grand to old Harold. I expect him to be absolutely magnanimous in his thanks."

"Christ, how'd they get to forty-two grand by bumping a pier?"

"The physical damage was about twelve thousand; the rest is down time, back shipping the catch, extra harbor fees, you know the drill. That's why Harold is going to be so thankful to me."

"You mean you think he's going to give you a raise—don't count on it."

"I don't want a raise—I want a transfer."

"You wouldn't like it out here, Bud, the booties are too focused for you."

"I didn't say I wanted a transfer for me. I want it for you. I'm gonna ask Harold to bring you back here to Portland, where we belong."

DR. SOCORRO

"How'd he do it? Doc, you really wanta know how my brother embezzled premium money from AmHull? Why? It wasn't me. I told you that a hundred times now."

"Yes, Arthur, I took notes on that—you said it wasn't you and you got it from Martin before he died in that fishing accident. But I'm thinking the details might be important for my report to Judge Hightower."

"OK, Doc, one more time. Pay attention this time. Premium checks from AmHull's clients landed on Martin's desk every day. It was another of Alice's little ways of irritating him. She loved it. His office desk faced the rear of the room. Toward the clearstory glass up high on the East wall. Here's the thing. She'd tippy toe in, hold the mail packet, properly rubber-banded, as high as she could, and drop it on his desk. He'd log them in, like Harold's father had done, way back when counting was done in longhand and inked into leather-bound journals. Nowadays, they do it on a computer. Which Alice also had some access to, remember? Anyways, the ninety-year-old login procedure hadn't varied in ninety years. The office procedure was the same, only with different people. Alice Blue Gown opened all the mail, even Harold's. Sorted out the checks. Took 'em to my brother. She was a real nitwit. Never even suspected she was playing a role in the Hide-and-Be money plan."

"All right, Arthur, what did Martin do with the checks when the clerk gave them to him?"

"The usual. I did it sometimes myself. Remember, I told you we'd cross-trained each other. Part of our thing. Martin would check the premium due. It was there, in the red leather account book. Every active dec page, arrayed alphabetically. Just match the dollar amount on the check to the right dec page. Simple. Yeah. Sure. It was ridiculous in the age of computers. Why?

Well, damn, Doc, didn't I tell you that before? That's why you are taking notes, right? It's the AmHull way. First check against an ancient analog document, the red leather notebook. Don't look in QuickBooks. That's digital. That was the way *we* did it—just like Harold's dad did it. Such a little thing."

"But, Arthur, then what would happen? I'm missing that part."

"For us, especially Martin, my brother the planner, it was perfect. That little mandatory login procedure. Martin knew no one would check if the numbers were different. He was the checker, not Mr. Hull, or Alice Blue Gown. And Martin was the man that logged data into the company's accounting software. That's where Appletree Accounting—and brother Martin—came in."

"Wait, how did the company's accounting software make a difference?"

"Ah, Doc, now you're thinking. Martin knew the dec sheets were entered into Quickbooks Pro by Alice Blue Gown. But the accounting software allowed the administrator, Martin, to hold off closing the books, whenever he wanted. Also, he controlled the file copies of the office dec sheets. Simple."

"Arthur, that's not what I really was asking about. I'm not clear on this scheme except that Martin cooked it up and you went along. I get that part. But how was it supposed to work? You talked about Martin's computer. Did you mean his office computer? He used that to cook the books?"

"Jeeze, I already gave you all that. It's in the red leather book. We gotta explain it again? No, of course he didn't use the office computer to plan it. He used our laptop, at home, the house on Brighton Lane. There was this attic room, you see. Up a steel winding staircase from the second floor. Not counting the basement. So, it was actually the third floor, and that little attic room was four floors up from the ground. A door off the upstairs hall led to the staircase, but it was always locked. I guess

Martin told Rosie that it was locked to keep the rats in. I dunno. Maybe I told her—gets confusing, don't it?"

"All right," she said. "Hold up a minute. I need to switch pens—this one is running out."

She fished a new ballpoint out of a drawer and tested it on a scratch pad. "OK, why did Martin use a laptop, why not just write the numbers down and then transfer them to the office computer system?"

"Doc, you are particular, aren't you? Why a laptop? You had to know Martin. He never learned cursive writing. He only printed. It made him feel bad, only printing. I don't know why. What difference does it make? OK, on with the story. No one except me had been up to that little room in our house in decades. When we first rented the house, the door was locked. No one had a key. The landlord thought it was a storeroom, never bothered to break in. Yeah. You bet we did. Picked it ourselves. Then bought a new lock, new key. Put tar and stuff on it to make it look old. Then repainted the door, and the wall all around it. Good place to hide. A little like the trap door in the broom closet when we were kids. Only this was up, not down. Same idea though."

"Arthur, is this when you first learned about Martin's scheme? And how did you learn this—by a phone call from here in San Diego, or when you went back that last time to Portland?"

"By phone. Yeah, just before the last trip and the accident. He was the paranoid twin, remember. So, he used a Radio Shack flash drive, which I never did find. I think he hid it somewhere and planned to tell me about it. But he died."

"Was his goal to make money for you *and* him?"

"His goal was to punish AmHull. Make 'em pay. He does it, then he hides. I'd get blamed, but I'd have the perfect alibi. Harold made me move out here, right? Hell, the way Martin figured it, the alibi was Harold's fault. It wouldn't have worked if I'd been in Portland."

"So, how did it work once he changed the numbers?"

"Once he changed the data in the company's Appletree Accounting program to match the one in the red notebook, the rest was easy. Both sets of records showed the same amount of premium. But it was actually 10 percent below the amount on the next premium check from that client. Here's how he got the money. He opened a bank account in the name of AmHull Insurance Agency across the state line. Down to Portsmouth. Phonied up a corporate resolution. Listed *me* as the corporate officer authorized to sign checks. Make deposits. All that shit. Used *my* driver's license and company credit card to open the account. Signed *my* name on the authorization card. Ordered deposit slips, checks, and a rubber deposit stamp. You know, the one with all the preprinted numbers, address, etc., etc."

"Arthur, how do you know all this? Some of it happened after Martin died, right?"

"Yeah, damn right. The FBI showed those documents to me when they interrogated me. But that just confirmed what Martin had told me."

"So, it was convenient that he died, is that what you're telling me now?"

"No, dammit! It's not convenient he died. It's Hide and Be. I told you that."

Arthur got up out of his seat and held his arms out, birdlike, and started shaking his head up and down, toward him.

Doctor Socorro slid open the right-hand drawer where the alarm buzzer was. Then, trying to talk in a low, soothing voice, she said, "Arthur, calm down. Don't make me call the guards outside."

"Calm down? We are calm. You calm down. You're not a cop. You're a shrink. Supposed to be figuring me out. So, figure this out. Write it down. The FBI never did. They just thought I was Martin. They were right. When I talked to them, I was Martin. But not before. We were each other before."

PORTSMOUTH, NEW HAMPSHIRE. A YEAR AGO

The First State Bank of Portsmouth looked like a bank ought to look, small, but imposing. Shiny white granite flooring, wrought iron, brass, and a security guard wearing a gun older than he was spoke to strength and safety. Just what I needed—a bank concerned with image, not size.

"May I help you, sir?" asked the five-foot-two purple-headed lady at the new-accounts desk. I couldn't tell her age—maybe late thirties or early fifties—lots of wrinkles around her eyes, but a burnished forehead gave her a no-nonsense air. Makeovers and hair dyes were not done in stoic New Hampshire any more than in Maine. I'd picked the day based on what Arthur told me last night—he'd spend his day on Mission Bay with two New England policyholders who were out there on West Coast business. He would be himself three thousand miles away, and I'd be him down to Portsmouth, on the same day. Course, he wouldn't know it. Soon, I'd say "Surprise, bro, you have a bank account in *New-By-God-Hampshire.*"

"Yes, you certainly may, Miss. My name is Arthur Cheshire, and I need to open a new account for my company up in Portland."

"It's Ms., not Miss. Ms. Partridge is my name and I'd be happy to open an account for you. It's a business account, is it?"

"Yes. Well, actually, it's a supplemental business account. You see, we do most of our business in Portland. Our main account is up there. We are starting to do enough business down here in Portsmouth to justify an additional account here. I think it will be small potatoes for you, but we hope to build it up—over time, of course."

"Oh, don't worry about size—we love new start-up companies, and we understand the needs of today's entrepreneurs. We're quite modern down here; we can connect your accounts, provide online services, add a line of credit, and make you feel as comfortable in our little town as you no doubt are up there in Portland."

This lady was just what the doctor ordered—someone who was more interested in what she had to sell than in what I wanted to buy.

"A simple business account will do for now. But we do need to order printed checks, deposit slips, and an endorsement stamp. I will open the account with one dollar in cash and then come back first of next week with our first actual deposit. How long will it take to get the checks and the deposit stamp? Oh, by the way, we are not exactly a start-up company. AmHull Insurance has been doing business in Portland for over eighty years. Of course, I haven't been with them for quite that long."

My attempt at humor was lost on this serious little lady.

"Well sir, I meant no offense. Of course, I've heard of AmHull Insurance, but I didn't know you had a Portsmouth office. In fact, my uncle gets his insurance from you—he has a tuna boat. That's what you sell, isn't it? Marine insurance?"

"Yes, indeed. What's your uncle's name?" I said, somewhat fearfully.

What if she's related to the Fontaine brothers? Good thing I didn't bring the Fontaine premium check with me. Good thing I played it safe and would wait for the endorsement stamp to come in.

"Frederickson," she said, waiting for me to respond.

She said it as though it were a question, not an answer, and I stupidly said, "No, not Frederickson, Cheshire. Arthur Cheshire is my name."

She looked over the edge of her little oval-shaped glasses, with the red sparkles on the earpieces. She gave me a disapproving look.

"Yes, Mr. Cheshire, I knew that. Frederickson is my uncle's name. I don't know his business name—it might be something else, but you insure his tuna boat. Maybe he has more than one, I don't really know. We're not that close, although my mother gets a wrapped piece of Giant Bluefin once a year or so. Now, sir, we'll need a corporate resolution to open the account and, of course, proper identification and signatures."

I handed her Arthur's Maine driver's license. He has a new California license, but he picks up the Maine one off the dresser when he's home. I also gave her the corporate resolution, which I'd cut and pasted from one I found on the Internet.

"These look to be in order, Mr. Cheshire. Just give me a moment and I will get the forms for you to sign. Then we can make your initial deposit—one dollar did you say it was? I will also get the book so you can select the style and type of checks you'll be needing. I'm sure we can get this done on a twenty-four-hour turn around, will that be sufficient?"

When she came back, I signed all the forms with Arthur's signature—the one I had perfected over the years—and convinced Ms. Whatever-Her-Name-Was that Arthur was who I said he was: the chief financial officer for AmHull Insurance. She assured me that the printed checks, the deposit slips, and the endorsement stamp would be delivered tomorrow. She'd mail them to my new PO box in Portland. Actually, she said that the endorsement stamp might not come in tomorrow, but I was not to worry, the bank would take my hand-written endorsement. Not a chance lady, I thought, you're not gonna catch me, or Arthur either, making the mistake of a handwritten endorsement on a check we were skimming. The stamp endorsement was critical to Hide and Be the Money. The look-and-see crowd would perceive the stamp as something it wasn't, while the Hide-and-Be boys would deceive them with what it was not. Clever, huh?

DR. SOCORRO

"Morning. Yeah, Doc, I slept as well as you'd expect someone in an eight-foot-square steel box to sleep on a steel spring cot hung from a wall surrounded by guys farting and belching all night. Wada you think?"

"And good morning to you. Let's pick up where we left off last session. I want to make sure I understand which of you decided and implemented the Hide-and-Be trick on AmHull Insurance—the one where Martin, your brother, went to banks and falsified the books at AmHull."

"Right, Doc, that was Martin, but using my particulars at the bank down to Portsmouth, and for parts of it in the AmHull office. You know he got a post office box in Portland too. It was one of those four-inch-square bronze boxes with their look-inside glass. That's how he got the mail from the bank down Portsmouth way. You know—monthly statements, confirmations, bank junk mail. All that crap."

"Yes, but I've forgotten the part after Alice whats-her-name gave him the monthly premiums to enter into the office computer software."

"We called her Alice Blue Gown. Her real last name was Singworth. She opened the mail and then gave premium checks to Martin for accounting. He'd stamp the back with the rubber stamp he got from the Portsmouth bank. You know, the *for-deposit-only* kind. Then he'd drive down to Portsmouth and deposit it. That would have been the first deposit. He'd have wanted to do it in person, to make sure it got in the right account. The FBI dicks said they had a witness against me who saw me in that bank down to Portsmouth. But they are wrong. I was never in Portsmouth then. I never opened a bank account then. It was Martin that guy saw and told the FBI about. I told you that. We look the same, remember? Cept, I'm Arthur—you know that for sure, now. Right?"

PORTLAND. A YEAR AGO

Martin parked his truck a block away from the bank. He got a coffee in a local shop across the street from the bank and watched the local traffic go in and out for a half hour before walking across to the front door.

"Good morning, Ms. Frederickson. Remember me? I'm Arthur Cheshire. AmHull Insurance, up Portland way."

"Why of course I remember you," she said, looking clerical in her little oval glasses, but wearing a suit coat and long pants this time. I liked her better in that silk blouse and black skirt she had on two weeks ago. But most of all, I liked telling her I was Arthur made her think I was. Hide and Be.

"I had some other business down here and thought I'd stop in and make our first deposit in person. And I need your assistance with a small matter as well. I need to deposit this check in our account, and at the same time, have you draw a cashier's check in a smaller amount for me. Can you do that?"

"Of course."

I handed her the Fontaine premium check for $3,480.00, properly stamped on the back with the new endorsement stamp she'd been so happy to send me last week. She took it, turned it over, saw the endorsement stamp, smiled again, and punched in the numbers, extracted a printout for the deposit receipt, and sweetly asked, "Now, Mr. Cheshire, about that cashier's check."

"Thanks. Please make it out to American Hull Insurance, in the amount of $3,132.00. It's a bit of a bother. A premium error actually. We'll be refunding some premium money to our clients for the next few months. But from now on, we'll do it via telephone with you, and do it all via wire transfer from our account here to our account in Portland. That is satisfactory to you, I assume?"

"Of course. We offer wire transfer services free to business clients. Now, Mr. Cheshire, your account does not have a sufficient balance yet to qualify for that service, but I'm sure you will build it up over time."

"Yes, I will. Do I owe you anything for the cashier's check?"

"No, of course not."

With that, I left Portsmouth. I couldn't wait to tell Arthur when he got up there next Friday night.

DR. SOCORRO

"Arthur, I don't mean to upset you like this, but I still do not quite understand your brother's scheme to get money out of your employer back there in Maine. I reread the reports the FBI gave the prosecution team here in San Diego and . . ."

"Doc, come on. This ain't fair. We been over this before. You have secret documents about what you say my brother did back there. You won't give them to me, my lawyer doesn't have them. This ain't right. I told you all I know."

"Arthur, I'd give them to you if I could, but they are restricted by the judge. I can read them for the purpose of identifying you, that's all. I am not reading them as evidence or anything like that. It's just personal, historical background. But they help me understand your relationship with your brother, and they also help me separate you *from* your brother. That's what this is all about, separating the two of you, so that I can tell the court that you're Arthur, not Martin. We discussed that, remember?"

"All right, but it ain't fair. What's the question again?"

"Question is about that first check—it was for $3,480. I only know that because it's in the doc's the prosecution offered in support of an arrest arrent in Portland."

"I haven't got the foggiest idea about that. I know the Fontaine client was a longtime client and always paid their premium checks on time. Who knows what happened? Not me. My guess? Fontaine Brothers gets the real check back, looks on the back—it has an AmHull deposit stamp. So, they are happy. They're paid up for the month."

"All right," she said, sounding skeptical. "How'd Martin work the switch at AmHull?"

"Doc, you got me. Dunno. But coulda been simple. My bro was plenty smart. Maybe he stamped the cashier's check back the other direction—in the real AmHull bank account in Portland. And let Alice Blue Gown take it to the bank. Hell, it was for the real premium. But she did not know that. As long as the premium check was hunky dory with the dec page, no one at AmHull would be the wiser. And Martin, yes Martin, not me, did the login at AmHull. All bases covered."

"So, it's your theory that Martin did this for the two of you—not just himself?"

"Him *and* me. That was his plan. But I never got a dime or knew a dime was missing. Wire transfers did the work. That's how Martin moved the cash. Hell, Doc, John Grisham did it in a novel. You read it? Slick—moved cash all over hell and back, in every book. But it was just fiction. Like the case against me."

PORTLAND. MARTIN AND MR. HULL. LAST YEAR

"What are you doing in the personnel files, Martin?"

I jumped at the sound of Harold's voice. At six-thirty in the morning, it was rare for him to be in the office. It was rare for anyone, including me, to be here at such an ungodly hour. "Morning, Mr. Hull, what brings you in so early?"

"I need something from the safe before I go to Boston on the nine o'clock shuttle. But I am surprised to find you here, particularly in our personnel files. Is there something in particular you need? I would like an explanation."

I had one all prepared for him last week when I started changing things around, but I never thought I'd get caught at six-thirty in the morning.

"Well, sir, the state insurance office called and wanted to know the certification dates of all our claims adjusters and outside sales reps; I figured it was here, and that you wouldn't want to be bothered with it. If it's something you want to handle though, I'll get back to the Accounting Department."

"At six-thirty in the morning; you're telling me they called at this time of day with a request that we give them the certification dates? That makes no sense, particularly since I just mailed our renewal forms in last week."

"That must be it. They called last week, and I forgot about it until about five o'clock this morning. I don't know why, it just hit me that I'd forgotten to tell you or do it myself. To tell you the truth I was a little embarrassed, and so I came down here and opened up assuming that you'd rather me get it done before you went to Boston. Aren't you going to be gone for three days?"

Harold harrumphed and wandered on past the file room to his office. Close call that—my snooping skills were getting rusty with Arthur spending his time on the beach with Marcella Wella. He and I used to do this sort of thing all the time, but I was losing my touch without him one step behind me. I closed the file drawer, secreted the two files under my sweater, and headed back to my office. Now I had both my personnel file and Arthur's. All I needed was a little time to massage them as soon as Harold left for Boston.

AmHull, like all regulated insurance offices, kept personnel files in accordance with state law on all employees certified by the state to perform certain tasks. Underwriters had to be bonded. Claims adjusters and sales reps had to pass a routine criminal background check. And, although it was not a state requirement, most insurance agencies had their employees take basic tests, like a psychological profile and a three-question polygraph exam administered by an outside security agency. I suppose that's why Harold seemed irritated when he caught me in the personnel files. They were supposed to be under lock and key, but that was a little ridiculous in an office of only four people. Harold was in Boston, Alice Blue Gown was out front filing her nails, and Arthur was marooned in San Diego. The key to the locked cabinet was kept in a drawer. The drawer was not a secret.

My desk, including the ink blotter, was three by five. Stacking the ins and outs on opposite sides gave me room for our staff folders. I found our computer-graded MMPI-II results, the ones we took when we first joined the company. The summary page said Arthur had a valid clinical profile. Ditto for me. But they said both of us "attempted to present a positive attitude, but became uncomfortable in situations involving confrontation, and the expression of anger." Damn straight! They got that part right.

What burned me was the bullshit about me exhibiting some "mixed personality disturbance with narcissistic and histrionic features." What's that shit? Arthur and I are as normal as any twins who live one life, right? Yeah, we have mixed personalities, but we're not disturbed—unless we're pissed off—like when you move Arthur three thousand miles away and stick me in the back office counting broken boat parts. I suppose we are narcissistic if that means what I think it means. We have high self-esteem, and we damn sure think a lot of ourselves—who doesn't? I mean who doesn't think a lot of us? Harold, Rosie, Alice Blue Gown? I'm sure I can speak for them all when I say they think the world of us—at least they do me. The thing is, they don't always know that it's me they are thinking of or talking to. Sometimes, it's Arthur. Like when I hide, and he becomes me. Is that narcissism or what?

I found my file, and Arthur's, but could not find one on Alice Blue Gown. I guess she didn't have one since she was not a bonded employee. Just as well, who would ever bond her, or bone her, for that matter? Alice damn sure wasn't narcissistic—Alice wasn't anything that took gumption. Her idea of high class was a cold salad fork at the all-you-can-eat buffet.

Looking through our polygraphs, something was fumbucked. No names. Just a control number assigned by the Ricci Investigative Agency. But mine was in my folder. Arthur's neatly stapled polygraph report was in his. Whoever did the original filing had the cross reference—names tied to control numbers. But mine was bullshit. According to Mr. Ricci—I flunked my polygraph, more or less, and Arthur passed his. Both of us got the same three banal questions. Have you ever stolen anything of value from your employer? Have you ever told a deliberate lie to cover up misconduct on the job? Did you answer all questions truthfully on your pre-employment interview?

Right. I remember it. Arthur gave the same bullshit answers I did. No to the first two questions, yes to the third—like who wouldn't answer them that way? But the so-called examiner labeled Arthur as "non-evasive" and me as "evasive, likely an intentional deception."

What a fumbucker that Ricci toad was. The only person on the face of the earth more deceptive than me was my brother. How could he pass their stupid test and I fail it? No wonder judges never let that shit in on Court TV. Unreliable—you bet! Arthur is living proof. If they were accurate, then they would have never labeled me as "likely intentionally deceptive." There was no *likely* to it. I out and out lied to all three questions, like Arthur did, like everyone did. Who in the world ever worked somewhere and didn't take something of value—pads, pencils, briefcases, whatever? And who on God's green earth never did anything that would be called "misconduct" and then told the truth about it? And if you are among the 100 percent that did, then you didn't answer all the questions in the pre-employment interview truthfully.

How in hell did Arthur pass? Answer me that. It was easy to see how I failed—who gives a shit anyhow? But finding this out gave me another idea. If Arthur was supposed to be the truthful one—according to Ricci, the polygraph god—then why not just switch his polygraph test with mine in the file? They didn't have names on them, just numbers. No one would know that my test was now in Arthur's file. That way when, and if, they ever tumble onto my Hide and Be the Money deal, they'll point the accusing finger at Arthur. But, thanks to me, he'll give 'em the finger right back. He will have his ironclad alibi. Maybe we'll be on Court TV and break the rule about not admitting polygraph tests in evidence. Who knows?

Speaking of "who knows" stuff, why did AmHull hire me if I failed their little polygraph test? As I thumbed through our files, the answer jumped out of the file. Arthur and I were interviewed *together*. Took our little short-form MMPI test in the same room, and then three days later we took the stupid lie detector tests. My results were mailed back to Harold the day after that.

That's when Harold called us in for the *real* job interview—I remember that's how he put it. He offered us jobs that day but he didn't even have the results on my polygraph until two weeks later. The postmark proved that. Somebody opened the envelope, but I bet nobody ever read the report. I was on the job by then. We told Harold when he interviewed us, it was both of us or neither. We only work together, as a package.

Come to think of it, I wish he had read the damn thing and refused to hire me. At least then Arthur and I would work somewhere else now—somewhere together.

MaRTIN'S PHaSe TWO

How can I explain Phase Two? Is it as bizarre as it sounds in my head? It's something only Arthur will understand. Phase Two was the ultimate Hide and Be. I would hide, that is, pretend to be dead, and Arthur would be my executor and close up my affairs. He would pretend to grieve. We'd find a little island down in the Caribbean and enjoy AmHull's hundred and fifty grand.

Wowser, bowser, wait till I tell Arthur about this. We have the same DNA!

I got the idea from the O. J. Simpson trial. Well, not actually the trial itself, I got it from a newspaper article in the *Boston Globe* on the scientific value and absolute certainty of DNA testing in all human beings, *except* identical twins. Some asshole speculated that maybe O.J. had an identical twin that did the dastardly deed. That explained all the DNA crime scene evidence. That got me to thinking. If one of us died and left nothing behind except some DNA tissue, or hair, or skin, or whatever, the authorities would never know which one of us died. Bamber! Our DNA is as identical as we are—or is it the other way around? Whatever. The point is that if one of us died and there was no body, like in an explosion, or something, then the DNA would only prove that one of us died, not which one.

DR. SOCORRO

"Arthur, you're sounding chipper this morning. The sound of the sea birds always brightens things up for me. Is it that way for you, too?"

"Nah, I ain't so good myself. Sleeping OK, but my gut's twisted. You know. Baloney sandwiches, day-old white bread— limp green beans—lettuce who knows how old, and milk. That's government for you. Kill you with processed food, let your bowels move with milk. Gotta love 'em."

Five minutes passed with easy questions about life in jail and did I have sleep problems. Then she asked about my brother's flash drive. I gave her that stupid look I use to distract smart people.

"No, I don't know nothing about a flash drive. Martin's flash drive? Sure, I guess he had 'em. Most guys who work with computers do. I never had one. If the FBI found it in Portland, I'd say yes, it was Martin's. Did you find that out from reading my file—Jeeze—when you gonna let me see my own file? But never mind—I'm only the one they think murdered his twin—don't show me something that might help us prove our innocence."

She asked something new.

"Phase Two? You already asked me about that last week. Remember? I said Martin never told me about any Phase Two, or any other number. You got it where? Goddamn, again. The FBI. What is this? They feed you stuff. You feed it to me. I get baloney in jail, and baloney from you, salted by the FBI, and peppered by the prosecutor."

"Calm down, Arthur," she said. Then she reached down to get something from a drawer in the desk. I could see her left breast tilt.

"Yeah, damn straight it riles me up, Doc. I told them everything I knew. They told me shit. Now they feed you stuff, a little breakfast, then lunch? Hell with it. I don't care. If it helps me, I'll answer whatever you want. The truth, not that baloney from jail, or the fumbucked FBI.

"Martin did what? He saved hair and tissue samples from us. Did I get that right? Oh. He didn't, but he wanted to. Why? What bullshit, pardon my language, Doc, can't you see what it is?

"Yeah, we had an old boiler down in the basement of the Brighton Lane house. Fuel oil burning boiler. Smoked things up some. Planned to blow up the house? Lady, either you, or the FBI is just plain crazy. He'd never do that. No matter how pissed he was at AmHull.

"He's not insane, he's my brother. Lemme get this straight. You say he laid out a plan on that flash drive that got the fire department to come to the house, check the furnace for an oil leak, find nothing wrong, and that would set up the accidental death of my brother? He planned to blow up the house, plant some DNA in the basement, but make sure it didn't get consumed in the fire, and then let everyone think he was dead? He's my brother, but he wasn't a criminal.

"All right, you got me a little bit. It's similar to my plan to disappear myself down in Mexico. But not real. You're saying he was gonna fake his death, just for money? No way. I only came to that after he died. Got that! After, not before. I did not do it for money, I did it for him, my brother. Yes, he is dead, but he died on the river. It was an accident. You know that. He didn't die of an explosion in the house. I killed him before he had a chance to kill himself? Is that what you are saying? Fuck the FBI. Who's sitting here right now? You or them? *You write down the truth, you hear me?*"

PORTLAND. EIGHTEEN YEARS AGO

"You boys get up—I've been calling you since seven—your breakfast is on the table. You wash your faces and get those clothes on right today. Yesterday Marty had his shirt on inside out. Arty, you look after your brother, and make sure he gets it right."

"Why does she always tell you to do things? It wasn't me who got the shirt on upside down."

"She told you because she thought you were me. She always does. I thought you liked that. Being me. You like it when I'm you and I get in trouble for you."

"See? My shirt is on right, just like yesterday. But does she care? Nooooo. She just cares about saying stuff. Mommy never mixed us up like she does. How long is she gonna keep us anyway? I don't like her sometimes."

"Your shirt is OK. I don't know why you don't like her, she . . ."

"I don't mean I don't like her. She's OK, I guess. I just wish she could be nicer sometimes. Like when she hollers at us and stuff and when she gets mixed up."

"Everybody gets mixed up. I think it's fun. We can do stuff, and nobody can tell for sure."

"Arty, why do we look the same? We're different people but we look the same. Did God make us the same so no one could tell us apart? Are all twins like us—do they look exactly alike, and they get blamed for being the same all the time, like us?"

"Dunno. But it's fun. No one else can play Hide and Be but us. No one at school can play because they look different. Let's do it again. Put your shirt on backwards and we'll tell her that you're Arty. She'll never get it. She never does."

"I told you boys to come down here and . . . Well, finally. Marty, I told you to get your shirt on straight. Don't you remember yesterday? Come here, I'll fix it for you—and you, Mister Arthur Cheshire, didn't I tell you to watch out for your brother?"

"I'm Martin—that's Arty. I did tell him, but I forgot to check myself. I can fix it myself."

"Oh boys, when am I ever going to find a way to tell you apart? I've had you for over a year now and you still fool me every day. Maybe I should tie a ribbon on one of you."

"But what if I untied it and then tied it on Marty?"

"Arty, you would not do that to me would you?"

"I'm Marty. He's Arty."

DR. SOCORRO

"Doc, neither of us took drugs or were drunks. Sure, we popped beers like normal guys. Sure, we had hangovers, but we never blacked out and we went to work every day. Our livers are fine, thank you very much. By the way, did you know that hangovers are not identical? They're fraternal. That's a bad twin joke. Speaking for both of us, I can say that we never quite understood why everyone else thought it funny enough to repeat."

"Arthur," she said as she closed the stiff back on the lab book and fished for a new one from a shelf behind her desk. "We've been over this before. This is our seventh week. You're making progress, but you cannot keep speaking for your brother. We are separating your thought patterns and trying to identify you for the court, right? You know that don't you?"

"Yeah, Doc. But sometimes it's hard. That's why I go over to your picture window on the bay. Blue sky, white clouds, gulls, pelicans, every which kind of seabird. They got no worries. Sometimes, I think moving around in your office will make you understand better. Did you know I almost never move around in my cell?"

"No, I didn't. What do you do, just sit or lie down on your bunk?"

"See, it's too small to move around in. It's not like in here in your office. In the cell, I sit on the bed, or the toilet, or on the little chair under the pull-down table. But no walking around. Makes the guards nervous and sends the wrong message to the inmates. Know what I mean?"

She nodded her head at him before taking a deep breath. "Let's talk about the first two days that you and Martin had in Portland before he died. I think you started to talk about that earlier, but it was too hard."

"Yeah, Doc, it was too hard. Still is."

"I want to know how you felt about being home, being with Martin again."

"I think I already told you, but maybe not. I forget sometimes. I got home from here on a Friday night. We went to Sweeties.

Rosie was already there, at the bar. We woke up the next morning with hangovers. All three of us. Mine worst. Then Martin. Rosie not far behind. As usual, Martin and I drank the exact same number of beers, which we used to wash down nearly identical amounts of food. Rosie drank half as much beer, ate slightly more lobsta, but only half of a sweet potato, without butter. She was sure she'd recover. No later than noon."

PORTLAND. THE DAY AFTER ARTUR'S WELCOME HOME PARTY AT SWEETIES

"Jeeze, Babe, do you feel as bad as I look?" Martin said to the image of Rosie behind him as he squinted into the mirror in the dining room. Rosie came from the kitchen carrying a platter of bagels, lox, cream cheese, red onion, and pickles. We always liked pickles in the morning.

Rosie looked far better than she felt. "No siree, sir, no one could feel as bad as you look, except possibly your brother, who looks exactly as bad as you do—and I haven't even seen him yet this morning. Or have I? Did you play another switch on me during the night? Am I going to have to wake up every morning and say, Martin, is that you? Jesus, why'd you do that to me? I admit it was fun at the time, but the more I think about it the more it pisses me off."

I was out on the porch, but the bay window was open. Could hear it all.

"We didn't plan it, Babe, it's just what happens. If I'd been the first through the door at Sweeties, I'd have introduced you proper-like. But Arthur is fast and expects me to back him up whenever he pulls one of those 'who's he' jokes on some unsuspecting victim. He means no harm and causes none, although it pisses off many people."

"No, Hun, you're missing it. I wasn't pissed at him. I doubt most people are when he does something like that. I laughed at him. I was pissed at you. You're the one who shouldn't fool me, not him. He doesn't even know me. It's OK, I guess, to play little jokes on me. I know he meant no harm and it damn sure proved the point. You guys got an invisible umbilical cord—why didn't they just leave you hooked up at the hospital and save the world a lot of doubt? They could have called you Pete and Repeat. Get it?"

Martin, Rosie, and I gobbled lox and bagels and enjoyed the crisp air from the porch. Mostly not talking much. Nursing full stomachs and aching heads. For me, it was a little unsettling for another reason. Martin was making nice with Rosie. He was more animated, and she was more receptive than imaginable, especially with twin hangovers. He talked faster than normal. She bounced answers, questions, and quips right back. A self-confident babe, but still a babe. An active participant in our effort to bring one another up to date, as though it had been two years, instead of just six weeks.

Rosie had no previous interaction with identical twins, and at first could only focus on our uncanny physical similarities. Then, by noon, she seemed even more struck by the apparent fact that we seemed to share the same phobias.

"I'm telling you, Bud, San Diego is no place for a Mainer. My apartment is designed for a hermit, and it's as big as $800 a month will buy out there. Three rooms. Seven hundred square feet—or so they say. But it's a mole hill compared to this house. God I wish I still lived here."

Rosie chimed in as though we wanted her opinion, "Seven hundred square feet? That's a lot to me. That's bigger than most of the student apartments around here. What's it like, can you see the ocean? What's the Pacific Ocean like? I've never seen it."

As she had noticed last night, when she posed a question to one brother, the other often answered. When she asked Martin about Portland, I answered. Now Martin answered for me.

I smiled while Martin said, "Seven hundred square feet is not big. As for the so-called Pacific Ocean, it's not bamber. It's aptly named; I'll give them that. Their idea of an ocean is mostly tied to the beach. They like long stretches of sand that sits there. Sitting sand, that's what they have out there. If the Pacific was a dog, it would be a lap dog. But the Atlantic! Our ocean. Pure pit bull—short—compact. With a hell of a set of teeth. San Diegoans, is that what they're called, Arthur? Don't answer that. They like to go to the beach, not the ocean. As far as I'm concerned, the Atlantic is the only real ocean—it has rivers and inlets, and good, hard granite on the shore. Granite doesn't just sit—like sand—granite is solid shit—it stands up. And our ocean is full of fish, which is where we need to get to, Bud."

"Yeah, but I've got something to do first. Harold called me once on Monday and twice on Thursday, and I promised him I'd stop by the office for a little personal visit this morning before we go up to the Dramiscotta camp."

"Ah shit, Arthur. Harold can wait till Monday—I already told him you and I were going fishing today, and he'd have to wait to get his little personal report on his boys. Tell him to stuff . . ."

"No, Martin, it'll only take a few minutes—load up the truck and I'll be back in twenty."

PORTLAND. THE NEXT DAY

I made it to AmHull's office in six minutes and walked into Harold's office where, as promised, he was waiting for me. Alice was out front. She waved me on through with a smile. I gave her a half-smile back.

"Arthur, I can't tell you how happy I am to see you," Harold said as I walked into his office.

"Good morning, Harold, it's nice to be back, although I wish it were on a more permanent basis."

"Arthur, please don't start with the transfer business again. I thought you understood our special need for you out there in . . ."

"No, Harold, I really don't. But I haven't asked for a transfer, I was just hoping . . ."

Like two cats in a sack, Harold and I kept stepping on one another's hisses.

"No, you haven't, my boy. But your brother has. He did a fine job unearthing that ridiculous scam that the Russians, the ones who bought out the Bellemear family down in Portsmouth, tried to pull on me. I gave him a nice raise, but he said all he wanted was a transfer—he wanted me to transfer you back here. I patiently explained why that can't happen, not just now, you know."

"Yes, Harold. Martin told me about that one. Wasn't it over a hundred grand he saved you?"

"Actually, it was probably more than that when you factor in that they'll have legitimate claims that they won't file over the next year. I'll be forever grateful to Martin—he's proved his loyalty, and he's earned my complete trust. I wish I had more like him."

"Actually, you do, Harold. You have me. I'm exactly like him."

"No, Arthur, there is a difference between you and Arthur. I can't quite put my finger on it but there's a difference. Of course, you're both loyal to the company, and Martin did thwart those Russians. But you're the one I count on to keep me informed on how my boys are doing out there in California. Now, what do you really think of our operation out there? The boys are, well, to be honest with you, somewhat vague about the *pro forma*, and whether we are on track, or not."

I gave Harold what he wanted—which was far from the truth. I told him the boys were working hard, the business was coming in, and life in California was good. Then, all bullshit over for the morning, I went back to Martin's, and we went fishing.

PORTLAND, FIFTEEN YEARS EARLIER

"Well, where are they, then?" Marty asked me.

"Dead, I already told you ten times. Marty, you know that already—the lady in the grey dress with the stupid hair told us that about fifty times already and I told you it too. Why do you have to keep asking me?"

"I know, Arty, I know you said dead, and the stupid hair lady said dead, but where is that—I mean is heaven and dead the same place? She said heaven first. Then when I said why, she said cause they are dead. That's where you go when you are dead. But you can come back from dead, can't you? I don't think you can come back from heaven, though."

"Who told you that you can come back from being dead?"

"The priest did, and so did Mommy when she read to us from her leather bible in her bedroom. Member? It was baby Jesus, I mean after he grew up, and he died, and he came back. I guess it was before he went to heaven, so . . ."

"Marty, you're sooooo stupid. Even more stupid than the stupid hair lady. Mommy and Daddy are dead, and they aren't Jesus. Only Jesus could do that—I don't remember that part too well, but I don't think it was before he went to heaven. I think they just thought he came back because they wanted him to so bad—that's what the priest said in catechism class."

"Well, so why can't we want Mommy and Daddy to come back real bad, and then maybe they will. But if they are already in heaven then they can't, so who is going to take us to school next month? Are we still going to school? Are we going to die too?"

"No, we aren't going to die. I will take us to school—you know that. I am always in front, and I know the way. It's not very far."

"Do you promise? You have to promise. I think I know the way, but I know we'll get there if you lead. What's a funeral,

Arty? Why do we have to go? Is she right? Will Mommy and Daddy be there—at the funeral, I mean? I thought they were in heaven. I don't want to see them anyhow if they're dead. I don't like dead things. You know I don't, Arty."

"The funeral is where everyone goes when someone dies—like when the guy that used to fish off our dock—he died when he drowned. He had a funeral, and we went, and you could have seen him in that big box they put him in if you hadn't been so chicken. Member, we were walking up there and . . ."

"It wasn't me that was chicken, it was you. I was walking right beside you, and you stopped, and wouldn't look in . . ."

"Not true. Not true! I was going to, but you wouldn't, and like always I stopped so you wouldn't wet your pants. I'm not afraid of funerals like you. I woulda looked. I wanted to. And I'm gonna look in the box when we get to the funeral for Mommy and Daddy too. I want to see them. Even if they are dead. Don't you?"

"Nope."

DR. SOCORRO

"So, Doc, the guard says you've got me booked for ninety minutes this afternoon. That's good. Does it mean you're starting to believe me, believe I'm Arthur and I didn't kill my brother? Are we there yet?"

"I don't mind telling you that you've convinced me that you are who you say you are. But if I'm going to be able to help you, I will have to convince others that you are Arthur. That's why, in fact, I've added thirty minutes to your session today. We have to talk about something very serious today, perhaps as serious as the boat accident itself. I know that was the worst day of your life, but now we have to talk about the next day. The day you drove back to Portland and pretended to be Martin."

"Doc, that was not the first time I pretended to be him, you know that, don't you?"

"Yes, you've given me many examples. But this was the first time, as an adult, you tried to convince someone who really knew Martin that you were Martin. That had to be very different. Rosie was no fool, I can tell that from what you've already told me about her. How did you carry it off, that first day?"

"All right, can I just talk you through it without a million psycho-nutcake questions? Like just talking, not answering questions?"

"Sure, Arthur, have at it."

Pulling up to their house, and my old house, I practiced that first sentence. The first lie—or the first truth. Hard to tell which. Whichever it was. It did not goddamn work. Not at all. Said it fifty times. Hi Babe. Watcha doing? Fishin' was terrible. Arthur? He's gone—rented a car in Somerset, headed north, up Bangor way. To see an old . . . Won't work. Won't!

Backed the freakin' truck out of the driveway. Went south on Brighton Lane twenty, maybe thirty blocks. Jammed the truck in park. Wrenched hard on the emergency brake. Get it together. It's all physical. No, mental. I got that part. It's touching her and looking back at her that's gonna fuck me up.

The truck? It's mine because Martin bought it for us. Everything in the back is mine. Not cause he's dead. Because I'm Martin—so why shouldn't it be mine? Hallucinations? Delusions? Freaky thoughts? Sure, all that and some you ain't mentioned.

Started the engine back up. Drove two more blocks, pulled a U-turn, and then over to the side in a small parking lot. Dental office. No one there on a Sunday. Figure it out. Got out. Jumped into the truck bed. Our fishing gear was there—two of everything—all the same. Except for one left-handed reel. Nothing distinguishable. My stuff.

You mean Arthur's? Boxed it up two hours ago. Stuck it in two one-dollar-a-day lockers at the bus station. Tomorrow, I'd send it to San Diego. Hold for Arthur Cheshire thirty days. Read about some guy on the lam doing that in a book. I wouldn't be Arthur for another week—when I went back to San Diego. That's Arthur. Here, I was me. Well, you know that, right? And you are writing it all down. Thank you.

PORTLAND. THE DAY AFTER MARTIN DIED

"Hey Babe, I'm home. What do I smell? Smells like nothing cooking. I get the hint, we're going out."

Rosie looked up from the dining room table where she'd spread this week's crossword puzzle collection. She was an organized mess. The *New York Times, Portland Press Herald,* and the *Maine Sunday Telegram* were strewed all over the table, but little cut up puzzle squares were lined up like miniature soldiers in the middle, beyond an oversized coffee cup, two juice glasses, two napkins, one used, the other not, alongside a cereal bowl, and half a bran muffin. What was it Martin had said about her word passion? Ah, comparison and time. She had some kind of invented scoring system, based on time. Finishing the hardest puzzles was a given. The real challenge was to improve on her time, measured weekly. She had a system, what was it? Factoring, or something.

Not answering my dinner question, she said, "I had a great weekend. I scored a 260, that's 25 points up over my high since last June. Where's Arthur? You haven't dumped your twin, have you?"

First test passed.

"Well, hell, you're not going to believe it. How could you? He dumped *us*—he went up to Bangor to see an old booty. Said he'd be back end of the week. Actually, it's a sore subject. We almost never fight but he wanted me, and you of course, to go up there with him. Seems he had this worked out with her on the phone last week, and just assumed we'd take the week off and go with him. I said, shit Arthur, we have jobs, we have stuff to do, we can't just dump everything and go to Bangor for a week. So, I told him no. Pissed him off. You know Arthur."

"No, not really. I know you and you say it's the same. But I don't know him. Hell, Babe, I'm just getting to know you."

"Well, this was gonna be a get-to-know-Arthur week, but he caught the bus from Brunswick to Bangor. I expect he'll get laid Maine style, and then be back here by Wednesday. Speaking of getting laid, how's your afternoon going so far?"

I took a deep breath and waited for her answer. It was odd talking to a woman who just sat there, not engaging you at the end of every sentence like Marcella did. With Marcella, I would never have gotten away with that story non-stop. She's the inter-rupting type. Rose apparently was patient.

"That's sensible, I guess. Who is the lady in Bangor? Is he really hot for her—maybe that's obvious, since he dumped you, his indistinguishable twin, for her? But why didn't he say anything last night? And why, is he a cheat? I mean he talked about Marcella a lot the other night. I thought that was a seri-ous thing for him. Is he a sailor with a girl in every port, is that your twin brother?"

And so, I passed the first two tests. Rosie easily accepted me as Martin, and as easily accepted Arthur's absence.

"You got me, Babe. Friday night was catch up time, and today was bye-bye time. It says a lot about the attraction of Maine women. You got me, and that booty in Bangor's got Arthur."

"What's the booty's name? She does have one, doesn't she, or is it a secret?"

"It's a secret. Arthur's goosey about names. He keeps them to himself until he's sure that a new girl is gonna accept both of us. You know, another twin thing. He's probably telling her about himself, or me, this very moment. Sometimes new girlfriends get a little bollixed up and can't keep straight who he's talking about. That usually ends things. Hell, maybe he'll show up tomorrow, depending on how things go in Bangor."

Taking a breath, I paused, walked on by her toward the kitchen. She had her head back down, carefully trimming an old puzzle, filled in, and scored on the margin. Apparently, she kept them after finishing them. What a good idea. Over my shoulder I said, "Of course, I do have a remarkable physical description, and could recognize her, without her clothes, of course, but he keeps their names to himself for the first few times he tries a new one on."

"You're kidding; I thought you two shared everything."

"Well, actually I accidentally stole one of his booties a year or so ago, and ever since he's kept the new ones hidden, at least at first. I expect he might bring her down here for the weekend and we'll meet her together."

"Hold the phone, Martin. Something doesn't compute here. How could he have a new girlfriend up in Bangor when he's been in San Diego for the last, what is it, three months now?"

"Yeah, right, he did go on a lot about her. But I'm not sure how permanent that deal is. California is famous for three-month stands, you know."

"But you said he was really into this Marcella and that she was mesmerizing him out there in the land of sandy beaches and money. Based on his Friday night regaling us with Marcella stories, I thought he was thoroughly smitten. I smell a rat. Is it a San Diego rat, or a Bangor rat? Does your brother usually have two girls on standby—is that a twin thing—two for the price of one?

"Beats me, Babe. He might be something of a rounder since AmHull moved him out there."

"That's no answer. Does he keep two girls on the string at the same time or not? If he does, what does that tell me about you? Who do you have on the side—someone in Portsmouth? You've been going down there a lot lately. Is that the real reason?"

This conversation had turned from easy to hard in a heartbeat. It told me two things, both of which were scary. For one, Rosie would not be easy to fool. More important, I would have to work out better stories, or I wouldn't be able to fool anybody. If I was gonna hide Arthur and be Martin, I would have to be more convincing, or limit the game to stupid people.

Life for us, or at least me, was all nerves until that night after dinner. I'd ducked her question about me having a side booty down in Portsmouth. Now, at the kitchen table finishing yesterday's pizza, I realized she was staring at me. Now, I had an answer. "Rosie, I really don't have someone in Portsmouth. And I'm guessing but I think the girl up in Bangor is Arthur's old girlfriend from maybe last year and that . . ."

"If she's an old girlfriend, you'd know her name."

"Well, not old like more than a year ago. Just old like maybe a few months. He met Marcella in San Diego maybe two, three months ago, and I got the idea that the lady in Bangor was just before that. So, I think what's really going on here is that Arthur is torn between two loves, just like he's torn between two coasts. It's all AmHull's freakin fault splitting us up and causing him and me to lead two separate lives—as though we could. He probably mentioned her name to me on the phone when he first started talking about Marcella, because I know he was worried about how Bangor would feel if he broke up with her. He's like me in every way, Babe, monogamous to a fault."

I turned back around and headed for the sink. But Rosie wasn't letting go that easy.

"Well, you're probably right, but you gave me a scare this afternoon. I had the eerie feeling that we were back in Sweeties on Friday night, and Arthur was leaning on the doorjamb pretending to be you. Maybe I'd better take you upstairs and give you a bedroom check to make sure it's really you. Arthur's kiss on Friday night was not at all like yours. I can tell you guys apart miles away, as long as we're under the sheets."

"Now you're talking. I'll race you upstairs."

THE NEXT MORNING

It worked. Sex with Rosie was just like Martin said it was. His description of what turned her on at the foreplay stage was perfect. She liked him to do the unbuttoning, the sliding down, and to do it with a smile on his face. That was the easiest thing I ever did. Unbuttoned and undone. What's not to smile about?

My god, this is a marvelously firm-feeling woman. As for my clothes, they were actually Martin's, so like Martin, I took them off myself. The late afternoon light was soft behind the screened window. A small breeze, coming in the harbor, the soft din of traffic on Brighton Lane, two floors down. Time passed in a flash but took hours—that is, the flash took hours. Time disappeared.

Once we got into it, I let her lead, like Martin said she liked. That was odd though. She was passive about a lot of things, or so he had said. But in bed, she liked to be in charge. That took all the thinking out of it for me. This was just what I wanted, two women who led in bed, and two women who thought I was good because of it. Life was sweet. As soon I said that out loud, in my head, I started to cry—again.

"What is it, Hun? Why are you crying? Why . . ."

Stop this stupid crying! But I had no idea how to do that. All I could think of was to lay it off on Arthur, that is, on me.

"It's Arthur. I miss him more than I wanna talk about—I don't know why he has to come home, stay two lousy days, and then run off to Bangor. What's that say about us—him and me? Maybe I should have taken the week off and gone with him. I don't know; things are pretty fumbucked."

Christ almighty. This is my first morning in Martin's bed with Martin's girl. I felt cold. Martin should have fired up that old monstrosity of an oil furnace in the basement by now. Rosie was still asleep or pretending to be. In time I'd be able to tell, but for now I just let myself believe she was asleep. Laying there with her, her left hip toward me, and her right foot tangled up in mine, I wondered how she slept without seeming to breathe. Marcella didn't exactly snore, but I could always hear her breathing. Rosie was as quiet as the blankets.

Martin and I used to wake up at the same exact second when we were little—well, not little—that started after we moved into our second foster home. Before that, he'd sleep, and I'd have to wake him up. Always it was me who had to do the waking. He never took his turn waking up first. But after they died, and we moved to the first foster house, then we'd wake up together. It was like, you know, a telepathy thing.

Shit. Rosie was moving. Laying there, it dawned on me. We'd shared each other's life like only twins can. Answering each other's questions. Telling each other's lies. Being ourselves one minute, and one another the next. But for now, I would have to be both—I owed him that much, didn't I?

What about that time in our senior year when he fractured his finger by jamming it into the ice wall? I was clear across the pond taking off my skates and I felt the pain in the same finger. I swear I did. But I never told anyone, except Martin. All he said was, "I know. That made it better."

Monday morning, I was back at AmHull. Harold. What a joke.

Harold believed what he saw. Skin deep—that's old Harold. A man with permanent blinkers—wore them through life like a bad haircut. He was absorbed in his life, his boy's lives, his father's life. Paid but scant attention to mine, or Martin's. That's why he accepted me as Martin.

Alice Blue Gown? She'd just turned twenty-two. Did she notice anything—is that your question? Yeah, everything. She didn't wear blinkers, like Harold, she just never blinked. I was who I looked like. That's Alice—look it over, look away. Busied herself with those little stacks of papers, notes, lists, paper clips, mailers, flyers, God knows what. After chitchat, she went back to sorting the markers of AmHull. All of it was there on her giant front desk.

Don't alter their expectations. They are not curious people. They are stupid people.

But. There was that one odd thing.

"Martin," Alice cooed to my back, as I walked down the hall, "did you get that premium check from the *Fontaine Brothers*?"

"Yeah, what about it?"

"Nothing," she said, "just wondered if they paid up."

I let it go. Harold was standing in his doorway, waiting. If he heard, he was quiet about it.

Nothing changes; well, nothing at AmHull. I did Martin's job. Walked the dock. Downed a couple pints at Sweeties. Ate lunch at Martin's regular places. No one noticed. Said hello to Martin's friends, including Jimmy the newsboy. Everybody knew Arthur was gone. In San Diego. Out of sight, out of mind. You know that drill, don't you? But they all saw me. In Portland. Martin was not hiding. I was Martin. Get it? Yeah, all the little things. I drove Martin's truck. Wore his clothes. Lived with his girl.

Explaining Arthur? Well, sort of. On Wednesday, I told Harold that Arthur had gone to Canada on a trip with a friend from Bangor. Took some work. But no prob. See, it's about sameness. Arthur never came back from Bangor. Maybe things didn't go well in Bangor. You know upstate girls. He caught a ride with her to St. John, Newfoundland. Something pissed him off. He flew from Newfoundland to California, by way of Chicago. Called me at work.

Harold was the only one pissed off. But easy fix. Called Harold from phone booth on the harbor. Put on my Arthur voice. Same voice. Water lapping on pier. Ship horns blowing. Sea birds screeching. Winches and back up alarms from forklifts. Same sounds, same coast. Said I was Arthur. He jumped me but gave him bullshit update on his boys. Things good. Sales slow. Both boys are hard at it. No, not seen 'em. Yeah, I know. They never call. Me either. Work first. Right, boss?

I told Rosie that Arthur had cut it off with the Bangor girl. He felt so good about Marcella that he'd agreed to meet her in Chicago.

"It seems, so my wayward brother said, that Marcella's family was gathering there for a wedding, and this would be a good time for him to meet them."

Rosie was twisting wires on the back of the TV. "Chicago? That's odd. I thought you told me that Marcella was a Latin girl, from Mexico, or Central America. Why is her family in Chicago?"

Rosie had that dubious look on her face, but I had learned not to look at her too closely when answering questions. She was far smarter than any other woman I knew.

"Chicago has lots of people from Central America. But I don't know anything about her family—that's all Arthur told me when he called."

"Why did he call you at the office? He has called you here at the house every time since I've been here—that's going on three weeks now."

"I guess it's because he can call collect to the office and our stupid office girl will accept it."

"You mean Alice? She called you today and I talked to her a little bit. She didn't sound stupid to me. But that's not the point—why is Arthur now starting to call you at the office? Once again, Hun, something is not computing here. I can't put my finger on it, but I get the sense that your brother is trying to put something over on you. Why would he do that? Does he have something to hide from you? Does Alice what's-her-name have anything to hide?"

As we talked, I got better at responding with half-facts. As long as we were talking about Arthur it was easy, but when we talked about me, that is, pretending to be Martin, I had more trouble.

What about the San Diego office? What do you mean, what about it? It morphed. From me into us. See. It was always a one-man shop. Harold's boys. Just figureheads. Right from the start. Ghosts. Office girl? Three in six months—one at a time. The ghosts and the turn-style office girls added up to freedom. Something I never had in Portland.

Two weeks in Portland. Then one in San Diego. Then I changed the routine. Half here. No, not *here*. This is jail, remember. Here in San Diego. Out there. Down at the harbor. Take I-5, south. Sheds. Warehouses. Ships. Boats. Trucks. Chuy's bar. Tattoo stands. Smells fishy there.

DR. SOCORRO

I got the last appointment in the afternoon. The good doctor was worn down from listening to other cons tell her lies. She told me to just tell her my story, about Rosie. I gave a little truth, a few guesses, and a paper sack full of opinions.

Rosie was complex. Damn smart, and very caring. No guile. Curious, yes. But a big-time skeptic. Born with an innate doubt about a lot of things. Don't know how I fooled her. Took nothing on faith and damn little for granted. Not like me and Martin. We lived in the past. She lived in the moment.

Born and raised in Eastport, bout 250 miles upstate from Portland. She said—or was it Martin that told me? Not sure now. Spent six years in Augusta working for a small but respectable accounting firm. Two years of accounting classes. Quit college at twenty. Couldn't afford it. Liked accounting and good at book-keeping. But never took to your standard liberal education. Too many old hippies at the University of Maine's Augusta campus.

Love life? Yeah. Several, I'm sure. More complex. That's how she wanted it. Passionate and in charge. But patient too, you know. I'd guess she moved slowly into a sexual relationship with a man. Martin? Prob an exception. Way I heard it, she fell for him the second time they talked. Not hard to get that story from her.

"When did you know I was the one for you, Babe? Tell me the truth or tell me a lie—just make sure it was the first time you saw me, or you'll crush my fragile ego."

She said something like, "Can your ego stand the truth? It was the second time—the first time I thought you were differ-ent. Then it turned out that there were two of you. You told me more stories about Arthur than yourself. Do you remember that? Once in a while, you got mixed up. It made you mysterious. I'm a sucker for mysteries, remember?"

Sounds odd now. Life with Rosie lasted four months. One with Martin, three with me. Never caught on, till the end. It wasn't just sex. Or just pretending. Ready for something stupid? Accounting. Yeah. Bookkeeping. We were both good at it. Better than Martin was. AmHull used Appletree Accounting. So did the university. Her job. My job. Something to talk about and avoid commitment. Worked for both of us.

Rosie called her mother every week, up in Eastport. She said my mom's my anchor. Protector. Guiding light. Best friend.

They lost her dad when Rosie was thirteen. He was a "sea-faring man," according to Martin, and "died doing what he loved," according to Rosie.

"He loved the sea most when it was at its worst. He talked, when on shore, about how storms welled up out of the ocean and grab the sky. A magnificent storm took his life and settled his legacy. She was a romantic; can you see that? I never meant to hurt her; can you see that, Doc?"

I got it. Death brings you closer. Her mom never remarried. She had gentlemen callers. How'd she feel? Just one parent. Anyone can handle that. One thing, though. Losing her dad made her sure she didn't want to marry anyone. Never marry—never be a widow. Something like that. But then she forgot her thirteen-year-old view. Married a Bangor-born sailor. He taught her about sex. Seems he was experienced. Decent living. Short marriage. Widowed her at twenty-two. A good man, but too much in love with the sea. Too much like her dad. She loved the sea, but only from the shore. Too young. Lost her dad at thirteen and her husband at twenty-two. Like twin deaths in a way. The sea took both men. I never knew this when I became Martin.

How'd I feel when she told me? Well? What do you think? I had to be Martin. Even God would not strike her three times.

PORTLAND. A MONTH AGO

"Martin, were you ever called 'Marty' or 'Mart'? What I mean is, did you have a nickname as a kid? Arthur calls you 'Bud.' Was that one of those words you guys made up, or just plain old American Bud? Get it?"

Me and Rosie were sitting on the back porch having a cup of black tea on Saturday afternoon. The leaves were in retreat, colors fading. The one-hundred-year-old maple in the backyard was showing its age—gnarling, curling, creaking. The ground was awash in burnt orange leaves. As we watched them drift down with every shift in the breeze, I tried to answer her question the way I thought Martin would have.

"Yeah, I was Marty and Arthur was Arty. 'Marty and Arty, smarty, smarty.' Sometimes, on the playground, it was 'farty farty.' I hated it, and so did Arthur, but I hated it more than he did."

She took a long slow sip of her tea, cocked one eye lid upward, and asked an innocent question.

"I'm sure you did. Is that what your foster parents called you?"

I sputtered a little. Almost dropped the cup. What had Martin told her? Fosters? The strap? The crucifix? Nah. Never. Tense fingers relaxed. This was exactly where I could screw things up. Rosie's a bright bulb. Don't get her to wondering.

"Well," I said, begging for time, and moving to the porch rail for distance. "When we were kids and lived in the first foster home, I told you about that one, right? Well, it started then. Our real parents never called us that, but the Paxtons did. Actually, it was Mrs. Paxton. She fixated on those cutesy pie nicknames. She must have thought it was creative. Mr. Paxton was beyond cute. He was a serious man—dead serious—way too serious to use nicknames. But who cares? As for 'Bud,' you're right, Arthur uses that a lot, but I don't. We're identical. That's just genetics. We're separate, you know? What about you, did you have a nickname as a kid—what would be the nickname for Rosie, anyhow?"

Soon as I said it, I regretted it. Careful. Don't ask about stuff she probably already covered with Martin, before I became Martin. Sipped my tea. Held my breath. Safe ground. Good.

"No, I never had a nickname. For me it was just the opposite. Kids at school never gave me one because they thought, I guess, that Rosie was my nickname. Every once in a while, I'll get asked at some government office for my 'real' name. When I tell 'em Rosie, they just look at me like I must hate my real name so much I have to keep it a secret. Once, at the driver's license office, they asked me that, and I said, 'It's Rosebehind.' I thought they'd laugh but they just said, 'How do you spell that?' I let it go and retreated to Rosie."

"I know about your dad, and his dying at sea, and that you don't like to talk about it, but I hope you don't assume my lack of questions about your family to be lacocare. You don't, do you?"

Mistake. Yeah. I was fishing. Did Martin use twin talk with her? Did he slip like I just did? Took another sip of tea. She gave me a look. Eye quarter-cocked this time.

"Lack 'o care? There you go again. That's the second or third time this week that you have said something like that. What is that? It sounds like a secret language that you and Arthur had. Something anonymous. Am I right? You know, I spent last Saturday morning, while you and your brother were fishing, at the main library on campus reading about twins. Didn't know much about twins. Still don't, actually, but I'm learning."

Holy shit, she scared me with that. I told her I needed to go to the bathroom. She gave me a scoot whisk with both hands. When I got back, she picked up right where she'd left off.

"My education on twinning started that Friday night at Sweeties when you and that rascal brother of yours fooled me with your little game, 'Hide and Be'—is that what you said you called it? One kisses me. The other shakes my hand. Pricks, both of you. But maybe that's the wrong word. Maybe it's tricks. I read one article about identical twins often developing their own language. Is 'laco' a word that translates into 'lack' for normal people? I mean people like me; we're called singletons in research books about twins. Did you know that? Twins you, singleton me."

"Yeah, it is. Arthur and I needed something to make life on River Road more interesting other than watching the leaves grow in the spring and fall in the fall. We were isolated out there.

Didn't see other kids, or adults very often. Our foster parents were pretty clueless about life in general. Not conversationalists. For some reason, Arthur started to talk to me in a way that he didn't want them or anyone else to get, so he started making up words. Before long I was doing it too. But he was always better at it than me. You called yourself a singleton. I know you didn't have any brothers or sisters, but what about cousins, or aunts, and such? Didn't you have much family?"

She gave me a squint, said it was her turn to go. I used her absence to take deep breaths and try to get my head into where this family inquisition might go. When she came back, she had that worried nelly look on her face.

"You asked me that before, over coffee after one of our Appletree sessions. Are you trying to change the subject? But, no, not much family. No siblings. Mom was an only child too. From New Hampshire. Moved to Maine after she met dad when he was in the Coast Guard stationed down there. Dad's family was originally from Nova Scotia, but they weren't close, so we were pretty much on our own. Now it's just Mom and me. That's why I call every week. She's still young and healthy, but you never know."

We lulled away another half-hour on the porch. I finished my tea, feeling soft and easy. Then, out of the blue, Rosie smiled.

"You know, you have become more of a gentleman this week. Whatever your brother did for the two days he was here, he seems to have had a positive effect on your sense of chivalry."

When we went back in to work on our separate weekend chores, I knew more about her, and she knew less about me. She went to her crossword puzzles in the dining room, and I went back to pretending to be alive.

"Martin," she said as I was stacking the dinner plates and clearing the breadcrumbs, "you're a thoughtful man, has anyone ever told you that?"

"No, but thank you. Harold thinks I'm thoughtless. Arthur thinks I think whatever he thinks. You're the first to suspect I have thoughts of my own."

"I wasn't talking about your thought processes, or your brain power. I was talking about your manners, and your concern for others—namely me. My husband was a loving man, but it never would have occurred to him to stack the plates or clear the breadcrumbs—that's the kind of thoughtful I had in mind. And this is the first time you've done that since I moved in. Good boy!"

We walked into the kitchen and started the hot water in the big stone sink. With wet hands, I encircled her waist and said, "Actually my thoughts are a bit more prurient than you suspect. By cleaning up quickly, we can move on into the evening—perhaps an early-to-bed night? Does that interest you?"

"You betcha. But I was just looking at you over the dinner table and thinking how nice it was to be here with you—a man I hardly knew just two months ago. Now I feel I'm getting to know you more intimately every day. I wish you didn't have to go to San Diego next week."

Neither did I. Well, mostly. I was eager to go back "home" because of Marcella. But I was making choices. Didn't know it then. But it's clear now. Marcella was exciting. Rosie too. But Marcella dramatized everything. Rosie smoothed life over, like a warm blanket on a cool night. Marcella hated covers. Martin was lucky to find Rosie. Me too. Me too with Marcella.

DR. SOCORRO

Another day just me talking, her taking notes. Sounds good, Doc. You wanta know bout Marcella. I'll give you Marcella. Martin never knew her, except through me. That worked. We knew her, Martin and me, remember?

Yeah, hell yeah. Where do I start, Doc? You up for truth or tell? How did I fool Rosie so easy?

Remember, I told Rosie that Arthur had gone from Bangor to Canada and then on to Chicago to meet Marcella. Well, right. But the first leg—Bangor to Chicago—I made up. The second leg—Chicago to San Diego was real. Marcella had asked me to route myself back that way. I did meet her family. Went to a family wedding there. Wow, what a party. Low budget but high fever. Six days after Martin's death, there I was in Chicago. O'Hare was packed, like always. But I found her; well, not exactly. Marcella walked up behind me. Just liked Martin always was—a step behind me. A week in Maine. Then two days in Chicago.

She picked me up at O'Hare. Two cousins with her. No chance to talk. Good for me. Did the wedding three hours later. Partied all night, almost, slept maybe three hours. Then a quick shower, sack breakfast in the cab back to the airport. Full plane. Couldn't really talk.

Biggest difference? Between Maine and Southern California? Maine is a wild forest. Even now. San Diego is tame. Maine's forest runs from Canada to New Hampshire. Solid. Continuousness. Uninterrupted. And quiet. Lindberg Field is noise. Freeways. People. Horns. Buses. More cabs here than in all Maine. Fighter jets five miles away at Miramar. But bits and pieces—not connected.

OK, now Marcella. You already know her California attitude and living the coastal good life.

Looks. You mean different, right? Right, thought so. How different could they have been? Marcella. Short but taut. Hair like silver but black as coal tar. Looked damp. All the time. A permanent tan, more tea than coffee, and opalescent. No one in Maine ever had that skin. Pronounced eyes, set well apart. Like she could look at you with one eye, or the other. Look through you. See your secrets. If she stared at you, you felt thrilled, or twitchy. Depends on why she's sighted in on you. Is she hunting, or just grazing? Man, those eyes. Some girls, most I ever knew, had eyes with some kind of light color. But Marcella had eyes like giant bruises inside milky white ovals. Livid eyes—black *and* blue. First glance—her best feature. Then, second glance— her lips. Like Rosie, Marcella's lips were full. But Rosie wore lipstick. Marcella's lips glistened. Probably something in a tube. But it never faded. She never applied anything. I watched her do her makeup, late in the afternoon. Six in the morning. Didn't matter. Liquid lips, like magic, you know?

Rosie was soft, soft everywhere. Marcella hard. Hard like sheet steel, only polished. Nothing matted. Slick, smooth but impenetrable. Temperament? Not sure what you mean. Marcella was a screamer, in or out of bed. Feelings ruled actions. Rosie was a planner. Slow to burn, tempered herself down. Took her time about it. Marcella flashed like a fit whirling out of a wasp's nest.

The doc switched pens, from the fountain pen to a ball point.

"Now, Arthur, I have a good physical image and a little about their temperament, but ultimately, your relationship with both women came completely unwound. I gather it started with Marcella shortly after the Chicago trip. Tell me about that, please."

Sucked in a double dose of Pacific Ocean air. Yeah, right— San Diego Bay. You being technical today, Doc? The air, sea air, was me breathing. I'd been breathing for Martin for two weeks. But stepping off the plane at Lindberg Field, just two days after the boat accident, after Martin died, I could finally breathe on my own. Being Martin was hard work. Being Arthur is a walk on the beach. Relished it. Different because I didn't have to spend every second reminding myself who I was supposed to be.

Marcella was suspicious? That's your question? How do I explain us? Me, her, *and* Martin. That's my explanation. I had a lease on my downtown San Diego apartment but was mostly staying in hers an hour away. Didn't we already cover this? Seems like we did.

She had her space. I had mine. Why not move into one place, or the other? Dunno. Guess I was reluctant. Guess she was glad. Except for what happened with Rosie, I'm monogamous. Maybe monotonous too.

Lemme give you a metaphor for Marcella. Fire and Ice. Like the house specialty drink at *The Blind Burro*. Tequila, a splash of habanero juice, a pepperoncino, over crushed ice. Crank your flame or cool you down. Up to you. That's why I just visited. Fire can burn you. Ice can chill you down. Give you a brain freeze.

A talker. That she was. Long talks about fidelity. My word. She called it cheatin'. I mistakenly called it a misdemeanor. Felony, she said. Banishment or castration. See what I mean? Different ways of looking at a simple reality. But no matter. She was in my face bout it. *You cheat—you die.* She told me she'd always know if I was cheatin'. Not the case. Three days at her friend's house in Chicago. Sleeping on the pullout in the den. She did not know. Not a hint of Rosie. So much for the famed Latina radar.

Other men cheated on her? Yeah, she talked bout that. Some ended up with high squeaky voices. Most others moved way far out of town. Best thing about her. She was predictable. Don't mess with her.

Switching gears on me, Doc? What about the hull insurance business here in San Diego? So-called business, I shudda said. Left Marcella's place and went to the office down on Broadway. Called Harold's boys right off. No answer. No surprise. Left my usual message. Should have taped it to save breath.

"Hi guys. It's me Arthur. Back from the home office. Had a good talk with your dad. Told him what you said to. Business is promising. Lots of possibility out here. Two fleet policies under active negotiation. Enough premium to support the office for half a year. And on and on like that. OK with you boys? Hope you are fitting in with the San Diego scene. Call me if you need anything. You know, policy forms, endorsement language. Anything technical. You know the number."

How's that for business development, Doc? Doing what Harold sent me out here to do. Taking care of the boys. Hell with business. It's about the boys.

Cynical? Who, me? Not a chance. I didn't volunteer for this. They didn't give a shit about business; I was the only one paying any attention to business. It was getting away that counted. Yeah, we had one. Four messages on it during the two weeks I was in Portland and Chicago. All from the day I flew back east. All from Harold. Asking about the San Diego branch office. Crap. It wasn't a branch. Not even a twig. Two-room suite in a barely decent downtown office building. Two blocks up Broadway from the harbor. Pricey real estate on the other side of the street. Pity, too.

Could have been real. You know why? AmHull was an insurance company in its own right and was also a managing general agent for three first-class carriers—Sunderland Marine, Atlantic Mutual, and Lloyds of London. We sold hull and machinery coverage on the vessel itself, protection and indemnity on the boat and the crew, and cargo insurance on both inland and ocean-going cargo. Specialized in commercial fishing. Plus, solid book of sport fishers, ocean-going yachts, and racing sloops. Harold Sr. was a smart old bastard. Knew something. Fishing people and yachters ignored their insurance coverage until a loss occurred. Then they obsessed about it. Most times they had too little coverage, or wrong endorsements, or just bad underwriting coverage.

Harold Sr. took good care of Maine boaters and fishers. Key is underwriting. Writing endorsements and policy agreements that'd pass muster when it counted. He took care of them. They stuck with him. Even when other companies quoted lower premiums and better coverage.

But that was a hundred years ago. And three thousand miles away. No Harold Sr. out here. Not even Harold Jr. Just the boys. Gonna be a long wait.

Back to Marcella. OK. Makes me happy, too. She's a corporate executive headhunter. Makes sure her clients know the ground before plowing begins. Hunted new executives like Blackbeard hunted buried treasure. Worked strictly for the potential employer. Charged 'em a flat fee to find and place just the right executive in their operation. Rich bastards. Save the out-of-work execs. Poor bastards. She got paid on the upside, or down. Didn't matter to her.

"Arturo," that's what Marcella Wella called me. Did I tell you about that? No? The only person to give me a name I liked. Promised it was not Mexican for Arthur. Her way. *Arturrrro.* She sort of sang it, spreading out all three syllables *aah . . . tour . . . o.* With kind of a Mexican jazz sound on the second syllable. I loved it and loved watching her lips move when she said it. You know, I felt it was a grown-up label, a West Coast name.

Well, now that you ask, I guess I'm not that sure she was of Mexican descent. Maybe some other Latin American ancestry. Yeah, she told me. But it was about Arturo. Sort of glossed over the rest.

"Did you miss me or what? You better have, or I will cut on you, and you know what a pipsqueak you are about pain."

"Yeah, sure I missed you." She could talk but she was better at kissing. She had a velvet tongue and knew more about lip sucking than any woman I'd ever known. She could make me wet by just kissing me. That first day back from Maine, by way of Chicago, was like the Rose Bowl parade way up in LA. Everybody happy. Game to follow parade. She pressed up against and almost into me and said with a grin, "Ah, I feel you did miss me, *mia wisa,* maybe I better get you home before you embarrass yourself."

We waited for the bags, and I told her my practiced lie about Martin.

"Martin's fine, but the job is getting kind of complicated. Business is down in Portland and so Harold is thinking about letting the office girl back there go. Her name's Alice. Martin can do her job. If that happens, he won't send Martin out here as much as he has been. Bullshit on that. Ain't gonna happen. We are not going to be permanently split up by some stupid insurance company. I'm going to look for a job here. A *new* job. Hopefully one that has some East Coast travel in it. I need to get back to Portland more often. Once this job folds up here."

"What do you mean, folds up? I thought things were just starting to pick up here."

"Shit, Marcella. Harold's boys are bagging it most of the time. They are never gonna cut it. No new business. Even Harold will catch on sooner or later. He'll pull them back and shut the San Diego office down. Wasn't his idea in the first place. Just the boys'."

As the cab lurched up the steep hill from the airport, the back way past Cal Western Law, I studied her profile. Worried? Stressed? What? She frowned, sunk back in the seat beside me, and exhaled.

"Man, that doesn't make any sense to me. If you and Martin have to be together and this AmHull job goes south, why doesn't Martin just move out here?"

"Cause he's tied up back there. He wants it his way. Just like always. I gotta move, not him."

"Not that I want it, but maybe that's not so bad. Maybe I'll go with you. I've never been there—in fact I've never been anywhere except Fresno, the LA valley, Chicago three times, Panama with my cousin, and here. Are you really serious? Do you think this Harold asshole will pull the plug on your job?"

"No, he won't, as long as his boys carry the con job. But they will have to produce some business, not just race their boat, and hang around the San Diego Yacht Club. But I'm saying that the money is getting tight. Harold is thinking about expenses. In fact, he just told me last week that Martin can't come out here every month. That means that I will only be with my brother one week a month, when I go back there. That's just not enough."

We drove on up the hill five miles to her apartment and quit talking one foot inside the doorway. Hard to talk and shed clothes simultaneously. After we gobbled one another up, Marcella mellowed down into the pillows, on her stomach and elbows.

"So, how's Martin, really? You told me about the job and all, but nothing about what a good time you had. What's up, you and he have a fight, or what—that'd be something."

"We fight; don't think we don't. We just keep it private, that's all. That's what everyone should do. Fight and then shut up about it. He's busy, I'm busy; he's got Rosie, and I've got you. Not much has changed."

"Well, you've changed, Arturo. You are a different lover than you were last week. You see a dirty movie where the girl does all the work or what? You acted like you wanted me to make all the moves. I'm not saying it was bad—I kinda liked it—but it was different."

"Well, Babe, whatever it is, we'll make the best of it, won't we?" I said, feeling lame and tame at the same time. Marcella gave me her look, the one that asks, you ain't cheatin', are you? This was the second weekend back from Portland/Chicago. We were in Dos Amigos Café, down on the boardwalk for lunch; didn't think about the irony in the restaurant's name.

"You want to know what being Martin's twin is like? Do you? Do you like metaphors? Well, he's my anchor. Safe in a storm. But in a calm sea? Still an anchor. I can't go anywhere. Not that I want to. Well, maybe that's what's changing. You see, now things are different. I'm here, you're here—that's different. Maybe I don't need an anchor—maybe there's no storm—maybe I want to sail out to sea on my own. But Martin seems to be like pulling me down, you know? He's been my anchor when I needed one, just like I am for him. But he sure as shit doesn't need one now."

"What are you saying, lover man? Why doesn't he need an anchor? Does that mean he's glad you're gone, glad that you're out here? Is he feeling free and easy without you—his anchor—it worked both ways, *que no*? That's what you always said before . . .″

"No, I didn't mean that. What I meant to say was he needs me now more than ever—trust me on that—his need is greater than ever. But it's like . . . it's like . . . my brother has been an anchor on me my whole life. Pulling me down. Even before the boat . . ."

My gut sucked in by itself. Squinting against the pain, I knew I was about to tell her. She can't know. She has no right to know. I'm the only one who can know. We know. But nobody else can. I tried to get her off the subject.

"Hey, Babe, enough of this high-level philosophy. What say we hit the beach?"

"Boy, you are one swift quick-change artist. One minute you looked like you are going to spill some deep dark secret that is making you all white in the face and the next you are all red in the face—like you're pissed at me. Then you back off and say, 'Let's hit the beach.' What's in your head?"

"I'm sorry, Marcella Wella. I'm just wound up and a little jet lagged. You're right about one thing—Martin and I had an argument. It's twisting me up. Has been two weeks. But it's a good thing. I need the space. I need some more rope to break the surface. To breathe. I'm starting to think that San Diego needs to cut a little of the cord from Portland, you know? Here I am, twenty-six years old. Still running interference for Martin.

Makes me crazy sometimes. Makes me hate him sometimes. I'll admit it. Well, maybe not hate, just pissed. But that doesn't mean that anyone else can badmouth him—nobody else better even look at him cross-eyed."

Marcella gave me the look again. One eyebrow up, the other down. Chin out, head tilted to the side. The one that said, hey man, you're talking stupid again. Man-oh-man, I am not good at this charade stuff. Back home we could hide and be whenever we wanted. No one caught on. Now, on my own, I can't even hide from myself. Out of the blue, she said it. Crazy, huh?

"So, why don't you get your butt tattooed—your brother doesn't have one. That will sure enough mark you as you. Everyone says you're so alike. They can't tell you apart. But you can just drop your drawers and there you'll be—your own man, at last. When they say, which one are you, you can say 'I'm the one with the tattoo on my butt, wanna see it?'"

I gave her a look, one that said, woman you take the cake for stupid—do I look like a California dope head? A sailor on leave? But I didn't say anything, I just thought about it for a minute. That was a mistake—it's always a mistake to think when Marcella is giving you a look.

"I can see you're thinking on it, Arturo. Good man. I knew you had some *cojones*. Tattooing is not for East Coast sissies, and it's not for everyone out here either. But in the barrio where I come from, it's a way to post your attitude, you know? Prove you are not just some gringo looking to score with the bikers and the prison gang. A high-class tattoo is a work of art. Ain't cheap either. My cousin makes fifty thou a year, mostly in cash—so it's like seventy-five thou in East Coast honest money—like you make."

"Your cousin? You have a cousin in the tattoo business? So why don't you have one on your tight little ass, if you think they're so cool? I have inspected you. Tattoo-less. Fearsome, but *sans* tattoo.

I bit you once on the behind, remember that? Besides, tattoos are not art; they are mutilation. I'm not into that—besides, I hate pain, and I don't have an attitude that needs expressing that way."

"My cousin is an artist, but I'm not. I don't like him, or his art. I don't have a tattoo because it's mostly a male thing—it's something you guys with attitudes do. Sure, chicas and valley girls and Irish U2 babes are inking up, and sure, I've been tempted—you know, maybe just a little one in a discrete place could be way cool. But then I think about those scabby guys with snakes and knives and crosses all over—they are freaks—that's their attitude—freakiness. But, Arturo, you have an attitude that is dying to get out—just dying to see the light of day. Or maybe it's the dark of night that your attitude is begging for. You know what attitude I'm talking about?"

Marcella, waiting for Arthur's answer, tapped a bright red fingernail on the Formica tabletop impatiently. Arthur crossed and uncrossed his legs, looking at first one bare ankle and then the other. They used these conversational interludes between sex, as both resting and arousing.

"No, but I bet you're about to tell me. What attitude?"

"The one that says my name is Arthur Cheshire and I'm not my brother. That attitude! Sometimes even twins need to sing alone, not in stereo like you and Martin do all the time."

"No," I said to Marcella, "that's you talking. That's your attitude about me, not my brother. Why would I want a California freak thing? I'm a Mainer, remember."

"Sure Hun, but how about those deep-water sailors in Maine? How about those famous guys who go way up north in those tiny little fishing boats with giant storms and all that shit? Are you saying those guys don't get tattoos? What about that guy in *Moby Dick* who was tattooed all over hell and went looking for a white whale? I bet they got tattoo parlors at the harbor in Maine, right? It ain't just a California thing."

Arthur got out of bed, pulled on his shorts, and went to the bathroom. When he came back Marcella was half dressed, like he liked her, and sitting at the window seat looking out over the freeway.

"I been thinking," she said more to the window than me. "Maybe you owe it to your brother, not yourself. Maybe it's time one of you did some little thing to stake out your own little place on this big ole planet. You're twins but you ain't the same person. I was thinking about 'La Bamba,' you know the song, right? Lots of guys sing it, but when Richie Valens did it was him, not somebody singing his song. A tattoo could be your song, not Martin's. No two tattoos are alike, you know?"

"But, Marcella Wella, we are identical. And we could get identical tattoos too. Hell lady, that might even give us more hide and be opportunities. Maybe I should. Just *maybe*. Lots of pain there. But I don't know if I want to put Martin through that."

Marcella squinted at Arthur, got up, pulled an orange tee shirt on over her head, and headed downstairs. Halfway down the stairwell, she stopped and said to a man she could no longer see, "I tell you what. When you guys decide on what you're going to do about your tattoo, lemme know. I'll call Maldonado."

MALDONADO

The next day, Monday morning, Arthur and Marcella made a pact. Arthur got Marcella to keep it a secret.

"Marcella Wella, let's go see your cousin before I lose my nerve. But you *got* to keep it a secret—something between you and me. I don't want anyone to know. Not even Martin. Shit, if he found out, he'd get one too and it would look just like mine."

Maldonado's Tats & Inks sported a bewildering display of photos, ink drawings, and not-so-famous figures in all their partial nude glory. Once inside the heavily barred door on lower

Broadway, the parlor loomed bright and airy. Three-tube fluorescent lights covered the ceiling in the twenty-by-thirty foot ground floor space. To Arthur it seemed odd—too much light for such a dark idea. Marcella stepped ahead, past the four tattoo cubicles, looking for Maldonado. Arthur, holding back at the entrance, held his breath. On his left, two girls sat close to another girl, who was having her butt-crack inked. The friends giggled, the tattoo artist, a grim Asian with a tattoo machine in his left hand, seemed frozen as he pierced the girl's skin. She seemed oblivious. Hardly even interested.

Spotless floor, brightly painted tables alongside reclining single beds—no headboards, a four-inch-thick mattress with dark blue sheets and a pillow. They also had armchairs with large wooden arms, like Stickley furniture, spar varnished, with soft Indian-style cushions. Six people ignored Arthur. Two were getting tattooed. Two were using little electric needles with slow, intensely deliberate movements, and the last two, the look-alike friends of the girl getting her butt inked with a bright green and yellow dragon, kept on giggling.

"*Que pasa*, Señor Arthur," Maldonado said, as he slowly walked from the rear wall toward Arthur. "Marcella says you got an itch to be different. Man, you come to the right place. I can make you Spiderman if you want. But maybe you don't want to be that different. What you thinkin' *compadre*?"

Arthur watched the human tattoo swagger slowly toward him. Here's a guy with attitude from ankle to top-not. Maldonado's knee-length Levis cutoffs were nearly the same color as his knees, calves, ankles, and thronged-feet. Lots of deep blues, red curvy lines, green slashes, orange animals, and most of all, silver knife blades slicing every which way. His baggy sweatshirt, with cut-off sleeves, raggedy neckline, gave way to hands, wrists, elbows, biceps, and sloping shoulders that told many stories, in black and red ink, letters, cursive lines, numbers, little heads, big-breasted creatures, and snakes. Lots of snakes, and even more flames and clouds. Maldonado was his own advertisement.

"Not sure what," I said. "Or why. Needles scare me. Are you licensed? I hate to ask, but I'd like to see it. Does it hurt a lot, or just a little? I only want something small, something not visible when I'm fully dressed, like I am now. Not a showoff person, you know. And, well maybe this is a really bad idea. Maybe I should wait a few months and come back."

"Hey man, chill. We got a license, and you can see it back there on the wall. Sure, it hurts a little, but a tattoo needle is an electric machine, you know. It's tiny and only goes less than one sixteenth of inch into the skin. That's not much, you know, maybe like a wrinkle on your forehead, not so deep, my friend. And we don't allow no drinking or drugs in here. You gotta be sober. We give you drinking water, that's all. But don't worry about being safe, we are 100-percent safe in this place. I got two other artists working here, but Marcella, she's family, you know. So, I'll do you myself, just for her. And give you a haircut on the price. OK?"

Marcella reached over and with her right thumb and forefinger, pinched the skin on Arthur's forearm.

"See, Hun, that's what it's like. Just barely into the skin, and it don't hurt much unless you are a baby or a weenie. You ain't' no weenie, Arturo, I know that. So, tell him what you want and let's get some color on you. You're turning even whiter than you already are; we gotta get on with it."

"Well, but I want to be careful here. I need to know exactly what it will look like. I don't know want snakes, or knives, or names. No skulls either."

Maldonado pointed out various designs on three of the four walls. The fourth, mirrored from floor to ceiling like a dance studio, reflected the pictures, drawings, and hundreds of satisfied customers. Before he could suggest anything, Marcella piped up.

"Hun, what you need is something to make you part of me, part of California—something that will make you remember me when you get tired of us and head back to the frozen north. You need me on your skin, and under your skin. *Que no?*"

"Babe, you are under my skin already and I'm not going anywhere. No names, remember? I just need a little design to make me a tiny bit different from Martin. That's all."

Maldonado would turn out to be as moody as he was talented.

"Hey, *compadre*, lots of guys want to be different, from their old ladies, or their hometowns. So, you want to be different and your brother lives in Maine or one of those East Coast places, right? I got an idea. How about a surfboard, or a seashell? Something like that?"

"No, we have seashells in Maine, and every once in a while some fool brings a surfboard to the Eastern shore. It needs to be something that says California, but not in so many words."

"Well, how about a little sea-urchin? You know, like the ones in the Scripps Aquarium. You been there yet?"

Marcella held on to Arthur like he was going to run away. "Yes, we went there. Arturo, remember we saw the ones that they said only live off the Southern California coast. An urchin from the Southern California sea. That's wild. It could be for me *and* California. Take that back and show it to Martin."

"Babe, you are into irony. Innuendo, too. How about an urchin with a tiny little tail? Your tail is always on my mind anyhow, might as well be on my butt too. But if it's on my butt I won't be able to see it except in the mirror—what does a little urchin look like in the mirror? Is it right upside up or upside down—which way is it swimming? Toward you or away from you?"

"Arturo, you are such a dumb shit sometimes. Or is it just another twin thing with you? You are always wondering about whether something is the same, or something is reversed, and about how things look. That's because you and Martin are always the same, never reversed. Well, a tattoo on your tight little butt will reverse you, but a little sea urchin will look like what it is head on, or in the mirror. Jeeze, are you serious?"

Arthur asked Maldonado if he could do a sea urchin. Maldonado said sure.

"You know skin sags over time. In a few years, your sea urchin might look like something that wants to slide down your leg. That's pretty saggy skin, butt skin. How about your ankle? If you wear socks most of the time, you can hide something small on your lower ankle. That skin never sags down there."

And that's the way it happened. Arthur ended up with a red, blue, and yellow sea urchin about the size of a quarter on his left ankle. As Maldonado was inking him, he showed them a before-and-after picture of a woman with a tatt of a butterfly on her right breast. The before picture was when she was twenty-five, the after, when she hit forty. The butterfly had become mottled butter, no longer flying, but looking a little on the rancid side.

"See?" he said, "Sagging skin ain't no good for tattoos. You will always see an ankle tatt, don't worry none."

As for the pain, Arthur's only comment during the forty-five-minute ordeal was to ask Marcella if her cousin was stitching a beach ball on to the side of his leg. Maldonado and Arthur ignored one another. He treated the tattoo artist like he treated his dentist. Never look at them, and they might go away. And he refused to look down at his ankle. Lock-jawed the whole time, he gamely tried to laugh at Marcella's jokes.

"What is the one word you never want to hear in a tattoo parlor? Oops. What do you mean you're all out of red and used pink? Oops. What's the difference between a bruise and a tattoo? Oops."

"Give it a break, Marcella. You're gonna give Maldonado the hiccups. Don't do that to me."

All Arthur wanted was a tiny mark, something to identify him-self, and differentiate him from his brother. But he got much more than that. He told Maldonado he didn't want to see it until it quit hurting and the little scab fell off. So, he and Marcella drove to her apartment. Three quick Tequila shots helped; a beer chaser mellowed him. Later that afternoon, sitting on the little porch overlooking I-5, he got up the nerve to look. The sea urchin was ornate and colorful. It had an innocent look but was no doubt noticeable. Looked bigger than a quarter. No, Marcella said, it's actually smaller. Just right.

But something else was there, something so small he didn't notice it at first. He asked Marcella if she had a magnifying glass. She beamed and said, "I thought you'd never ask." On close inspection, he discovered Maldonado's little surprise, his trademark, so to speak. The magnifying glass revealed a tiny little "m" in red ink imbedded in the urchin's blue tail.

"Your bastard cousin put his own initial on my tattoo! That is against the law, or it ought to be. He has no right. What a bastard . . ."

Marcela burst out laughing.

"Ah Arthur, it's not an em for Mal. I mean, it was Maldonado's work, I mean he inked it, but I told him to."

"This was your idea? What were you doing—we never talked about this. And besides . . ."

"Sure, we talked. Or at least I did. I told Maldonado some-thing about his blue urchin needed another color. You were busy chomping down your jaws and grinding your teeth. You kept drinking bottles of water and trying not to cry. I said to Mal, why don't you put a little m in there in red ink so Arturo will think of me whenever he sees it. Mal was trying to be funny and said yeah, cousin, whenever he looks down, there you'll be. So, I got pissed at him. Don't you remember that?"

"No, I don't. But what the hell, you're my girl now. It's so tiny you have to have a magnifier to see it, maybe it's a good thing. Come to think of it, why shouldn't you be on my ankle as well as on my mind? This is sort of like a California chica brand, right?"

"Brands are cowboy things, Arturo. This is not my brand; it's my hex mark. If you cheat on me, this little red m will become like a hot needle and will cause you much pain."

To prove his loyalty, and to test her conviction, they went to bed—at three o'clock in the afternoon. To sleep. Really.

PORTLAND. SIX WEEKS AGO

As Arthur steered the Hertz Ford 500 out of the turnabout at the Portland International Airport and onto I-95, his hands hurt from gripping the steering wheel so hard. Coming home from San Diego had always been a thrill. But this return was a series of firsts. First time in a rental car. First time without his brother at the gate. First time to live the lie his life had become in just two months. And the first time he talked out loud to himself.

"Freaking ridiculous—this is doubly stupid—I cannot keep this up—I'm me in San Diego but Martin here? Get ahold of yourself? Which one? Yeah right—I'm as rational as any two guys I know."

He punched the power button on the radio, releasing a fifty-decibel blast of Portland's AM560 news/talk. Pure drivel. Punching the preset buttons one by one, he waded through four rock stations, a Spanish station, a so-called new country music twang station, and landed on FM 90.1, Portland's NPR affiliate. An interview of some guy who had written a book about the deep-seated desire in everyone to sing, sounded just stupid enough to take his mind off himself, and his brother, for the twenty-minute drive into town. But it turned out to be the most bizarre drive of his life. He started talking to himself about his dead brother.

"What about your brother's corpse that you buried without his duck boots—you remember, the duck boots you wore back to town the day after you killed him—the duck boots you kicked off on the side of his bed when you fucked his new booty because she thought you were him. What about that?

"What the fuck you talking about? We agreed to that, to all of it, the goddamn rock just offshore killed you, not me! Shit, man, there are lots of identical twins and sometimes one of them dies. The survivor is no longer his brother's keeper. That's what they say when you lose a brother, even an ordinary brother. Not that anyone said that to me—why would they? No one even knew I'd lost my brother. We fixed that, remember? I been in California four weeks now. Out there, I had only myself to listen to. But now that I come back, you show up. So, we are back, you say? We? Fumbuck that. There ain't no we. There's me, Arthur, in California. And there's me, being you, in Maine. You're hiding under the floorboards up there at Camp Cheshire, and I'm being you down here in town. Just like always. I'm ain't your keeper no more. No, sir! I am you. How's that for being my brother's keeper?"

Arthur turned off the NPR drone, turned onto Brighton Lane from 14th Street, and eased the Ford through the one-car hole in the hedge. Parking behind Martin's beat-up blue pickup truck, covered with rain spots, leaves, and a plastic newspaper wrapper caught in the radio antenna, he tried to lower his pulse rate. Couldn't hold it. Broke out into another crying jag, his third since he left San Diego nine hours earlier. Backing out onto Brighton, he drove three blocks down before pulling over into a carless parking lot next to his dentist's office.

Remembering the time he and Martin had fooled the hapless Dr. Donshire when they played Hide and Be in his dental chair, one with cleaned teeth and the other with a missing tooth next to number thirty-two, Arthur collapsed over into the passenger seat.

For three weeks now he'd been telling himself to say "so long" to the single life and hello to the double life. Except it was really a triple life—Marcella, Rosie, and him. Blathering to the dashboard. That ain't it either. We were twins; now we're quintuplets. Mine is a quadruple life—me, Marcella, Rosie, and Martin. Grab a page out of our book; somewhere on it, you'll see all four of us. But I'm the only one of the four of us who has read the prior page. And none of us has read the goddamn next page. Take it from the surviving twin—the guy who beat the wrath of the river and saved his brother's image. But not his life. Goddammit it, Martin, why didn't you just drive the goddamn boat yourself! Now see what you got us into?"

"Rosie, hey Babe, I'm home, what's for supper?"

"Hey yourself," she said, coming down the landing encircling him with hungry arms, and separating him with her even longer legs. They rubbed each other up a while and then unhooked. Ignoring the inane question about dinner, they shed clothes all the way up the central staircase, barely making it to the bed before collapsing into one another.

"Is Arthur aright?" Rosie asked two hours later.

Looking at his reflection in the bathroom mirror, standing beside her at the sink, she continued, "You seem sort of distant and you've been home two hours and you've not even mentioned his name. Everything OK in sunny San Diego?"

"Oh, sorry Babe. Sure, everything's fine. He's living the good life. Sun, surf, babes, life's a bowl of cherries out there. But I'm not sure he realizes how much he misses the way life ought to be, the way it is here at home. Maine. This is real. California is a fiction created by the Disney people. I mean, it's fun and all that but it's deceptive. I'm an expert on deception. You can get addicted to it, you know."

Rosie toweled off, pulled a pair of grey sweatpants on, added a black tee, and padded back into the bedroom. "Deception? Yeah, I guess you qualify as an expert."

Rosie finished banding and weaving her hair, bent over to stick something in the lower drawer and mused, "I wonder if maybe your little trips to California aren't turning you into your brother. You seem more talkative but that's just the half of it. The thing is, you talk more about abstract things. 'Deception.' 'Disney people.' You're philosophizing—do you realize that?"

"So, I've always been a philosopher—maybe a hick one—but a philosopher none the less. Maine does that to you—you're pretty good at it yourself. That's what attracted me to you in the first place, Babe. Did you think I was just a hick? Wrong, I'm a hick philosopher; that's an upgrade."

Later, at their first quiet dinner on the rear deck, Rosie posed what she likely thought was an innocent question. "What's with the rental car, Martin? Your truck, your once-beloved truck, has been rusting away in the drive waiting for you. Didn't you see it looked like crap? All dirt and rain spots. I thought you'd taxi home and jump into that beater and head for the car wash. Why the rental?"

"I'm gonna sell the truck. Too old and beat up. Breaks down every winter. Arthur has got himself a new ride out there in la la land—a Ford 500—a businessman's car, he calls it. I like it. So, this guy next to me on the airplane says that he only rents from Hertz because they have the Ford monopoly, and he tells me about how solid and reliable the Ford 500 is. Quick decision. I'm selling the truck. And then when I come back, I'll buy a Ford 500. Did you know that Hertz sells their rental cars when they get thirty thousand miles on 'em? They have a web site that's only a few months old now. They let you look at every aspect and . . ."

Rosie reached across the little two-foot diameter cocktail table and took hold of his wrist. "Martin, slow down, my man. We were talking about philosophy and abstraction, now here you are going on about Fords, and Hertz, and changes that surprise me. How come you never mentioned this to me on the phone? And by the way, how come you're too busy out there in San Diego to take a moment and call me? You know we only talked two times in three weeks; what's going on with you, Martin?"

"Nothing. Like I said, I'm pretty much a hick at lots of things. And I think my life deserves some changes every once in a while. That's all. Jeeze, it's just a car. What's wrong with shucking that old truck and getting a shiny car?"

"Well, you're anything but a hick. But come to think of it, and since you bring it up, I was first attracted to you by your lack of guile, by your simplicity. I don't mean that you're simple. Don't frown at me that way. I mean simplicity as a virtue, not as a judgmental thing. You had a way of making life simple—now you are sort of, I don't know, expanding things somehow. You talk about California as though it doesn't really exist, but you go there and come back all different somehow. You talk about concepts that are complex and you don't simplify them like you used to. Don't get me wrong—I like you—particularly the new you. But I'm not sure you're the same smart and simple guy I fell for three months ago—you seem to be a smarter and more complex guy that I am really falling for now. Does that make sense to you?"

"Nope, but I like it just the same. Well, I spoke a bit soon—is that still where we are—liking one another? I could get all-gooey on you, get down on one bended knee with a rose in my teeth. Let's say I did—would that move you from merely liking me to more than that?"

"Oh, Martin, I think you know my feelings—better than I do maybe. But, darling, don't make me say something sooner than it ought to be said. We are still in the learning phase here—although we're on a fast track. I do care about you, and I hope what we're building is real. But I just can't say what I think you're asking me to say—at least not today."

Arthur's hangdog look worked, although not the way he hoped. Rosie got up, moved around the cocktail table, clasped his head with both hands, and gave him a nose kiss—followed by a real kiss. Not a kiss of passion, but a kiss of compassion—one she hoped told him maybe I love you, but for now let's take things one day at a time.

Arthur almost lost it; almost gave up. But gathering himself, remembering he was not Martin, he said, "Sure Babe, whatever you say. Speaking of one day at a time, I'd best get myself into the study. I've got a pile of paper to read before I face Harold tomorrow. He'll have lots of questions about his boys, and what he thinks they are doing for AmHull in San Diego. Harold never changes, never philosophizes, and never gets it. Neither does Alice Blue Gown. At least I hope they never do."

A MONTH AGO

"Morning, Martin, how are things in our San Diego branch?" Harold said about an hour after Arthur got to the office. An hour! Arthur, wearing his best Martin smirk, was pissed but tried to restrain himself.

"Things are just dandy, Harold. Business is still slow but we're doing some underwriting out there—no claims to speak of but that's good, right?"

"I meant how are my sons. I didn't hear from Arthur at all last week and the weekly report from the boys was not very informative."

"Well, Arthur's very busy—he's doing all that you asked of him. But he's not trying to develop new clients—you said that was the boys' job. So, he sticks to underwriting the risks they bring in, and he's ready to deal with the claims on the business that they produce, but as I said, there's not much new business. Of course, it could pick up, that all takes time."

"Yes, but how are the boys? I mean on a personal level. How do they look, are they happy? You know I get very little from them."

"Well, I don't know about the boys; I didn't see them. But Arthur is looking well, he's happy with his life although he still would rather be here full time. Who wouldn't, right?"

Arthur tested Harold almost daily by asking him questions that he'd asked before—as Arthur—but that Martin probably wouldn't have.

"Harold, why do you think our reinsurance companies pay so much attention to the age and condition of diesel engines in commercial fishing boats? Why do they make us get so much technical information on that before we can quote a premium?" That was an underwriting question, one that Martin paid no attention to. Instead of giving Arthur a puzzling look—which he would have had he thought Martin was Arthur—he gave Arthur the answer he thought Martin deserved. A short, over-simplistic answer suitable for accountants and claims adjusters, but woefully inadequate for working "underwriters."

Arthur's testing of Alice Blue Gown was problematic. Despite the density or clarity in the question, she just gave him that odd look, obviously picturing him in her mind as Martin, but which Arthur took for, "Are you wasting my time or yours?" But when he moved to something she should have no interest in, no matter who she thought she was talking to, she surprised him.

"The Fontaine brothers? You asking me about them? Those boys are your problem, Martin. Keep me out of it."

He'd been standing while she sat. Both the little stack of papers on her giant desk, and her nails were perfectly propor-tioned. But he could not understand why his mention of the Fontaine brothers account should irritate her. What a nerd.

Arthur tested their casual acquaintances even more indirectly. He asked old Fred, at the hardware store, if he'd seen Martin lately. Fred, moving the gumball on a stick from one side of his mouth to the other, answered like he was on a game show. "Yeah, he was in on Monday, but he didn't buy much. I guess that old relic of a house of his is getting snuffed up to suit him."

He posed a tricky one to Patsy at the main information counter in the library. "Liz, I forgot my library card. I been out in California a few weeks, did you know they have digital signatures for book checkout—can you look up my number for me?"

"Sure, Martin," she said, looking through him rather than at him, "it'll just take a sec."

"Whoa, if you look up Arthur's number, I still won't be able to check out this book. Look up Martin's, I'm the reader in the family, remember?"

"Damn, Martin, when are you guys going to give me a break? You've been coming in here for four years now and you constantly expect me to tell you apart. I'm going to make a print of the books you check out and then compare it with your brother's list; maybe I'll get some clues from your reading habits."

"How do you know we don't use each other's cards just to make sure you cannot label us by comparing our reading lists? Have you ever thought of that? Besides, I never knew you kept a list of what people read. Isn't that a crime or something? I mean, who is the head librarian here anyhow, George Orwell's prodigy?"

He didn't mean to piss her off and didn't realize his tone was harsh. "Mr. Cheshire, you know that's not in the least bit funny. Now, if you want me to look up your card number, give me your driver's license. If you don't, well, have a nice trip to California, and don't forget to get your card so we can omit this little conversation next time."

Tricking total strangers had been fun since they were little kids, and Arthur hadn't lost his touch. He asked the checkout girl at the Pop N' Stop if his brother had been in that morning. "No, I don't think so," she said. Arthur retorted, "My twin brother."

She looked at him like he might have been a little off. They get lots of nut cases in that fast food joint. Ratcheting it up, Arthur said, "He looks just like me—we're really identical twins."

She said something like, "Nope, you're one of a kind as far as I'm concerned."

Moving close to home, Arthur, while rearranging Martin's lockbox in the bed of the pickup, at the Winston Super Mart, tested a cocky looking teenager sitting in a '95 Mustang. "Cool car, man, how long you had that ride?"

"A year, man. You a Mustanger?" the kid replied.

"No, but my brother is. He owns this truck, but I was wondering if maybe you had ever let my brother drive your car? I been out in California for a while, but he told me he drove one just like yours a week ago. He even talked about that cool silver stripe on the fender panels. Black and silver are his favorite colors, and he sure does love Mustangs."

"Nah, man, if your brother's a boy, he never drove this chariot. Only me and chicks drive this baby."

Pimple face, in the passenger seat, thought that was hilarious. His teen age shrieking almost drowned out Arthur's retort. "Hey man, you oughta let boys drive. A real chick would probably make a hard left, pop open your door, and dump your dumb ass out on the street."

The more Arthur tested his acceptance in Portland as Martin, the more convinced he became that Martin was still there. Arthur knew his physical reality, but playing Hide and Be with himself took on a virtual reality that mirrored his physical world. At the new mall on the north side I-95, he tried one of their oldest Hide-and-Be tricks.

Walking into the Payless Shoe Source, Arthur said, "I'm looking for a pair of Reeboks, black in an eleven. You got those?"

"Yes, we do. You sure about the size, or should I measure your foot?"

"I been wearing elevens since I was eleven. Too old to change now."

The clerk, a girl of maybe seventeen, brought two boxes, knelt down in front of Arthur, and slipped the left shoe on him. Arthur stood up and frowned. "This is too tight. You sure it's an eleven?"

"Yes, sir, see it's right here on the box. And it's also on the tongue in this brand, see?" she said, picking up the right shoe from the floor and pulling out the tongue. Arthur frowned, put his loafer back on, and got up. Over his shoulder as he walked out, he said, "There is something wrong here, I know I'm an eleven."

Two years ago, when they'd tried this same trick, Martin had been waiting outside, dressed in identical clothes except for a bright orange pair of socks. He'd let Arthur walk down the mall about twenty feet and then he ran back into the store. But today, Arthur picked the closest bench on the walkway, took out the glaring hunter's orange wool socks he'd bought at K-Mart, changed his brown socks, and walked back into Payless Shoes. Swinging open the double-wide glass door, he spotted the young clerk.

"You know, let me try those on again, maybe they do fit."

"Sure, I didn't even put them back in stock. Here they are."

He sat down in the same seat, she opened the box, and Arthur pulled off his left shoe.

"Did you just change your socks?"

"What? These orange jobs? No, I had 'em on when you tried to fit me two minutes ago."

The original trick took two boys wearing different socks. But this version only took one boy changing socks. It validated Arthur's growing belief that he could be himself and his brother, just by changing his socks.

Their favorite Hide-and-Be trick was at the one-barber barber shop on the corner of Forest Avenue and Congress in downtown Portland. The barber, a woman named Trudy, began her career as a stylist, but discovered better money in leaning up against men in a barber chair and cooing at them while she charged eight bucks more than most barbers. A busty woman can attract a lot of business that way. Among her many talents was a sensitive sense of smell.

Martin and Arthur had great fun with her because she always commented about how a customer smelled when he got into the chair. Like, "Did you enjoy those onions on your hamburger for lunch?" Or, "Sweetie, did you just pop out of a bubble bath or what?" Their best trick on her was on their fifteenth birthday. Martin went in, she cut his hair, and noticed, predictably, the minty smell of the mouthwash he gargled in the car before going in. Arthur had his hair cut fifteen minutes earlier at a Chop the Locks shop two blocks away. There he'd told the barber to lather on some bay rum that smelled awful—you couldn't miss it. As soon as Trudy finished with Martin, he popped out the door. Arthur, waiting outside, jumped back in, saying, "Hold up, lady, would you mind clipping the hair in my ears?"

"OK," she answered, not looking at Arthur as he jumped into the chair. The bay rum hit her as soon as turned toward her. She leaned closer and said something but backed off and went about clipping his ears. When she finished, Arthur asked, "Hey, do you by chance have any bay rum after-shave? Because my brother likes it."

Trudy, wearing her best frown by now, said, "Honey, I know this is a trick, but I don't get it—what's going on? You got a bottle of the stuff in your pants pocket, or what?"

Arthur couldn't quite figure out how to run that barber shop trick again. But his new game made all the old ones pale by comparison. It had been good practice, although neither of them could have known it before Martin died.

PORTLAND. FIVE DAYS BEFORE THE FISHING BOAT ACCIDENT

"So, what did the lady at our bank tell you about my check, Martin—are they gonna prosecute us or not?"

Martin gritted his teeth and gave Arthur that palms-up gesture he used whenever his brother started in on him about money. "No, Bud, they aren't going to prosecute us. They never were going to prosecute *us*. It was you they were thinking about because they told you two days ago that our account was overdrawn, and you wrote the check to Abe's Liquors anyway. That makes it an intentional overdraft—that's what they said. But I talked them out of it with a little Hide-and-Be stuff."

"Really, how'd you do that?"

"Man, you should have been there. It was sweet. I just told her, 'No ma'am. I assure you that's not my signature on that check. I told you, it's my brother's. We have a joint account, and he can sign checks just like me. It was me you told about our account being overdrawn when you called day before yesterday, but I couldn't tell him because he was up in Augusta delivering groceries to our aunt, who has cancer, and, well, I know that's no excuse, but . . .'"

"So, how does that make it OK?"

"It's not OK. It's still an overdraft, but it's not intentional because they believed me when I said it was me that they called. Why didn't you tell me they called? More to the point, since it was you they called, why did you write the check to Abe anyway? Did you think the bank would just loan us the money?"

"No, I thought we were out of beer. First things first, bro. I thought I'd get my paycheck tomorrow and deposit it and everything would be fine and dandy. I didn't count on Abe cashing the check before I even popped the lid on the first brew. Man, that guy is desperate for money."

"Well, I covered us with my check from two weeks ago. Good thing I still had it in my wallet, or we'd been paying a big, humongous check charge and you'd be facing a warrant, or something, for an intentional overdraft. They tell me it's a crime, but I think they might be shitting me there. Why is it a crime if you don't know that you're out of money? It's just an accident, right?"

"Yeah right, that's why when they call me next time, I'll answer the phone—Martin speaking, is this the bank calling?"

"Hey, Arthur smarter, I got a better idea. First you deposit your paycheck, then you write checks. Like everybody else. Like me. Why can't you be more like me, and less like yourself?"

"I'm more than like you, Bud, I am you. Isn't that what you told that nice lady at the bank?"

DR. SOCORRO

The walk with Officer Martinez down the brightly lit, slick lino-leum flooring made Arthur feel a little queasy. Seven weeks in jail, nine sessions with Dr. Socorro, and they still didn't seem to get it. He was Arthur, why was it so hard getting them to see that?

"Good morning, Mr. Cheshire, I hope they are treating you OK in the cells. And by the way, thank you for giving me those tips last session about how San Diego County could make this facility more bearable for people awaiting trial."

Arthur had taken his time arranging himself in the arm-chair across from her. He moved the chair a little to his right so that he had an angle view of her and could still see Mission Bay through her window to her right. Her fourth-floor office, at mid-morning this time of year, produced a dazzling light. No clouds today, so the sun was behind the building and wafting out onto the water and the low ridge of hills separating the bay from the ocean. Perfect.

"You're welcome. But those weren't tips, really. More like complaints. Right? I guess I don't have reason to complain yet.

This is still only jail, not prison, right? So, Doc, how are we doing? Have you got a handle yet on who we are? That's still the point of me getting out of the cells three, four times a week to talk, right? We are complicated, but truthful—that's my story."

"Mr. Cheshire, well, Arthur, if you please, I am making progress because you are letting me inside the life you and Martin led in Maine. But it's today that I have to understand before we can hope to understand how you got here. I don't mean just to California; I mean how you came to be living two lives at once."

"Good start, Doc. By two lives, I sense you are going back to Rosie there, and my life with Marcella out here. I love both of them. I surely do. And they both love me, even if they ain't sure which one I am anymore. It just occurred to me that you should talk to them. Have you called them? They will tell you the straight-up truth, I know that because I loved them, and they loved me. Me, not my brother."

Dr. Socorro scribbled a long note, shifted her chair sideways, causing Arthur to scoot his to keep her profile in view. She'd noticed this before but was not sure what to make of it. Was he uncomfortable with being face to face, or was it something more prurient? And why did she feel odd when talking about death of a loved one with him?

The seventh anniversary of her life as a widow was coming up. A day she hated and made sure to always spend with close friends. Somehow, despite four years in medical school and two more in residencies followed by six months of intense psychotherapy, the day her beloved Norman was murdered flooded back and swamped her like a rogue wave. The fact that she was an eyewitness to his death and had her own gunshot wound in her left calf made her sick all over, every seven years. Norman had spent his life after college as a San Diego police officer. The story they told her was still gritty, still obscure. Something about getting out of his marked police car in their driveway, when a murdering bastard opened fire from the driver's side of his truck parked in front of their house. He had a machine pistol and spent a full magazine at Norman. One bullet ricocheted off the driveway and hit her as she got up from pruning a rose bush, near the driveway. Every seven years, that god-awful day came back, in full color.

"Arthur, you say both Rosie and Marcella love you, but don't you know they might also be terribly angry with you? You tricked both of them, you know. And as far as I can tell from what you've told me, Rosie doesn't write to you. Marcella is right here in San Diego, and hasn't visited, has she?"

"No, she has not and that pisses me off. I was never anybody but Arthur to her. I guess I did trick her a little about my brother, but you know that's just us. We had to trick people to save ourselves when we were little kids. I never told her that but whatever. You know, love me, love my brother. She knows that. We made it clear to her plenty of time. I don't know if she's changed or what. Tried calling her. No luck. Changed her number. And they don't offer 411 service in the jail, ya know."

"I'm glad you brought that up, Arthur. Don't you think they suspected something was wrong? How could you possibly believe that you could engage in sex with two women, in two different cities, without one or both of them catching on? You told me about your game, Hide and Be, but that cannot work for very long. These women, from everything you've told me about them, were very smart. How long did you think you could carry on the charade of being two different people, loving, and making love to two different women?"

Arthur did what he'd always done when challenged by the game. He became his brother. "Now, just you hold on there. Rosie loves me, Martin. It's that simple. Marcella loves me too. Even if she thinks I'm Arthur. She's right technically speaking, but we have our own lives to live. We had to combine to survive. Don't you get that? You are making too big a thing out of the sex part. What in hell difference did it make in bed? Both of us liked it—me and Rosie—me and Marcella. I bet that if I'd died, Martin would have taken care of Marcella for me. That's all I did for Rosie. Take care of her. We owed that to both of them, don't you see? It was just sex; quit making such a big thing out of it."

"Arthur, I get that's your view of sex. But I wonder if you think that sex was just sex for the two women you slept with. Have you thought of it from their side of the bed? Rosie fell in love with Martin. That's what you told me. Then you tricked her into thinking you were Martin and started having sex with her. Now she knows Martin died, or at least she knows that's your story. Your new story. Have you thought about what she thinks, if you are only now telling the truth? Maybe she hates you for lying about the death of a man she loved. Maybe she hates you for sleeping with her; that's a kind of rape, isn't it . . . ?"

Arthur jumped up, turned his back on her, and screamed, "Officer Martinez, you out there? Get in here right now—I want out of this room!"

As Officer Martinez closed the door with Arthur in tow, Dr. Socorro called the judge's clerk and asked her to schedule a chambers conference with the judge and both lawyers.

CHAPTER THREE
WHO ARE WE?

US DISTRICT COURT—San Diego, California

Judge Eli Hightower's chambers consisted of his desk, a huge
Cordovan leather executive chair, six smaller black leather arm
chairs, a court reporter's stand and swivel chair, two flags, one
book-lined wall, one oversized poster-board wall complete with a
thirty-inch combo-calendar and docket list, a three-by-five foot
picture window with a better Mission Bay view than Dr. Socorro
had, and the wall that faced his desk with two other doors, one
leading to his private bathroom, one to the courtroom hallway,
and the third to his antechambers. And of course, since this was
a federal facility, not a state-owned building, solid hardwood
flooring. His robe hung on a hook next to the American flag.
His umbrella stand doubled as a holder for the California flag.
Overshadowing everything, the twenty-four-inch official pho-
tograph of President George W. Bush set the tone.

Sitting squarely in the middle of the room, behind his cross-cut oak desk, and looking as bewildered as the president, Judge Hightower said, "Come on in" to the soft knock on his door by the bailiff.

"Good morning, Your Honor," the lawyers and Dr. Socorro said, almost in unison.

"Have a seat, do you need a record, or can we do without the court reporter?"

Assuming to speak for everyone, Cabelson said, "No, Your Honor, we'd like to keep this informal. I don't think anybody needs a record."

Kemper nodded, and Dr. Socorro smiled uncertainly, but said nothing.

Judge Hightower flipped open the thin file on the middle of his old-fashioned leather-bordered ink blotter.

"This file is almost as thin as it was when you all were last in here. My clerk says you have something to tell me, which I took to be a kind of status conference on where you are on identifying the defendant. Who wants to start?"

Both lawyers looked at Dr. Socorro, signaling to the judge this was her idea in the first place. "All right, Dr. Socorro, you're up. What's going on?"

"Well, Judge, I called the lawyers on the phone yesterday, after my session with Mr. Cheshire. I gave them a sense of where I think we are. They thought you ought to know about it, so your clerk kindly gave us an appointment with you."

"Yes, Doctor, I gathered that. And I allowed it because this is a rather unorthodox criminal case in the first place. But I don't want any of you to get in the habit of discussing this without the preliminary step of written reports, and a proper motion for the record that tells the reviewing court, that would be Judge Garrison, how we are proceeding. This is his case, but he asked me to conduct a hearing to find out, if that can be done by a psychiatrist, exactly who is headed for trial. Mr. Cheshire's been charged, so having his lawyer here is appropriate, but I think we need a record. So, if you don't mind, let's get the court reporter in here."

Within three minutes, the court reporter swished in, set up her digital steno machine and her notebook computer, and nodded to the judge, who intoned, "All right, let the record show that we are in chambers on Docket Number 2003-CR-218519-FJM, *United States of America v. Martin Cheshire*. Present are US Assistant Attorney Stran Cabelson, US Deputy Federal Defender Gordon Kemper, and Dr. Lisbeth Socorro, from Court Psychiatric Services. Doctor Socorro, will you give us an update on your consulting sessions with Mr. Cheshire? And if you don't mind, I'd like you to supplement this record with a written report for the court file, if you please."

"Yes, Your Honor. Since we are on the record, I should tell everyone that Mr. Cheshire has signed a waiver of any physician-patient privilege. I'm not sure he has one, since I made it clear to him that I am not treating him as a patient. My role is limited to assessing him for a narrow purpose and reporting my findings to all parties in the case. So, he clearly understands that there is no confidentiality to what he tells me.

"Now, the reason I asked for this conference is to let everyone know that the problem of who he is, is more complicated that I thought initially. If I might, Your Honor, let me give you a psychiatrist's view of the question rather than a legal view. In my brief conversations with the lawyers, they emphasized the ambiguity of charging or defending a man whose name and identity are in question. But from a psychiatric perspective, the problem is not who is sitting in the chair in my office telling me about his history, but rather who that person in the chair *believes* he is. They, pointing to the lawyers, asked me to identify him. But now that I've had seven fifty-five-minute sessions and two ninety-minute sessions with him, I don't think it's that simple. From what I know now, I can offer you a professional opinion. But it might not help anyone."

Judge Hightower held up his hand. He closed the flap on the file folder, got up slowly, and went to the bookshelf on the far wall. No one said anything while the judge was in motion, given his reputation for using quiet moments to ponder what someone says. He picked a book from the shelf and returned to his desk.

"Dr. Socorro, this is an old courtroom manual on criminal procedure. It's no longer in effect, but I was looking in it the other day pondering a different issue, and something struck me that might apply to this case. Let me read this to you. Quote, where the proponent seeks to offer opinions, conclusions, or inferences to assist the factfinder in determining a fact in issue, and such opinions are beyond the ability of the factfinder, the proponent may offer such opinions, conclusions, or inferences from a witness qualified as an expert in the relevant field. Where the expert is proffered to testify regarding a novel scientific principle, the trial judge must make a preliminary determination that the novel scientific principle has sufficient bases that the opinion will be helpful to a jury determination of some issue in the case. There is no need for the trial judge to find that the principle is generally accepted in the field to which it belongs. End of quote.

"So, Dr. Socorro, that long-winded rule is giving me a headache right now. Let me ask you two simple questions. First, are you about to offer me something that is akin to a novel scientific principle? And second, is your opinion going to help me, as I sit as a factfinder for Judge Garrison? I am like a one-man jury. I must decide who Mr. Cheshire is. I'm mindful that you said that your opinion might help no one, which would include me. Did I hear you right?"

"Judge, I don't know legal rules of procedure, and might not have said what I intend to say. The lawyers want me to tell them the identity of the man in jail. He comes to my office twice a week and tells me that he is not Martin Cheshire, the name on his jail ID card and the name on the arson-murder charge. He says his name is Arthur Cheshire. I believe he is both, at least psychologically. Well, Your Honor, he's both. He's Arthur sometimes, Martin sometimes, and has lived for a few months now as both himself and his brother. I'm not saying he's crazy, to use a non-psychiatric term, only that he has mastered the role of being two different people at the same time."

Judge Hightower wheezed and used a Kleenex to rub the tip of his nose for almost a full minute. Then, tucking the Kleenex into a drawer on the side of his desk, he nodded his head from left to right and started talking.

"Remember, all of you. I told you at the open court hearing that identity was not the only issue, mandated to me by Judge Garrison. I think I said there was also a sanity issue. Now I'm thinking there is a third issue—one that maybe Judge Garrison will want to answer on his own, as a matter of law, not of fact. That is, whether a defendant can be charged criminally with being his brother."

Stran Cabelson was visibly nervous. He'd been taking rapid notes and underlining things on his yellow pad. Gordon Kemper didn't even have a legal pad and seemed almost amused by what he was hearing. He alternately grinned, nodded his head, and tapped his knee, as the judge settled himself deeper into his giant leather chair.

Cabelson spoke first.

"Judge, if you please, this is getting a bit far afield. I mean our office has no intention of charging the defendant with being someone else, brother or not. We believe he murdered his brother. He may think he's his brother, or even act like him. But his brother is dead. That's our case, and we'll prove it. All we agreed to was, a psychiatric evaluation to determine his identity. I object to expanding Dr. Socorro's brief beyond that narrow issue."

Kemper took the pause in Cabelson's monologue to jump in.

"Your Honor, this is part and parcel of both problems. I think, given the informality of this conference, and the fact that Dr. Socorro obviously has something to tell us, that we should hear her out. Nothing she says here is binding on the prosecution, or the defense. But I have a feeling we can all benefit from listening to her."

Judge Hightower waved them both off.

"Proceed, Dr. Socorro."

She leaned forward in her chair after looking down at her lab book and took a deep breath.

"OK Judge, sorry to have gotten off track. Arthur and Martin are monozygotic twins, meaning that they were born at the same time from the splitting of a single egg after it has been fertilized. Consequently, the DNA is identical in both twins. We have to start with that. Foster parents may have abused these boys. That abuse likely created in them the deep need to protect themselves by acting as if they were just one child, instead of two . . ."

Cabelson stood up and raised his right arm up toward the bench. "Objection, Your Honor, irrelevant and immaterial and outside the scope."

"Overruled," Judge Hightower said. "This is an in-chambers discussion, not an evidentiary proceeding. You may continue, Doctor."

"Thank you, Judge. This is a vital element in understanding how and why identity is so important in this case. The Cheshire twins invented an involved game they called *Hide and Be*. It began as pure self-defense, but over their childhood became something quite different. Not merely a game, but a way of life. If the man I'm seeing twice a week is Arthur, and I'm leaning in that direction, and if his brother died in Maine, which is entirely plausible, then there is no murder in a fishing cabin in Mexico. On the other hand, if the man in my counseling room is Martin, and if his brother Arthur did not die in Maine, but in Mexico, then maybe the arson-murder charge is viable, but that's a legal question which I'm not qualified to answer. From my perspective, neither question can be answered without first figuring out who the man in jail *believes* he is. If he believes he's Arthur, then someone has to determine if he is sane, that is, whether his belief is the product of normal rational thinking or is he delusional to the point of impairment. If he is lying about being Arthur, then you have to ask the same question. Is the lie deliberate and the product of a sound mind? Or is it psychiatrically true, that is the product of an unsound mind?"

Dr. Socorro pursed her lips and let out a long slow breath. The lawyers had stopped their frantic notetaking, and the judge continued to slowly rock back and forth in his bench chair. There was a rustling noise at the rear of the courtroom where two young women got up and hurried out of the courtroom.

"Judge," Cabelson asked, "is it OK for me to ask the good doctor a couple of questions?"

Turning toward her without waiting for a formal reply, Cabelson said, "Doctor, there are lots of maybes and inclinations in your preliminary assessment. Can you give us some sense of *when* you think you will be able to tell us whether you believe the guy or not, and if so, how both sides might be able to test your thesis?"

"Sure. I think that another three weeks will be sufficient. And as for testing, I would think that both sides will want to interview two very important witnesses—Rosie Anderson in Maine and Marcella Munoz here in California. As the defense lawyer already knows because he's been talking to his client all along, the man I *think* is Arthur, has been living in Maine for a few months as Martin, and sleeping with Martin's girlfriend, Rosie Andersen. Remarkably, at the same time, he flies back and forth between Maine and California and sleeps with Marcella Munoz here in San Diego. Those two women, if what Arthur is telling me is true, have been intimately involved with *both* Martin and Arthur, because they were duped into believing that both were alive. Their suspicions, beliefs, doubts, hunches, and so on will be helpful in assessing Arthur's truthfulness. Or Martin's lies."

Judge Hightower nodded again and asked the room a question, not looking at the people in the leather arm chairs in front of him.

"You know, it might help if anyone knows whether either Martin or Arthur Cheshire was ever fingerprinted. Might that help you, Dr. Socorro?"

"It would, Your Honor. Then, I could engage in some confrontational therapy."

"Well, choice of therapy is up to you. But in court the precedent is clear. Identical twins have different fingerprint patterns, notwithstanding they share a common DNA. And while it's not allowed in court, polygraphs can be helpful in determining identity. In fact, polygraphing the two women and the defendant might be a good idea. Lastly, dental records for both boys might be available to compare with the body found in the fishing cabin in Mexico.

"Dr. Socorro, while the lawyers are following those areas, you ought to keep talking to the defendant. We know one thing for sure. He *is* the defendant, and he *says* he's Arthur Cheshire. It's odd in the extreme for you to interview a man in your medical office with a name tag around his neck that says he's his twin brother."

With that, the chambers conference ended with both lawyers promising the judge supplemental reports about the investigatory path everyone thought would produce some answers.

san DiEGO. FOUR WEEKS BEFORE ARTHUR WAS ARRESTED.

On the Friday after he got back to San Diego from Portland, on what turned out to be his last trip, Arthur had lunch with Harold Junior at the elegant lobby bar in the Del Coronado Hotel. Marcella had driven the day before up to Fresno for a two-day visit with her family. So she said. But inexplicably, there she was, coming down the main staircase in the hotel—the one that wraps up around the vintage iron cage elevator to the left of the open bar area. She had a small overnight bag in hand and wore oversize sunglasses and a beautiful grey and white sun hat. Arthur was mystified as he watched her cross the lobby, past the registration desk, and step into the foyer. She maintained a steady gaze straight ahead, not glancing right or left.

"Hey," he said, more to himself than to her, as a tall, prematurely gray-headed man stepped away from the cashier's desk, caught up with her, took her bag, and then her arm. First reactions to such a thing are always physical. Bile moving up from the stomach cavity to the throat. A burning sensation building up in the frontal lobe. And sweaty palms. But all of that pales in comparison with gut pain, the searing ache under the rib cage, and the inexplicable loss of breath. Arthur felt it all. But his own guilt magnified at the realization she was doing to him exactly what he'd been doing to her from three thousand miles away. She was cheating on him eight miles from her apartment just over the Coronado Island bridge.

"Wasn't that Marcella?" Harold Junior asked.

"No, I thought it was at first, but my Marcella is taller, classier and, as it happens, out of town today."

"Well, from the look on your face, I thought I was about to see a confrontation between you and that older distinguished dude that the not-so-classy babe spent the morning with upstairs in a suite. At least that's my assumption based on her spiffy little overnight bag. He's checking out at the crack of noon on a weekday, Arthur."

"Well, Harold Junior,"—that always irritated him but never to the point of actually commenting on it—"you're probably right about the assignation but you got the wrong lady. Besides, you would have hated it if I had to kill that distinguished dude right here in the lobby. Your father would have disapproved."

"Well, you could have used your brother as an alibi—Christ almighty—I'm sitting here with you, but I could never swear that you, Arthur Cheshire—is here, while your brother, Martin, is alive and well in Portland. You guys have always mixed me up, you know—sometimes I think you do it on purpose."

"Harold Junior, we'd never do that to you—what would be the point of us mixing you up? It's us we want *you* to mix up."

They went back to the small-talk drivel they'd been at since ten-thirty that morning. Just then the ornate grandfather clock struck its deep bass chime twelve times.

"Did you know that clock is signed by Pemberton and Cooke?" Harold Junior asked Arthur.

"No shit," Arthur said through pursed lips, as he watched Marcella and her too-tall gentleman friend walk through the crowded lobby to the front entrance. He lost them for a moment, as the man held the door open for Marcella, who tipped the brim of her hat down, and stepped out onto the pebbled circular drive.

"Yeah, man, Dad told me to look at that bloody clock when I called him from the lobby the first day we got here, what was it, six months ago now? He said those guys, Pemberton and Cooke, were making clocks in Bristol when his great-grandfather made the trip from Bristol across the Atlantic to start the business in Portland. Funny how that ancient stuff gets to Dad."

"Yeah, right, Harold, your dad is a sucker for the old days. Hates change more than I do."

With that, Harold Junior mumbled something about his dad hating tennis, fished underneath the small table for his tennis bag, and took his leave out the door and down to the dazzling tennis courts between the hotel and the ocean. Arthur took a deep breath, then a sip of water. The waiter came back with the bill. Arthur paid the bar bill with AmHull's business platinum credit card and went out front to nail down the obvious.

Palming a twenty-dollar bill, Arthur asked the white uniformed bell captain, in an intentionally secretive tone, "Did you see the tall, gray-haired man in the tan with a flashy babe in a pale green come-get-me dress?"

True to form, the always solicitous bell captain lowered his voice, mouthed sideways that he didn't get the dude's name, "But he's from Los Angeles. Drives a coal-black Porsche 911. Sweet car."

"How about the babe? Know her by any chance?"

"She's a local."

Arthur stood there, as though there was more. Fifteen seconds went by. Arthur took the hint. Fishing out another twenty, he learned how the bell captain knew the man was LA and the woman local.

"Simple," he said. "He's got a Beverly Hills license plate holder on his personalized plate and a Los Angeles Country Club decal on his windshield. She, on the other hand, drives an old beater with no license plate holder and a stack of San Diego PD parking tickets up over the visor."

Yep, Arthur said under his breath. That's my Marcella— parking tickets and all.

"Well, I guess I was wrong about them being together, if they left in separate cars, I mean."

"No, you were right, man. They drove off in different cars, but they were definitely together. He paid her parking bill, and she patted his skinny butt before he drove off to the little wife and family in LA—they were an item all right."

The next day, Arthur confronted Marcella over the phone. She admitted she'd been in the lobby of the Hotel Del and that an older man had walked her, arm in arm, across the lobby. But, she insisted, it was business.

He raised his voice. "You're lying, Babe. You should watch out for rich guys in Porsches, one of them might steal you away from me."

Her voice spiked up as she spat back a response. "What the hell you talking about, Arturo? You accusing me of something or what? If you got something on your . . ."

"No Babe, hold the phone here. I was just making talk. I meet with Harold's boys over there at Del Coronado and I always see fancy cars, like Porsches. Guys that drive Porsches are inherently suspect to guys like me. I didn't mean anything by it. Are you overreacting or did I just innocently discover something I shouldn't have?"

DR. SOCORRO

"Arthur," Dr. Socorro said, "is that all that happened? She just left and went to Coronado Island? You didn't follow her to make sure she was cheating on you?"

"I ain't a stalker, Doc. I ain't no killer either. We never hurt anybody with the game. People, plenty of them, tried to hurt us, but we never meant no harm. When Marcella brushed me off like that, giving me a flat kiss and a wave of her hand, I knew it was happening, I just didn't know his name, not then anyhow."

Arthur turned away from Dr. Socorro and toward the plate glass window looking out over toward Coronado Island.

"I guess it was that bridge that got me to thinking. I was all heated up because Marcella was cheating on me, but at the same time I was living with two different women. Bridges, Doc. That's what it was. See, me and Martin, we always lived around bridges, all our lives. And sometimes we were on the other side of the bridge, know what I mean?"

She finished her note, turned the page, and set the pen down. Her black skirt rustled as she adjusted her seat.

"I'm not sure what you mean, but I think you saw the irony, even then, of your girlfriend having a thing with an out-of-town man, while you were pretending to be Martin back in Portland."

"Yeah, you see, that was it exactly. I was Arthur here and Martin back there. Arthur was faithful to her here. Martin never even met her. How could he be unfaithful to her? I don't think you see how it really was—you know me here, and then living Martin's life back there. It started out make-believe you know, just to protect Martin—to keep his life going—after the accident and all. But it was my own life, the one I was in here in San Diego, which had to come to an end. Marcella pissed me off at first when I found about the too-tall dude. But she actually did me a favor, you know?"

"How's that? I'm not sure I'm following you."

"Remember what I told you about what Harold Junior told me in the lobby, just before Marcella came down the stairs? It sunk in pretty deep. You know, about him saying that Martin was alive and well in Portland. He didn't know what he was talking about, as usual. But it made me think, right there with a Bloody Mary in my hand. Jeeze, Doc, I was not living two lives, I was living one—it was our life. But then when Marcella went south on me, I knew I had to pick a life—mine, his, or ours. It led me back to Portland, and Rosie."

"Arthur, think back for me, please. When did you decide to give up Marcella in San Diego and make a permanent life with Rosie in Portland?"

"Doc, you surprise me. Didn't we go over this last time? I mean I told you about Marcella and her tall dude from LA. That was it. A hellva predicament. Now, that I'm in an even worse fix, I can see how stupid it was. But at the time—flying business class, back to Portland—with the seat next to me empty, it seemed so clear, so easy, so fitting. Somehow the fact that I was above the earth and sitting alone made the decision to stage my own fake death an easy one. I was Martin in seat 6A, next to the window—and I was Arthur there in 6B, on the aisle. It was the first time I imagined the two of us not together, but apart—it was almost as if there were three of us—Martin, Arthur, and me. I was going to kill the Arthur in 6B while saving the Martin in 6A. It was like I was squished in the middle but facing backwards looking at the two seats and seeing my brother and myself outside myself. I can't describe it in any other way. I guess the psychic hotline would call it an out-of-body experience—but whatever it was, it was eerie—clear but eerie. And, as I said to myself over and over flying across one great river after another, and then seeing the Great Lakes, remembering that Martin died on a river, it came to me. The right thing to do is let Arthur die so Martin can live."

"Well, Arthur, you knew you could not bring Martin back to life. And you knew that pretending to take your own life was not real either. You were twins, but I don't see anything in your life that was psychotic, let alone pathological. You speak of one death as though it was not real and the other one as though it was. I mean, you do understand, don't you? Martin died. You lived. You still live—you are here, in my office. You are not confused about that, are you?"

I heard her. I did. But it was like she wasn't talking to me. So, I told her the truth, and hoped she'd write it down.

"Martin should have never died. He was the younger twin, remember? He was the little brother that I was supposed to protect—to save—to nourish. But I didn't do that. I let him down—strike 'down'—I out and out killed him. I drove the damn boat, I hit the damn rock, and I let him drown to death, or bleed to death, or whatever the fuck it was that took him instead of me. It was me that should have drowned, or bled, or suffocated. It was fumbucked from the start, don't you see? Now, through the magic of DNA testing, it would be me. Arthur *would hide*, and Martin *would be*. Permanently."

Dr. Socorro looked at her watch. Whenever she did that, I knew my time was almost up. She never looked at the damn watch if we had time left. She only looked when it was time for me to go back to the cells. I tried one last time.

"Doc, you know about all those Marines they have over there, training on the beach, with the Seals and all that macho stuff?"

"Well, there are some Marines over there, but mostly sailors and naval airmen. Camp Pendleton, up the beach about fifty miles from here, is where the Marines are."

"Whatever you say, Doc, but my point is what they always say, you know, 'Once a Marine always a Marine.' Ain't that right?"

Dr. Socorro had seen the bumper sticker. She gave him a palms-up answer with a question on her face.

"Well, that's it, see. Once a twin always a twin. One of them dying doesn't change anything. They still got one another."

HIGH IN THE SKY—ESCAPE FROM ROSARIO

Arthur's head felt like a racquetball slammed at fifty thousand feet as they flew over Lake Michigan. He'd been intermittently dozing off and then startling himself as his dropped forward onto his chest. Fishing a pass-the-time-away magazine out of the seat pocket in front of him, he was surprised to find a two-month-old copy of *The Atlantic Monthly*, opened to an article about detecting suicide as a defense to life insurance claims. Sipping the now-warm beer on his tray, he skimmed the article. Suicide—Met Life fraud investigations—telltale signs in fake deaths—non-death DNA.

Page 58, center column: "DNA is something of a cultural icon. Everyone talks about it, especially after the O.J. case."

He'd forgotten the tabloid speculation about O.J. having a twin, which accounted for the blood match at the crime scene. The main point of the story, how DNA and testing for genetic identity would greatly influence culture and society in the twenty-first century, hit home. "We," the global society that is, "need to deal with the vast implications of research into our genetic makeup." That's because, the article proclaimed, "Medicine, privacy, insurability, ethics, patents, and other business issues, matters of paternity and immigration, criminal investigations, and even military applications, will become matters of scientific fact rather than mere opinion. Knowing for certain who did this or that, who lived, who died, who ought to be out of prison, and who should be locked up, will all become clear in the bright light of genetic testing. No one can hide from his DNA," the article concluded.

Except us, Arthur thought.

He wasn't interested in the military applications of DNA but the words "privacy, insurability, ethics, paternity, and criminal investigations" caught his eye.

"All individuals can be distinguished from each other at the DNA level. This is because the DNA of each individual is different, at several different levels, from all other individuals (except for *identical twins*, whose DNA sequences and patterns are *identical*). These so-called genetic signatures can be identified in the laboratory by Southern blot and Polymerase Chain Reaction based assays which exploit DNA polymorphisms."

Arthur spilled his beer when the captain announced that they would shortly begin their descent into Portland and cabin staff would soon come by to pick up the lunch trays. He patted his jacket with the little paper napkins and tried to settle his racing pulse. God almighty, it's that simple. Twins are one.

They'd always known that, he thought, but here it is inside of little parenthetical markers in plain font. At first, it made him a little sick, reminding him of how Martin's blood had oozed in with the rainwater, the engine oil, and the saltwater in the bottom of the boat. This asshole, he thought, punching the name of the author in the text box running down the right-hand pane on the page, thinks we are genetic freaks of nature. It pissed him off but moved his mind away from Martin's real death to faking his own. The nerve. The real point of genetic testing is to pinpoint something, something important, like who you are. To say that all individuals can be distinguished from each other by DNA testing and then sort of slide in the fact, *in parentheses*, that *all* does not mean identical twins. Fumbuck. It's like saying identical twins don't count, aren't important, aren't genetically significant in the global sense. Well, he's important, he thought, so's Martin.

If he faked his own death by using Martin's DNA to establish with scientific accuracy that he died, well, who'd know? His DNA is mine, it says so right here. He's already dead but nobody knows that. All I have to do is switch his DNA for mine. *Hide* my DNA and let his *Be*. The game continues.

San Diego—Marcella's Apartment

Arthur and Marcella were enjoying the Sunday morning sunshine. The *Los Angeles Times* and yesterday's *Boston Globe* were scattered between the lattes and cranberry scones at the Starbucks overlooking Mission Bay, three blocks down the street from her apartment.

Marcella seemed incredulous. "Arturo, why do you want to go across the border and fish the Pacific from inside Mexico? The California coast has the same fish as the Mexican coast and you speak the language here—down there on the Baja, they fish for gringos, ones that are easy to catch, like you. Do you want to be caught, or do you want to fish?"

"Because everyone says that surf fishing is better the further down the coast you go. I don't speak the language down there, but you do. You could help me find a little beach shack where I can fish in the day, and you can cook the catch at night. We need some time together, like a little vacation—so humor me. Help me find a place. Maybe AmHull will finance the weekend. I'll tell Harold that there is a premium to catch down there—that's all he cares about."

"Why do you need a little vacation? You just drove all the way here from Portland with that U-Haul trailer strapped to your car. I still don't see why you needed that thing just to bring your records and your stereo out here. You could've packed them and shipped them. Jeeze, Arturo, three thousand miles driving just to bring your non-funky East Coast CDs?"

"Like I said, Babe, my CDs are irreplaceable. Martin and I spent half our time and half our money collecting the best of the eighties and nineties. I was just tired of Martin having all of them back there, that's all, and I damn sure wasn't going to let some airline baggage guys lose them or rip them off. Besides, I needed my fishing stuff, tackle boxes, waders, you know. And here's the bonus. I never drove that far before. You should have come with me. I never knew every state was that different."

"I would have but you never asked. You just called from Martin's house and said you were leaving early, by three days, but would arrive on time—since you were driving, not flying. I think it would have been nice for you to fly me to Portland to meet Rosie, renew my feelings for your brother, and then spend three days driving and motelling with you across America. By the way, do you know that the only time you call me 'Babe' is when you first come back here from Portland? Is Babe what Martin calls Rosie? I hope it's not what you call Rosie. I am getting jealous of that babe and I don't even know her. When is Martin gonna bring here out year for a beach party?"

"I dunno. Maybe this fall. She works, you know, and can't take any time off."

As Marcella continued to verbally meander around his life in Portland, Arthur tried to get the U-Haul trip out of his head. Getting Martin's decomposed body up and out of the floorboards at their camp on the Damariscotta River had been a lot tougher than he'd thought it would be. The physical part was bad enough; his brother's body was decomposed, but still intact and didn't smell too bad. He'd aired it out in the boathouse. A winter in Maine will do that, he thought. It'll freeze away any smell. But it was still hard—secretly digging up your brother seemed ghoulish, almost as bad as secretly burying him had been.

DR. SOCORRO

"Arthur," Dr. Socorro said, dropping her pen to the desktop, "you are either the most accomplished liar I've ever met, or a man who is so immersed in his dead brother's personality, that he has lost his own. You tell the story about digging him up under the floorboards of that fishing shack, so abstractly, so . . ."

"No, Doc, it wasn't a shack. It was a camp. We kept it real neat, and it had good paint, and as good a boat winch as anyone on the river."

As he turned away from looking out her window, she could see the quick blaze in his eyes. Every time she challenged him, she saw the squint, as he poked his chin at her and narrowed his eyelids. So, she tried to apologize.

"Wait, I'm sorry, Arthur, I didn't mean it disparagingly. Out here, we don't have camps, but we have some lovely beach shacks along the coast for miles north and south of here. My point is that when you told me a few weeks ago how Martin died, it almost killed you to tell the story. Now you tell me how you dug up his body a few months later, and it sounds like unpacking old boxes looking for collectibles to sell at a garage sale. How did you feel while all this was going on?"

"I did not feel anything. We knew that this was just clinical. It was about our DNA, not a body. Somehow, I retreated back into time and rationalized it the same way I did the last time I pulled up those floorboards. I got through it by telling myself over and over, it's just a body—it's not really Martin—Martin is alive as long as you are in Portland. That's what everyone thinks and what they think is what counts, right?"

"Yes, I can see that. But you cannot put life events into little boxes, like shoes."

"We did. We did it our whole lives. We, me and Martin, shared our life, we lived one or the other all the time. Sometimes I didn't really know I was Arthur because Martin had taken over for me in some tight spot. So now, when he died, I had no choice, I became him. We proved that millions of times. I would hide somewhere. Martin would be me. But they thought it was me, see?"

"But Arthur," she said after taking a note in her lab book, "I don't get why you hauled Martin's body all the way from Portland to San Diego."

"Come on, Doc, you're a scientist. It's because we had the same DNA. If I died, though, that'd be real because the DNA said so. They would have a body with my DNA, so nobody could argue with that."

"But Arthur, don't you see now, that is exactly why you are here, facing a murder case? The police believe you. They believe you are Martin and that you killed Arthur. I want to help you, but I just can't say that you outsmarted them with the DNA trick. You've got to give me something to confirm that the body down there in the fishing shack was not yours, because you, Arthur Cheshire, are alive. See?"

THE MEXICAN BORDER—TIJUANA

Arthur's first trip into Mexico, with Marcella, was a glorious fake. He pretended he didn't know about her LA lover. She pretended she liked Mexico. Like many Mexican Americans, she was proud that she was born in America and never thought of herself as hyphenated—Latin-American. He felt terrible about fooling her into thinking this was all for fun—death was no fun, even a fake death. But, at the same time, he felt exhilarated by the deception.

"What is your destination and your purpose of travel, please?"

Marcella answered from the passenger side, "We're going fishing down past Ensenada to Rosario. Is the road still good, Señor?"

The border guard quit scowling at Arthur, beamed at her, and said, "Si, Señorita, the road is good, but you know it's not too good at night. It will take you the rest of the day to get to Rosario so maybe you better get going. Have a good fishing, *por favor.*"

Arthur had crossed the Canadian border hundreds of times but thought that Mexico would be different—more foreign somehow. When the guard had asked what they had "to declare," he gave him a blank look.

"Nada, Señor," Marcella said sweetly.

Arthur had never seen her act coy before; it was enticing. They pulled over to the side and two other border guards looked in the back of the car at the fishing gear, the large ice chest full of dry ice, and the assorted camping equipment. One of them said to her—as though he didn't even exist—"You know you have to be cautious below Ensenada. There are some bad people down there sometimes. What's all this dry ice for, *por favor?*"

Arthur piped up, partly to practice talking to a border guard, even if it was in English, and partly to prove that he was there in the car.

"The dry ice is for the fish we are going to catch. No one told us it was not safe below Ensenada. Do you mean that the road is not safe or what is it that's not safe?"

The man looked at him as though he should let the lady do his talking.

"I didn't say it was not safe—I said you should be cautious below Ensenada. Sometimes *Norte Americanos* do not respect the road and sometimes the wild ones, the banditos, like to play some games and scare you. It's safe anywhere in Mexico as long as you are cautious. I hope you catch some fish, so all your dry ice don't go to waste."

They pulled out of the inspection area and back onto the road through Tijuana, and on down through Colonia Vicente Guerrero to Rosario.

"Well, that was easy enough. It's just like Canada. You don't need a passport, just your driver's license. I thought they would be worried about us smuggling something, but they didn't even search the car."

"Arturo, Arturo—it's smuggling things out of Mexico that they search for. The only time the Mexican side searches you is when you fit their profile of someone they don't want in Mexico."

"Profile? What's that? I always thought I had a nice profile and you sure as hell do. That's what that border guard was so interested in—watching your profile. But seriously, what kind of a profile? What do they look for?"

"They look for people who are likely to bring in contraband— you know guns, liquor, computers, things that are dangerous."

"Guns will kill you and liquor will thrill you but what's the danger in computers? Why are they dangerous down here?"

"I don't know, but there are lots of stories around about dumb shit gringos who try to take computers into Mexico—I think it's because they are still rare here and so can be sold for a lot more money than they cost across the border."

"What would happen further down the coast—say, all the way to Cabo San Lucas? Do they stop you on the way—like checkpoints or something—or is it like Canada where you can go anywhere in the country?"

"It's like Canada, I guess—I've never been there. But going all the way to La Paz is not as easy as it sounds. There is a paved road now all the way, or least a good graded one, but it's pretty sparse, and a long way between gas and potty stops. Are you thinking of driving me to Cabo, Arturo? Why, if you want to go to La Paz, don't we just hop the Aero Mexico flight at Lindberg Field and we're there in an hour or so. Driving is for adventure, not love. La Paz is a place to love."

"No, you sweet thing—I don't want to drive you to La Paz, I was just asking because it shows on the map as the furthest place you can go on this road. At the end is the Pacific Ocean."

"Actually, lover boy, at the end is a town called Cabo San Lucas. That's where the Gulf of California spills into the Pacific Ocean. They say it's more American than Mexican—big fancy airport, big fancy golf courses, and big prices too."

"Marcella, you never cease to amaze me. Where else have you been in Mexico that you haven't told me about?"

"Mexico is very big, so big I can't tell you all the places. But actually, not that many. I don't like Mexico very much. I like Panama better."

"Panama? Why? That's no place for someone unless they are into running drugs. You're not a drug runner, are you?"

"No, Arturo, I'm not. But my family does a little business in Panama."

"What business?"

"Well, let's just say that they know about making things disappear."

"Like what?"

"Like money, and good times, and gringos."

Arthur realized the conversation was going in the wrong direction. He turned his attention to the road. Marcella went silent as well. The rest of the drive was uneventful, if you call traversing the Sonoran Desert uneventful. This part of Mexico is wild—beautiful, but wild. Just what Arthur was looking for.

They found a small hotel in Rosario that night and woke up in a wonderfully bright little town. Small shops and cafes, a plaza that was well kept, at least by Mexican standards. There was a good tackle shop with cheap bait, and helpful people. Arthur spent the day surf fishing, and Marcella spent the day wandering around wondering what the attraction was in surf fishing. He didn't catch enough to justify a hundred pounds of dry ice in that oversized cooler in the trunk. But the purpose of bringing the ice was not to preserve the fish; it was to see if they would look under the ice at the border. They didn't.

Arthur was hopeful he could establish some sort of custom and practice. Another trip or two, to let himself be seen, but in three weeks, he'd drive down with Martin's body tri-folded into a bigger chest packed with dry ice. It was safe enough for now, in the Azteca Self-Storage Company, off I-5 near the industrial piers in south San Diego.

As they were clearing the breakfast plates from the little outdoor table at the hotel, Arthur pointed up to the top of the hill on the south end of Rosario.

"Wadda yah say we go for a walk up the hill there before we start back?"

"Why? It looks like just another hill to me."

"Just because it's there. Where is your spirit of adventure? I think I saw some old shacks up there when we drove in yesterday. Maybe we can find one to buy and renovate. We could turn it into a bed and breakfast, and I could cook the omelets, and you could mop the floor and . . ."

"No sir—I ain't mopping no floors. For you or anyone. Besides, are you crazy or what? B and Bs are strictly gringo things, Arturo, they don't have such things down here."

"I'm just kidding. It's just that AmHull has got me by the throat. It makes me think about other ways to make a living. I've always fantasized about owning my own business and it seems like everyone is quitting corporate life and opening snazzy little B and Bs in remote places."

"Well, this is certainly remote, but I wouldn't call it snazzy."

She gave in. They walked up the hill, for about a mile. Marcella was tired and wanted to go back but Arthur pointed to two shacks another half mile up the road. One on the ocean side and one on the other side of the highway. They went back to the hotel and got the car. He joked her into letting him stop and look at the one on the ocean side. One room, clearly deserted, but not trashed. There was an aluminum table with a green Formica top and one chair—at least it had three good legs. An apparently dysfunctional wood stove was in one corner. Wooden planks were nailed into the wall for shelving. A sink drained directly into a hole in the floor below it, and from there, down to the ocean. He didn't get too good a look because Marcella honked the horn.

"Let's get the hell out of here before one of those Baja banditos comes along and offers to help us out—that is, out of our money."

DR. SOCORRO

Officer Martinez always thought it was a good day when he pulled the assignment—delivering Arthur to Dr. Socorro's office. He liked her looks, it got him out of the cell block for an hour, and everything in the clinical section smelled better than the cells.

"So, Cheshire, they figured out who you are yet? You know we started a pool in the guard breakroom. Each guy puts in five bucks, and when Dr. Socorro figures it out, the guy who picks the right name wins the pool. Course there are only three names in the hat, so it'll be a split pot."

"Three?" asked Arthur, as they cleared the cellblock double doors, and headed into the short hallway before reaching the clinic.

"Yeah, man. Three. You say you are Arthur. The DA says you are Martin. But the way you talk, some guards think you are both, so we made three little slips of paper—Arthur, Martin, and Them. I ain't on that pick, but the captain is. Hell, man, he wanted a fourth pick. He's way, way out there on you. Says you coulda been one guy all along. There was only one of you, but you convinced everyone you had a twin brother, who never even existed. There was a movie like that, he says. You can't put money in the pot, but if you could, which one would you bet on?"

"We don't bet," Arthur said, as they got to the clinic entrance and Martinez fished for his digital ID at the scanner to open the door. Once inside the medical complex, Martinez stopped at the vending machine. He bought two Pepsis, gave one to Arthur and knocked on Dr. Socorro's door. He kept Arthur's change, like always.

"Good afternoon, Arthur. I'm sorry I had to change the time on you, but they gave me two new cases this week, and I had to reschedule everyone to fit them in. What should we start with today? Unless you feel strongly, I'd like to get a deeper under-standing of how you managed to get a body across the Mexican border, and what happened after the fire in the shack at, where was it, oh yes, Rosario. Can we talk about that?"

Arthur stood at the window looking at Mission Bay.

"Doc, did you know the guards have a betting pool on your clinical decision about me?"

"A pool, you mean like the NCAA college basketball tournament?"

"I guess, but that's sixty-five teams. This pool only has three names. They are betting on who you end up telling the judge I am.

The guy who picks the right name wins the pool. Which of the three you leaning toward, Dr. Socorro? You and I can't bet, but maybe you could throw me a little hint and I'll try to help Martinez win the pool. Maybe he will give us each a little slice of the pot."

Talking to his back, she said, "Three? I don't understand. You are either Arthur or Martin. Why do they have three names?"

"Arthur, Martin, and 'Them.' Martinez says the captain is betting that I never had a twin. So he wants a slip in the hat that says 'them.' He thinks I made it all up. "

"Why don't you sit down, Arthur? We have lots of work to do. Please tell me how you got across the border with a body in your car."

"It wasn't that hard, not like this chair," he said, as he squared himself in front of her. "It was easy. See, I knew they would not look under the dry ice on top of the chest. I'd made the trip three times. Most of the guards were more interested in the hot chica in the car, not the gringo and his chest full of dry ice. The body was under the dry ice, on the last trip."

"How big was the ice chest?"

"Four feet wide, three feet long, and two and a half feet tall. A real monster when it was full. When I buried the body a year ago, it was in a pretty small space, below the floorboards, like I told you. I doubled his knees up against his chest to fit under the floorboards. So, the body was stuck like that when I brought it out here in the U-Haul. It fit in the four-foot box just right, with plenty of dry ice around it."

"It? You know you never said Martin's name. Does mentioning his name bother you when you talk about his body?"

"It was just a body to me. It wasn't Martin. I told you plenty of times. I became Martin that day. I had to. Otherwise, he'd be dead. I owed him that much, didn't I, Doc? He'd have done the same for me. I know you're trying to help me, but I don't want to talk about the body anymore."

"OK, then tell me how come Marcella didn't go on this trip with you."

"I picked a Thursday when I knew she had to be at work. She pouted, but like always, made me feel that she could do just fine without me. That made it easier to leave—she could do just fine without me for the rest of her life. She was still cheating on me, you know."

"Did you think she would be that easy to fool?"

"Sure, I was careful to leave the things that were valuable and important in the apartment in San Diego—just as though I were coming back the next day like I said. I left a paycheck on the dresser, my laundry in the bag, my favorite Maine hat on the hall rack and, most important of all, the framed photos of Martin and me."

"And just like before, the guards at the border didn't bother with you?"

"Nah, I had two thousand dollars in cash in the bottom of my tackle box and a change of clothes and my passport, that is, Martin's passport, stuffed into the bottom of the sleeping bag inside a canvas flight bag."

TIJUANA, MEXICAN BORDER CROSSING

"Good morning, Señor," the uniformed border guard said. His whispery mustache hardly moved on his upper lip as he eyed Arthur, his car, the rear seat, and the trunk.

Arthur had pulled into the same lane as last week, naively hoping for the same guard. No such luck. The border crossing connecting San Diego to Tijuana was thirty miles south of Mission Bay. It was always busy—twelve lanes, a two-story collection of government buildings with dual inconsistent missions. They guarded against visitors bringing in contraband to a poor country, but hoped they'd spend their money in a poor country.

The driving lanes headed south into Tijuana are busy eighteen hours a day, in daylight with two lanes on the west side marked "Nothing to Declare." The locals, those who travel back and forth daily, use that lane. Passports or driver's licenses checked, names mentioned, and a simple set of perfunctory questions asked of driver and each passenger. This was Arthur's first crossing alone. He tried to act calm and collected hoping for what Marcella had called *no tenga pena,* no penalty.

Arthur had to pay a permit fee of 180 pesos because he was going beyond the *adena* area, the twenty-two miles roughly containing the city of Tijuana.

"What you got in the trunk, Señor?"

"Just my fishing stuff, you know, poles and hooks, some dry ice to keep the catch, a few groceries, that's all. Same as last week. I'm going fishing down at Rosario again. Be back mañana," Arthur answered, hoping his single Spanish word would ease the tension in the guard's wandering eye.

"No knives, guns, or illegal or dangerous drugs, Señor? You been across before?"

"Yes, sir, I mean, Señor, I was here last week with my girl-friend, Marcella Munoz. The fishing was pretty good."

"Could you tell me please where you're going and how long you plan to visit Mexico?"

The guard pronounced it *meh he co.* Arthur handed him his driver's license, the real one, which the guard handed to younger man in a black uniform shirt, with no insignia. He took it inside the building and handed it to another older man, with a bigger mustache, at a desk, who appeared to scan the license and then look carefully at his screen for a few minutes. Returning to the traffic island, the younger man handed the license to the still stern-faced guard, said something is barely audible Spanish, and looked away. The guard pondered a moment.

"OK, Señor. You got to pay your fee. Park over there and go inside. I hope the fishing is better for you this week in Rosario. They will look into your trunk over there, then you gonna be on your way. Adios."

The inspection was perfunctory; two other guards opened the top to the cooler but didn't ask about, or even seem interested in, eighty pounds of dry ice. They poked the sleeping bag and lifted up the tackle box but didn't look inside anything. Arthur felt queasy as one guard stuck a screwdriver into the ice. The other guard seemed fixated on Arthur's face. It only took a few minutes, but it seemed much longer to Arthur. He wiped his brow when the guard said adios. He was on the way to Rosario in five minutes. The start of a new life.

He drove a little faster, a little more confidently down the paved, pot-holed road to Rosario, arriving before dark. The fishing shack on the rocky outcrop overlooking the south part of the village was still abandoned. All the way down from Tijuana he mulled his plan over. Ridiculously easy. He traced the steps out loud for twenty-thirty miles before rounding the curve down into the town plaza.

One, I do the deed—fire, not too big, but enough to burn the body. Two, I catch the bus from Rosario to La Paz. Three, take the Aero Mexico flight to El Paso, switch to Continental Airlines to Boston. Four, take the bus to Portland. Simple. All in cash. Use Martin's passport in Cabo, and if they ask, in El Paso. Once I get back to the US, keep using Martin's driver's license. After all, I am Martin. Arthur was the body in the fishing shack.

Arthur's plan came down when he could not imagine how to start the fire. As he rolled up into the rocky path from the highway to the shack, he reverted to how he and Martin had planned their game for years. They asked themselves questions. "OK, how to burn a body," he mouthed standing outside the shack. "We'll figure it out," he said aloud to himself.

One substantial worry was that his fake death would be discovered within minutes of the fire in the fishing shack, which might cause someone to call the police in San Diego within an hour. Would they call Marcella? How would they connect her to him? If they did, she'd probably rush to Rosario, but would accept as true what they told her—that Arthur was dead. That was where it got dicey. Her first call when she got back to San Diego would be to Martin in Portland. He had to be there when she made that call—or at least soon after it was made. Traveling on two buses and three airliners clear across the country would take twelve to fifteen hours—if he made every connection. The last thing he wanted was for Marcella to tell Rosie that Arthur was dead. Arthur, switching to Martin, wanted to do that himself. It occurred to him that rich people were installing car phones but no one he knew had one. So, if he could get to Portland in time, no one would dial the phone in Rosie's apartment.

Arthur's plan made an easy assumption about Mexican bureaucracy. Less efficient, less suspicious, and even slower than American bureaucracy. They'd find his car outside the shack. He'd leave his wallet and his passport locked in the glove compartment. That'd slow them down. They'd want to know whose body was inside the shack. But it would not be a simple matter of recognition. A gringo? A local transient? Was the car outside connected to the body inside? Hoping that the Mexican officials would take some time to confirm that it was really the gringo whose car was parked outside boosted his chances. He needed at least an hour's head start before the Federales started investigating. He left the keys to the car in his pants on a hook by the stove. He put the body, after de-icing it, in the sleeping bag.

The only tricky part was igniting the fire. He'd given that a lot of thought.

After changing pants, Arthur sat on the small chair in the middle of the shack, looking at the sleeping bag with "a body" in it. Success depended on everyone concluding that it was his body. The wind rattled through the loose boards on the ocean side of the shack. He studied the small cast iron cook stove in the lee side of the cabin. A shelf about four feet off the floor was a hand's width away from the stovepipe. He separated the stovepipe about three inches below the wooden shelf. Then he put the open can of kerosene on the shelf.

Then, as the wood fire in the stove got hotter and hotter, and as his carefully built woodpile caught, his newly defective stove pipe would vent very hot air upward to the sky. But some of it would escape through the small separation in the stovepipe onto the wooden shelf. The kerosene fumes from the open tube would catch fire, helped by the paper cup full of kerosene he placed in front of the can. The top of the can was also ajar, so the fumes would suck in the flame from the paper cup. Once that happened, the tinderbox of a shack would devour the night and everything in the shack. Including the body with his DNA in every bone. With a little luck, some skin, muscle, or bone would escape the fire. DNA. Martin's DNA. Also, his DNA.

He left the shack on foot ten minutes after midnight. He was a quarter mile down the hill when he looked back. The kerosene fire had consumed the shack. A funeral fire, he thought.

He was careful to walk down the rocky shale trail that he'd driven up, placing one foot and then the other outside the tire tracks, on the rock, not the indentation made by the car. He reached the highway, looked back, and saw a light glow. Jogging to the south on the pavement about a mile, he waited for some sound, some bright flash of light. Nothing. He stopped at another outcropping, another faded path to the ocean cliff and settled into a small bunch of Mesquite trees.

The first sound was an ominous whoosh, followed by a crack that sounded like a piece of good China hitting a marble floor. Then the entire shack erupted. His timing was a little off. He thought it would take five or six minutes for the heat to build up and catch the kerosene fumes, but it was more like fifteen minutes. But his timing error was advantageous. He was nowhere in sight of the shack when Martin's body, his body, their body, blew.

The nearest occupied house was about three miles south. The fire was visible from the road but there was no traffic. He headed north, alternating between a jog and a fast walk, making the three-mile trek in just under fifty minutes. Then, standing across the street from the Rosario bus station, in a darkened and apparently abandoned storefront, he squatted on weak knees, sipped water from a small bottle in his jacket pocket, and sat remarkably still as the time passed the time before the 5 am. bus hit town, for all destinations south of Rosario. Actually, it arrived early and left exactly on time—5 am.

"Hey, Gringo, watcha doin' here?"

Small man. Deep voice. I knew he was speaking to me but thought for a second that maybe if I ignored him, he'd give it up. The man leaned against the window on the other side of the bus aisle. A local, I thought. We were the only two to get on the bus in Rosario. It was full up front but had five empty rows empty in the back. I took a window seat on the driver's side; he picked the aisle seat one row behind me. Didn't think much of it.

"I'm on my way to La Paz, " I answered, looking at him sideways. Not wanting to seem suspicious, I worked up a smile. "How about you, where you headed?"

"Why are you going there? You think the Federales down there are gonna pay you no attention? Those hombres are pretty smart, Señor."

He lowered his head a little, which caused the brim of his off-white straw hat to drop down almost to his eyebrows. No one up front was paying any notice to him, or us—they were asleep, mostly, in the dimly lit bus. I involuntarily stiffened my neck. Probably made me look scared—surprise, surprise—but he seemed to pay no attention to what I did. Just sat there. Waiting for my answer. Didn't look like off-duty Federale, although I had no idea how they looked on, or off duty.

"Why would I have any interest in the Federales—there, or here for that matter? I'm going to visit my brother down there—he's had no trouble with them so why should I? Besides . . ."

"Hey, Señor, I don't think you're telling me the truth—I think you are running from somebody, maybe a woman, I don't know—but it don't make no difference to me. I know Baja and I know the Federales. I think you need me, Señor. But let's not talk about it anymore in here. We stop in Las Donde in a little bit—we can talk some more then."

"But I told you . . ."

I stopped in mid-sentence because he turned to the window, turned up the collar on his old leather bombardier jacket, smashed his straw hat against the seat cushion, and sniffled loudly. I got it. It was warmer in the bus than out. I got it. Turned toward my window, zipped up my LL Bean fishing jacket, and held my breath, all the way to Las Donde.

Who was this curious little son of a bitch? Did he know me? Was he from Rosario? Is that why he is suspicious—had he seen me with Marcella on our earlier trips? I spent the ninety minutes alternating between thinking about how to get away from him and thinking about how to use him. It was full light when we got to Las Donde.

Everybody got off the bus. But he was never more than ten feet from me for the next twenty minutes. I picked a stall—the only one—in the men's room. He took his piss into a rusty steel piss rail, with a plastic water tube running in from one end. I washed my hands in the sink—he wiped his hands on his pants. I ordered coffee and a burrito—he bought a Pepsi and a chocolate bar.

Coffee was strong and sweet, with three hard cubes of brown sugar. Been three hours now but the taste of smoke was still there, about an inch down my throat on the way to my tonsils. And my hands still had a faint kerosene tinge on them. Didn't remember spilling any.

Standing at the side of the bus waiting for the driver to tell us to board, I confronted the little bastard. I talked; he put his finger on his lips. So, I waited. Like him.

We got back on the bus, and I took my same row, but the window seat. He walked past, to the last row, and sat right behind me. Close enough to hear him sniffle, wipe his nose, wheeze. He lit a cigarette. Didn't notice that before. Ten minutes of a long uphill pull on what I took to be a graveled goat road, noisy, and just wide enough for about five goats. I was thinking about the body in the fire; how much would the fire eat before it went out? God knows what he's thinking—but probably still bout me. Then, effortlessly he moved around and slipped into the seat beside me.

"Hey Gringo, watcha doin' here?" he asked again.

"I already told you, I'm going down to La Paz to visit my . . ."

"Gringo, *por favor*, maybe you should tell me your name. And maybe you should think about what I can do to help you—you need a little help, don't you?"

"Everyone needs a little help. But right now, I don't think I need any. My name is John and . . ."

"OK, John, that's what I will call you. You can call me Juan. If you tell me your name is Joe later on, then you can call me Jose. Like I already told you, it don't make no difference to me. Now, Señor John, how can I help you?"

"Well Mr. Juan," I said, trying to sound confident, "about the only help you can give me is to tell me the best way to get to the airport in La Paz."

"Watcha want to go to the airport for? I thought you were visiting your brother down there?"

"Well, I am visiting my brother, but you see he doesn't actually live in La Paz , he just ships in and out of there a lot—he has a charter boat. We were going to go fishing tomorrow, but he got a charter, and so I'm going to fly over to the mainland and meet him for our fishing trip."

"OK, John. I can help with you that. Maybe I can even help you get a private plane for the hop across the Gulf of California to the mainland. That's quicker and more private than Aero México but maybe you already got that lined up. Do you, Señor?"

"Do I what?"

"Do you have a charter already lined up—to go see your brother on his fishing boat—that's what you said, right?"

"Yeah, that's right. But no, I don't have a charter plane waiting. I thought the Aero México flight left at ten every morning—that's what my brother told me—do you know about that?"

"*Si*, John, I think you are right, but a charter can take off thirty minutes after we get off this bus in La Paz. The charter pilot—the one my cousin knows—he don't ask no questions of his passengers. He's not like me, I ask a lot of questions, but I assure you, Señor, I don't give no answers unless you want me to. You know, I can be a good friend of you. Maybe you should give me a small sum of money, to assist with the charter, *que no*? Then I could forget I ever saw you. So, when the Federales come to me and ask me who was on this bus, I can say what I always say—nobody was on the bus—nobody talked to me about nothing. So, I can be a pretty good friend of you, *si*, John?"

"Let's say I did need a little help, how much would a little help cost?"

"*Bueno*, Señor, the truth is easy. A little help will cost you five hundred dollars, American. It will be very good for you, Señor, to have such help—then you can finally get some sleep and leave all the worrying to me. I could be a Greyhound, *que no*?"

Looked away from him out the window into the graying sky. Dawn would be in full bloom in fifteen or twenty minutes. Needed time to sort this guy out. Should I bribe him? Keep him quiet? From who? What does he know that five hundred bucks will silence? He just sat there beside me. Like he was asleep with his eyes open. Noisy breather—heavy smoker. But relaxed. Man knew his business. Whatever 'n hell that was.

"I am pretty sure I don't need five hundred dollars' worth of help, but maybe I could use about one hundred dollars' worth— can you take over my worries for one hundred dollars?"

"No, but I can see you like to lie first and then bargain a little. Maybe you're not in as much trouble as I thought. I will help you, Señor, for two hundred fifty, American—see, you got me for half-price—not too many Gringos have bargained that well with me. OK? When we get there, I will call my cousin—you can call him Jose. He'll pick us up and take us the airport and give you over to the charter pilot man—he's a gringo like you. But that don't include the charter flight. You got to pay the man who owns the plane for that. It's extra."

I gave him one hundred dollars, promised to give him one-fifty more when we got to the bus station in La Paz.

"But I want to go to the airport—in a cab, alone. Just tell me where the charter service is and I will consider using it, or maybe I will just wait for the ten o'clock Aero México flight."

"You still don't have much trust, Señor John. I will arrange for two cabs to the airport, one for me and one for you. You can pick whichever one you want. Is your brother going to meet you when you land on the other side?"

"What brother?"

"*Si*, Señor, that's what I thought."

Juan, or whatever his real name was, got his two-hundred fifty dollars American. I got a charter flight across the western side of the Baja to Phoenix, no questions asked, for fifteen hundred dollars. Like he said, the charter pilot had no interest in my name, or my life story. I was with him for three and a half hours. He only said two words. He took my cash, pointed at the back seat, and said, "buckle up." It was a big change in my plan—Phoenix instead of El Paso, but it was quicker, and a lot more private.

DR. SOCORRO

"Arthur," Dr. Socorro said, looking up from her notepad, while twirling a green and silver Cross pen between her fingers. "I'm not following why you made the change of plan in La Paz. Who did you think the little man you called Juan actually was? A policeman, a bandit, what?"

"Hell, Doc, I didn't know then, or now. They say everyone in Mexico is out to make a buck on American tourists. That's what he did, I guess. I haven't thought about it since then."

"All right, we can come back to that again. What were the arrangements from Phoenix to Boston? How did that work? Not another Juan, I hope."

"Nope. Uneventful. No one paid any mind to me. But scary because I had no idea what had happened in Rosario. The charter guy from La Paz dropped me off at a big private hanger. Big sign over the building said *Swift Transportation*. They had a small customs office in there. Lady in government uniform and little green cop-looking hat. She asked for my passport, asked where you are flying from, on business or pleasure. Said fishing. In Mexico. Worked just fine. Got a cab to the other side of the runway to Terminal 3. Caught the American Airlines flight direct to Boston. Left there ninety minutes later. Lucky, eh?"

"So, you gave them your true name, Arthur, is that right?"

"No. I thought I was clever as shit, if you'll excuse my French. When she said *name* as though it was a question, I mumbled my name as Mortin Esser in what I hoped was a sort of cowboy Texas accent. My plan was, stupid as it now sounds, to claim that I actually said Martin Cheshire and to speak like a proper Mainer if they asked for identification. She wrote Mortin Esser on a little pad on the desk. I gave her Martin's passport. She looked him up—that is, me—in the computer. Waved me on goodbye with a bored 'Welcome home, Mr. Cheshire.'"

"I thought you told me you left your passport in the glove compartment in the car at the fishing shack?"

"Right, I did. It was mine. But the passport I showed the customs officer in Phoenix was Martin's. And my name, remember the Mortin Esser thing, was Martin Cheshire. It really was—in both their minds and mine. It was Hide and Be. Arthur going across the border into Mexico at Tijuana. Then, switch identities and *be* Martin coming back into the United States at Phoenix. Simple, right?"

"Yes, Arthur, simple. Do you realize now why the prosecutors here think you are Martin, and that you killed your brother in Mexico? It's no game to them, Arthur. I need more details for my report to the judge."

"Sure, more details on the way. But first, about that report to the judge. You already told me you were going to do that. I gave you my permission, right? But I forgot to ask. Am I going to get a copy of it? Seems like I should."

"Ask the judge. I'm sure your lawyer will get one. It's an official court filing. Ask him."

"Right. So, I went to Terminal Three. Took American Airlines to Boston. Rented a car there with Martin's driver's license and drove to Portland. It was natural, really. I was Martin on the East Coast and Arthur on the West. We never saw it any differently."

"So, when you got to Portland, I take it no one had called Rosie about the fire in Mexico."

"No, see, it was after midnight by the time I got to Portland, what with a three-hour time change, and a five-hour flight, Rosie was in bed. I crashed in the downstairs guest room but put a note on the bathroom mirror upstairs. She was a sound sleeper, I guess."

PORTLAND, THIRTEENTH BIRTHDAY (FLASH BACK)

"But Arty, today's the day—the day! We're thirteen and we can smoke and drink and all that stuff—just like in the movies. Get up you, lazy bastard, it's our birthday."

"If I'm a bastard then what are you, Smarty Marty? Answer me that, will you? How could I be a bastard if you aren't? Are you calling yourself a bastard? I'll tell you what a bastard is. A bastard is a turd like Joe. Why did we have to get stuck with a bastard like Joe—he's more than a bastard, he's an assy-fucker. I hate him and I am going to take you and run away . . ."

"We can't run away today. It's our birthday. Thirteen, I never thought we'd be this old."

"We may not get too much older if Joe the Bastard has his way. How many times do you think he's gonna whack you today? Thirteen whacks maybe?"

"I told you, Arty, he doesn't hit hard, and besides he thought I was you. I told him he was hitting the wrong one again and he said . . ."

"Yeah, I heard him from under the crack in the bedroom door—'You little shit, whichever one you are don't mean jack-shit to me—you're gonna mind me and do what I say you little shit, now bend over and . . .' I couldn't see you, but I heard it—I was scrouched down at the door. Did you even hear me? Why didn't you answer me?"

"Quit it, Arty, he is stupid, but Sherlene says he's got a weak heart, so's he can't hit very hard. You hit a lot harder than him. Besides, you said that when we turned thirteen that we'd . . ."

"I said a lot of things and starting today things are gonna change—for one thing, we are grown up today. We can Hide and Be from everyone

but Joe, cause Joe don't give a shit. So, from now on we'll be adults; at least we'll have adult names. So, I'm Arthur and you're Martin. That's what we were named; and that's what we should be called, Arthur and Martin. Sounds good, don't it?"

"Sounds OK, but I bet Joe won't go for it. He can't tell which one of us is Marty or Arty, how's he ever gonna start with Arthur? Christ, he's likely to whoop you just for telling him you got a new name. You go first—I dare you."

"I will, I'm gonna go right down there and tell him my name. I'll say, Joe, my name is Martin and I want you to call me that from now on."

"Yeah right, Arty, try that—he knows you're Arthur cause you still got that black mark on your arm from where he whacked you out back last Friday when you came through the fence instead of the gate."

"Yeah, I got the black mark still. But he thought I was you—member, I screamed at you and said Arty, Arty, stay back!"

"You shit! You did that! I almost died. I was coming through the gate anyhow. Did he really believe you—did he think you were me?"

"I dunno. He's been living here for two months now, and he hasn't got it right once. Shit, Sherlene can't even tell which one you are. She knows me cause I smile more, but she's afraid to tell Joe anything. She's as afraid of him as you are. That's a whole bunch of afraid. But Joe doesn't really give a shit which one he hits, and he doesn't give a shit what you say when he hits you. I tell him I'm you, you tell him you're me and he says shut up, you little bastard and take your medicine like a man. Like a man. Thirteen is old enough—we're men today. So, . . ."

"But, Arty . . . Why did Sherlene have to marry him anyway? We were getting on OK, weren't we?"

"They ain't married. Shacking up. That's what. They just told the caseworker they was married to get the checks for taking care of us."

"Well, why does the judge or whatever he is, keep sticking us with someone new?"

"I don't know what he is. What's a magistrate? You tell me. But you just remember what he said in that hearing in town at the courthouse.

He said when we're fourteen then we can say who takes care of us, and who lives in our house, and stuff. So today we're thirteen. In one more year we can say, Judge, give Joe the Bastard his walking papers. We don't want him living in our house anymore. This is our house—our folks left it to us when they died, and we want Joe the Bastard out of here. He ain't married anyhow. Shacking up son of a bitch, that's what he is."

"But Sherlene's nice, can we keep her if Joe gets run off by the judge?"

"Sherlene is nice but she's just a foster parent, you know that. She's the third one we've had. We have to have one they pick until we turn fourteen and then we have a say. I say let's tell him to tell Joe the Bastard to go to hell or wherever he wants as long as he gets out of our house. But that's next year. For now, we need to be grown up, Marty, I mean Martin. Remember that. I'm Arthur. You're Martin. Get it straight, will you?"

"Why? No one else will."

PORTLAND. POLICE CALL FROM SAN DIEGO

"Martin, Martin darling, I hate to wake you but it's the police in San Diego—I assume it's about Arthur."

Arthur looked at Rosie with what he hoped was a blank stare. He'd been expecting the call but couldn't show it. The elapsed clock hours between the time he left Rosario and when he stepped into the house in Portland was only nineteen hours. About right, he thought.

He hadn't slept all night, but he pretended to be coming out of a deep sleep by shaking his head from side to side, and mumbling.

"What'd you say, Rosie, who's calling? Is it Arthur?"

"No, it's the San Diego police department. They want to talk to you."

Picking up the bedside phone in the guest room, Arthur said, "Hello, this is Martin Cheshire. What's this about, my brother Arthur? My God, did something happen?"

"Mr. Cheshire. I am sorry to inform you that there is a possibility that your brother, Arthur, died in a fire yesterday, or the day before, we're not sure. We just got a call from the Federales in Mexico. They have his car, his wallet, and his passport. They were found in a small house south of Rosario, Mexico."

"What? Why do they think it's him? He's not in Mexico. He's in San Diego, with his girlfriend. I don't understand."

"Mr. Cheshire, we don't know all the facts yet, but the Mexican authorities are assuming that, for now, your brother died in the fire. Either that, or someone stole his car, his identification papers, and tried to make it look like him. There is a body in the house. It's not identifiable, but they will be doing genetic and dental tests very soon. Meanwhile, maybe it's best if you call your brother's girlfriend in San Diego. Then, you can call us back and we can go from there. Or, if you'd rather, we can call her. Either way, we'll want to talk to her. Can you do it, and call us back just as soon as you can confirm your brother's actual whereabouts?"

Arthur hung up the phone, told Rosie what they'd said, and they both collapsed.

They held on to one another for a moment, then Arthur pulled away.

"I've got to call him. What time is it?"

"It's six-thirty, Martin, but it's only three-thirty in San Diego. Let's have some coffee. Maybe you should not wake them up. It can't be Arthur. You'd know if he went to Mexico, wouldn't you?"

"Not always. He told me last week that he and Marcella had gone to Mexico a couple of times fishing. Marcella will know where Arthur is. But we can't wait," he said, turning to dial the phone.

Rosie's face turned ashen as she listened to Arthur's call. Hearing only his end, she began to shake at the news. What do you mean, he's in Mexico—I thought you were going with him—No I don't know anything more than what the police told me three minutes ago—Yes, I'll call the police in Rosario—No I don't, how would I even find the number in a foreign country—Yes, absolutely, I'll call you back when I get more information—Sure, call the San Diego police—That's a good idea—No, I haven't given up on him—it's just coincidence—I'll call soon as I know.

She held him for almost ten minutes until he gathered himself. Then, muffling his voice and wiping away a tear, he jumped from the bed.

"I've got to call the Mexican police. But I'm afraid. What if it is him? Rosie, what if it is? Who do I call? Why did he go to Mexico, by himself? What was he thinking? Goddamn him! We always went fishing together, he never went fishing alone."

"Let me call," Rosie said, trying as best she could to stifle her own cries. She called 1411, got a local operator, and asked for the police department in Rosario, Mexico. No, she said, she did not know which Mexican state; "It's in Baja, I think."

They gave her a number, complete with an international dialing code. As she asked preliminary questions, apparently of someone in Rosario with some English, Arthur left the room. She found him ten minutes later, on the back porch, with a beer in his hand.

She gave it to him straight—they have a body, mostly burnt up, but definitely a human body. The glove compartment in the car said it was a rental from San Diego in Arthur's name and address. The body is in a local mortuary—but it will go by ambulance up to Tijuana, to a special morgue for an autopsy.

"OK, OK, I'll go today. I'll get a flight and be there in the morning. Even if his body is burned, I'll know. I always know."

She sat beside him, asked him if he wanted coffee. He didn't. So, she tucked herself under his arm and locked it around her.

"No, Martin, you cannot go—the body is almost cremated, they said. It will take days to know for sure. They will extract bone marrow DNA, that's the best way, they said. They will know for sure. Do you know if Arthur ever had a surgical procedure, or for whatever reason, had his DNA extracted? They will need that to make a match."

Arthur swallowed slowly, unsure how much to say. Since he had no ready answer, he said the first thing that came to his mind.

"Well, they can match me. We have the same DNA, you know, identical twins and all. If the DNA in that body in Rosario matches mine, we'll know it's Arthur."

"Yes, love, I'm sure that's what they will do. But there might be fingerprints there, in Rosario, and they will want to look at his dental records. They will be here in Portland, right?"

"I guess, but the DNA will be the key, won't it? And besides, if the body is cremated, they won't be able to take his fingerprints from him. And dental records might not be accurate either if his teeth are burned up. Oh, God, how could this happen? It's all AmHull's fault! They never should of made him go out there. I'm quitting them today, right goddamn today, you hear!"

"Well, sure, but first, we have to make sure. They say his car was there, parked at the house that burned up. They'll take fingerprints from the car, won't they? Maybe there are other things they do. They would in the United States, but I don't know anything about Mexico. It's very poor, and the police on TV are always fat and stupid. If it's Arthur, he would be the last one to drive the car. And maybe there will be hair follicles in the car too. That will help them identify the body."

"Wait," Arthur said, "I know something. If it's Arthur, he would have given his ID, at the border, in Tijuana, that's how they will know he's in Mexico."

"Yes, Martin, it will, but it might not show where he went after he crossed the border. They are saying Rosario because that's where they found his car and a body. But please, darling, you have to be calm about this. Wait until the autopsy is done and they have scientific evidence. I'm afraid it is him, but we don't need to guess. It will only be a few days, I hope. Then, we'll know."

Rosie insisted that Arthur call Marcella. He pretended to be so grief stricken that he could not handle it. She understood, and said she'd call. Rosie called, while Arthur paced the living room floor. He heard Rosie's end of the call and imagined Marcella's.

"No, he's doing OK, really. He's probably in shock but he seems to comprehend. I think . . . Yes, I'll tell him . . . He will want to make the arrangements, but he can't, you know. I'll get us together, and I'll call the airport and then . . . Marcella, that's so kind—I don't know why we never met either—they talked about it, but you know them—big talk and no follow through. Life is so cruel—they had no parents, no real friends, except you and me, and now, well, oh God, I just can't imagine how Martin is going to get through without . . . What about the boys—Harold's boys, do they know . . . ? No, Martin will call Harold, but it can wait. The first thing to do is to get out there and . . ."

They talked for another fifteen, twenty minutes. Rosie's organizational skills rose to the occasion. She worked out travel arrangements, asked about burial and getting the remains back across the border, talked to Alice at AmHull about work details at their office in San Diego, and gave Martin a sleeping pill crushed inside a glass of V8. She made two logical assumptions. Martin's grief would last for a long time. Second, she'd be there when it subsided.

As the day wore on, Rosie did all the calling. Arthur woke up mid-afternoon, frantic all over again.

"Please, Martin, try to calm down. Listen to me, I talked to Alice and to Mr. Hull. They will handle the office things in San Diego. I talked to Marcella again. She's a total mess, of course. But she's a very smart girl."

"What'd she say? I mean does she believe it, herself?"

"She says he went surf fishing in Rosario two days ago. She expected him back today. I can hear it in her voice, though. It was Arthur, she can feel it."

"What'd Alice say? What'd you call her for; she's just a clerk. You talked directly with Harold, right? Should I call him now? I mean, what'd he say, the bastard? Did he know he caused this?"

Rosie went over to the doorway, where Arthur had been standing the whole time. She took him in both hands and said, "Let's sit on the porch. You need some air. Me too. Want anything, some eggs maybe? Should I put a pot of coffee on, how about tea? You like tea too."

"Beer. I need a beer. I need somebody to quit bullshitting me. Is my brother dead or not? Jesus, why don't they just say it? Marcella knows it. I know it. Fucking Harold knows it."

"Martin," she said when she'd led him to the porch, handed him a cold beer, and sat beside him on the swing, "Alice was obviously hurt and afraid for you. Mr. Hull, whom I've never met, sounded distant, distracted almost."

"Not surprised. Alice's a simple girl, not a bad girl, just not ambitious, and never curious about anything. But she knew us a long time. Harold's life, his only real life, revolves around his boys. For him, Arthur's death will be an unfortunate turn of events for the company. Who will look after the boys, which is the only fucking reason to even have a San Diego office? He won't care one way or the other about Arthur. Or me."

The next day, compliments of AmHull, Arthur and Rosie flew first-class to San Diego.

DR. SOCORRO

Officer Martinez walked Arthur from his cell to the medical complex. The nurse ushered him into Dr. Socorro's office.

"Sit down in the chair, Mr. Cheshire. I've just talked to your lawyer on the phone. He said to ask you about attending your own funeral, here in San Diego. What is he talking about? Did you actually do that? And no, before you ask, you cannot look out my window for half our session. Sit right there."

"Hey Doc, you seem mad at me. Maybe it's me that should be mad. Why are you talking to my lawyer without my permission? Why is he talking to you? So much for attorney-client privilege. He told me that you would be writing a report on my true identity, for the judge. Remember, we talked about that too. I don't recall anything about the two of you having private conversations *about* me."

"That doesn't matter right now. What does matter is what happened at the funeral or memorial service. Did you go, or not?"

Her jaw was set. She tapped incessantly on the pad with the upside of her fountain pen.

"Yes, of course I went. How could I not? Don't you see? We had to do that. Else, how could Martin live? I owed him that. I owed Rosie that."

"Well, we'll talk about who owed who what. For now, just give it to me slowly. Start with who arranged it, and what role you played in it."

"It was something I considered as part of the plan, way before the thing in Rosario, you see . . ."

"Let me interrupt, Arthur. By the thing in Rosario, you mean burning up your brother's body so that it would look like you died in the fire, right? It wasn't a *thing*. It was your funeral. Up to now, you've told me what happened in Rosario and how and why you burned up Martin's body. You did that, you claimed, so that so could live your brother's life. That was factual, even though it was of the most bizarre things any patient has ever told me. But going to your own funeral? With both of the women that you lied to? My God! That is audacious in the extreme."

"OK, Dr. Socorro. OK. But I had no choice. Neither of us did. I'd thought about it a lot, long before Rosario. You think of it is such simple terms. Faking my own death, for you must be some kind of sickness, or maybe even a crime. But for me, it was permanently hiding so that I could be Martin. Don't you see that? I had to get out of being me, here in San Diego, in Portland, and everywhere. But Marcella wasn't gonna let me go that easy."

"Arthur, you are not saying this was *her* fault, are you?"

"No, not exactly. But think about it from my side for a minute. If I just broke up with her, quit my job with AmHull in San Diego, and moved back to Portland, what might happen there? I was Martin there. I could not be Arthur there, not ever again. Arthur had to disappear permanently; don't you see? It wasn't suicide, homicide, or any kind of *cide*. It was the most important game of Hide and Be we ever played. But to carry it off, I had to go to my own funeral, which wasn't even a funeral, it was just a memorial thing."

"Arthur, I can see that you believe what you did was right; but that does not make it right in a mental health sense. It tells me you are still deluding yourself about your brother's death. You cannot let him go by becoming him; that's what you pretended to be in San Diego at that memorial service. You pretended that you were dead, that you were Martin, and that everything was going to be all right."

"Wrong, Doc. We did it plenty of times. We did it in San Diego. The only awkward part of it was that Marcella invited her cousin Maldonado. I thought I'd never see Maldonado again, but he was there. Can you believe it? Well, in retrospect, I guess it was predictable. Marcella's family was up in Fresno and Maldonado was the only family she had in San Diego. Rosie and Marcella both thought I was Martin, and they did the memorial thing to help me deal with what they thought was my brother's death. Like I said, how could I not go?"

"Tell me. Tell me all of it."

"It was the day after we got there, six days after the fire in Rosario. The Federales told the American consulate in Tijuana that the body would be released in a week or two. I could not stay that long, and neither could Rosie. We had our lives in Portland, after all. I even talked to the consul general himself. He told me my brother's remains would be held in Mexico until the official investigation was complete. But he, Señor Garcia, I think he said was his name, had personally talked to the investigating officer about the case. They thought it was an accidental fire, just like I thought they would. But they had to investigate anyhow. Cops are like that everywhere. He said the investigation would confirm the obvious—that my brother died in a fire that started accidentally in the cabin he took refuge in for the night."

"Arthur, were you ever interrogated by the Mexican authorities?"

"Sure, it was at that same meeting the morning of the service. The one with Mr. Garcia. A senior officer was there asking questions and taking notes. Just like you're doing. The questions were routine, why did he stay there—why not the little hotel where he stayed the week before—why did he have the kerosene on the shelf—he wasn't using the kerosene stove. I told Mr. Garcia, if that was his name, that his questions were troubling, but I had no answers. My brother was dead—that was final. His body was important but was, after all, just a detail. I accepted his official condolences and his assurances that nothing untoward happened and that there was no suggestion of foul play and that the Mexican authorities were acting in a very professional way, and yada, yada, yada."

"OK, get back to the little service. I want to know what happened and how you felt about it."

"Sure. It wasn't much. Kinda like a delayed lunch, about three in the afternoon. Everyone was dressed up, more or less. There was me—coat and tie. Marcella—long dark dress, long, almost to her ankles. Rosie wore . . . what? Yeah—a dark red pantsuit with a yellow silk shirt. Hair in a tight bun. I remember that. I'd never seen her like that before—you know, all somber. Between her and Marcella, real melancholy. Harold Junior was there— black long-sleeved shirt. Just to fit in, I suppose. Maldonado, damn him, he wore a jacket, but he'd had the sleeves cut off in the middle of his forearms, so that his tattoos showed. We had little snack sandwiches, flavored tea, lemonade, nothing alcoholic. Marcella said we could go for beers later, but she wanted this done right. That's about it."

"Where was it?"

"At the apartment—it was small, you know. Maybe nine hundred square feet. But only five people. So, it was comfortable. Marcella had put flowers around in little blue bottles, with water. She had candles everywhere, and my picture, with her, of course, in a little frame on the table, with a rosary and a cross. Goddamned cross. Made me nervous. We're not religious, you know. What else? Oh, I guess you want to know what people said. Everyone talked but me. They were talking about me. I could not."

"Do you remember what Marcella said?"

"A little. What you'd expect. Loved Arthur like she'd never loved anyone before. Made me think of the tall dude at the Del Coronado. Pissed me off. She read from a little book, not a bible, thank God, but just something where she wrote things down. I don't remember all of it—pretty short. Something about love being an act of forgiveness and that my death made her realize what it means to die for love."

"How did that make you feel?"

"Bad. Bad for her. It would have been really bad except that I kept thinking about her and the guy with the black Porsche. I mean, what was all that about love being forgiveness and dying for love, if she's got two boyfriends at the same time? And in addition . . ."

"Hold on, Arthur. She was talking about you. In loving terms. Was she crying when she spoke to the little group?"

"Yeah, a lot, actually. She's a very emotional person."

"Did you cry?"

"No."

"Well, what I think we should talk about today is why you think it was wrong for her to have two boyfriends and mourn your death, while you had two girlfriends and had faked your death to get out of her life? I'm not being critical. I'm just try-ing to get you to let me see a little of what is inside you—then and now."

"It was just that Maldonado was there. He was her cousin, but not my friend. Hell, I only seen him once. He was a creepy guy. I guess maybe I didn't want him to see me cry. Otherwise, I probably would have."

"Arthur, did you and Maldonado have some sort of falling out? You said he had lots of tattoos. Did that bother you? Do you have some kind of dislike for tattoos, or guys that wear them?"

"No."

"All right. What did Rosie say? She did not know at that time that you were actually Arthur. This is when she still believed you were Martin, right? So, what did she say about the brother that she thought she'd only met once, the day before the boat accident?"

"I wasn't listening close. She just said a few things. About how much Martin loved his brother and how much they were alike. She even told the story of how we fooled her at Sweeties bar in Portland, the first night I met her. Everybody laughed."

"Is that all? From what you've told me this memorial service must have lasted less than five minutes. Did you black all of it out, or are you holding something back on me?"

"No, it lasted a half hour, I guess. But I don't remember things word for word, like you do. I didn't take notes. I didn't want to be there at all, remember? So, when we were all there, and I was being myself—like I had to be in San Diego—it was just hard, you know. In one way it was like we were all strangers, you know?"

"Strangers? I'm not sure what you mean."

"Can I go over to the window now? I'm answering as best I can."

"All right, but tell me why the word strangers popped into your head just now."

The bay was rippled with white tops because of a strong wind coming in from the southwest. It looked like my head felt. Just rolling over and over, never getting anywhere. She said nothing for a while. I started to shake my head up and down, like I was remembering something. Then I went back and sat down in front of her, but I didn't look at her.

"Strangers is what we used to call everyone when we were playing the game. A stranger is someone that doesn't know you. At least they think they don't. That's the way it was. Rosie thought I was Martin. That day so did Marcella, for the first time. Rosie and Marcella thought Arthur was dead and Martin was alive. Both wrong. Maldonado only knew one me—Arthur. He never met us together. Harold Junior didn't give a shit one way or the other. He was only there because he was afraid his dad would close the office and make him come home if he wasn't respectful. So, there we were, five strangers."

Dr. Socorro stared at Arthur for a long time. Three, maybe four minutes. He sat there, looking down like the floor had answers. Then, without another question, she pressed the little buzzer on the telephone, signaling the clinic floor receptionist to have Martinez come back and take me to the cells. It was the first day she didn't tell him to take care.

MARCELLA. A WEEK AFTER THE MEMORIAL SERVICE

Early Monday morning, Marcella packed Arthur's clothes, shaving kit, two photos of him and Martin, and one with Marcella. She took them to the closest UPS store and sent them by ground to Rosie in Portland. She called the rental agent, canceled her month-to-month tenancy, got her security deposit back, and moved out—on Wednesday afternoon.

In their last conversation, Arthur told her to keep his car. She did, thanking Martin for his generosity. After all, as Arthur said in that last phone call, "It's what Arthur would have wanted."

"Thank you, Martin," she said, "I'll get Maldonado to go down to Rosario and get it, whenever the authorities release it." She promised to let him know when the Mexican authorities in Tijuana were ready to release the remains.

"No, Marcella, don't worry about that," Arthur said. "I'll take care of it. I talked to them this morning and they will work everything through me. I'm Arthur's executor, you know."

"OK by me," she said. "But just for the record, I don't want anything from his estate. I don't even know if he has one, but you should have whatever he had. I had his love, for a little while, that's enough."

Arthur gave her a bill of sale for the car, which he signed *Martin Cheshire*, Executor of the Estate of Arthur Cheshire. He promised to keep in touch. She said, "Likewise."

Arthur's only concern was a small, needling worry that Marcella might say something to Rosie about Arthur's tattoo, but she never did. That tattoo was the last tangible thing left of Arthur. He was sure Rosie would spot it soon, but he had a story ready for that. Rosie, a proper New Englander, was a romper in bed but liked the dark. He'd become adept at keeping her out of the small shower stall and keeping his left leg under the covers. He dressed in the bathroom and wore socks all the time, even in bed—New Englanders did that in the winter.

CHAPTER FOUR

WE ARE WHO WE SAY WE ARE

DR. SOCORRO'S OFFICE

When Officer Martinez steered Arthur into the clinic waiting room that Thursday afternoon, he said, "Sit. Stay," and pointed at the bench closest to Dr. Socorro's office. Sitting on the other bench, opposite Arthur, Martinez thumbed through a new "rules book" the DOC had passed down through the jail chain of command. Normally, they'd only sit a few minutes before her door would open, another inmate slash patient would come out, and Martinez would usher Arthur in. But not today. Through some snafu, Arthur wasn't on the schedule. But neither knew that, so they sat there for an hour.

"So, Cheshire, what's the deal with the two women? I been hearing bout you from the guys at the mess hall. You got two chicks on the line—one here and the other on the Atlantic? How do you do it, man, you a super dick, or what?"

Arthur's instinct was to duck. But since Dr. Socorro was not in any hurry to fit him in, he answered Martinez's question.

"Well, it's kinda complicated. But I got caught up in the situation. Wasn't my fault, at first, but I kept it up too long."

"So, it's true. Two babes. Wow, man, I'm jealous. Must of wore your ass out, though. I got one lady in my life and she's gonna kill me. I mean she likes it more than any chica I ever knew. I heard one of your babes is a chica. Is that right? What's the other?"

This was ridiculous, Arthur thought, but couldn't resist.

"Yes, one lady was a chica, her name was Marcella. The other lady in question was an Irish lass from the great state of Maine, 3,500 miles from here. Different ladies from different oceans, you know. But they loved us and felt the need to share that love and their mutual grief—Marcella over me—and Rosie over how she thought my death would affect the man she thought I was."

"Whoa, bro, you are talkin' some shit here. Who's us? I thought you had two babes, now you say some other guy's involved. You pitch for both teams, my man?"

"Officer Martinez," Arthur said, "I'm sorry. Like I said, it's complicated." While I didn't know it back then, Rosie and Marcella were talking over the phone to one another, even before the meltdown. You know when I faked my death in Rosario. They each had their doubts, unbeknownst to me. My lawyer interviewed both of them three weeks ago. He filled me in. See, they shared anecdotal stories—about the little clues that bothered them both—about the little flashes of light—about the little mistakes I made and, most importantly, about the gnawing feeling they both had—I wasn't what I seemed to be. Gordon Kemper, he's my lawyer, you seen him in here, right? He says both girls were plenty suspicious. I thought they were totally fooled. But it was not that tight. They came up with some wild-ass theories."

"Like what, man?"

"Like, maybe we were identical triplets, not identical twins. Maybe there was a third guy. A guy kept coming back into their lives in place of the one they thought they knew. They laughed it off as too bizarre. A third twin—making us identical triplets? Impossible. But it was closer to the reality I had created for them than the real truth was."

PORTLAND. TWO MONTHS AGO

When Arthur and Rosie stepped off the plane and into the Portland terminal, Arthur felt free. Thinking he was shed of California forever and believing his life as Martin was now fixed in stone, he encircled her waist and tried to kiss her. She slapped him.

"Martin, you act like a teenager sometimes. What is going on with you? Three days ago, you learned that your brother died, now you act like nothing happened. We need to talk as soon as we get home."

He tried to get her to talk while they were waiting for the bags. But she would have none of it. As he watched the bag carousal go around for the fifth or sixth time without spotting her small peach-colored suitcase and his duffle bag, he realized how happy he was, and how sad he was supposed to be. For once, being Martin and hiding Arthur caught him off guard. How long, he thought, could he carry this off?

When they got home, Rosie started in on him.

"Let's unpack later, Martin. We need to talk. How about I make a pot of tea, and we'll sit on the back porch? You go on out, I'll just be a minute."

She started by apologizing for slapping him at the airport.

"I don't know what got into me, really, I don't. But when I looked at you, not thinking of anyone but yourself, I could see Arthur. When you put your arm around me and tried to kiss me, I thought of Arthur. Remember that first time we met at Sweeties? It was his face, there at the airport. The same face I saw at Sweeties. And you've been so happy the whole trip. As though Arthur weren't dead. What you two morons did to me at Sweeties was fun, sort of. But now, can you understand my reaction, Martin? It was as though nothing had changed. It was just fun and games again. So, help me out here. What's going on with you?"

"Guess I don't know what's going on. What's expected of me now? I mean, today is not real, not to me. I'm trying to make sense of it, I guess. Put the worst day of my life behind me. You were never around us; that is, Arthur and me. I'm the only twin you know. But, as we tried to tell you before, we're different."

"Different? I thought you two gloried in your sameness. Know me, know my brother, you always said, or something like that."

He sipped his tea. So did she. Herbal tea usually soothed him. But today, out on the back porch, it scared him. His stomach churned like an industrial washing machine. She said something, but he put his forefinger to his lips, warning her to let him explain. A minute passed. Then another. The crows seemed to sense something and quit cawing. Then they flew from the giant oak off the porch to a telephone line across the back alley. He took it as a sign.

"No, you don't understand. Nobody could. I didn't mean we were different from each other. Only different from everyone else, including you. For twenty-nine years, we breathed the same air, together, at the same time, in the same way. Our thoughts, our plans, our fears, our dreams were not merely alike; they were in every sense identical. Or so I thought. The memorial in San Diego was not just for Arthur. It was for us. *We* died!"

Her face paled and she leaned back into the cushion on the swing, crossing her arms and tilting head sideways. Inexplicably, she started clenching and unclenching her fists.

"Hey Babe, I know how stupid that must sound to you. But Rosie, I hate how I feel now. He's dead, that's what they said. But is he? There's a body, they said. It matches our DNA, they said. And the wallet and the fingerprints on the wheel. That's science. So, I guess it's correct. But it's fumbucked."

Arthur got up, walked out to the fence at the end of the lot. Rosie followed, tried to take his hand. He shook her off. Motioning to her with his head to come on, just walk with me, he continued.

"That stupid memorial service in San Diego—what was I supposed to make of that? Everybody there, even that freak Maldonado, accepted as fact my brother's death. Science rules, right? Cops are always right, even Mexican ones, right? But what about me, the twin? Am I a survivor, or a victim? Is the death of a twin not the other's twin's death too?"

"Martin, I know how much you hurt inside. What don't I understand is how you're feeling about it. None of us there, including Marcella, had known Arthur for very long. Me probably the least of all. But we are not important. We cannot understand your loss, or define it, or make it better."

Rosie stopped, picked up two handfuls of decaying leaves, and let then trickle out of her fingertips.

"But there are things that don't add up here, things that don't make sense. You seem to have some doubts about whether Arthur died at all. That's the message I'm getting. Do you believe that Arthur is still alive? Is that what you are questioning?"

Arthur couldn't stand it. Not one second longer. He was afraid if he didn't bolt, if he said anything, Rosie would never forgive either of them. She was no fool. So, he tapped his forefinger on his lips again, then moved his hand to cup her chin. He kissed her so lightly that she hardly felt his lips. Then he got up, walked through the back door to the front yard, and ran as fast as he could down Brighton Avenue. No coat, no plan, and no brother.

He called two days later, when he knew she'd be at work. The answering machine picked up.

"Rosie, it's me. Sorry about bolting out on you. I'm in Boston, thinking that maybe I'll take some time off. Alone. Find myself. You are the loveliest woman I've ever known. Don't want to hurt you but I got some things to work out. It will take some time. Don't wait for me. Do what's best for you."

PORTLAND—ROSIE

Secrets don't die—people do. Martin's secret plan to get even with AmHull didn't die with him. It survived under the floorboard in the third-floor attic of the Brighton Lane house.

Rosie trusted herself, but no longer trusted Martin. His phone message triggered a growing concern about him and Arthur. The gnawing feeling that Arthur's death was another awful game of Hide and Be would not leave her. She decided to move out. She began gathering up the stuff she'd stored in the attic storeroom, the only room in the house Martin had been secretive about.

Feeling secretive herself, she climbed the metal winding staircase from the third floor to the attic. Martin had reluctantly let her help him move her unopened boxes into the small storeroom. The rest of the attic was an unfinished, filthy dirty, open space. Finding the door locked, she went back down to the kitchen, hoping the key would be on the rack by the back door. It wasn't. She looked everywhere, including Martin's desk in the library. No key. What the hell, she thought, it's my stuff in there. I have a right to it. So, she got a large claw hammer from the basement tool chest, trudged back up four flights of stairs, and busted open the door, lock and all.

It looked worse than it smelled. A layer of dust was everywhere, even on the single naked bulb hanging by three inches of electrical wire from the seven-foot ceiling. There was no wall switch, just a fifty-year old knob switch on the brass receptacle above a forty-watt bulb. She hated dust. Sweeping would not be enough. The four boxes with her name on them, plus her mother's two oversized suitcases, coated with dust, and something that suspiciously looked like mouse droppings, beckoned from the far side of the room. She hoped it was mice, not their larger and more menacing cousins.

Deciding that sweeping would not make the room safe enough to work in, she headed back down the staircase for a mop and a bucket of very hot water. She'd give the creaky old boards a good mopping before she tackled the job of moving her boxes and cases downstairs. She'd only been up here the one time, when Martin moved some boxes in. She could not remember what he'd said, a joke or something, about goblins in the floorboards. Noisy ones, too. Each board seemed to have its own creak, as she walked around the room. The eighteen-foot square room had her boxes against the far wall, Martin's winter clothes on a rack covered with plastic sheeting on the near wall, and a shamble of stuff piled on top of a gargantuan sofa, on the other side. The inside wall, next to the door, was decorated with newspaper clippings dating to the fifties.

Once she got the first bucket of water up the stairs, it dawned on her that mopping the floor would be futile if she didn't sweep the dust off everything first. So, she got a small hand broom, two old towels, and a large spray bottle of Lysol. The floor, an ancient mix of nine-inch-wide fir planks, gave way and spoke to her in their goblin language with every step.

"Shut up, you little bastards," she said.

With the first few swipes of the dust broom, Rosie had a sudden image of Martin's actual words, some three months ago.

She'd asked if he would mind bringing down one suitcase, the smaller one with the red strap holding it together.

"Sure," he'd said, "I'll get it this weekend."

"No, Hun, I'll get it myself."

"Right, Rosie the adventurer. But take care not to wake the bat. He's small but quick. I don't think he's a vampire, but his bite would be uncomfortable."

"Bat? Are you crazy? You got a bat up there, with my stuff, and my mother's suitcases?"

"Nah, but it's creepy and dirty up there. Can it wait until the weekend? I always take a bottle of Windex with me when I go up there. Windex kills bats; you knew that, didn't you?"

She took it as a joke then, and even now still thought it was. Still, she was cautious about where she stepped and studied the low ceiling, especially the corners of the room. No bats. But the floorboards were uneven. Originally nailed down with three-inch tapping nails, they were now loose everywhere. Each board covered half the distance to the wall, loosely fitted to another board, which completed the span. But the center of the room, directly below the light, had three boards instead of the two long ones on either side of the center. Two were about six feet long with a three-footer in the center. The pattern was odd. As she walked over the board, it seemed less stable than the others. And once she put a foot on it, it seemed to slightly tip upward at the far end. And it sounded hollow.

A bat in the floor, she mused, with a smile to herself. Bending down, she pushed down on the close end, and the opposing end rose up about a quarter of an inch. Reaching to it, she could just get her fingernail under it. Lifting up carefully she was surprised to see the whole board lift out, like a coffin lid. Underneath, in an oiled paper basin, was a double plastic baggie with a zip lock closure. Two floppy discs were inside. Rosie knelt silently for a moment. She could make out the writing on the top disc.

A chill went through her as she read the bright red ink on the first disc label.

"*Phase One—Hide and Be the Money—Fumbuck AmHull.*" She collapsed to the floor when she turned to the label on the second disc. "*Phase Two—Hide Martin and be Arthur—A Fake Death Plan.*"

She took the discs down to Martin's little home office in the library on the second floor—a place Martin jokingly called the "Brighton Lane Branch of AmHull Insurance." She powered up her notebook, inserting the disc in the floppy drive, and let Word automatically open the file. The document on her screen, a blue-bordered, two-page document written by Martin, said: "*Hide the Real Premium and Be Rich.*" Rosie read it once, went to the bathroom and took two spoonsful of Pepto-Bismol.

She spent the rest of the day, and half of Friday, trying to fathom Martin's plans. The floppy discs were the easy part—two word processing files, one document on each disc. The file names were scary enough, but the second file was bone chilling. *Did I ever know this guy?* she thought. Phase One was simple—Martin had engineered a way to embezzle money from AmHull—to get back at Harold Hull for moving Arthur to California. The details would likely be clear to someone in the insurance business, as Martin was, but were incomprehensible to her. She would call Mr. Hull and let him work it out. That could wait until after lunch, if she could even eat lunch.

Phase Two was another matter. Martin had apparently been planning to make everyone think that he'd committed suicide. Then, he and Arthur would run away to some secret island half-a-world away and live in luxury on AmHull's money. More Pepto-Bismol.

Dialing AmHull's number from the little yellow sticky pad next to the phone, she held tightly to the other disc, the one marked Phase Two. That one frightened her; the phone call to

AmHull was a welcome distraction. Next, she'd call the police. Or not. She'd tell Mr. Hull about Phase One, and then think about how to deal with Phase Two. Martin was on a walk-about in Boston, or so he said. She'd have time to figure this all out, she thought.

"AmHull Insurance," said the cheery voice. "How can we help you today?"

"I'd like to speak to Mr. Hull, please, is he available?"

"No, sorry, but he's out for the weekend. Can anyone else help you today?"

"Well, no, I don't think so. This is Rosie Anderson, I'm a friend of . . ."

"Rosie, oh Rosie, I'm so sorry for you and Martin. This is Alice, you know, we met once at the office party when Arthur was getting ready to move to California. What terrible news it was that—well you, know. How are you holding up? How is Martin . . . ?"

"Alice, yes, I remember. I'm sorry I don't know your last name, but I need to speak to Mr. Hull. It's about Martin."

"Alice Singworth, that's my name, but the Cheshire twins called me *Alice Blue Gown*. You know that, right? They were big kidders, the boys were."

"Yes, Alice Blue Gown. I never got the meaning. But I hate nicknames anyhow. Martin, and his twin, Arthur, were into lots of games. I guess naming other people was part of it. Alice, somehow, I feel I can trust you. I've just learned something disturbing about Martin. And he's not here. I know he's not at work. But this thing, the thing I just learned about Martin, is something that Mr. Hull needs to know. Do you have a number for him that I could call? I mean is he here in town?"

Rosie thought the line went blank because for twenty or thirty seconds there was no sound. Then, she thought she could hear breathing from the other end.

"Alice, are you still there?"

Another few moments of silence.

"Yes, Rosie, I'm still here. I have a terrible feeling about what you just said, you know, something disturbing about Martin. You know I'm the office manager here, right? The boys, I mean Harold's boys, not to mention Arthur and Martin, always marginalized me, and my job. But I know a lot about this old place. No, I don't have a weekend number for Mr. Hull, but maybe you could tell me what this is about? I could come over to your house; it's not that far, really. I can hear in your voice that it is really troubling you. Could I do that?"

Rosie crumbled. Crying into the phone, mumbling words like lost, alone, what in bloody hell do I do, life is such a bitch, you know, and so on.

Alice, in a calming voice, said, "Please let me come over. You shouldn't have to carry this by yourself. You're sure Martin's gone away? He won't be at the house?"

"No, he's in Boston. OK, I guess. Come over. I don't know what else to do."

Twenty minutes later, Alice used the antique brass knocker. Rosie saw her through the leaded glass and let her in. The perfunctory handshake collapsed into a smothering hug. Alice cried for Rosie. Rosie cried for herself. They went to the kitchen, Rosie made tea, and they took the tea upstairs to the library. Rosie showed Alice the freshly printed copy of Phase One.

"What do I do, Alice?"

"I can help, Rosie."

Sunday morning, Rosie decided that Martin's Phase Two plan was so bizarre that he really could never have meant to carry it out. She had not shared Phase Two with Alice, and now rethought that. She wondered if Martin had confided in Arthur before he died in Mexico. He must have, she thought. But the plan itself, called for secrecy, *especially* from Arthur. How crazy, she thought. Keeping Arthur in the dark seemed a key element in Martin's mind. Something about protecting both by keeping Arthur in the dark. Martin may have been ready to start Phase Two, or maybe he gave it up. Maybe it was supposed to start next month, or next year. But whenever it was, he intended to cut her out of his life. So, it seemed unlikely that he had told Arthur. If he had, Marcella would know, right? Oh, my God, did she? Did she know about Phase Two? Is that why she acted strangely toward Martin last week in San Diego, at the little memorial service they had for Arthur?

Rosie had not talked to Marcella since they left San Diego the prior Wednesday. She needed to call her anyhow and felt bad about taking five days to check in. Digging out Martin's Rolodex, she found Arthur's San Diego number.

"Marcella, it's Rosie. Look, I feel terrible about not calling you sooner, but . . ."

"Rosie, oh God, don't worry about me. I'm a tough Southern California chica, remember? I'm OK. How are you? How's Martin?"

"He's gone, Marcella. A lot has happened. I don't know where to start."

Rosie's confidence in Martin, not to mention herself, was gone. Or was it more than that? Fear—was she afraid of Martin? How could she converse with a woman she hardly knew about something so ominous she didn't know how to start. She'd taken notes from Martin's Phase Two memo. As the conversation moved on, Rosie kept glancing back and forth at her notes, and outside through the large plate glass window that faced the street. Hoping, but dreading, that Martin might drive in from the street.

"Hey, girl, start with Martin. Watcha mean, he's gone? Gone where?"

"We had a fight. He stormed out the door on Thursday. He left me a message on my phone saying he was in Boston. He had to think things over. I guess he will come back someday, but he's pretty messed up."

"Yeah, of course. That actually makes sense to me. Arthur's death hit him like a fifty-foot wave. He was scared of the water; did you know that? Raised on the Atlantic coast and living in San Diego. It took me over a month with Arthur, but one thing I know for sure. Death for twins is different, know what I'm saying?"

"Marcella, it's not just that. There's more to this. I hate to impose, but could I ask you some questions about Arthur? Please? I don't have anyone else to call."

Marcella had her own questions to ask about Martin but hadn't thought of an excuse to pry into it with Rosie. In a way unbeknownst to Rosie, Marcella welcomed this call.

She said, "Sure, fire away."

No, Arthur said nothing about getting even with AmHull. No, nothing about premiums, or shaving a little AmHull money off the top, either. No, they never had any disagreement I know of, and for sure, Arthur didn't talk about death to her. After almost a half-hour of dancing around softball questions and sidestepping vague answers, both Rosie and Marcella came together on common ground.

"Rosie, are you as worried about Arthur's death as I am? Does it smell funny to you?"

Rosie's sigh into the mouthpiece turned into a wail.

She screamed into the phone, "Oh, Marcella, thank God for you! I thought I was the crazy one. I don't know anything, but yeah, it stinks. There's some hiding going on. I do not know what your twin, Arthur, or mine, Martin, were up to, but we are in the middle of it. Arthur is dead, Martin is AWOL, and God knows what else is gonna happen. I know you have a job and all, but maybe together we could figure this out. Have you ever been to Maine? It's still a little crisp here, but we could talk better in person, couldn't we?"

"Yeah, we could. But all the way across the country? And what about Martin? You expect him back, and what if he came back and walked in on us puzzling all this out?"

"You're right. But maybe there's a middle ground. It's pretty easy for me to get to Chicago, I've had some education meetings there. It's a great convention town. Maybe we could meet there. It's about halfway, and we could have a long dinner or something."

"You got it, girl. But let's do it quick. How about next Saturday? We could each fly in the morning and then spend the afternoon and dinner talking. I'd catch the red eye back here. I sleep on airplanes, you know?"

"Done, I'll fax my flight information to you; you do the same, OK?"

The following Saturday, Rosie met Marcella in the lobby bar of the Chicago Hilton O'Hare Hotel at 5:00 pm. They found a table on the far side of the room, not close to anyone else. The waiter couldn't wait to get to them. Marcella ordered a glass of white wine.

"Yes, that's what I thought you'd order," Rosie said, turning to the waiter and ordering a Jameson's neat.

They'd both had a long flight and dreaded the upcoming conversation. The waiter asked about *hors d' oeuvres*, pointing to a little menu propped up in a Hilton hand in the center of the glass table. They smiled a no thank you. He headed for the bar to place the order, no doubt thinking there was no big tip at this table.

Rosie broke the ice.

"Marcella, this is so nice of you, coming all this way. I know you're heart-broken over Arthur. How are you holding up, you know, all things considered, even though I hate that phrase."

"It's the things that are not being considered that bother me. Let me put it this way. I loved Arthur, in a way, you know, not like getting married and moving to the suburbs or anything. But he was very fun to be around, except when he obsessed about being a twin. It kind of got in the way of things. I'm sure you saw the same things in Martin, right?"

Rosie took the first sip of her Jameson's, a tiny one, and frowned.

"I don't know how to ask you this, cause you are gonna think I'm nuts. But I'm afraid there is a good reason why we both saw the same things. You know, how unerringly my man and yours did everything exactly the same? We both got all the childhood stories about their little game of Hide and Be. You know, how no one could tell them apart and how they used that to give themselves a life, despite the foster homes, the spankings with a belt, you know all that, right?"

"Yeah, sure, I got the whole nine yards on that. Then I got it even more when I'd listen to Arthur's side of phone calls about how much he missed Portland, or how much they missed each other. They were one and the same, that's for sure."

"How long had you been with Arthur before he died? I forget."

"Let's see, I met him a week after he moved to San Diego, then he went back and forth to Portland for, I dunno, maybe two months. That's when he went back for their fishing trip, and they pulled that dirty trick on you in a bar, what was it called, Eddies or something?"

"No, it was Sweeties. It was kind of dirty, but kind of nice too. Jesus, they fooled me totally. I'm glad it was only once. You're lucky you didn't meet them together like that. You never saw them together, did you? They were a real hole in the boat, those boys."

The table next to theirs filled. Two women and a man with brief cases, talking about a judge. They were focused on themselves and their judge. The waiter took their order, with a smile, no doubt smelling a larger tip. All the same, Rosie scooted her chair close to Marcella's.

"So, let me ask you an awkward question. After Arthur came back to you in San Diego, after that fishing trip and my mixing them up in the bar, did you ever hear them talking on the phone to one another again?"

"Sure, I guess. Hell, I don't know. Maybe not, now that I come to think of it. Why do you ask?"

"Well, I never heard them talk either, not to one another, not after the fishing trip."

Marcella went blank, and pale. Picking up her glass, she drained it, and held her palms up to Rosie.

"What exactly are you saying, girl? Were they on the outs; is that what you mean? What, did they have a fight or something?"

"I don't know what I mean. I am just scared, and I don't know why. Little things have been bothering me for three months. Why no phone calls between them after the fishing trip? Why so much obsession on twinness, I mean wasn't it worse lately? Did Arthur talk more about them than either himself or Martin? Martin did. He focused on Arthur a lot, and their life together. But he didn't say much about himself. I stopped learning about him and got lots of lessons about Arthur."

"Rosie, I gotta tell you something. Arthur and I finally came to an understanding about that. I got tired of listening about life in Portland. I tried to get him to start thinking about life with me, life on the West Coast, you know?"

"Did it work?"

"Yeah, well, at first it worked. But now you got me thinking about it, he went back to talking about Martin all the time, and you too. I know he liked you a lot."

"Well, Martin only talked about Arthur, but he didn't say much about you—of course, that's because he never met you. Marcella, remember when we talked on the phone? I asked you if you felt anything was funny about Arthur's death?"

Marcella caught the waiter's eye, motioned him over, and ordered another round, plus peanuts or something. He asked again about *hors d' oeuvres*.

"No thanks, cupcake," she said, "I don't like French food."

He went away unhappy, again.

"You did not ask if it felt funny, you asked me if it *smelled* funny. I didn't get your meaning then, but now I do. I been trying to add some things up. It don't add. And Arthur was really good at math. So, yeah, it feels funny, smells funny, but it's not funny. What bothers you the most? Maybe we can start there."

"Well, something happened on the fishing trip. That's what I think. They were so excited about spending a week together, Arthur comes in on a Friday night, kisses me at Sweeties, and then drives off up north the next day. I only saw him once. Martin saw him after that, when he went to San Diego, but nothing was ever said about him coming back. You saw Martin out there, what was he like around Arthur?"

Marcella turned ashen. She clicked her teeth together and scratched at her throat as though something was caught.

"Rosie, I've been thinking about that. That's what smells funny to me. I never saw Martin on either of those two trips. He was always so busy, Arthur said, and he was in hurry to get back to you, so we just never got together, you know the three of us. Arthur had already told me how he tricked you in the bar. I was kind of hoping for the same experience from Martin. I never got it. But here's what really hit home after your phone call."

"What?" Rosie interrupted and leaned forward in her leather swivel chair.

"Arthur was real proud to be with me—a Latin booby prize, he called me. He liked to show me off, you know to the Hull boys, to new people we would meet. But he never showed me off to his twin. What's up with that?"

"Martin was equally proud to be with me, but even more so after the fishing trip. Why do you suppose that was? And I still can't get over Arthur leaving so abruptly. He told Martin some story about wanting to see an old booty in upstate Maine, that's what they called us, booties. Did you know that? Anyhow, now I'm thinking how strange that was, seeing that you and Arthur were hooked up by then. Now you say you never saw Martin in San Diego, and I know Martin talked about you when he got back from there. I can't say he said he actually saw you, but I just assumed that the three of you had dinner every night, you know?"

"No, that was not it. Arthur and I had dinner every night, but Martin was only here two, maybe three days."

"And you never had dinner with him?"

"Nope."

Rosie pursed her lips, nodded her head slightly, and slid her chair around the little cocktail table a little closer to Marcella.

"If you don't mind, I'd like to know some things that might be a little sensitive, you know, about sex. Sex with Arthur there in San Diego. I'm not just prying. And I know Arthur's dead, so this might seem morbid to you, but I have a reason for asking. Do you mind?"

For a moment, Marcella withdrew. She looked taken aback, but not repulsed. With a little twist of her wrist, she pushed her wine away. Looking around, as though to make sure what they said was private, she looked hard at Rosie.

"No, go ahead. But you should know, California girls are tough. Serious women, like me, from the East Valley in LA are especially tough. I am glad you asked that question. I'm no prude. Arthur was. Did you know that? You're not either, I can tell. But Martin was your man. Arthur was mine, at least for a little while. You too, right? My Arthur is dead. Your Martin is alive. But gone, *que, no?* You want to talk about sex. *Si*, it's

OK. When you came to my apartment in San Diego for the memorial, I could tell you really cared; Martin, I'm not so sure. Didn't you think so, too? I mean Martin is so like Arthur, he could be Arthur. So, it was weird when Martin said he didn't want to talk—no eulogy—*nada*. Maybe that's why your Martin is acting weird. Maybe it's just the same thing, *de ja vu* all over again, as they say. What's he doing that's weird?"

"Well, like I said, part of it is sex. When I first met Martin, he was a pretty wild man in the sack, you know. Pushing limits, experimenting, game playing in bed, you know. Nothing kinky, always fun, but still a little out there on the edge. Was Arthur like that?"

"No, he was what church people say is traditional. You know, the missionary position, not enough foreplay, a little prudish, even. But I don't mean to make it sound boring. He had tons of energy, could go all night, and was very considerate. But please don't think I was unsatisfied. He was a very nice lover."

"Christ," Rosie exploded, quickly looking around to see if any one heard. "Martin was like I told you, pretty much a wild man. But then after we'd been together a month or so, he just changed. Not a bad change, still good in bed. But here's the thing, you just said it, he became 'a very nice lover.' It's hard to pinpoint it, but after a few nights I could tell he was different."

"So, I'm missing something," Marcella said, sipping on her third glass of Chardonnay.

"Oh, God. I don't know how to say this or even if I should. But you just said that 'Martin is so like Arthur; he could be Arthur.' That's what I am afraid of. That's what's so weird. I have the feeling that maybe he is."

"Is what?"

"Is Arthur. I know it must sound nuts and it's really me that's weird—not Martin. But, Marcella, I am starting to think that Martin is Arthur."

Drained, both women sat back and went mute for four or five minutes. Marcella said she had to pee. Rosie did too but didn't want to walk with her to the rest room at the far end of the restaurant. When Marcella got back, she pushed her chair closer to Rosie's.

"Rosie, you're not nuts. God, I have been thinking the same thing! But I don't know why. Martin has called me a few times, as you know, but each time the voice is the same—it's Arthur's voice. Like I said, I never was with them together at the same time. But I talked to him, Martin, on the phone three or four times. He always sounded like Arthur. I just thought it was part of the twin thing, you know. But even though it was only the one time, after Arthur died, at the memorial, when he hardly talked, I hear it. You know, could it be? Could he be Arthur? Oh, God, what the fuck is going on?"

Their conversation had been back and forth, neither interrupting the other. But now Marcella was on overdrive.

"Did you know that Martin called me that morning, about an hour before the memorial? He asked what time you guys should come over; you know. He said that one of the boys, one of the sons of the man that ran the company, would be there, to 'show the flag,' he said. Then he asked if Alice had called. I never heard of Alice. He goes, she works for the company. I go, beats me, I never heard of her from Arthur. Who is she? He goes, you know, business stuff. He asked if I heard anything from the coroner, or anyone in Mexico about the fire, or the autopsy, or anything like that, just routine stuff. He was nice, like always, asking if I needed anything, and can he send me some money, or anything? He's real generous that way, you know."

"Marcella, that's not right. I mean I believe you and all, but I have to tell you that he never said anything about calling you or offering you money. He never talks about Arthur—well, I mean he never talks about Arthur's death. Why would he ask you about things like the coroner, or the autopsy, and not ask me? Why would he send you money, and not tell me? I don't mean that he has to, or anything. We keep our money separate, so I guess I'm not surprised about that. He is generous. But asking *you* about Arthur's death while ignoring it with *me* is really odd, don't you think?"

"Odd ain't the word for it, girl. I can't believe what I'm hearing. Fuck him! Do you suppose that neither one of us really knows who he is? I mean, it's like you said—is he Martin, or is he Arthur? That's really scary. I mean how can I even be asking you the question?"

"Marcella, I'm so sorry. I hate to involve you in this, but I can't tell you how glad I am I called you. Let me ask you about Martin's tattoo. It's so out of character for him. I can't get it straight in my head. Let me tell you what it is, maybe you can . . ."

Marcella jumped up from the table, hitting the glass edge with her legs, and knocking the glasses over. Both drinks were dry, but the waiter had brought two small water glasses with the peanuts. Marcella's glass slid across the table.

"What are you saying, girl! You saying Martin has a tattoo? You sure?"

"Marcella, what's wrong? Yes, Martin had a little tattoo on his ankle. But what's the matter with that? It just a tattoo, right? Not so popular in Portland, but he got it in San Diego. At least that's where I think he got it. He tried to hide it from me. I started to kid him about it once, but he was enraged, and sort of guilty, I thought. So, I didn't press it. I pretended I never saw it. He pretended he didn't have it. What's this about?"

Marcella tried to wipe up the water with a cocktail napkin, but the waiter rushed over and used a towel to wipe it up.

"Sorry, Madam, would you like a refill, on the house?"

"No, bring me one of those Jameson's. And one for her too," she said, pointing to Rosie.

"Be back, Rosie. Got to go to the little girls' room. Hold on tight. Be back."

The waiter brought two Jameson's, straight up, two fresh little glass containers of peanuts, and a worried look on his face.

"Is your friend OK, Madam?"

Rosie asked for the check, sipped her shot glass, and waited.

Marcella took her time. Ten minutes later, she came back to the table, said she was sorry, sat down, and laid it out.

"Tattoo? Wait, don't tell me. It's on his ankle, his left ankle, a little sea urchin, with a tiny red m in the middle of it. Right?"

"Right. But how did you know? The little red m is like a monogram—it's for Martin. He said he got to identify himself—sort of 'to himself,' I guess. But he only talked about the one time. Two minutes' worth. From then on, he bristled if I even looked like I was gonna bring it up. So, I didn't. What's the big deal? Martin could have a tattoo if he wanted, couldn't he?"

"Rosie, Oh God, Rosie—you're not gonna believe this! That tattoo is one that Arthur got in San Diego. I designed it. I took him to my cousin Maldonado and watched him needle it in—the little red m is *not* for Martin; it's for *Marcella*! My cousin put it on Arthur's ankle cause I told him too—Arthur was pissed about it. He only wanted the little sea urchin, not the m."

DR. SOCORRO

The air handling equipment in Dr. Socorro's office was on the fritz so some government genius decided that all the windows in the clinic could not be opened until the AC was restored. That made it muggy inside, which meant that Dr. Socorro took off her usual crisp white doctor's jacket for the session with Arthur. He'd been locked up for eleven weeks, and she was the only woman he saw the whole time. Seeing her undone was a special treat.

"Wow, Doc, this air handling thing is a real mess, isn't it?"

"Yes, Arthur, it is."

"But you look nice, I mean more comfortable, without your coat, and all."

As the first five minutes of their session proved, Arthur would stare at Dr. Socorro's chest the entire session. She wasn't what you'd call busty, but she was a delight to watch move forward and back, taking notes, breathing, all the usual stuff obscured by that hospital-issue white clinical coat. If she was aware of Arthur's prurient interest, she never let on.

"Arthur, do you remember the last time you saw Rosie in Portland? I'm curious about that because I noted something in your Portland FBI arrest file that she was either there, or close by, when you were arrested, is that right?"

"Why you asking about that?"

"Because I'm a psychiatrist and am working for the court. You're charged with a crime for killing your brother. But if you're Arthur, not Martin, then you could not have killed Arthur. That's why. Now, do you remember the last time you saw Rosie in Portland? It could be important."

"OK. Remember I told you that Rosie and I had a difficult talk on the back porch at the Brighton Lane house? Well, I left that day, drove to Boston, and just sat there in a cheap motel north of the city, but right off I-95, I could see a little sliver of the ocean there, just like I can see Mission Bay through your government locked-down window right now. Anyhow, I stayed six days. After that, while I was still in a fog and trying to sort out my life, I got a call from her on my cell. She wanted to talk, right away, she said. She sounded scared or something. I wasn't ready to go back, but I did anyhow. Three hours later, I was back in town, where she told me to meet her."

"Meet her? You mean not at your house?"

"Yeah, she said to meet her at, well, lemme see. It was at a little drive-by place, with little white tables outside. I can't believe I can't remember the name, but it was on the bay, just off I-95. I remember that I went from the motel north of Boston on the same freeway all the way to Portland, turned off the freeway and there she was, waiting for me at one of the little tables, outside, watching the boats and birds in Portland harbor."

"Did you talk on the phone, during the drive I mean?"

"Nope, she just asked if I could be there at four and I said yes. I got there before four, but she was there, waiting. Boy what a set-up that was."

"A set-up?"

"Well, here's how it went. She had a glass of white wine on the table. I ordered a beer. I could see her car, maybe twenty feet away, parked next to my truck—that is, Martin's truck. I remember that when I pulled up and parked next to her car, she could see me. She waved at me. A little wave, that's all it was. No smile, no hug when I got to the table. The little wave was sort of symbolic—I thought it meant hello. Turned out, it meant goodbye."

"I gather it was a short conversation. How'd it go?"

"Bad Doc, real bad. She sounded OK on the phone. But no sooner I sat down, she started in on me. Martin? Is that your name? Or is it, Arthur? I'm not sure you even know. All I know is that you're not who I thought you were a year ago and you're not anybody I want to know any longer. Funny now that I think about it, Doc. She was like you in a way. She didn't know who I was. Neither do you."

"Well, that's why we are talking. What happened next?"

"She said what she said. Got up. Turned around. Walked back inside, through the bar and outside to the parking lot. I watched her go to her car. And that was it. I never saw her again?"

"So that was the end of the conversation? She just walked out?"

"It was the end of her talking, but I was there at the table; it was actually part of the parking lot, with just a little fence up on the short deck separating the tables from the cars. I screamed at her. I know she heard me, but she didn't say anything."

"You screamed at her? Why?"

"I wanted her to know the truth. She was mad because she thought I was Martin and that I had done something wrong, I don't know what. But she was confused too. I couldn't blame her. So, I just screamed the truth at the top of my lungs. Never thought a minute about other people being there, you know, at the other tables. I am Arthur! Martin is dead! I killed him but it was an accident. Oh, God, I . . ."

"Arthur, you know she must have been furious with you, whichever twin you were. You had fooled her, humiliated her, raped her, stole her love, you know that don't you?"

"Wait a goddamn minute. I never raped her. What are you saying?"

"You had sex with her under false pretenses. She thought she was making love with Martin, the man she loved. You were not Martin; you just pretended to be. That's rape. Don't you see it, even now? She never consented to sex with Arthur, if that's who you really are. It's no different than sneaking into her house, wearing a mask in the middle of the night. You may be the most confused man I've ever seen as a psychiatrist, but don't tell me you think she consented to have sex with you. You duped her into it. That's why she was furious. Yelling the truth out at her in the parking lot must have killed her."

"Yeah, I know it now. But you have to understand. I did it to save Martin. I only thought about him, not me, or Rosie or Marcella or anyone. It was about Martin. Now, sure, it's easy to see how stupid it all was. But then, it seemed the right thing to do."

"The right thing to do? You knew Martin was embezzling money from the company to get even for sending you away. You knew that . . ."

"NO! I only knew he had a plan of some kind. He called it Hide and Be the Money. I told you all that, but I never knew how it worked, or even if he actually did anything. It was always just something he was working on and would tell me about whenever, but then he died, and we had to find a way to live. You know, both of us had lives, it wasn't just me."

"Arthur, please remember that my role in your case is not to investigate the case back in Portland—embezzling money from AmHull. I'm not investigating the murder arson case here in San Diego, either. I'm only trying to help you see all of it in context, so that I can in good faith, tell the judge that you *are* Arthur. Most of what I am finding out from you convinces me of that. But too often you say things about *we* this or *we* that. That's delusional thinking. Maybe you can't help it, but you have to accept the reality that Martin died back there in Portland and that everything that happened after that was *you*. Not *we*."

"Doc, I sometimes say *we* because that's the way it was when Martin was alive. When he died, and I know he died, I had to find a way to accept his death. Keeping it the same way. That's what did it for me. It's not delusional. It's just us. He is alive in my mind. Can't you see that?"

"Yes, I can. But sometimes it hurts you more than it helps you. This is a legal case, not a coping mechanism. Let's move past that last meeting with Rosie. What did you do next?"

"I drove down to AmHull's office prepared to tell Harold the truth. I had no plan after that although I vaguely thought I might go to California and explain everything to Marcella in person. As it turned out, I would never see her again, either. When I pulled in the parking lot at the AmHull building, Harold's parking slot was empty. No sense going in if he's not there. So, I started to back out, and all hell broke loose. The front door of AmHull burst open and the guys in the dark suits ran out, flashing guns, and badges, and hollering shit like 'FBI, you're under arrest.' It's crazy what you think of at times—I thought, who's under arrest? Me, or were they looking for Martin? You say I'm delusional, Doc. Well, not then I wasn't. I was Arthur—they were looking for Martin. I had nothing to worry about, right?"

PORTLAND. ARTHUR'S ARREST

"I already told you why," Arthur said to one of the two gray suits on the other side of the table.

After his arrest in the parking lot at AmHull, he was taken to the federal building, searched, photographed, fingerprinted, and placed in a holding room, pending his first appearance before a federal magistrate. They read him his Miranda rights, he waived them, and now it was time to talk. He could not wait to explain "all this," he said.

The older FBI, with the scraggy grey mustache and loosened tie, asked the questions while the other one, a younger FBI maybe twenty-five, took notes. They seemed perplexed that Arthur had come to AmHull's parking lot.

"I was gonna tell Harold that I'd been pretending to be Martin for months, but that I never took anything from him, or the company. If there was embezzlement, it was Martin, not me. And if it was Martin, it wasn't much. He was hugely pissed at Harold, but he's not a thief."

"You are Arthur?" the gray suit said incredulously. "It is our understanding that Arthur Cheshire died in a fire in California ten days ago. You spent the last week with your girlfriend, Rosie, who told us she was worried about you—Martin Cheshire. You were booked in here as Martin because your driver's license and everything in your wallet says you *are* Martin Cheshire, your boss and your girlfriend identified you, in person, and . . ."

"No, that's what I'm trying to tell you. I'm not Martin. Martin died a little over three months ago. I've been pretending to be him because, well, it's complicated. I can explain, but I don't know where to start. First, I just want to clear up the question of who I am."

"Mr. Cheshire, I'll call you that just for convenience. I'm not the agent that you should explain all this to. I'm just working on one case—an embezzlement case against you because you wired money that didn't belong to you to an offshore bank. That money came from insurance premiums paid to AmHull. That's your job, right? You were the accountant at AmHull? You worked there last week, five days ago. We actually saw you there. We were onto you by then. Alice Singworth, AmHull's office manager, told us that she discovered your embezzlement plan three weeks ago. We've had you under surveillance since that time. I saw you myself in person, and we have videotape of you coming in and out of the office, and going in and out of your house, with your girlfriend. We lost track of you for a few days, and later we heard you were in California, at your brother's funeral. Now, I don't know what you are trying to pull about changing identities and claiming to be your dead brother, but it's not going to work."

"This is crazy, you saw me *acting* like I was my brother, that's what I'm trying to tell you. I know it was stupid, but you've got to listen to me."

"Let me ask you this, Mr. Cheshire. When is the last time you visited Panama? As I'm sure you know, the bank down there won't give us financial information, but we will be able to get your exit and entry information. That much they will give us."

"Panama? What's Panama got to do with this? I don't know what you're talking about."

The second gray suit held his ball point up and chimed in.

"Panama, Mr. Cheshire, is the little banana republic where you wire-transferred $263,000 out of AmHull's money market account here in Portland to the *Banco de Fontana National.*"

"OK, I know only one thing, and it doesn't include Panama. Martin told me once on the telephone that he got $26,000 from AmHull. That's all. He didn't say how, or when. But I remember the number. He did not have a money market account, just a joint checking account, with me. We always pooled our money. You can check on that. We never had a money market account. Now I can see that you are talking about Martin's Hide and Be the Money plan. I never got any details, but he probably put it on his computer. And he always backed up stuff on floppy discs. He was like that, always the computer. Call Rosie, she'll tell you."

"We did that, Mr. Cheshire—two hours ago when you first mentioned it. Rosie knows of no floppy disk and the search team found nothing but a loose floorboard in the attic. It was loose just like you said an hour ago, but it was also empty, just like your story."

Grey suit number one subbed back into the game.

"Do you know how bizarre your story sounds? Do you really expect us to believe one word you've said for the last two hours? Why don't you take Agent Bacon's advice and call a lawyer? You really need one, you know that, don't you?"

They had me for not reporting Martin's death—a misdemeanor "if true" they said. They had me for faking my own death—a felony "if true" they said. They had Martin for stealing from AmHull—a big felony "if true" they said. But nothing I said was "true" at least as for them. It was Hide and Be in reverse—this time I was telling them who I was and not hiding anything.

"Look, I've told you over and over. I didn't steal it, my brother did. I'm not him, how many times do I have to tell you?"

Finally, Arthur woke up from his nightmare. He did what he should have done two hours earlier. He invoked his right to remain silent. They quit asking him questions. He quit incriminating himself. During the booking session, he told the magistrate he was unemployed and had little savings.

A federal public defender was appointed, who summed up his status succinctly.

"Mr. Cheshire, if you are telling me the truth, they got you on a felony fraud case for faking your own death in Mexico. If you are lying, they got you on a felony embezzlement case for stealing $263,000 from your employer. Your girlfriend is thinking about rape charges. And my guess is that, if you are Martin, then you could be looking at a murder investigation. Somebody with your DNA and fingerprints burned up a body in Mexico. Or killed somebody in Mexico and then burned up the body. Either way, you are looking at criminal charges. If I was you, I'd figure out who I am. And go from there. No more pretending, OK?"

PORTLAND—SECOND INTERVIEW WITH FBI

Three days later, against the advice of counsel, but with his public defender present, Arthur gave a second interview to the FBI in Portland. He'd been transferred from the holding cell in the federal court building to a jail cell in the multi-agency detention center north of the city. The room was utilitarian, not uncomfortable and well equipped. A four-by-six-foot metal conference table, with two armless chairs on each of its four sides, held the basic hardware of FBI investigations. Pens, pads, a paper clip holder, six bottles of water, a four-sided clock, and a reel-to-reel tape recorder with a small box of blank tapes. After the usual preliminaries, repeat readings of Miranda warnings, repeat waivers of same, the older, mustachioed man in the black suit laid it out.

"Mr. Cheshire, my name is Scoopmire—Special Agent Douglas Scoopmire—here are my credentials. I am in charge of the Portland field office and have talked to Agent Bacon. It is, if you don't mind my saying so, a rather far-fetched story. While I can't say that any of us believe you, I am going to give you a chance to prove yourself. You can do that two ways. First, you can give us permission to search your fishing camp on the Damariscotta River. If we find the remains of Martin Cheshire, that will tell us who you are and give some credence to your story about his accidental death. But what we find there can be used against you as well; you need to be warned of that. Second, you can take a polygraph test. If you pass it, it can also lend credence to your story. But it is not without risk. While polygraphs are not admissible in a court of law, we in law enforcement use them to establish probable cause in criminal cases. Of course, it can't be used against you in court, because as I said, it's inadmissible evidence. So, you have little to lose on that one. What do you say, do you want to give us permission to examine your property and take a polygraph? And, for the record, you do not have to do either, or you can stop this interview anytime you want. Your lawyer is here with you, and everything we say to one another is being recorded. Your lawyer has agreed to that. What's it going to be, Mr. Cheshire?"

"Call me Arthur, Mr. Scoopmire. Agent Bacon claims not to know who I am, but you seem to. I understand why you need permission to give me a polygraph and I know what they are. You can go up to the fishing camp and look in it without my permission. I hope you do. My brother's body is not there, as I told Agent Bacon. So, I'm not sure what is there to help me but there's nothing there to hurt me so, by all means, go ahead. I'll sign whatever you want—including a polygraph consent. I wish they were admissible in court because mine will prove I am being truthful. Where do I sign?"

"Thank you, Mr. Cheshire. I will call you Arthur. We will have the forms drawn up in a few minutes. In the interim, I'd like to go over a few things from your interview with Agent Bacon."

"It was hardly an interview. More like a third-degree, I'd say, but fire away."

"The first thing that is confusing is why you didn't report your brother's death last spring. You must have known that eventually it would be discovered, and your deception about it would make it appear as though you were guilty of more than just failing to report it. Motive is an important thing in criminal cases, Mr. Cheshire, I mean Arthur. Can you help me out here and tell me a little more about your motive? What exactly did you hope to accomplish and why?"

"Did Agent Bacon tell you about the game my brother and I played for the last twenty-five years? Did he tell you about Hide and Be? Did he tell you about how guilty I felt about not being able to save my brother's life even though the accident wasn't my fault? What more can I tell you that I didn't tell him?"

Agent Scoopmire proved to be a patient man. He didn't answer questions but held his arms out with his palms up, as though he were on a pulpit asking something of God. He rolled his smallish eyes over the rim of his rimless glasses as if to say, I don't know, just keep on talking, maybe you'll convince me. So, Arthur tried.

"Martin should not have died that day. If anyone should have, it was me. I was the one driving the boat; I was the one who wanted to stay out all day on the river. I was the one who looked right at where he was in the water and didn't see him. All that was my fault and I just thought I could make it up to him by being him. You don't have a twin so you can't know. I've wished a thousand times that I died, and Martin lived, but each time I thought things maybe could be the same. He would have to become me—just like I became him. Can you understand that? My motive—that was your question, righ?—my motive was to keep him alive. Can you understand that?"

"Yes, Arthur, I guess I can. But how does keeping him alive square with faking your death out there in California, if that's what happened? That seems very different to me."

"No, sir, you still don't see it. I discovered that I could be Martin here in Portland, but it became obvious that I couldn't do that and still be myself, that is Arthur, out in California. So, as stupid as it sounds now, I convinced myself that to keep Martin alive here, I had to do away with myself out there."

"Arthur, I hear you but I'm not sure you are listening to yourself. Of course, your DNA is the same as that of your identical twin brother. But that's the problem, not the solution; don't you see? How can it help you prove you're Arthur if you and Martin do, in fact, share the same DNA? I think you're going to have to give us something else. We have your fingerprints, but since you have no criminal record, we can't verify them. Are your prints on file somewhere? That might help prove that you really are Arthur."

"Well, maybe the university has them, or the MVD, or the guys that issue hunting licenses. I don't know. God, I never thought about these things before. Wait. Come to think of it, I can tell you one quick place to look. AmHull was always very security conscious. They took fingerprints and polygraphs from all employees. That's how I know about polygraphs, like I told you. Just get my prints out of my file and compare them with the ones Agent Bacon took yesterday. Then I'm out of here, right?"

"No, Arthur. If those prints do confirm you are Arthur, then that lends some credence to your story, but there is one other thing you haven't even started to clear up. That's the money that you say Martin stole from AmHull. You say it was only $26,000 but we know of at least $263,000 that is missing. You say Martin put it in a bank in Portsmouth—we know most of it was wire-transferred to Panama. If you and your brother were so close, how is it that you never knew what he was doing? And why in the world would he implicate you?"

"Actually, Mr. Scoopmire, that's easier than you think. The plan to steal AmHull's money was entirely Martin's. He did it to get back at them for separating us—that is sending me to San Diego and leaving him here. But he intended to tell me about it the weekend he died. He wrote it all out on his computer. It's probably on a floppy disc. I told Agent Bacon about that yesterday. Get it and it will prove my innocence."

"Yes, we tried that. It's gone—if it ever was there."

Arthur stayed in the multi-agency lock-up another night. The next morning, Agent Bacon came back, and more or less rearrested him. This time it was formal—quiet but formal.

"Martin Cheshire, you are under arrest for theft and embezzlement of money from your employer under Title 18, Section 655, of the United States Code, and international wire fraud. The state authorities here are detaining you in Maine pending an extradition hearing in the State of California. I believe it is likely that you will be charged with the felonious murder of your brother Arthur Cheshire. I want to read you your rights and then Mr. Cabelson here, who is with the US Attorney's office in San Diego, will have some questions for you regarding your status in San Diego County. You have the right to . . ."

The rest of the morning was a blur to Arthur. His federal public defender was a year younger and had only slightly more experience in legal affairs than he did. As Arthur put it, "I have none and he has none plus one year."

"Martin Cheshire? Is that your full name? I'm Steven Bell, call me Steve. I've been asked to see you about your extradition hearing."

"No, Steve, that's not my full name—it's only half. The other half is Arthur. My full name is Arthur Cheshire. How old are you anyway? Are you here on the embezzlement charges too? And please, tell me you've read whatever it is that says I am being deported to California on felonious murder charges. I can't believe how truly fumbucked this is. And why are you here at all? I thought Mr. Chase was my federal public defender; he sat with me when I talked to Agent Bacon and the other guy, Scoop something."

"Well, I'm here because your case has changed since yesterday. I've been with the office for six years now and have handled more extradition cases than almost anyone in the office. You case is the first of its kind that we know about, because of the name thing."

"Name thing? My name is Arthur Cheshire, I only used my brother's name for a little while, and if that's a crime, I'll cop a plea. But extradition to California? I don't know anything about that."

"I do. The prosecutor gave me a copy of Agent Scoopmire's interview with you, along with Agent Bacon's. I also talked to the state police officer that arrested you. Here's the status as best I can figure it out. Although you claim to be Arthur Cheshire, the authorities have a certified copy of a Mexican death certificate on Arthur Cheshire. It will take some time to reexamine the DNA that you think will establish your true identity. The FBI checked, as you apparently asked them to do, your fingerprints in your employer's file against the ones they took from you the day before yesterday. I must tell you they match. Your fingerprints are the same as those in Martin Cheshire's personnel file. They say you are Martin Cheshire. Your employer, AmHull, also has a file on Arthur Cheshire, and they checked the fingerprints in that file. They are different from the ones taken from you at the Portland police department the day before yesterday. So, as you can see, it looks to them, and frankly to me, as though you are who you have been saying you for almost six month; that is, you are Martin Cheshire."

"Steve, what did you say your last name was? I have already forgotten it."

"Bell, Steven Bell."

"Well Mr. Bell, if you are going to take the word of the police department over mine, then I'd best call you Mr. Bell, not Steve, since it doesn't appear you're my friend. I don't know how in the world my fingerprints got put in my brother's file at work, and I don't know how to prove to you who I am other than to promise you that I am telling the truth. I don't suppose my words are worth much these days. But you're here and it looks like you're all I've got for now. So, let's both make the best of it. I haven't been charged with anything in California so how can they force me to go out there? What are they going to extradite me for exactly? I guess faking my death was probably a crime of some sort but the fed—Mr. Scoop something, said something about murder—whose murder? My own? How can you murder yourself? I know about suicide, but homicide yourself; what's that?"

"Mr. Cheshire, I understand your confusion. I only just read the departmental reports on this case this morning and they are a bit sketchy. But here's a brief outline. The official records in California confirm that Arthur Cheshire died in Mexico and that you were appointed to be your brother's executor. You established a probate estate under California law. The DNA testing confirmed it was Arthur that died. They confirmed that with the hospital here in Portland, when you were first tested in an identical twins study twenty-six years ago. You told Agent Bacon the first day and Agent Scoopmire yesterday that your brother, Martin, died here in Maine last October. Then you said that you moved his body to California in December and burnt it up so that people would think it was you. But there is no evidence at the fishing camp, no body, no evidence of foul play; no evidence there ever was a body there and, finally, no DNA. The only body is the one out there in California, three thousand miles from here. That body appears to be that of

Arthur Cheshire. The fingerprints in your file at work match the ones taken here in the police department. You have been telling everyone here, including your girlfriend, Rosie, that you are Martin Cheshire. So, to make it short, you appear to be who you have always said, until this week, you were. They believe Arthur died because DNA testing scientifically confirmed it, beyond any reasonable doubt. They believe Martin is alive and here in this jail because the fingerprint analysis scientifically confirms that. Do you have anything to prove that you are Arthur, not Martin?"

"Goddammit! This is ridiculous. I'm Arthur Cheshire. My brother is dead, and I didn't kill him. What possible evidence could they have to the contrary? There is none because it never happened."

"Actually, they have no intention of looking into what you say is an accidental death on the Damariscotta River beyond what they've already done. They don't think Martin Cheshire, or anyone else for that matter, died on the Damariscotta. They think you killed Arthur Cheshire because they think you are Martin Cheshire."

"Well, what about this, Goddammit? Isn't this good enough proof?" Arthur pulled up my left pant leg and showed him the little sea urchin.

"A tattoo? Is that what you mean? I must be missing it, Mr. Cheshire. How would this prove who you are?"

"Because I got this tattoo months ago, before I faked my own death in California. I got it in San Diego and my girlfriend Marcella was with me. In fact, it was her cousin that did it—hurt like a son-of-a-bitch too. He'll admit it, and so will Marcella. Martin never had a tattoo—only me. Well, I told Rosie I did but that was when she thought I was Martin."

"I have to ask you, sir. If you are Arthur, why does this have a little m in the middle of it? Doesn't that stand for Martin?"

"Good question. Marcella got her cousin Maldonado to put this on as a sort of a brand—it stands for *Marcella*, not Martin. Maldonado is a walking ink spot. I didn't know it was on there—I couldn't look. It hurt too damn much. I just downed tequila shots and then found out later when the skin quieted down enough to really tell what was there."

The extradition hearing got put off for three weeks—Stevie Bell was good for something. But when it finally happened the testimony was short and compelling—that's the word the prosecutor used, compelling. It compelled Arthur to throw up.

The US government, represented in person by Assistant US Attorney Stran Cabelson, summed up his case after putting on three witnesses and offering three documents in evidence. He droned for the magistrate.

"One—Martin Cheshire is in fact the person named in the extradition warrant. We know that because his fingerprints at the time of arrest match those in his personnel file at his place of employment. Two—the man before the court, whom we have proven to be Martin Cheshire, admits to burning up a fishing shack in Mexico in which he claims to have placed the body of his brother. That body has been scientifically confirmed to be that of Arthur Cheshire. Three—the state police and the district attorney's office have carefully investigated the claim by the man before this court that Martin Cheshire actually died last year. No proof whatsoever was found to give any credence to that story. Four—his employer and his significant other have, under oath, identified the defendant as the man they believe to be Martin Cheshire. He lived with one and worked for the other witness. Both were credible. The fact that he's an identical twin, while interesting, is not probative, and does not establish sufficient rebuttal to the *prima facie* case presented here. We ask that you execute the warrant of extradition, Your Honor."

After the hearing, Arthur talked to conversed with Steve Bell.

"What do you mean Rosie is confused? Confused about what?"

"Mr. Cheshire let's start at the beginning. I spent almost two hours with Rosie. She, as you well know, is a bright young woman. But she's either confused about the facts or is lying; you'll be the best judge of that. She is quite convincing when she talks about her life with Martin, and she remembers well her first meeting with Arthur here in Portland. She told me the story of kissing Arthur and shaking hands with you."

"No, it was the other way around. She kissed me thinking I was Arthur."

"Actually, she confirms most of what you've told me about that first meeting. She admits that she was intrigued and even somewhat skeptical about Arthur—she says she suspected that Martin might try to trick her somehow at the first meeting of the three of you. She had some vague understanding of your game of Hide and Be. She admits to having doubts about Martin; that is, his love for her. She had doubts also about who he was? But she ultimately comes down on the side of believing you—she says you are Martin. She does not believe you killed Arthur. She believes that Arthur died an accidental death out there in California. She admits to talking to Marcella, who she says she doesn't really know, or trust. But she says she knows nothing of any floppy disks, and not surprisingly, any money. But that's not the worst of it, Mr. Cheshire. You and I have talked a fair bit about the importance of the tattoo on your ankle, and how easy it will be to prove that it was Arthur, i.e., you, who got it out there in California. Rosie says Arthur never had a tattoo. If he had, Martin would have known about it and told her. She saw it, and you had it. You, Martin Cheshire, that's what she told me."

"Damn, damn. She's lying, Steve. She knows who I am, I told her. I don't know if she knows anything about embezzling money from AmHull. But she should have found the floppy disk. I don't know who else could have been in the attic. She was starting to figure me out and she damn sure knew about my tattoo. That much I know for sure. As for the tattoo, she's right—Martin never had a tattoo. I was the only one that did. So, she is telling the truth there. But she saw me with the tattoo long after Martin died, and just before the feds busted me in the parking lot at AmHull. Doesn't that prove my case?"

"No, sir, I'm afraid it does not. You see hearsay evidence cannot be used unless it substantiates an admission against interest. She admits that the guy she was living with had a distinctive tattoo—you have the one she describes. But she says you got it here in Portland and that it was recently. You say it was months ago and that you got it in California. She says you said you were Martin—you admit that too. She says she would take a polygraph test and they will give her one—eventually. You say you will take one but that will be done in California. So, for now, neither you nor she can contest or confirm. But it's you they've charged with a crime. So, it's your problem not hers. The case is circumstantial, but it rises to a *prima facie* presentation. All I can do now is to follow the case from here and assume that the polygraphs will at least suggest that prosecutorial discretion will allow them to decline prosecution. That assumes, of course, that you pass your polygraph, and she flunks hers. And here's one last problem, Mr. Cheshire. If you are Arthur, then you lied to her about who you were for three months. You had sex with her only because she thought you were Martin. If she comes to accept that you are Arthur, like you say you are, then you are looking at rape charges here in Maine. So be careful of what you wish for."

"She'll flunk it, that's for sure. She's a truthful person so if she lies about my tattoo and about the money the machine will go off and ring bells or whatever it does, won't it?"

"Maybe, maybe not. She can say what you told her—that is you, Martin, got the tattoo here in Portland. If she believed it at that time, the machine might record her answer as truthful. But, on the money thing, if she denies that, she ought to show up as a liar there; so, you ought to be OK. Time will tell."

San DieGo—New LawyeR

Arthur's California lawyer was twice as old as Steve Bell. They met for the first time in Arthur's holding cell in the San Diego federal detention center. Arthur was in freshly laundered jail clothes, loose-fitting cotton pants, matching shirt, white socks, and his own shoes, the ones from Portland.

Kemper looked the part. It's always summer in San Diego, so he wore a JC Penny white, long-sleeved shirt, dark Paisley tie, black belt, clunky black shoes. Grey hair, cut in a 50s style crew cut, not a 90s style buzz. Tired, but friendly eyes peered out through oversize black plastic glasses, topping off an easy smile, and a ready opening sentence for new clients of the federal public defender's office.

"Good morning, my name is Gordon Kemper. I've been appointed to your case, and we need to go over some things. To start with . . ."

"Shouldn't we start with my name? Do you know what it is? Or are you taking the word of the guys in Maine just like your counterpart back there did?"

"I have read the file, sir. I know you claim to be the man that you're charged with killing. But I assure you that I am not taking anyone's word for anything. I simply . . ."

"Who does anyone include? I mean if you're not taking anyone's word, I guess that includes me. Your client. You're not taking their word—the guys in Maine—and you're not taking my word. Is that it? If so, we're off to a poor start."

"Mr. Cheshire, I want to take your word, but I also want you to get the benefit of my objectivity and my knowledge of the law. If you prefer, I'll call you Arthur. I'll try my best to prove that you are Arthur. That seems to be the linchpin in your case."

"Mr. Kemper, that's a better start. I'm sorry if I sound rude or cynical, but I have spent three weeks locked up under a false name. I can prove who I am if I can just get someone to listen."

"Let's start there, Arthur. While we're at it, call me Gordon. I was an engineer for a lot longer than I've been a lawyer and I'm comfortable with first names."

"Just how long have you been a lawyer? I'd say by your hair color that you're fifty or so."

"Thanks for the compliment, I am fifty or so—fifty-nine to be exact. I've been a lawyer for five years. I was riffed out of the engineering field ten years ago, so the law is a second career."

"It took you five years to get through law school?"

"Yes, it was a night law school and then I spent a year taking and studying for the bar before I got my license. But tell me about you, Arthur, I must admit to being fascinated by your story of living two lives at once."

"It's not a story, Gordon, it really happened."

Arthur told him what happened. Kemper took notes, like an engineer. He diagrammed everything on graph paper, as though getting Arthur's tangled history lined would produce a defense squared to scale. Arthur took an hour to relate the story, from foster homes to the boating accident last October, to his life-switching, cross-country charade on two coasts.

Kemper then went over his diagram with Arthur, connected as many dots as he could with circular lines, small neatly formed arrows in the margins and red circles connecting events with blue lines forming angles up and down the carefully printed, outline form, legal solution.

He recommended crosschecking factual sources, telephone interviews with "the women involved," legal research on the "identity issues," consideration of polygraph testing to establish a "baseline credibility," and ultimately, a plea bargain.

"Not a case we'll want to try to a jury, Arthur. Any San Diego County jury would have a majority of young women on it. Not likely to be favorable to your side."

San Diego—Polygraphs

Arthur's only experience with polygraphs was at AmHull, where all bonded employees had been given routine polygraphs.

In their second meeting, Kemper cut that part of the discussion short.

"Arthur, you can forget about that polygraph that your old boss in Portland gave you, it was probably illegal anyhow, but the point is now you are in California and facing a capital murder charge. So let me tell you how a polygraph might work for you here, or how it might cook your goose. Polygraph testing is scientific to some and voodoo to others. The term polygraph literally means 'many writings.' But it's not the writings that are important, it's what the examiner *says* about the writings that's important. See the difference?"

"No. I don't. What do you mean by 'writings'?"

"The writings are essentially the little squiggly lines on the paper tape that the machine produces. Let me tell you a little about how it works. A polygraph instrument, what I call the machine, records cardiovascular, respiratory, and electrodermal activity. That's the lesser half of it. The greater half of it is the testing procedure and the scoring system. That part is subject to the skill, or caprice of the examiner—the guy that operates the machine. I don't know why they are almost all men; women don't seem to have gravitated to the polygraph field. I've used a lot of polygraph tests, mostly private ones, on my clients. And . . ."

"Aren't they always private?"

"What I meant to say was that I arrange for the client to take the exam without the prosecutor knowing about it. So, it's private between me and my client."

"What good is that? I mean if it's just private how can it help the case?"

"Sometimes it doesn't help the case—that's why it's best to start off with a private test. But there is a problem there too. You see if we get a private test, and it helps the case, then we tell the prosecutor that we are willing to take one. They always ask if we have already had one done privately, and if I say yes, they know it was helpful and so they aren't too interested in having another one done at state expense. If I say no, I'd be lying, first of all, but more importantly, it's a lie that sometimes comes out in the second test, the one done by the state."

"I don't follow you. How does it come out?"

"Well, the state's polygrapher often gives a sort of pre-test and one of his favorite questions is, 'Have you ever taken one of these before?' If the subject says no, the machine records that as a lie, more or less. And if the subject says yes, then the examiner guesses that the lawyer for the defendant has already arranged for a private test. So, it's hard to win—one way or the other."

"OK. I get that part. But how accurate are those things? Science versus voodoo. I've heard of people failing them that tell the truth. That bothers me cause I'm one of those guys. I am telling the truth here. I'm Arthur Cheshire—my brother, Martin Cheshire, is dead, but I didn't kill him. Will the machine say I am lying when I say that even though I'm telling the truth?"

"Arthur, I think you have put your finger right on the problem. They aren't charging you with killing Martin—they're charging you with *being* Martin. Since they think you are Martin, they think Arthur is dead. That's because you did such a good job of faking his death—too good in fact. But your point is very insightful. I think we might be able to have our cake and eat it too."

"How's that?"

"We'll have to stipulate to the admissibility in evidence of a polygraph on not only you, but on the only two people who can save you. Marcella and Rosie. That can be done in California. But there is a huge risk that you may not want to take. If the machine says you lied and that Rosie and Marcella are telling the truth, then your goose is cooked."

"Well, that's not gonna happen. I know them. They may hate me for what I did to them, but they know I didn't kill Martin. They know it was an accident—at least Rosie does. Marcella really doesn't know one way or the other. Besides, how could they answer yes or no to a question like did I kill my brother? They couldn't answer that as a fact question, and you told me that opinions don't count in polygraph tests."

"That's so. But the prosecutor won't have the examiner ask them about the death as such. He will ask them about who you are. Maybe he will concentrate on your tattoo. You told me it is the only physical thing you have that distinguishes you from your brother. You say that both Marcella and Rosie know the truth about that tattoo, and how you got it. So, seems to me there is not too big a risk there. If either one of them lies about the tattoo, then you will look innocent, at least in the eyes of the prosecutor. If they tell the truth about the tattoo then the prosecutor will have to accept your version, that is the one that the examiner will say is truthful. You are telling the truth about that, aren't you?"

"As God is my witness, I am. Here look for yourself."

Arthur pushed down the white sock on his left ankle and pointed out the little red m, for Marcella, in the yellow tail of his sea urchin. Kramer said he'd be back to take pictures of the tattoo. He wanted to show them to some local tattoo artists to see if there was a signature there.

"Signature?" Arthur asked.

"Yeah, some of the better tattoo artists in San Diego are well known enough to have identifiable signatures on their tattoos. The experts can tell. Sailors have been docking here for more than four hundred years. Wherever you find sailors, you find tattoos. If your Maldonado did it, maybe we can get somebody other than him to identify his work. You know, now that I think about it, there is another angle here."

Saying he'd be right back, Kemper left the room to make a telephone call. When he returned, ten minutes later, he had Pepsi for Arthur and a small cup of machine coffee for himself.

"You know the examiner will be told your name is Martin because that's how you are booked in here. He will ask for a driver's license with your picture on it. That brings up a tough issue. The state can't make you take a polygraph—in fact, they can't even ask you to take one because of the Fifth Amendment."

"What's the Fifth Amendment got to do with it?"

"The state can't compel you to give testimony that might tend to incriminate you. When it comes to polygraphs, no one can say in advance that your answers will be truthful so they might, in a worst-scenario case, incriminate you. That's why the state can't ask you to take a test."

"Wait a minute, are they reliable or not? I mean, why can't we just tell the prosecutor we want one? I'm the one who's telling the truth. How can I fail if I tell the truth?"

"Because of what they call 'false positives.' That happens when a truthful examinee is reported out as being deceptive. That can happen where the guy taking the test wasn't properly prepared to take it, or the physiological data on the polygraph charts can be wrong, or even misread by the examiner. Sometimes your emotional state when you take the test can throw things off. Sometimes it's physical—you know, heart conditions and the like. Some people are just overly nervous—others are overly responsive. All kinds of things can happen to screw up the test. Then there are false negatives—that's where a liar is called a truth teller by the machine. Same deal there. Things happen, you know."

"Well, here's what I know. I didn't kill anyone. I can say that a thousand times and if the machine is turned on, it ought to show me telling the truth."

"Arthur, long before they get to that question, they will ask you a much simpler one. They will start with, 'Is your name Martin Cheshire?' When you answer that one, will the machine record your answer as truthful?"

"Nope, that's not my name. That was my brother's name—he's dead, remember?"

"Well, Arthur, we are going to have a problem. You see there is an association, sort of a national trade group, and all the good polygraph examiners belong to it. The first thing they do when they give a test is to require the subject to produce a photo ID—a driver's license is preferred. Then they check it with the name of the subject on their little form. Do you have a photo ID that says Arthur on it?"

"Sure, mine. I also have one, or at least I did, with my brother's name on it, and it has my picture on it too. I had both drivers' licenses. Mine out here in California and Martin's from back in Maine."

"I'm missing something here. Why did you have two driver's licenses with two different names on them but the same picture?"

"Actually, they are two different pictures, but we always wore the same clothes when we got our driver's licenses—a blue button-down with a moose tie. That way it looks like the same person even though mine was mine and his was his. Get it?"

"Was that a variation of the Hide and Be game that I read about in your file?"

"Yep. Funny thing, though. When I got my California license and wore the moose tie, the MVD guy asked what that was. It was like he'd never seen a moose before. No one in Maine ever asked that question."

"OK. Let's give it a shot. I'll set it up. I will have to stipulate to ultimate admissibility though. That means we will be stuck with the results. You sure you want to take the risk of a false positive?"

"Which one was that again?"

"That's where you tell the truth, but the machine says you're lying."

"As I see it, I don't have much to lose. They don't believe me anyhow."

"I'll set it up."

The nerdy looking guy, who said his name was Creighton Ralestead, set up his machine on the table in the interview room and spent twenty agonizing minutes fussing with it. Then he did the predictable. Arthur looked on from the opposite side of the table. Officer Martinez had brought him a Pepsi. Ralestead, dressed in a brown tweed jacket, a knotted black tie, and an even darker brown shirt, did not approve.

"You should not drink sugar drinks before the test, didn't they give you my recommendations about food and drink?"

"Those were yours? I thought they were from the dietician at clinical services. She's opposed to soda drinks too. But I did avoid anything that would upset my stomach. I ate everything on my plate. Bland is in at this facility, you know."

"May I see your driver's license, please?"

"Sorry, my driver's license is in the prosecutor's file. I left it in the glove compartment of my car, down in Mexico two months ago. I have my brother's license, the one I used in Maine, would you like to see that one?"

Ralestead said yes.

Kemper said, "I've got it. As you know, Creighton, prisoners turn in personal belongings to the jail staff on arrival. I got permission to bring it to this polygraph session from the desk sergeant. I'll return it after you've seen it. Here it is."

Ralestead compared the license with the booking form they gave him downstairs when he checked in.

"There seems to be some confusion here. Your lawyer filled out the form and said your first name was Arthur. The booking form says Martin. This driver's license says Martin—so is this your license, or your brother's?"

"Yes."

"Yes, what? I don't understand."

"That's because you asked a compound question. I answered both parts truthfully. That's what this is about right—the truth, the whole truth and nothing but the truth so help me polygraph. The license is the one I used when I went home to Maine. It's got my brother's name on it, but my picture. My driver's license, which he occasionally used, has my name and his picture. We're identical twins, didn't they tell you that?"

"They said you did have a brother—in fact I understand it's him that you're charged with killing. But no one told me the victim was your identical twin. They didn't say identical, or younger, or whatever. I must tell you this is pretty bizarre. I've never tested identical twins before."

"Well, today won't change that. You are only going to test one of us today—your mission, if you accept it, is to tell which twin am I. Do you accept, sir?"

"I'm afraid I don't get your humor, but then I never do. Your lawyer has given me three questions that he thinks I should ask you. I believe the prosecutor has approved them; but I have the final say on the actual form of the questions. So, I have modified them somewhat—they have to be yes or no questions, you understand. Now, let me explain my machine before we start, and then I have three different test questions to set up the machine for you."

He explained physiology to Arthur, stressing how important it was to remain calm, that he shouldn't think too much about the question, and to try not to be nervous.

"Nervous," Arthur said aloud, "what's to be nervous about? It's not like proctology, is it? I mean, no wires below the belt, right?"

Ralestead did not approve of the little joke. He put a blood pressure cuff on Arthur's left arm, a breathing measuring cup on his chest, right over the sternum, skin-conductive measurement wires on his right hand, and a suction-cup style breathing wire above Arthur's belt to measure breathing from the abdominal cavity. After asking about his comfort level—"Everything all right, sir?"—he asked Arthur to deliberately lie to the first three questions.

"I need to examine the writings you create on my graph when you lie on purpose, don't you see? Are you a resident of Russia?"

Arthur said, "Yes."

"Are you more than one-hundred years old?"

Arthur lowered the tone of his voice and said, "Yes."

"Are you nervous?"

Smiling, Arthur said, "No."

Mr. Ralestead had positioned the graphical interface close at hand so Arthur could turn his head to the right and with a little effort crane his neck far enough to see the squiggly lines on the paper feed.

"Well, thank you, Mr. Cheshire. You see these little lines here—they are all alike—all suggest an effort on your part to be deceptive. We'd don't call it lying, even though you did exactly as I asked you to do. This gives me a reasonable baseline to work with. Now, let's go with the three questions your lawyer and the prosecutor have agreed are pertinent to your case."

"Before you do that, Mr. Ralestead, can I ask you how come the machine says my three test answers were deceptive when I only lied about two of them?"

"I'm not sure I understand you. I asked you to give me a false answer to all three."

"Yeah, but I messed up. I lied about my age and my mental condition at the moment—but it sure feels like Siberia here to me—get it?"

"Mr. Cheshire, I will now have to recalibrate the machine. Please do me the favor of only answering the questions that I put to you."

So, he recalibrated, which required repositioning the catheter style leads and the blood pressure cuff. Then he asked his same please-lie questions. Arthur lied. Ralestead seemed pleased.

All right, sir. Here are three new questions. Pausing as for effect, Ralestead asked, "Is your brother alive?"

"No."

"Did you kill him?"

"No."

"Was his name Martin?"

"Yes."

"I've got some bad news for you, Arthur," Gordon Kemper said, an hour after Ralestead packed up his box, and left the room.

"What? Was it a false positive?"

"No, the examiner is quite adamant. He says your three test answers proved that you are a valid personality type and that your three real answers were based on reliable physiological data. He says you lied when you said your brother was dead, you told the truth when you said you didn't kill him, but lied again when you said his name was Martin. He said it's one of the clearest sets of writings he's ever examined. He gave the prosecutor and me the results together. He cannot, for the life of him, make sense of the three answers. If your test is not a false positive then only one conclusion can be drawn: Your brother is alive notwithstanding the fact that you killed him, and his name is not Martin."

"So, who is nuts here, me or Mr. Ralestead?"

"Lots to talk about, Arthur. Let's start with the fact that most other polygraph examiners would have labeled your test as inconclusive based on inconsistency alone. But this guy says it's conclusive. He's confident that you lied in response to *all three* questions. I argued the obvious: how could it be that your brother, whose name is not Martin, could be alive if you killed him? And get this, the prosecutor agreed with me. So, we essentially agreed, the prosecutor and me, that as far as this case goes, we are going to ignore Ralestead *and* his opinions. But I gotta tell you, this is something I never saw coming. What did you do to his little squiggles?"

"*Hide and Be.* That's the answer, Gordon, *Hide and Be.* The data is misleading—at least to him. The nerdy little professor with his machine says that I lied when I said my brother was dead, told the truth when I said I didn't kill him, and lied again when I said my brother's name was Martin. The overzealous prosecutor layers a new conclusion on top of the polygrapher's false assumption—he concludes that I'm lying about killing Martin because that particular lie fits his theory of the case. But here's the truth—I didn't kill Martin. He's dead. It took me a long time to accept that as fact—especially during the time I was living *as* him. I know that's absurd to you, and everyone else I know, but it's the truth. For a while, I *became* Martin."

"But Arthur, while I follow your logic, that still doesn't explain the test results, or Ralestead's certainty about the result."

Arthur told his lawyer how valuable the facility's library could be at a time like this. He explained that a little reading was good for the soul, the blood, and one's respiratory system.

"You see, when I said Martin's still alive, my emotional state, my blood chemistry, and my respiratory system recorded that as a true answer. Just like it did when I said I didn't kill him, which was true too. When I said my brother's name was not Martin—the machine treated me as Martin and so rejected my answer that my brother's name was Martin. So, the long answer and the short answer are *one and the same*. Don't you see? My physiological reaction, as recorded on the machine, is entirely consistent with my lifetime of playing Hide and Be with Martin. All that happened here this afternoon was that a nerdy little professor believed his machine, even against the logic of the answer. Martin's name was Martin, no one can dispute that. Get it?"

"No, Mr. Cheshire, I can't say that I do. But here's my take on your present legal risk. The prosecutor has all the narrative reports from the FBI interrogators in Maine. Even though we are not at the discovery phase in the case, he gave them to me this morning. I read your long explanation of that game you and your brother always played. I can also tell you that the prosecutor on your case thinks you are either a pathological liar or a full-blown nut case—in either case, he intends to convict you of murder one."

"Well, what does that actually mean? The polygraph says I murdered my brother. The prosecutor thinks so too. Where do we go now, coach?"

"I'll let you know next week. They are going to give Marcella a polygraph on Monday. I'll get the report on Tuesday. If you're guessing right about her, she'll flunk the test, which just might balance things out. We still have a chance at getting a plea to a long prison term here—it will save your life. Or the judge could decide that you are Arthur Cheshire, as a matter of law. That means they cannot charge you with murdering Arthur. But they could regroup and charge you with murdering Martin."

"How do they explain away my tattoo? That's the ticket, isn't it? No one says that Martin had a tattoo, except when I lied about it to Rosie."

"Arthur, you're an intelligent guy," Kemper said. "But what if Rosie lies and says you did not have the tattoo? What if Marcella lies and says that you never had one either? Those women are very mad at you for lying *to them*. What we don't know is, are they mad enough to lie *about you*?"

"Maybe they are. Mad enough, I mean. But being mad at me is not enough. They get nothing out of lying except making me go through a trial. And their lies would get found out at trial, wouldn't they?"

"Arthur, they would have to testify *for* you to make any difference. Just lying on the stand is enough for the prosecutor. You need them *on* your side. We will have to see how Marcella does in her polygraph. She's agreed to take one. Let's wait it out."

Marcella Visits Arthur In Jail

Marcella made it clear to Arthur—in the only visit she made to him in the San Diego County detention center—that she hated his guts for what he did. Faking his death was bad enough, she said, but coming to his own memorial service, was *"pensar lo peor en el mundo."* The worst thing in the world.

"So, if you hate me so much, why did you ask to see me?"

"I'm here to give the cops a polygraph test. But I asked to see you while I was here so I could spit in your face and tell you what a piece of shit you are. Only, I won't spit because I want the guards to know I'm a lady—ladies don't spit, right? Besides, I wanted to see you sitting in jail clothes behind bars where I hope you spend the rest of your fucking life."

As she was leaving the table and the guard was coming over to escort her out of the room, Arthur said, "Marcella, please wait. I know you must hate me for what I did, but come on; we both know that you were not exactly faithful to me either."

She waved the guard off and sat back down. At first, Arthur assumed she would deny it again. But he had badly misjudged this little lady.

"Goddamn you, Arthur, or Martin, whoever you're pretending to be now, don't you try to accuse me after what you've done! I was with Leandro long before you came along. In fact, that day you saw me with him in the lobby of the Del Coronado was going to be our last time together. I was dumping him for you, you bastard."

"So, you did see me!"

"Sure, I saw you—how could I miss you sitting twenty feet away in the bar with Harold Junior, as you call him? I tried to be discreet and move on through the lobby. At the time, I thought maybe you might understand—that morning was the morning I said goodbye to Leandro. He's my third cousin but I loved him since I was a little girl. It's just too bad for you that my other cousin, Maldonado, told him about your tattoo. God, what a mess and besides . . ."

"Marcella, please, slow down. What does Maldonado have to do with this? I'm lost."

"You're lost all right, you piece of caca. Maldonado is a cousin to both of us from different branches of the family. He thought he could shake down Leandro for a few bucks by telling him about you and me. He told Leandro about the tattoo he put on you so that Leandro would believe him. Maldonado double-crosses everyone, and he thought that

Leandro could use the tattoo somehow to get back at me—
you know, then Leandro would have something on me. That's
what a scum ball he really is. Leandro told him to piss off.
He knew about you and me; I had already told him about the
whole deal at the hotel. You know, the tattoo with the little
m, and everything."

"What do you mean by everything?"

"Maldonado had already told him that the little m in the
sea-urchin was your first initial—m for Martin, right? So, I
told Leandro the same thing—that it was for Martin—your
brother, the one you killed. Now Leandro goes to the cops and
says that the little m was your first initial because that's what
he got from that scummy tattoo freak. I just didn't tell him any
different. Now the cops think the little m is your first initial. So,
that makes you Martin because all three of us, me, Maldonado
and Leandro said so in our statements. Maldonado and Leandro
are telling the truth—at least they believe it to be the truth. I'm
lying, but they don't know that. The head detective told me our
testimony wraps up the case against you. You can't be who you
claim to be—Arthur—because Arthur would not tattoo an m
on himself; he'd put an 'a' there, right? It comes down to who
are they gonna believe. Me or you?"

"Marcella, please, for the love of God. You told Maldonado
to put that little m there without me even knowing what the
shit he was doing. The m was you; please, please tell the truth."

"Here's the truth, man, you cheated on me and now you're
going to prison for killing your brother, either back there in
Portland, or down there in Mexico. Either way, you're dog meat."

And that's the last Arthur ever saw of her.

Gordon laid Marcella's polygraph answers on the table in
front of Arthur.

"Let me read the Q&A out loud for you, Arthur. Question
Number One. Did you know Arthur Cheshire? Answer—Yes.

Question Number Two. Did he have a tattoo on his left ankle? Answer—No. Question Number Three. Did his brother Martin have a tattoo on his left ankle? Answer—Yes."

"Gordon, what the fuck is going on here? Marcella did know me; that's true. I have a tattoo on my left ankle; she knows that, so her answer is false. Shit, I told you, she got her cousin to tattoo me. But she had no way of knowing whether Martin had one or not. So that answer is false also. Are you telling me that Ralestead said she passed the test, on all three questions?"

"Yes, he did. He was just as confident about her results as he was about yours. Now let me show you Rosie's results. She came in from Portland just for the test—at the expense of the State of California, I might add. What they usually do is give all the subjects in one case the same questions. Take a look."

I looked at Rosie's Q&A and nearly lost it. Question Number One asked whether she knew *Martin* Cheshire—she said, "Yes." Question Number Two asked whether he—that is, Martin—had a tattoo on his left ankle. She said, "Yes." Question Number Three asked whether his brother—that is, Arthur—had a tattoo and she said, "No."

"Oh, God. That little nerd and his lying machine. Are you telling me that he believed Rosie? Did he report her out as telling the truth on all three of these trick questions?"

"Yep. Reliable profile. Accurate data. Three non-deceptive answers. Matches Marcella to a T. So, here's the deal. Your polygraphs are out, Rosie's and Marcella's are in. You are in the bag. That's pretty much it."

"Oh, God, Gordon, where does this leave me?"

"Well, it's not good, I have to tell you that. Remember we arranged for your polygraph because we thought you'd test truthful, and we agreed to accept Marcella's and Rosie's for the same reason—we thought they'd tell the truth as well. But your test says you lied—when you *say* you told the truth. Both of their tests say they told the truth—when you *say* they lied. I just don't think you have any choice but to accept a plea."

San Diego—Lawyer Visit

Gordon Kemper's fourth visit to the detention center was on the morning of Arthur's final visit with Dr. Socorro. He was to see her right after his lawyer visit at 2 pm. Gordon Kemper explained a possible plea bargain to Arthur.

"A plea of guilty to second-degree murder with a recommended sentence of twenty years to life—it looks to me like that's the only way to save your life. I've mentioned this to you before, but you seem to block it out when I start talking about it and . . ."

"Wait, hold the phone here. Don't they have to prove I killed somebody before they can either kill me, or lock me up for life?"

"What they have to prove is that Arthur Cheshire is dead. That won't be hard. Next, they have to prove you had a motive to kill him. You gave them that in Portland by insisting that you were Arthur, and that Martin stole the money. Next, they have to prove that you are Martin—you gave them that, at least part of it. They have a lie detector test and Ralestead to talk about it in court—they have your fingerprints from the AmHull file—they have Rosie and Marcella both ready to swear that you are Martin. And they think that if they put enough pressure on you to save your life in the murder case, you will eventually tell them about the $263,000 that's missing from AmHull's bank in Portland."

"I'm Arthur Cheshire—you tell them that. I didn't kill anyone—you tell them that too. I am not going to plead guilty to any degree of murder. And what the hell happened with my identity hearing before the magistrate? I thought the deal was that the case would go forward only if the judge found that I was Martin. He has not done that. I think Dr. Socorro believes in me. She really does. What about her?"

"Well, she has yet to finish her work, but the prosecutor is pretty cocky on that point. He says even if a shrink believes you and testifies to her belief before the magistrate, that won't cut you free. It's up to the District Court judge to make a final ruling. Magistrates only get to make recommendations. Let's see, while we are waiting for Dr. Socorro to write her report, whether the prosecution is willing to cut a deal. Think about it, Arthur, you bet on Marcella, then Rosie, and they slammed you hard. Now you want to bet your life on Dr. Socorro? She's only talked to you. Even if she says, under oath, that she believes you, that doesn't wipe out the testimony from Marcella, Rosie, and whoever else the government has in its back pocket."

"Whoever else? Who could they have that you don't know about? I thought they had to tell you about all the witnesses."

"They do. Eventually. But remember this case is not on the docket, or before the grand jury, because of the identity hearing. They don't have to reveal anything yet. They've been cooperative with me as a defense lawyer because they want me to convince you to take a deal. The identity hearing, from their side of it, is a sideshow. The polygraphs and the forensic evidence from Mexico are the main event. And they have real motive—you killed Martin to get the $263,000 that he stole from AmHull. Don't forget that. It's the missing link—the motive to kill Martin."

"Damn it all to hell! My brother was not really a thief. He skimmed off $26,000 in excess premium charges. That's all, and that was only to get back at Harold in a stupid way. It wasn't me anyhow. How can they blame me for what Martin did?"

"Because Martin made it look like you did it. His plan was to fake *your* death, only it was a different fake than the one you came up with. But when the feds decided that you did not fake your own death, and that you murdered Martin, your plan went up in smoke, so to speak."

The next day, Arthur woke up in his jail cell thinking it couldn't get any worse. It could. They had another witness.

Gordon Kemper called a quick meeting for later that morning. Officer Martinez arranged the interview room and stood outside during the meeting.

"No, I have no idea who they have as a witness in Mexico," Arthur said. "When did they tell you this?"

"This morning. They say that we can have another week to check out the witness, and negotiate a plea bargain, or they will indict you."

"Tell 'em to go to hell. They can't have a witness to something that never happened. How could some guy in Rosario be a witness to my brother's death? He died in Portland, Maine."

Kemper shook his head at Arthur like he was a troublesome child.

"But Arthur, by your own admission, you moved his body from Maine to Mexico, and burnt it up to make everyone think it was you that died in the fire. Don't you see how it might look to some local resident down there? And besides, I didn't say that they have an eyewitness. What they apparently have is a witness who says you told him you killed your brother. This witness claims he talked to you after the killing. Do you know a man named Diego Cortez? His address is listed as Rosario, that's just three miles from the fishing shack where they found your brother's remains—at least his DNA."

"No, I don't know anyone named Diego Cortez. What does he say I did? Aren't you entitled to take his deposition or something? How can he just say something, and we don't get to . . . ?"

"Yes, I am allowed to interview him. But they don't have to produce him here in San Diego until just before the trial. I can go down to Rosario and talk to him, but I doubt I'd ever find him. They gave me his written statement—course it's in their words—they typed it up, but it has his signature on it. He says he rode the bus with you from Rosario to Cabo San Lucas and that you confessed."

"Oh God, it was the little shit who saw a business opportunity. He was on the bus with me from Rosario to La Paz. I was *John* and he was *Juan*. I never told him anything. I couldn't have confessed to something I didn't do, and I sure as hell wasn't going to talk to any beaner on the bus about faking my own death; that's what I was doing, remember, and . . ."

"All right, tell me what you did say. Be specific."

"He hit me up for money right away. He said he had connections and that he could see I was running away from something, maybe a 'woman,' he said. He had a leather bombardier jacket. He said his name was Juan, or Jose, or something fake like that. He wanted five hundred dollars to help me get a private charter plane from Mexico back to the US."

"So, did you? Did you pay him to get you back across the border without a customs stop?"

"No, I did not pay him five hundred, I paid him two fifty. And I also paid for the charter flight separately, and we went through customs at the private plane terminal in Phoenix. I used Martin's passport. I had to because I'd left mine in the glove compartment in Rosario, remember, I told you all that. Martin's passport was legal. I was pretty proud of myself at the time because he scared the shit out of me at first, and then let me bargain him down to two hundred and fifty bucks in bribe money. He said it was for his 'help' in La Paz , but I knew it was a bribe. My original plan was to take the Aero Mexico flight to El Paso and then on to Portland via Houston, but the charter guy got me to Phoenix just in time to catch a non-stop to Boston. That got me to Portland four hours earlier than my plan and then . . ."

"No, slow down, Arthur, you're losing me. Let's go back to the bus in Rosario—did this man get on there with you, or was he already on the bus?"

"I'm not sure. I remember wondering about it at the time. He said something sort of ominous to me a little while after we got out of Rosario, and I didn't . . ."

"What'd he say?"

"I don't remember but it was something about the Federales and was I running from them, or some such shit like that. Later, on the plane ride to Portland, I convinced myself that it was mostly my imagination and that he was just your typical Mexican opportunist trying to make a quick buck—in fact, a quick five hundred bucks."

"So, you don't remember telling him anything about your brother, and what had happened at the fishing shack?"

"No, well actually, I did tell him I was going to visit my brother, but I used a fake name and I'm sure he did too. We really had very little conversation—all he wanted was a little money. He could probably sense my nervousness; that's all there is to it."

"Well, he remembers a lot more than you do. He told the FBI in his second interview that you admitted on the bus ride that you burned up your brother in the fishing shack and offered him a pile of money—five thousand dollars—to keep quiet about it."

"Second interview? What does that mean—what was the first interview, and how did they find this guy anyhow?"

"They didn't find him—he showed up here in San Diego saying he had information about the guy that burned up in the fishing shack down in Mexico. He said he read about it in the newspaper and wondered if there were any rewards for information. They told him no but sent him upstairs anyway to talk to the FBI. That's when he gave his first interview. He didn't say anything *then* about seeing a man run from the fire and jump the bus in town. All he said was he rode the bus with a guy who smelled like smoke and kerosene and the man got on the bus with him in Rosario.

He wasn't sure of the day but placed it in the same month as the fire. They showed him some mug photos of the usual suspects for everything that happens around here, but he couldn't make an identification. That was the end of it for a while."

"Then what happened, how did the second interview come about?"

"Well, after you were arrested in Portland, and extradited here they called him in Rosario. Arrangements were made for him to go to the local police district office. The FBI office here faxed your booking photo to the Federales down there. He identified you as the man he'd been talking about in the first interview. But here's where it really gets interesting, he told the Federales something new. He told them that he saw you running down the hill from the shack right when the fire erupted. He followed you into Rosario and then got on the bus with you. The Federales told the FBI, who flew down, and recorded their second interview with him. He's a quote 'smoking *gun*' unquote. That's what the prosecutor says about the FBI report."

"What day was that?"

"Well, let's see—it was Thursday, a week after they flew you here from Portland."

"That's the same day they talked to Marcella. I know that because she talked to me the next day—Friday."

"Are you saying there is a connection here? Does Marcella know this Diego Cortez?"

"No, I don't know. I don't know whether she knows him or not. I doubt there's any connection. I only know that the little shit comes in and volunteers all these incredible lies about me the same day they interview Marcella—and she also lied her head off about me."

"Well, Arthur, you can see why the cops don't believe you— too many people are saying the same thing. Their story is fairly consistent and it's very different from the one you're telling."

"Christ almighty. Any good lawyer ought to be able to blast that kind of bullshit apart. It's totally irrational. Why would I tell some total stranger that I just killed my brother back at the last bus stop and then offer him money to keep quiet about what I just said? That couldn't happen even in the movies. No jury would believe that. There must be more to this than . . ."

"Well, Arthur, actually there is. He isn't saying you offered him five thou to keep quiet about what you said on the bus. He says you offered him five thou to keep quiet about what he saw you do when he was watching you at the fishing shack, and when he followed you into Rosario before you got on the bus."

"Goddamnit, Gordon, why are you giving me this in little bits and pieces? Whose lawyer are you anyway? Are you cross-examining me with this beaner's statement? You told me just a few minutes ago that this Diego Contez guy was going to testify about something I said on the bus—now you're telling me he is going to testify about something he says I did *before* I got on the bus. What's the story here? You want honesty from me—how about giving me the same courtesy?"

"Calm down, Arthur, I apologize for misleading you a little when we first started but I wanted to see how you would handle this accusation about confessing on the bus first. What he says he saw is entirely consistent with your own statement and does not directly incriminate you. That part of his statement is not the part I'm worried about—it's what he says you said on the bus that worries me. He says he was getting ready to go fishing and was standing up in the back of his truck when he saw the fire explode in the fishing shack. He says he saw a man running down the hill as fast as he could toward the village—toward Rosario. He ran over to the fire and then decided there was nothing he could do so he drove down the road after you, but couldn't find you and then . . ."

"Well, if he admits he couldn't find me, how does he know it was me that he saw leaving the shack? It was pitch dark and I can't imagine he says he saw my face."

"No, he admits he didn't know the man he saw running away from the shack was you until you admitted it to him on the bus ride down to La Paz."

"Oh, right. I just picked out a total stranger on the bus and told him I had set fire to a fishing shack back at Rosario and offered him five thousand dollars to keep mum. That's real believable."

"It gains a little believability when he adds the reason why you so readily admitted the fire."

"What, pray tell, is this mysterious reason that made me so cooperative with a total stranger?"

"He says he sat next to you and could smell smoke on your clothes. He says when you got off the bus in Las Donde you washed your hands in the sink in the men's room and he could smell kerosene in the sink. So, he claims he asked you about it and you told him that your brother owned the fishing cabin and that you set the fire so your brother could collect on the insurance. Even though that part of his story seems plausible—the FBI doubted it at first and then Mr. Diego Cortez—it is *Cortez* not *Contez*—gave them some physical evidence to corroborate his story. What he gave them is not only corroboration, but it also directly incriminates you."

"What physical evidence—what could he possibly have that incriminates me?"

"He gave them two thousand dollars in crisp US fifty-dollar bills. Bills that were recently printed in a federal mint on the East Coast. Those bills are not readily available out here on the West Coast. He says he spent the other three thousand. Turning that money over to the cops makes him very credible. Can you imagine a local con artist giving the FBI two thousand dollars?

He has no motive to do that. He seems genuine. The FBI believes him. Where would he have gotten two thousand dollars in fresh East Coast bills in Mexico, except from you?"

"It's a frame job, Gordon. I never did any of that, except start the fire and run from the shack, and give him $250. He's making all the rest up."

"Why would he do that, Arthur?"

"Dunno. But he did."

US DISTRICT COURT—San Diego, California

Judge Eli Hightower's courtroom gleamed. The bench shined from anywhere in the thirty-by-forty-foot space, and the lawyer's tables were cleared, except for discreet computer cords and the standard shiny stainless steel water pitcher on a tray with four glasses turned upside down, each resident on its own circular paper doily. As was his custom, he moved quickly from the side door to the bench, catching the gathered lawyers off-guard.

"At ease, gentlemen, and Dr. Socorro," he said as he reached his swivel seat, lowered himself down gently, and picked up the now slightly thicker folder on the bench.

"For the record, we are here today for the identity hearing to establish the true identity of the defendant charged as Martin Cheshire, but who contends that he is Arthur Cheshire. This hearing was at the call of District Judge Fontaine, we've had one open court session, and three chambers' meetings, all on the record, I might add, and now we are gathered here to examine Dr. Socorro regarding her report, which everyone has read. Did I miss anything on my summary of status, Mr. Cabelson, Mr. Kemper?"

Both lawyers rose, said "No, Your Honor," and sat down.

"All right, then, Dr. Socorro, if you please, would you mind stepping over to my clerk's bench? She will read the oath to you, and then you may take the stand there," he said, gesturing to the

witness box. "Remember to speak into the microphone. The report-
ers in the back appreciate that. They seem quite fascinated by the
first-ever identity hearing in a federal court, as far as I can tell."

Returning his attention to the twin tables, which bookended
the advocates podium, he took a deep breath, let it out slowly
through pursed lips.

"Mr. Cheshire, I'm sorry for not acknowledging your presence
at the start. The record will note your presence. Mr. Cabelson.
Normally you'd go first, followed by Mr. Kemper, as we work
through Dr. Socorro's testimony. But not today. That's because
the government does not have the burden of proof on the probative issue. Now that I've looked into it myself, neither does the
defendant. The issue is, in lay terms for our reporter friends in
the back of the room, 'who's the man in the dock'? Of course,
we no longer have a dock, having severed our ties with the
United Kingdom some two-hundred and thirty-three years ago,
this coming July the fourth. But we kept the *Magna Carta*, due
process of law, and made a few new rules of our own—namely
the Constitution and its many Amendments.

"I start with this because we have two issues to resolve
today. One, the psychological evaluation of Dr. Socorro and her
insights into the *persona* of the man in the figurative dock. Two,
the constitutional power of this court to say, as a matter of law,
who the man actually is, *persona* or not. Questions from counsel?"

The prosecutor looked over at the defense table. Kemper sat
passively as stone. Both slowly shook their heads. There was a
good deal of scribbling in the back and rustling from the first
row, where four senior law clerks had gathered along with two
of Dr. Socorro's colleagues, appropriately attired in white lab
coats, and a well-known law professor from Cal Western School
of Law, Addis Blakey.

Taking a sip of water, wheezing in, and smiling, Judge
Hightower continued.

"All right then, given the *sui generis* nature of this hearing, I will assume a role too infrequently taken in courtrooms. I will ask a few preliminary questions of Dr. Socorro and see if counsel wants to take the matter further. That's all right with counsel, isn't it?"

Although Arthur couldn't see it, both lawyers nodded their heads at the judge.

"Right, I thought as much."

Turning to Dr. Socorro, he motioned to the folders on his desk and on hers.

"Dr. Socorro, I have your thirty-six-page psychological profile on the defendant, the two excellent articles from your trade journal, *Psychology Today*, and your separately penned conclusion. Those four documents make up your written report, do they not?"

"Yes, Your Honor," she answered, having been warned not to volunteer anything, especially not in Judge Hightower's court.

"I take it, since you wrote this with obvious care, that you included everything you felt pertinent to your task, right?"

"Yes."

"You've nothing to add, nothing oral, that would expand, or modify your written analysis, right?"

Dr. Socorro, now gun shy, nodded her head.

"Fine," turning his attention to the lawyers, he continued. "Both of you have no doubt read her report, its appendices, and maybe even her articles, haven't you?"

Both lawyers rose as if on a pogo stick, affirmed the judge's statement, and sprang back down. Hightower was drilling down, they no doubt thought to themselves, so don't get caught in the bit.

"Fine, we are all well-briefed and well-read. So, rather than proceed by testimony, let me tell you what I think. Then, when I've had my say, you may argue with me, instead of the witness. Lean back, gentlemen, this will take a few minutes.

"You will recall my reluctance some weeks ago to convene a hearing to establish the identity of a man charged with a federal crime. Here's why I was reluctant. No indictment. Only a holding charge in the form of a written complaint against a man the government believes to be Martin Cheshire, of the great state of Maine, on the other coast. The public defender on this coast *demurs*, believing that the man charged by the government is actually Arthur Cheshire, formerly a resident of the other coast, but now residing here on the West Coast, with all its natural beauty. So, we know Mr. Cheshire to be a wise man, whatever his first name may be.

"Lacking any precedent, I've turned to one of the law's most cherished, and occasionally abused procedures—*habeas corpus,* known as the 'Great Writ.' I see we have media folk in the audience today, so I'll define habeas corpus. It's a Latin phrase meaning, literally, "you shall have the body." In modern usage, habeas corpus refers to the right of a detained individual to be brought before a court or judge to determine whether the imprisonment is legal and justified.

"You've both participated in *habeas* hearings, but neither of you designated this identity hearing in those terms. I think you should have. For the benefit of both the record and our friends from the press, let me state the matter succinctly. It is, at its core, every citizen's right to personal freedom since that right never lapses, cannot be waived, and must be on the mind of every judge in every case. It's certainly been on mine since this saga began some twelve weeks ago.

"Dr. Socorro's report is a marvel to read because she limits her analysis to family history, mental status, the possibility of confusion, states of mind, and what she calls 'human awareness of one's reality.' She recorded her conversations with Mr. Cheshire. She looked for clinical signs of trickery, misrepresentation, self-delusion, and a variety of psychotic and neurotic diagnoses.

She dug deeply into the psyche of the defendant and thus into the factual underpinnings of what we lawyers call *mens rea* and *actus rea*. In this case, the prosecutor has to prove the defendant committed murder and had the right mental state to commit the crime. Lacking either, there is no case.

"Now, I have a few questions for Dr. Socorro. Do I assume correctly, Dr. Socorro, that you have arrived at the scientific conclusion that the defendant in this case *is* Arthur Cheshire?"

Snapping her head up toward the judge as though his mesmerizing oral essay on criminal jurisdiction had lulled her to sleep, Dr. Socorro answered.

"Yes, Judge, that's correct. You see . . ."

"I don't mean to cut you off, Doctor, but I was only asking for your confirmation of the correctness of my assumption. It was merely foundational, for my next question, which is, what is the scientific margin of error that you might be wrong, can you quantify that for me?"

"Well," she stammered, "ah, you see, I haven't actually thought about quantification. I mean of course there is a margin of error. That is always the case in scientific, especially psychological diagnoses but . . ."

"Is your belief in his correct name a diagnosis, Doctor? And if so, what is the diagnosis?"

"No, it's not a diagnosis, it's . . ."

Judge Hightower held up his hand. "You've answered my question, no need to amplify a simple 'no.' What is it then, a clinical finding? A brain marker of some sort? How would you describe your conclusion? And feel free to amplify on this one, Doctor, a simple yes or no might not do."

"Judge, you asked me to conduct as many sessions with the defendant as I felt necessary and to give you a written report describing my findings. That is what I did. I'm afraid I don't quite get your meaning as to exactly what I found as a consequence of my sessions."

"Excellent. Excellent, Doctor. I think you've got it exactly right. Your report is very compelling because it is an ordered, careful study of how you reacted, and how you judged the accuracy of what the defendant told you. Based on all you learned about his social and clinical history, his familial relationships, his work ethic and standards, and his reactions to customary norms in society, you *found*, which is a way of expressing one's belief, that this man, the defendant, was *truthful* in all respects, when he told you he was Arthur Cheshire. You also spent quite some time dispelling the prosecutor's notion that he could be his twin brother, Martin Cheshire. While you found him remarkably deceitful, even duplicitous, you believed him on the basic question—that is, who is he? Do you accept my summary of your accomplishment in this matter?"

"Well yes, of course, but I hope you will take into consideration the many qualifying factors involved in his very unusual upbringing and his deep symbiotic relationship with his twin brother."

"Ah, yes indeed. I did that. As to the relationship between Martin, who may be dead, and Arthur, I think you were extraordinarily insightful. Let me cut to the chase, Doctor, if I may. I accept your findings as scientifically sound and am keenly aware of the many qualifications you mention in the report. I am persuaded that Arthur Cheshire *is* the defendant before the court, but I make no finding as to his brother's current status, dead or alive. That is not necessary at this point. If it were my jurisdictional charge, and I hasten to add that it is not, I would not proceed with the pending charge against Martin Cheshire, because I do not believe he is properly before the court. Arthur Cheshire *is* before the court. But he is not here charged with any crime, or civil misdeed whatsoever. As my literary friend Hercule Pirot might have put it, 'By George, I think they've nabbed the wrong bloke.'"

Turning his gaze directly at the prosecutor, Judge Hightower recentered himself in his big black leather chair. He squared his shoulders and waited a moment for the prosecutor to catch his eye. Then he spoke in measured terms.

"Let's start with the government. Given my acceptance of the scientific reliability of the report, my agreement with it, and my specific finding that the defendant in this proceeding is Arthur Cheshire, what is your proposed course of action, Mr. Cabelson?"

As though he had been told he had a terminal illness, Cabelson rose to his feet and held up his copy of the report.

"Judge, I only got this report yesterday. I have yet to cross-examine the witness, and I will of course have to consult with the US Attorney on any future course of action."

"I got it yesterday as well. You have no burden of persuasion in this case since it is not your issue to prove. And given what I hope is clear—that is, my belief in the factual integrity of Dr. Socorro—independent witnesses or even cross-examination by you, won't aid you. As for talking to the man upstairs, that is entirely your province. What I'm asking for is whether you too are persuaded by this report and now believe, as I do, that the defendant you extradited from Maine is in fact Arthur Cheshire. Do you agree or not?"

"Judge, with all due respect to the court, I have not yet formed a belief one way or the other."

"Fair enough, Mr. Cabelson. Take your time. In the interim, let's hear from Mr. Kemper."

Kemper rose, moved to the podium, and grasped it on both sides as if it were a life ring.

"I agree with Dr. Socorro and the Court."

He then moved back to his seat.

"Not so fast, Mr. Kemper, if you please. Agreeing with either of us does not get us very far. I'll pose the same question to you that I did to Mr. Cabelson: what is your proposed course of action?"

Stepping back to the podium, Kemper said, "I move to dismiss all charges against my client, Arthur Cheshire."

"Motion denied," said the judge with a wry smile. "There is no charge against Arthur Cheshire, so there's nothing to uphold or dismiss. The fact that I believe the government has the wrong man, at least the wrong man on *these* charges, does not solve the problem, no matter what order I enter in the case. Congress specifically designed the statutory *habeas* action to add it to the other due process rights guaranteed by the Fourteenth Amendment. Are you contemplating that kind of action, Mr. Kemper?"

"Well yes, Judge, now that you mention it, that is exactly what I will do."

"You are welcome, Mr. Kemper. Now as to the government, You agreed with Mr. Kemper to abate the normal indictment process pending my review of the *identity* question regarding Mr. Cheshire. I've resolved that and made a finding that he is who he says he is, Arthur Cheshire, late of San Diego, California. That's the extent of my ruling. Neither side should take that finding as probative of guilt or innocence on the charges here in federal court. The government did not lose. The defense did not win. All I've done is accept Arthur Cheshire's statement that he is who he says he is. Court adjourned."

ARTHUR GETS A NEW LAWYER

Arthur did the smart thing. He got a new lawyer, a new plan, a plea deal, and a free trip back to Maine.

After Judge Hightower found that he was Arthur, and following the judge's hints from the bench, the feds dropped all pending charges against him *as* Martin Cheshire. That was the good news. In the next breath, Arthur learned that he was target of a new grand jury investigation on a surplus of new, *albeit* less serious charges.

Kemper tried to explain Arthur's new legal risks to him and filed a *habeas* proceeding for him. But the government's voluntary dismissal of the old charges made the *habeas* inquiry moot. Kemper was forced to withdraw as Arthur's publicly provided legal counsel because his office had only been appointed to defend him on the now-dismissed charges. They could not, he said, represent him on new charges until they were actually filed. But Kemper assured him, "That is a formality. If they file new charges, we will be back in court on your behalf."

"What can I do now, just sit here?"

"No," Kemper explained, "you will be released pending a new indictment. And they might try to put a hold on you for the embezzlement, and related, charges in Maine. It could get tricky, you know, the timing and everything. Want to know what I'd do in your situation?"

"Kill myself? Ask Rosie for forgiveness? What?"

"I'd hire Donald 'Rat' McGrath the Fourth. He's a killer lawyer, always goes for the jugular, and might get you a walk, at least here in California. Maine's a different matter."

"Do you know him? Why would he take my case?"

"Yes, I know him. More importantly, Dr. Socorro knows him. Quite well, I'm told. In fact, she called me this morning and suggested I talk to him on your behalf. He called me five minutes later. As I understand it, Dr. Socorro gave him the basic details."

"OK, now I see. Dr. Socorro called me this morning—Officer Martinez came to my cell and escorted me to the phone bank. It was really short; she was between patients, she said. Anyhow, she said she knows a lawyer that maybe can help. Could she talk to him about my case? I said sure, being that she's already saved my life once."

Kemper nodded his head, smiled, and said, "Actually, I only know *of* Mr. McGrath. Everybody in San Diego does. He's done a lot of trial work for big-name private clients, but he's also been a public prosecutor. He knows both sides and all the angles. Strong lawyer and smart politician, I hear."

"Why would a big gun like that take my case? I can't pay him."

"If he takes your case, the government will pay him. He's a contingent fee lawyer. He defends people in trouble, like you, and files Section 1983 actions in civil court, and . . ."

Arthur interrupted, "What in hell is a Section 1983 action?"

Kemper said, "It's a civil lawsuit you can bring in a federal court for deprivation of your civil rights. Federal law gives individuals the right to sue under color of state law for civil rights violations. Mr. McGrath, if he takes your case, would charge you a percentage of what he collects for you from the government. Shall I set up a meeting here in the interview room, for you?"

Arthur took Kemper's advice. Kemper called McGrath, who met with Arthur in Dr. Socorro's office. She kindly obliged a meeting in her office to help with the retention of a new lawyer. McGrath agreed to represent Arthur *pro bono* on any new criminal charges the feds might bring. Arthur also agreed to pay McGrath a 40 percent contingent fee on the civil case he might file against the federal government.

As it turned out, it took only one meeting between Stran Cabelson and Don McGrath to wrap up the California side of Arthur's legal troubles.

Cabelson told McGrath that the government was calling a new grand jury into session and that he intended to indict Arthur on federal charges of illegally transporting a body across state lines, fraudulent representations to US border officials, and an illegal entry into the United States at Phoenix, based on Arthur's use of Martin's passport. Cabelson explained that the government now accepted Dr. Socorro's report as factual and did not intend to pursue its murder/arson theory either here, or in Maine. But, he said, the state authorities in Maine are still very interested in charging Arthur there on several counts of embezzlement, wire transfer fraud, and sexual assault charges related to Rosie Andersen. There might, he softly suggested, even be a civil action in Maine by Rosie herself. It seems, that she too, has hired a big-name contingent feel lawyer in Portland.

McGrath listened patiently but sprang on Cabelson like a bobcat on a packrat.

"Tell you what, Stran, I'll try to persuade my client *not* to sue you, your office, the detention officers, the lawyers who drew the extradition papers, and the facility that held my client against his will, under color of law, in violation of Section 1983 of the Civil Rights Act of 1964, for both compensatory and punitive damages.

"While I've got your attention, I think the government wrongfully withheld critical information about a man named Diego Cortez, conspired with him to allow a massive fraud on my client for the paltry sum of $5,000, illegally engaged in taping my client's phone in Maine, and illegally acquired his financial records without bringing the matter to a judge for a search warrant. Even if you had a warrant, which is not a part of the record in this or any other case that I'm aware of, you did it based on Diego Cortez's deliberate lies.

"He didn't see shit in Mexico. He only rode the bus with my client. He's a good speculator, but not an eyewitness. And you'll never see his corrupt ass on this side of the border again. I'm sure you know his criminal connections in Mexico; he has protection from some very influential Mexican citizens in Los Angeles.

"I'm also sure you know that your polygraphs will never see the light of day if you make the god-awful mistake of indicting my client. And lest I leave anything out, you got no case at all of illegally transporting a body across state lines. Who could you possibly call to prove that case? My client? Not a chance. Fifth Amendment, remember? Dr. Socorro? No chance there either. Classic hearsay testimony. The girls never had a clue. You have a legal *theory* but no evidence. I'll dust your ass on any criminal case you file, and I'll do it *pro bono*. I'm in this for a contingent fee in the civil case I'm getting ready to file in federal court. I'll send you the first copy because you are the first named defendant.

"You say the government accepts the findings in Dr. Socorro's report. Yep, I bet you do. And you are stuck with a federal judge's stamp of approval on that document. She is witness number one in our civil rights case. Judge Hightower's order is document number one in that case. And you will be the second witness I put on the stand. I understand you even went to Maine and signed for a prisoner you called Martin Cheshire, then cuffed and transported him here to California, without making sure he was Martin. Martin had been dead for months by then. Very weak investigation, Cabelson, don't you think? You let the state boys in Maine work up the case. They spent less than fifteen minutes looking for evidence at the fishing camp. What the hell did you think they'd find with a drive-by investigation? What do you think I'll find with a full forensic team digging up the floorboards and finding DNA all over the place? Remember the color-of-law language in Section 1983?

"So, my friend, here's the deal. Release my client within twenty-four hours. We'll sign a covenant not to sue you, or anyone else in the federal government. And then, I'll take the show on the road to Portland. I hear it's a nice town."

Cabelson took the deal to his boss, who agreed that the civil rights case was weak, and that an indictment was unlikely.

Once the deal was inked, Arthur walked out of the federal detention center a free man. McGrath negotiated a temporary stand-off with the Attorney General's office in Maine by agreeing to submit his client for voluntary arrest in five days in Portland.

Arthur reported as agreed. Meanwhile, the state prosecutors in Maine filed a direct information with the Portland County District court, charging him with multiple counts of embezzlement, theft by wire, illegal transfer of funds, fraudulent conduct with both state and federal banks, assault, battery, sexual penetration, and theft of Martin's salary and employment benefit plan from AmHull.

The jail in Portland was not nearly as nice as the one in California. They stuck Arthur in a holding facility, waiting for trial on all those charges. Maine is not in love with plea bargains. They try them as they see them, as the Portland County district attorney likes to say.

Arthur spends his days waiting for lighting to strike and the heavens to open and the light to shine down on him. He's looking for answers. How could he flunk the polygraph? How could Rosie and Marcella both lie and yet pass the test? More importantly, why did they lie so blatantly? And where in the hell is Alice Blue Gown? Not that he was worried about her but because he hoped she'd be a helpful witness on his side of the story. She probably guessed about Martin's Hide and Be the Money plan, he thought.

McGrath declined to represent him in Maine.

Last anyone knew, Alice had quit AmHull and moved away. Rosie was not at the Brighton Lane house. No one was calling. His new public defender told him the case would take some time. The bail was $50,000 cash or bond. He did not have it, but someone did. A mysterious stranger posted his bond. His lawyer said nothing would happen soon.

Arthur's only hope was that Harold Hull, Sr., would tell the truth about how much Martin skimmed. Hull, Arthur thought, would admit that Martin only took $26,000. What Arthur didn't know awaiting trial was that the trial evidence would confirm that AmHull's bonding company had already reimbursed Harold to the tune of $291,000. Harold Senior's reconstruction of the loss was thirty grand larger than originally calculated. After all, Mr. Hull was the fourth generation of men who knew something about bonding, embezzlement, and profit.

CHAPTER FIVE
WHO ARE THOSE GIRLS

Panama's *Executive Hotel* in Panama City is a modern high rise business hotel in the heart of town. While not quite the Four Seasons, it's elegant and private simultaneously. Known for its easy acceptance of travelers of every sort, it is especially open to clandestine meetings or sitting at its expansive outdoor bar, waiting for the sun to set over the Panama Canal.

"Well, Rosie, I can't believe we're here. Panama! Us. Sitting here on this gorgeous porch drinking . . . what'd you call these?"

"Tequila Sunsets, Marcella. I thought tequila was a major drink out there in California."

"Yeah, it is. But we call them Tequila Sunrises there. But I'm still a LA chica—I'm a white wine lady, don't you know—and don't think I'm the Chablis type. For me a nice dry Chardonnay, well chilled, in a stem glass *por favor*. No plastic cups for me. But I could get used to these sunsets colored by tequila that costs nine bucks a glass. Who'd ever have guessed?"

"I can tell you one man that didn't. Arthur. He never guessed."

"Yeah, for sure. Arthur was a man of the moment. He thought I was a fool, you were a fool. In fact, all the world's a fool where Arthur was concerned."

The women sat close together, to ensure prying ears close by would not overhear or think they were loose women waiting for a pickup. And because they were obvious Americans, they kept a watchful eye on men walking by from one side of the large lobby to the other.

"You know, *Marcella Wella*, that is what he called you, wasn't it? Arthur really believed that Martin wanted him to live his life for him after the boat accident. He never doubted it for a second. What I still can't figure out is how in hell he thought we wanted him to be Martin. God, what a brother he was."

"Me neither. Of course, I knew Arthur longer than you did. Seems to me he lived Martin's life even before Martin died, you know. They were a pair of one—and not just inseparable, more like two cut into one without the cut showing. They were living one life that had two sides to it."

"I can buy that," Marcella said. "You know we never really had a chance to talk about their game—Hide and Be. I think we might be the only two people in the world who figured it out *while* the game was going on. What was your first real clue? When, deep down inside, did you know that Arthur was living the life of Martin—back with me in Portland? I'm dying to know."

"Bad metaphor, Rosie. Arthur's the one dying. But, even now, I'm not sure I can pinpoint the day. I told you in Chicago about the clue that made me start doubting my own sanity—it was that Arthur was really himself only when he was Martin. Crazy, *que no*? It was the second trip Martin made out to San Diego after the October fishing trip. Remember, I told you on the phone that Arthur would disappear so that Martin could show up. Since there was only one of them, Arthur arranged everything so that Martin would be down at the office when Arthur was at the house, and then when Martin was at the house, Arthur would have created some excuse to be away."

It was hot and humid outside, but the girls hardly noticed. Dressed for both the locale and the weather, they mirrored one another in brightly colored blouses, white linen slacks, and sandals showing off their new speckled toes, fire engine red, with little stars and moons in white. They'd selected a table where they could easily track the front lobby and newly arriving guests. The flowering Mango tree, with branches out fifty feet, gave them shade. The cocktails gave them pause.

"OK, Marcella, once you got the tip, what'd you do?"

Putting her drink down, picking up a miniature chip with a lovely chocolate pate on it, Marcela munched and talked.

"There was this one time when Arthur was supposed to be inspecting a boat down at Ensenada. Martin came to the apartment allegedly to wait for Arthur—then after an hour of chitchat, he claimed to have to go out on a call from one of the boat owners up at Dana Point. It was part of the game, but I hadn't scoped the whole thing out yet. Anyhow, Arthur came home an hour after Martin left and went through the routine of asking where he was, when's he coming back, yada, yada, you know. I mistakenly said Newport instead of Dana Point. He corrected me, saying it was Dana Point. I said yeah, you're right and then it hit me. How did he know Dana Point when Martin just said it was a new client who just got to Dana Point that afternoon? Arthur would not have known that."

"That doesn't sound too suspicious to me."

"Well, maybe you had to be there—but it just didn't ring true. That was when I started planting little things for him to bite on. In three weeks, I knew. Well, I didn't know everything. I didn't know Martin was dead. No, all I knew was that Arthur was pretending to be Martin. I didn't tumble to the reason until Arthur faked his death down in Mexico. That was the clincher."

"What'd you mean?"

"Arthur hated surf fishing. So why all of a sudden this passion for surf fishing? He always pooh-poohed those guys standing in the surf pulling in those tiny little fish. He said in Maine, those fish were only used as bait. My first thought was that he had a chica down there. But when they called me and said he was dead, my immediate thought was that it was really Martin who was dead."

"No. Really? That was your first thought! Marcella, I wasn't as suspicious as you were. I don't know what my first clue was, but I can tell you when I got scared. See, Martin gets the phone call about his brother's death, and he breaks up and all, you know sobbing, and almost screaming, but he does it all standing up. Who cries standing up? Tell me that! Looking back on it, it's almost funny. Your first thought was that Martin is the one that died, and my first thought was that Martin doesn't really care that Arthur is dead. Either way, those guys played Hide and Be one too many times."

Rosie tapped on the glass table, looking around at the two other occupied tables, twenty feet away. They were men, who kept looking over at them, but still seemed intent on some business deal. They kept reaching down into black shiny briefcases and pulling out documents to show one another. Some deal going down, she thought.

Marcella leaned back in her chair and adjusted her wide-brimmed straw hat. Then, waving her hand in front of her, she asked a new question.

"What were they thinking we were thinking? Whoa, there I go again. There never was a *they*. It was always only one of them. Now the cops are convinced that one twin was murdered by the other. Arthur faked himself out. Funny, huh? Serves the bastard right for screwing us both to death. God, he couldn't get enough. Did you see that too?"

"Let's hope that the FBI keeps thinking that way. Martin was a nice scoundrel, but you couldn't trust him any further than you could throw Arthur."

Marcella tapped her glass with a bright blue fingernail.

"Call the waiter, this Tequila Sunset has done set. See if he has another one before I lose the mood. How long before she gets here?"

"Oh, probably any time now," looking at her watch, Rosie continued.

"Her plane should have landed about two and a half hours ago and you know how stupid their customs are here—of course you do—you're the one that told me how to get through. Tell me again, Marcella, what is it that your family does down here?"

"Insurance. Life insurance, actually. One of my cousins lives here—not that he wants to, exactly—but there is no extradition from here back to the states. So, he pretty much lives here because it's better than jail. Hey, maybe my cousin will hit it off with her when she gets here. They do have a common interest, like insurance and money."

"You never know. I think she's sweet and all, but I sure never thought . . ."

"Wait, don't tell me. Is that her coming toward us? She looks like someone from Maine—no make-up, no nonsense, just like Arthur said all the women there were—except for you, I didn't mean that."

"Don't worry about it. You're right on both counts. That's her."

The short woman, wearing black cargo pants and a rusty brown long-sleeved shirt, moved toward them from the lobby. Reaching the table, she held her arms open. "Hi Rosie, I made it! Can you believe it?"

"Marcella, meet Alice."

"Oh Marcella, it's so good to meet you! I've been on that airplane for hours and hours trying to guess all the way down here what you hafta look like. Martin—or Arthur, or whichever one he was—talked about you a little, but since he hardly recognized my existence, I never got much from him. But Rosie told me you were a for-sure-California-looking-woman, and she was right."

They hugged one another, then melded into a three-woman hug. Pulling out the third chair, Marcella said, "Alice, have a Tequila Sunset. It's the kind of drink that will mellow your soul but don't drink too many of them—we have a lot to talk about. Thanks to you, that is. We were just exchanging stories about our twins, and their insane little game of Hide and Be."

"Well, girls, as you already know the Cheshire twins didn't pay much attention to me. Never tried to get into my pants, although they gamed me a time or two. You know, I never could tell them apart, even when they were playing it straight."

"I couldn't either," Marcella said. "Except for the tattoo. That was my Arthur's downfall—his tattoo. Poor Arthur. All he wanted was a little marker. My cousin Maldonado inked him just right. It made him different from his twin, once and for all. But he just could not let well enough alone. Now that little ink marker has gone and turned him into the brother he was trying to distinguish."

Ping-ponging back and forth between her two new best friends, Alice said, "That's another thing that I still don't get. Marcella, how did you ever talk Arthur into getting a tattoo? Arthur was really squeamish about pain. He got a paper cut once when he was looking through something at the front desk and screamed like a little baby."

Rosie added, "Well, that's just like Martin. He wouldn't even go the dentist to get his teeth cleaned except for once a year, and he dreaded it like it was surgery."

"Actually, it didn't take any talking from me. He was into the idea of something, anything actually, that would distinguish him from Martin—I don't know why. In fact, he denied that was the reason. But the more he denied it the more I knew that was the real reason. I still remember telling my cousin Maldonado about putting the little m inside the sea urchin. I probably wouldn't have thought of it except that Arthur was so adamant that this was gonna be his mark, his own ID—I thought well, *mui hombre,* wait till you get up the nerve to see this and see that sweet little m in red on your little ankle. I thought he'd either love me or hate me for putting my initial on him. But you know what the first thing he said was?"

"No, what? Wait, before you tell me, is this tattoo guy the same cousin that is here Panama in the insurance business?"

"No, a different one. But back there in San Diego, after Arthur got tattooed by Maldonado, he said, 'Shit, Marcella, Martin's gonna wish he could have got one—he'd have put an A on his—part of the game, you know.' I said, 'Well, he can just come on down to Mal's the next time he's here.' And he said, 'No, that can't happen.' And he got all quiet on me, when just before he was bouncing off the walls, from the pain, from the shock, from what I don't know. Then, he just got all down—that happened several times and it was always about something Martin could do or might do someday—that's when I started to think something was wrong with Martin. You know, like had the big C or something. But Arthur wouldn't talk about it—mostly we just talked *around* it. After a while, I noticed that it was only when the future was the issue. Martin in the past or Martin now was no problem. It was Martin in the future that depressed Arthur."

"Alice, tell Marcella how you tumbled to the Hide and Be scam that Martin was running on AmHull. I got part of it, but even now I'm not sure I really know what happened." Rosie sat back and sipped her Tequila Sunset.

"Ladies, it was just luck," Alice confessed. "You know Martin always thought I was a nitwit. But it worked for me. No one thinks a nitwit can outsmart them, you know. It was the first time he did it—the first time he took 10 percent of a customer's premium check. I remember the name like it was tattooed on me—*Montora Swordfish, Inc.* The Montora family is very old and respected in Maine. I knew the young ones from school. I even dated one of the uncles when I was only sixteen and he was about thirty, or even older. They liked their women young. Anyhow, Martin picked them to skim the first 10 percent from, and I spotted it only because Ginsella Montora called in to say their $3,480 premium check was in the mail. She said to watch for it since they were about five days late. So, when it came in, that very same day, I took it to Martin, and he skimmed it. Two days later Ginsella called me back and asked if I got it. I checked the register in QuickBooks and lo and behold the premium dropped from $3,480 to $3,132! I knew something was up. But the deposit slip that Martin had already brought back from the bank said $3,480. I just put two and two together and came up with $348."

"I don't get it. What's $348 got to do with it?"

"That's 10 percent of the real premium, $3,480.00. I mean, duh. The customer we insure pays us $3,480 for a monthly premium. Martin records it as that on AmHull's books but gets a bank slip for that amount. He cops the 10 percent. AmHull gets *screwed*. So, I just started watching and watching. Pretty soon, it only took a few weeks, the 10 percent skim job Martin was running amounted to over $25,000. Customers ain't getting screwed. They are getting insurance just like the policy says. But AmHull's getting boned by Martin. He's giving himself a 10-percent bonus."

"But how did you get any of it? I thought Martin was getting it?"

"He was, but he was a piker. He figured out how to skim the first 10 percent and I just followed his lead and sloshed the remaining 90 percent right off the table. All I did was open a money market account at our bank by going in and telling them that Mr. Hull wanted a better interest rate since there was so much building up in checking. I told them to complete the forms and the signature card, and I'd get him to sign it in the office. Then I forged his signature by scanning the real one and then digitizing the image onto the signature card. It's actually pretty easy if you're just a little bit good at computers."

"Well, that explains how you got the money out of AmHull's checking account and into the secret money market account, but what happened then?"

"That's when Rosie called, and we started talking about how strange Martin was acting. Then you called Rosie. You were just as bewildered as we were. But you knew something we didn't. You knew that Arthur was the one that got the tattoo and that Martin, according to Arthur, would never do such a thing."

"Alice, don't forget what else Marcella knew."

"Oh right, there was that little additional intel. So, tell me now that we're actually face to face, Marcella, how did you ever learn how to get a Panamanian bank to accept a wire transfer from an American bank and then give you the money in cash?"

"That's the easiest part. My cousin's been making a living down here doing stuff like that for ten years or more. He walked me through it. You know all they care about is good liquid funds. They charge an outrageous processing fee of 15 percent on deals they know are shady. So, when I gave you the account number that I opened in Portland under the name AmHull Insurance Brokers, using my cousin's Panamanian connection, they couldn't wait to get the transfer from your bank there in Portland and then give me the money ten minutes later—minus their 15-percent processing fee, of course. It's time for truth, ladies—have you ever seen $201,195 in good ole U-S-of-A currency before?"

Marcella reached down underneath the table and placed her oversize, zebra-striped shoulder purse in her lap. Unzipping the bag, she pulled the flaps open just far enough to let Rosie and Alice see inside.

Alice, who'd been happy but reserved until now, whooped, "Hot damn—would you look at that! I never thought I'd see that much money all at once—but is it safe to show it to us, even inside a zebra skin, right here in front of everybody?"

"Well," Marcella beamed, "it's safe enough to let you peek inside the zipper. But we better go up to my suite, it's got two bedrooms and a couch. Just right for dividing up the loot into three equal piles. And, girls, see that hook-nosed little felon, standing over there at the edge of the lawn? He's my cousin—not so patiently waiting for his 2 percent. He sells out pretty low. So let me tell you how I see the split. The 90 percent that Martin missed in Portland came to $236,700. The wire transfer fees and other bank charges knocked it down some, but it was a wash because of the money market interest it earned in the six weeks that it was there till they caught up with Arthur."

Rosie—"I remember seeing him out in the parking lot when the FBI guys nabbed him and slapped those new fangled handcuffs on him, they were black and looked like some hard plastic wires, not shiny chrome like the ones you see in the movies. Anyhow, they cuffed him and took him away. So, I called Marcella, and . . ."

Marcella—"I typed up a quick fax. Then, I called the bank to expect a wire transfer from us. I told them to expect it the next morning—then I called Rosie back, and . . . "

Alice—"Yeah, she called me. It took a few weeks, but then Rosie called and said, 'Alice Blue Gown, get your little behind on a plane for Panama. The money is on the way.'"

The waiter brought a fresh round of Tequila Sunsets. The girls hadn't ordered them, but the split could wait a few more minutes. They toasted Arthur again, but this time Marcella added Diego Cortez's name to the toast—"And here's to Diego Cortez—a little man in a brown bombardier jacket at the right place at the right time—and it cost us a mere $5,000 to make him credible."

Alice, feeling a little tipsy after two drinks, leaned into the table and said, "That's another connection I don't have straight in my mind. Rosie told me that your other boyfriend, Maldonado, knew this Cortez guy somehow, but I still don't get how he knew you."

"No, you got the players mixed up a little bit. Maldonado, the tattoo artist, was my cousin—Leandro, although he was a cousin too, but only a third cousin—he was my other boyfriend. Leandro was the one I was going to break up with until I got suspicious about Arthur. Leandro knows a lot of guys down in Baja who do favors for him from time to time. He was using Diego for some small-time stuff and was buying him beers in Tijuana one night and Diego told him the story about the bus ride. Cortez told Leandro that he got a few hundred bucks from some gringo on a bus from Rosario who smelled like smoke and kerosene. Leandro knew about the fire and assumed, like I did, that Arthur was dead. But the description Diego gave made it clear that Arthur didn't die in the fire—he was on the bus to La Paz *with* Diego an hour after the fire started. So, Leandro helped me put it all together. When Arthur got arrested in Portland and returned to San Diego, Leandro remembered the odd conversation he had with Diego a few weeks before that."

"Well, whose idea was it for me to FedEx five grand in East Coast bills out to you?" Alice asked.

"Leandro suggested that maybe Diego could be the icing on the cake for me to fix Arthur for lying to me—he doesn't know anything about the Hide and Be Fund. He thinks I got the five grand from you, Rosie—I told him you were as pissed as much as I was about being laid and made the fool by the Arthur/ Martin duo. I told him you came from a rich family on the East Coast—a real trust fund baby, I said. Anyhow, he said if we paid Diego Cortez three grand to make up a new story, one the cops would buy because of the money he was returning, that would make it freakin believable. That would be the final nail in the coffin for Arthur. He said the cops would buy it hook, line, and sinker, and they did."

"So, this Cortez guy didn't really see Arthur running down the hill from the shack? He just made it up?"

"Si, Señorita, do you know what five thousand American dollars is in Mexican pesos? It's enough for Diego to sell his soul."

"Wow, Marcella! That's fantastic. You're a magician—here's to you."

"No, here's to us. But before we get too many of these in our heads, there's still one part of this I don't get. Alice, you're the one who made the most important part work—the money itself—how in the world did you get the Portland bank to wire-transfer all that money to Panama?"

"Well, it wasn't me. It was Harold Hull. At least that's what they thought. All I did was invent my own Hide and Be game. It was his company, his money, his account, his signature, and his loyal servant—yours truly—that communicated with the bank. Of course, they now know that Harold did not really open the money market account—they think Martin did it. That's because I told them that Martin gave me the fax from Harold and gave me the signed signature card in the first place. So, they connect Martin to the phony money market account in Portland—then they trace it to the bank here in Panama—and *viola*, you and your cousin make it disappear. That's the end of the line for the feds—and for Arthur."

Marcella flashed her eyes at her two new closest friends and said, "Well, that brings everyone up to date. God, you know I never trusted anyone like I trusted Arthur."

Rosie chimed in, "Talk about trust—how about the way I fell for Martin?"

Alice closed with—"I never trusted either one of them—course I never slept with them either."

That brought on the final toast of the night: "Here's to the Cheshire boys and their wicked little game of Hide and Be."

Marcella and Rosie looked at Alice. Alice answered their unspoken question.

"They all think Martin did everything—burn up his brother—steal over two hundred grand and screw you two ladies in the process. What a guy! Where will we ever find another one like him?"

"What do you mean another one? We need another two."

The End

ABOUT THE AUTHOR

I am a retiring lawyer, a working author, and a preserving blogger. I was a full-time trial lawyer for thirty-two years in a large Phoenix firm. I was a part-time law professor for the last twenty-nine years. As of summer, 2023, I am writing, publishing, and blogging full time. My first book was a textbook published by the Arizona State Bar Association. My first novel was published by the University of New Mexico Press. I've written ten novels and eight nonfiction titles as of July 2023.

From the day I entered law school, I've been reading cases, statutory law and writing about legal conundrums and flaws in our criminal and civil justice systems. I've always read novels, nonfiction, and historical fiction by great authors who were never corrupted by the staid habits of trial lawyers. I write long-form, interspersed with the occasional blog, op-ed, or essay. One of the unexpected benefits of reading the law is learning how to write about it. Somewhere along the trajectory from a baby lawyer to a senior one, I became intoxicated with blending nonfiction with fiction in books, rather than legal documents. After spending thirty years in courtrooms trying cases, I started writing about them. That led to writing novels while borrowing from famous historical settings and lesser-known characters. My courtroom days were chock full of ideas, notions, and hopes about ultimately becoming an author. I organized and memorized critical information for judges, juries, and clients. Now I use that experience to write vivid fiction and immersive nonfiction. I moved away from trial practice to teaching law students how to use creative writing techniques to tell their client's stories, in short form.

F. Scott Fitzgerald said, "All good writing is swimming under water and holding your breath." The same could be said of my transition from trying cases to writing crime fiction. I've been holding my breath for twenty years waiting for galley proofs and book reviews. Anais Nin spoke for all of us when she said, "We write to taste life twice."

My first novel, *The Gallup 14*, won a coveted starred review from *Publishers Weekly*. I won a Spur Award from *Western Writers of America* in 2004 for my first nonfiction book ("*Miranda, The Story of America's Right to Remain Silent*"). I won the 2010 Arizona Book of the Year Award, The Glyph Award, and a Southwest Publishing Top Twenty award in 2010, for "*Innocent Until Interrogated—The Story of the Buddhist Temple Massacre.*" My third nonfiction title ("*Anatomy of a Confession—The Debra Milke Case*") was highly acclaimed. My nonfiction title "*CALL HIM MAC—Ernest W. McFarland—The Arizona Years*" was widely and favorably reviewed. My latest nonfiction crime book, "*Nobody Did Anything Wrong But Me,* was published by *Twelve Tables Press*, one of America's most distinguished publisher of law books about important legal issues. No New York Times bestsellers, yet.